My
Stratford
Friend

booke.I.

Dominick Reyntiens

Anna

Best *[signature]*

Valley Press

MY STRATFORD FRIEND: Book 1

First published 2014 by Valley Press
www.mystratfordfriend.com
info @mystratfordfriend.com

National Library of Australia Cataloguing-in-Publication entry

Author: Reyntiens, Dominick, author.
Title: My Stratford friend. Book I / Dominick Reyntiens ;
               illustrations: Caro Liddell.
ISBN: 9780992592202 (paperback)
Series: Reyntiens, Dominick. My Stratford friend; book 1.
Other Authors/Contributors:
               Liddell, Caro, illustrator.

Dewey Number: A823.4

Also available as an ebook:
ISBN: 9780992592219 (ebook)

Project patron: A P Lywood
Structural editor: Laurel Cohn
Copy editor: Carol Campbell
Art work and cover design: Caro Liddell

Typesetting and design by Publicious Pty Ltd
www.publicious.com.au

Published with the assistance of Publicious Pty Ltd
www.publicious.com.au

PREFACE

I do not see myself as a literary man; I believe I am more of a storyteller. Academia gives great insights into Shakespeare's life and work on which I could never cast a shadow. However, I longed to read about the man, the child, and what drove the very deep humanity that gave rise to the greatest writer ever.

The facts of Shakespeare's life are thin on the ground and, although academia's stock-in-trade, facts are not always related to truth. To elucidate: Fact: schoolteachers in Zimbabwe are members of Mugabe's ZANU-PF party. Truth: salaries are more likely to be paid consistently to members. Loyalty to State is not always brought about by personal principles and the Tudor era was no exception.

The only way to weave facts and truth together is by conjecture, and this is the responsibility of the storyteller. This responsibility is as deep and as serious as it comes, which is why I dismissed writing about Shakespeare in the first person; you cannot put oneself inside the head of a genius. With conjecture as my tool, I have taken the few bones left to us and gently built flesh upon them.

My Stratford Friend is my humble attempt to reveal the human side of the Bard through the observance of a fictional friend, one whose stature in society was low but, nonetheless, pivotal in the life of this great man. I embraced this idea after reading about Neil Aspinall and his relationship with the Beatles. A school friend who became manager of their recording company Apple, Aspinall was there from day one; near but far, close but unseen. What an evening over a bottle of wine, beside a warm fire, one could have spent listening to the tales of his life with the Fab Four. So please, sit by a warm fire with a glass of Madeira (or wine) and enjoy the tales of Tom Wickham's life.

DOMINICK REYNTIENS

Text references

Page 60
Original text: *Coventry Mystery Plays*. Published 1817.
Courtesy Wikipedia: http://en.wikipedia.org/wiki/Coventry_Carol

Page 91
Original text: *History of Mad Orlando*, Robert Greene. Published 1594.
Courtesy Luminarium editions:
www.luminarium.org/editions/orlando.htm

Pages 147, 152
Original text : *Metamorphosis Publius Ovid Naso*,
translated by Arthur Golding. Published 1578.
Courtesy Internet Archive: http://archive.org/stream/
shakespearesovid00oviduoft/shakespearesovid00oviduoft_djvu.txt

Page 288
Original text: *Passionate Century of Love*,
Thomas Watson. Published 1582.
Elizabethan sonneteers: http://www.sonnets.org/minto5.htm

ACKNOWLEDGEMENTS

I have many people to thank for their support and inspiration to see my publication through to this point. First, my late father-in-law who read everything I ever wrote and commented with wisdom, compassion and generosity, but sadly did not live to read *My Stratford Friend*; Clare Asquith, whose ground-breaking book *Shadowplay* ignited the fire in my heart for this project; my dear spouse Caro, whom for the past four years has listened patiently to endless Tudor diatribes over the breakfast table; Melissa Lucashenko, who gave me a much-needed sense of self at a very low ebb in my writing life; my father's endless Bard-related cuttings from English newspapers sent post haste; Laurel Cohn who assessed the original manuscript and gave me the necessary strength and confidence to push on through to the finished work; Gail Hartnett, who jumped into the breech at very short notice; and thank you, Carol Campbell – like the perfect midwife, your experience and knowledge was essential, whilst I pushed.

For Adrian

CHAPTER I

Iam seventy-nine years old and the year is 1644. In these times, the attainment of this age is an impressive achievement and, indeed, in the locality of my modest dwelling, quite a talking point. Neighbours often ask what my secret is to this long life. I tell them the only reason I can think of – that the greatest extravagance I ever made is the heavy wooden bed in which I sleep. Whilst enclosed by drapes from four posts, for womb-like warmth, a feather mattress cradles me in flax sheets; their cool touch soothes a tired body at the end of a hard day.

This gentle April morning, I stood erect by way of a walking stick in one hand; with the other I gripped the cold iron bollard to which my horse, Prospero, is tethered. In front of me an open area that used to be alive with refreshment traders surrounded by a throng of people, smiling, loving and laughing. Positioned in the centre stood the tall white walls of an almost circular building that once launched the greatest fountain of human merriment ever! The original building had burnt to the ground some thirty years ago; however, this replacement was well built and it remains in good condition. The spirit of the old building was still there, its heart intact, its soul alive, and it was still called 'The Globe'.

Lurking nearby a bunch of thugs casually dangled wooden clubs. I assumed they had been hired to deal with any rash thespians who thought they might be able to stop this impending act of abomination. Various people had assembled, some just curious, some supporters to witness 'justice' as they saw it; whilst others, on the southern side, sat beneath the oak trees. They had gathered, tearfully, to bid farewell to their home of so many years. We waved cautiously at one another, for I knew most of these dear actors.

Suddenly a chorus of birds flew from a tree, heralding 'their' approach, and around the corner of Maiden Lane, 'they' arrived – an imperious little lot dressed from head to toe in black, save their white collars. Puritans, in whose grip the country now found itself. Oh my goodness, did I not want to hurl abuse at them from the top of my lungs! Pure of what? Pure of authority, of God, of thought, of deed, of goodness? To what did their purity refer? Surely not even they dared claim purity of love? But yes, they did. These little black beetles moved like one pious entity of God-given authority. I, however, like many others, knew they were nothing short of inhuman usurpers, tolerating no opinion other than their own, no doctrine other than their own, no interpretation other than their own; thus their ignorance was total and their arrogance complete.

Up to the theatre they marched and stood facing the onlookers. The thugs, too, turned around and stood at the ready. Sir Matthew Brend, the landlord and owner of the site, rounded the corner ahead of a column of eight large cart-horses, ready and yoked. The rear was brought up by two other wagons full of well-tooled carpenters. There must have been twenty in all. They assembled at the south corner, thirty feet from the oak trees and to the right of the Puritans, one of whom took position in front of his horde and pulled out a scroll.

'By the ordinance of Parliament, made on the second day of September in the year of Our Lord sixteen hundred and forty two, I; here; on the fifteenth day of April in the year of Our Lord sixteen hundred and forty four, am summarily invested with the authority to order the Globe theatre, this house of Baal, this den of iniquity, depravity and all things ungodly, shall be demolished.'

The Puritan's compatriots smiled complacently. There was a sad silence, but then someone broke wind from their arse in a long, loud and demonstrative fashion. It cut across their sanctimonious ritual like a heaven-sent bird dropping. We all burst into laughter; even the thugs could not contain themselves. It certainly wiped the smile off the Puritans' faces. The speaker quickly rolled up his scroll and, with a nod to Sir Matthew, they all left, bar one; he to bear witness to their crime.

Sir Matthew's limp hand waved to his men and they sprang into action as two actors rushed up to him pleading, but he simply raised his hands in submission. Thugs approached with clubs, and the actors, knowing discretion be the better part of valour, also raised their hands in submission and backed away. The carpenters entered the building and, within moments, hammering, sawing and shouting were heard within. The horses were expertly lined up on the western end and harnessed to the large draw bar.

Sir Matthew caught my eye and I his. He looked from side to side, loosely received a glance from little Mr Puritan, then, as the sawing continued, he looked back to me, crossed his wrists in a sign of bondage and pathetically shrugged his shoulders.

Ropes were slung out of the third-storey windows and lashed to the drawbars. Orders were shouted; men made large hand signals to each other, and then, with incredible synchronicity, eight powerful horses pulled in unison. A section of wall started to move; there was a crack, the tiled roof split, the great white section of wall took motion towards the ground, but it stopped and lolled at an angle. It looked like some pale maiden with head shaved for punishment, trying not to faint in the face of her death. Another shout, another pull and, swooning, the wall landed on the grass with a deathly thud, releasing a waft of dust like a final exhale of breath.

When the dust cleared, there was our beloved 'Globe', split to the heart by the executioner's sword. Its innards spilt like the guts of pathetic victims of religious righteousness – of which I had seen far too many in my seventy-nine years. Had my Stratford friend seen this, I doubt he would have borne it; he surely would have died of a broken heart on the spot.

Unable to stomach the quartering of this dear old friend, I opted to leave. I loosed my horse from the bollard and he obligingly lowered his head down for me to lie across his neck; on cue he picked up his head and, with a small swing of my leg, I landed in the saddle. I headed for the inn at Bankside, not far from the livery stable I owned on the southern frontage.

It was a weary walk down the road; the continuing noise of the destruction stirred great memories in my heart and forced tears from my eyes. Though it had always been a possibility, I never thought I would live to see the day that poets and play actors would become direct targets of the State, let alone witness their wholesale suppression.

Leaving Prospero tethered to the water trough outside the inn, and with bones creaking like old cart timbers, I walked into the still-empty establishment. Two dogs with folded paws glanced at me as I made a bee-line for the coved wooden seat beside the fire, which was putting out a welcome heat. I asked Bill Pearson, the landlord, who knew me well, to bring me a glass of brandy rather than my usual small beer. As he placed my glass on the table beside me he whispered, 'Tom, I didn't think they would do it.'

I looked Bill in the eye and whispered back, 'Bill, for self-preservation, the ends to which religion will go are infinite.'

Some other fellows walked in and took service at the bar. I sat quietly sipping my brandy, pondering the twilight of my life.

'Old man, you were there, were you not?' called a young man, across the empty room.

I saw three men propping up the bar, one probably only sixteen years old.

'To which "there" are you referring?' I replied guardedly to the cocksure youngster.

He replied softly, 'Pulling down that theatre.'

Pulling down 'that theatre' I wondered, repeating his words to myself. I looked at him as I did all men, with a swift and penetrating honesty. In my life, I learnt that mistempered words took more men to the gallows than ever did mistempered deeds. In harsh political times, the best tool of security was ignorance on the part of your interrogator. Sadly, we were indeed in harsh times once more.

'You refer to the Globe?'

'We do, Sir.'

'Your observation was correct,' I replied.

The three men picked up their bottle and glasses and walked over. Surrounding me, they poured themselves more Madeira and engaged in the warmth of the fire.

'We just wondered why an old man such as you would want to see that theatre destroyed,' said the youngest man.

I wondered if these men were government ruffians, the type of which I had spent my entire life avoiding. Or were they just innocents alive with a fascination for everything unfolding around them.

'You first,' I said to the young man. 'Why were you there?'

'Witnessing history,' he said. 'The very subject I am to read at Oxford this year. Rarely does it occur on one's own doorstep.'

He introduced me to his companions, James and Samuel. His name was Phillip. I, for the moment, retained my name. They declared they were all off to embark on their studies and had decided to attend this historical event for nothing more than its unrepeatable significance. The playhouses were the most persistent targets of the Puritans, as too were the universities. Only the continual intervention by Oliver Cromwell himself was preventing the Puritans from shutting down both Oxford and Cambridge.

I became concerned that I could well be in the company of spies.

'So, old man, why were you there?' James insisted.

I thought for a moment and then drained my glass and placed it on the small table beside me. 'I have seen robbers, rapists thieves, poets and priests executed, but never a building,' I told them.

'Agreed! Who's next? The king?' snorted Phillip, which drew shocked looks from his friends. 'A jest! Even Cromwell wouldn't do that to the king,' he murmured unconvincingly.

I disagreed, but this was not a good discussion to get involved in. I said nothing. There was a pause.

'You have been to many executions?' Samuel asked quietly.

'Young man, in my day, you could not avoid them,' I replied.

Filling their glasses once more, Phillip called the landlord to refill mine, at their expense.

'So, old man, tell us, who in "history" would you most like to meet?' asked James, trying to steer this social intercourse in a lighter direction, and putting his engaging smile to full effect.

'Jesus Christ,' I answered without hesitation.

'Oh! Very interesting, but for why?' inquired Phillip, revealing a hitherto concealed naivety.

'On the account that no man in history has ever inspired greater devotion or bloodshed,' I replied. 'That is a singular man, with a singular enigma, whom I should like to meet.'

'Very good,' retorted Phillip, clearly impressed.

There was a silent pause.

'The builder of that theatre,' said James, quietly.

Another pause and a slightly awkward one; this told me it was they who were now wary of me.

'I would like to meet Mr William Shakespeare,' he whispered, purposefully lowering his voice.

An acolyte of Thespis. Relief! I was now convinced these men were benign. His friends nodded approval at his choice, and then looked to me for my reaction.

'What would you like to know?' I asked, sitting back to rein in their intrigue with the slick experience of an old horseman.

The three men looked at me, their glasses frozen in silent suspension.

'You knew him?' whispered James. His eyes beamed a glow clearly betraying a love for my friend.

I nodded and took a sip from my freshly arrived brandy.

'Tell?' grinned Samuel.

I took another sip.

'Come on, tell,' said Phillip.

I placed my glass down and seductively stroked the rim. The tension in their smiles was truly a delight.

'We were born on the same day, in the same house; I was there at his death and at practically every event in between. I ate with him, drank with him and slept with him. No one, not even his beloved Anne, knew him better than I.'

There was total silence as they puzzled what question to ask next. James broke the silence, and grinned. 'By heavens, my friend, you have quite a story to tell. And, by the time this day is out, you are going to have told it.'

Before I could formulate any response he turned and called for a fresh bottle of Madeira, a bottle of brandy, some bread, fine-cured ham and three-dozen oysters.

And indeed, by the back of midnight, I had. And this is the story I told.

CHAPTER 2

Will and I were born on April 26, 1564, at the Arden family farm in Wilmcote. His mother was Mary Shakespeare, an Arden prior to marriage. She, with her husband John, had temporarily moved out of Stratford, due to an outbreak of plague. Because Will was their first child to survive birth, their caution was well placed. My mother, Perdita, also the Ardens' young cook, died pushing my frail body out of her own into the world. Desperately needing nourishment, I was in decline but Mary lost no time sending for me and subsequently placed me on her free breast. *Fratres in lacte*, John was heard to muse with a smile as Will and I relaxed in the security of Mary's milk. 'Brothers in milk'. And this was what Will called me in times of solitude and reflection.

My strength rapidly picked up in the following days and, after a few long weeks, the plague outbreak abated. My still-grieving father engaged a wet-nurse and the three of us went to live at the Stratford stables, where Father was employed as livery master. However, due to the expense and, I suspect, the quality of our dwelling, I was quickly weaned and the nurse released. Inevitably, my father found the responsibilities of fatherhood and the livery threatened to overcome him, but rescue came from his sister, Grace; bless her soul. She left a very comfortable position of housekeeper to a physician in Coventry and moved in with us.

From my earliest days I spent more time on a horse than on the ground. Father and Grace often placed me on a horse whilst going about their daily duties. If the back of a horse seems a bit of a precarious place to put a small baby, this was no ordinary horse. This was Heavens Gate, a six-year-old Percheron war-horse, originally from the stable of Lord Lucy. Not only had Heavens Gate been his personal mount for heavy armour, but a formidable challenger in the peacetime war sport of jousting, or tilting as it was more commonly known.

At eighteen hands, Heavens Gate had a back as wide as a banqueting table and withers like the buttress of a great abbey. He was as placid as a fireside dog and as strong as Atlas himself. He had been retired by His Lordship due to his 'ill-health'; locally, this was correctly known to be His Lordship's fear of tilting.

My father had bought Heavens Gate on behalf of the livery for the purpose of rescuing carts stuck in the mud; he never failed and the charge was a monstrous two shillings, payable in advance. However much the cart owner complained, my father always pointed out it was cheaper price to pay than a spoiled load. Most mornings I lay in a basket on Heavens Gate's back. If a horse whinnied, kicked or reared in the yard, Heavens Gate would turn his massive head and catch my eye, as if to say, 'You're safe with me'. Since I had no mother, and Heavens Gate was more often my baby maid, my affinity for Equus arrived as naturally as song to a young thrush.

The central aspect of Stratford life was Sunday and the accompanying religious observations. Attendance of the Protestant Church of England was, by the Crown and State, required of all of us. In Stratford, the old faith of Rome did still have some loyalty and many only paid lip service to the Crown's religious decrees. My late mother had been old faith but my father cared for neither. Since his employer was a strict observer of State edicts, there was no question of him, my aunt and me going in any other direction other than with the political flow. Without question we observed the new Mass and took communion. The Shakespeares, on the other hand, came from solid old-faith families and, though they did refuse communion, they found it hard to sidestep attendance.

The six years following Will's and my birth were surprisingly good to both our families. Outbreaks of plague were fortunately few, though one never knew quite when or where it might return. Stratford prospered. John Shakespeare, a glove-maker by trade, presided over his own exceptional business and, as a result, was invited to become an alderman of the town. This wealth was reflected in the fine furniture and wall hangings purchased by Mary to adorn their home in Henley Street.

My father and Grace turned the Ely Street livery into a model trade, carving out a fine reputation and significant income for its owner, Owen Trentham. Though my father was paid adequately for his position, it seemed to be the story of his life: fine at making money for others but no good at making it for himself.

The Shakespeares celebrated 1566 with the birth of a fine healthy brother for Will, whom they named Gilbert. The house was quite full for that christening and celebrations spilt out into the street back and front. Years later, when I was in my fifties, I used to reflect on this time, wondering if life was actually that good and why it suddenly all turned. However, the fleeting and fractured visions of sound and image that were my infantile memories, made me suspect they were only a series of moments, gloriously enhanced by my young years. As I grew older and understood more, I saw what was happening and acknowledged why.

The year after Gilbert was born, Mary took on a new maid, Christine Bodicome, from Plumtree near Nottingham. Whilst Mary only ever called her 'maid', we knew her simply as Bod. She seemed grown up to us but, in fact, she was a slip of a thing of nineteen. Her parents had died of plague in the year of our birth, and since then she had been in service to a Catholic family who had been fined an enormous sum by the Crown, forcing them to sell up their entire estate. This is all I know of the background of the exceptionally charming maid that was Bod. She had long black hair, green eyes and a smile that could melt the harshest frost, not to mention a touch that could soothe the wildest beast.

The first time I met her, Will and I were playing in the garden at Henley Street. The garden was a very pretty affair. Mary had it laid out with myriad flowers, herbs and light vegetables – a gentle mix of discovery, beauty and necessity. We, of course, had ignored the patches of beauty in preference to the area where there were three piles of composting garden cuttings and kitchen waste. The watery aspect of the older compost made a great malleable substance, which was excellent for building castles. It was on one of those occasions when the beautiful Bod turned up. Mary walked over carrying the fledgling Gilbert. 'William,' she called.

Will's lips pursed at the sound of 'William'. He ignored the call and we carried on playing in our pile of warm mud.

'This is Miss Bodicome. She is our new maid,' she said.

We took no notice. 'Oh dear, they are utterly filthy,' Mary muttered.

'It's healthy,' grinned Miss Bodicome.

'All very well but we have to attend an alderman's family meeting this afternoon,' Mary groaned.

'I'll wash them both,' said the new maid, turning to Mary optimistically.

'Good fortune to you. That's all I can say to that!'

Miss Bodicome came over and knelt down beside us. 'Hello,' she smiled.

As filthy as a pair of gutter-snipes, we both turned to her.

'Which one of you is Will?' she asked.

Will limply raised his hand.

'Very pleased to meet you, Will. Now, who's your fine friend?' she beamed.

'Tom,' he whispered.

'Hello, Tom,' she said sweetly.

When I looked at her I felt I had always known her, even though I was only three. She had that touch.

'I'm Miss Bodicombe. But you can call me Bod!' she said with a bright giggle, as if only *she* would allow us to call her by this nickname.

'What have you been doing?' she asked.

'Building a castle,' I said.

Bod looked down at our pile of compost studded with stones and surrounded by a moat with a bridge of box timber. Either side of the bridge were two quite definitive entrance towers made from discarded seedling pots.

'That is a magnificent castle. Did you build it for the fairies?'

We hadn't but it seemed like a good idea, so we nodded.

'Fairies like a flag on their castles.'

'We haven't got one,' said Will.

'To make a flag, you need a fairy to breathe on the castle,' Bod said, looking around as if to search for a fairy.

Totally believing that a fairy was what we needed, we both started to look around, too. When we looked back down to our castle, there was a tiny flag made of a straw and little square of fabric on the top of it.

'Fairy breath – wonderful stuff,' exclaimed Bod.

'Where's the fairy?' asked a very impressed Will.

Bod looked perplexed.

'Can't you see her?'

We both shook our heads.

'Oh?' said Bod.

A tad concerned for us, she put her finger out into the air and then reacted as if something, or someone, invisible landed upon it.

'They can't see you,' she whispered to the air just above her finger-tip.

Bod then proceeded to listen to the invisible fairy very carefully, nodding occasionally. In a state of hushed hypnosis, we watched the exact space where the invisible fairy was.

'She says that is a wonderful castle and she and her other fairies want to live in it.'

Will and I looked at each other, flattered that a fairy would want to live in our castle.

'Would that be all right?'

We both nodded hypnotically.

'The boys say that would be fine,' Bod told the still annoyingly invisible fairy.

'Why can't we see her?' whispered Will.

Bod became pensive. 'Fairies only reveal themselves when they want to,' she said.

'What's her name?' asked Will.

Bod listened to the fairy once more. 'She says it's Tatania, and she is the queen,' she whispered.

'I want to see her,' Will whispered back, intensely absorbed.

Bod listened to the fairy once more, and then watched as the invisible fairy flew away. She gazed into the distance for a few seconds, and then looked to us with the most beguiling smile.

'I think maybe if you cleaned up to go with your mother and father this afternoon, Tatania might reveal herself tomorrow.'

Desperate to see a real fairy, Will nodded. Taking each of us by the hand, Bod walked us effortlessly to the washroom.

While the Shakespeare family went to the family meeting of the aldermen, I found myself getting filthy again by helping muck out the twelve stables. One of my main tasks was ensuring the water trough was replenished. I would stand on the thick stone trough and pull up the great iron pump handle, but pushing it down took all my weight. The spout would disgorge probably half a pail of sparkling water. I did that about ten times, sometimes more if the horses had been thirsty. That was tough for a boy of three and I reckoned it was what was meant by 'pulling my weight'.

Closely followed by the dogs, little bob-tailed tikes we had for ratting, I would poke and prod things and flip buckets or empty sacks to disturb any hiding rats, which our lightning-fast little tikes would kill in a second. After that, I searched each horse stall for eggs left by chickens that wandered freely around the yard. I would take the eggs and put them in the water trough, any that floated I threw out because they were old and rotten.

This particular day was also my introduction to one of life's realities. Two men came in with a handcart, followed by three others: a clerk, a physician and the sheriff. On the back of the cart, there was the corpse of a man with an arrow through his neck.

'What happened?' asked Grace, running across the yard and crossing herself.

I stood atop the trough and stared at the bloody face of the man's head hanging over the edge of the cart. His mouth was open, thick with blood and spittle; his eyes were blank, white and rolled back in his head. There was a sack-cloth on the corpse but it was pulled back. When the sheriff saw me, he gesticulated to the clerk, who pulled the sackcloth back over the poor man's face.

'Accident at archery – Mr Stafford. God rest his soul,' said the sheriff to my father as Grace ushered me away.

That was one of the other jobs we often did at the livery, the moving of the dead, unless it was plague, in which case the most destitute owner of a cart suffered that one. Mr Stafford was a target-maker for the archery butts, and it would seem some idiot thought he was the target rather than the target-maker. In order that Her Majesty had a capable army to repel marauding French or Spaniards, archery practice was still required of every able male. Father did his practice regularly, but was careful. He said there were some right-blind loose-fingered idiots out there masquerading as marksman.

From the hay loft door of the stable, I watched father take poor Mr Stafford off in the direction of Clopton Bridge. That meant he had no kin and no money and the paupers pit just out of town was his lot. The whole scene impressed on me that, in real life, there probably weren't any fairies but they were nicer to think of rather than that dead man's face. If the archers wanted a marksman, they needed my aunt Grace. Many times I watched her with a slingshot strike down rooks from the eaves over the feed hods; she had a keen eye and a savage arm. With some spices and a mug of beer, she would pot-roast them a treat, too.

I don't know if it was intentional, but I seemed to spend my childhood with the Shakespeares at Henley Street. The Ely Street livery only ever meant things that had to be done; I actually have no recollection of ever playing there. I do, however, recall that my father, Grace and Mary Shakespeare made quite an effort to see that I spent time at Henley Street. Whatever the reality, it was a strange combination that suited well. At an early age, I understood the importance of work and paying your own way, but also I saw the importance of stopping now and then to absorb pleasure and let the soul regenerate.

The other great social occasion of Stratford was, of course, shopping. On a Friday, I used to accompany the Shakespeare family.

We were quite a smart little convoy, always in clean clothes. Mary walked proudly with Will in hand but with Bod, Gilbert and me leading the way as we meandered through the drains, mud, puddles, spittle and animal poop. The shopping was done in order: first dough for bread to bake at home, then vegetables and, finally, fish for the Friday supper. Despite there being no papacy any more, old habits die hard and most people still ate fish on Fridays.

Bod's arrival was quite an asset because Mary was very particular about the quality of the produce she bought. But not being of an even temperament, she could upset the merchants. The baker, however, was a little so and so, and pulled a stunt of thievery on certain customers of which Mary was one. She had never noticed what was going on, and though Will did, she would never listen to his protestations. Regardless, Bod was as sharp as a tack, and when Will told Bod what the baker, Mr Chandly, was up to, the smile of a most mischievous fairy appeared on her face. When we arrived at the shop, Bod was ready.

Mary asked for a five-pound lump of dough, which Mr Chandly gouged out of the large barrel of the prepared mix. He placed it on the scales and weighed it accurately in front of us. When weighed, he placed the lump on the counter and turned to get a handful of flour for rolling it into a clean round ball.

Mr Chandley's ruse went like this, 'How is Mr Shakespeare, mistress? Mistress Chandly loves her gloves, such a perfect fit,' he would ask over his shoulder in his smarmy way.

At this point a counter trapdoor would open and Mr Chandly's brat of a son would put up his little hand and swipe a chunk of the dough, maybe half a pound, back under the counter. In timing worthy of a street acrobat, Mr Chandly would quickly turn around, pat flour over the dough, roll it into a ball atop the trapdoor and thus disguise its existence.

Well, this day, as the door started to open, in the twinkling of an eye, Bod picked up Will and sat him on the troublesome trap door. There was a mighty squeal as the Chandly brat found his fingers caught, followed by a bump as he pulled them in, and then muffled whimpering. Mr Chandly snapped round and saw us all standing there smiling, as if butter would not melt in our mouths, and none more so than Will, who could barely contain himself. Mr Chandly smiled the obsequious smile of ignominious defeat.

'Fff … farthing today, Mistress Shakespeare,' he said, struggling to maintain his composure. That morning the word went around and Mary was given a good price for her purchases from then on.

When we got home to Henley Street that day, all the shopping was placed on the table in the kitchen and Mary turned to Bod.

'Well! Mr Chandly, the very idea! Maid, I'm obliged to your quick thinking and smart action,' she exclaimed.

'Tis your son to whom you are obliged,' said Bod. 'Young Will put me wise to the rotter's little game.' Bod gave Will a big smile and stroked his hair.

'That may be, but it's time to get these herrings salted and ready for Mr Shakespeare's supper,' said Mary.

I saw the instant flash of pain cross Will's face. For months he had tried to tell his mother she was being robbed and, even when he managed to thwart it, she still would not give him his due. Bod knew it, too, but did not let it sit. She ushered Will and I to the back of the kitchen to help stoke the fire. The approval of both his parents was the one thing that Will would desperately desire all his life but sadly, it was the one thing he would never get.

The following years of my childhood were, in many ways, the same as any other. Fractured recollections of people, family and dramatic events, marked by sounds and images the significance of which could not be accurately resolved in a child's mind. For a long time, I wondered if we were actually all one family, because some impressions were harder set than others. Bod was one who definitely imprinted herself on my memory. When later in life, I had an eye for a lady, the woman she had to measure up to was Bod.

There was another person who lit up our lives with a constant fountain of joy, love and life, and that was John Somerville, always known as Cousin Johnny. His wife, Beth, was Mary's first cousin. She, too, was perpetual fun, never ceasing her infectious giggle. She only ever saw good in anything or in any situation.

Will simply adored Johnny, and I remember one specific Christmas at Henley Street. We had all joined up for the day and

Grace had roasted a goose over the fire. There were all kinds of breads and other meats with stuffed parsnips. I had never seen such a feast.

Cousin Johnny arrived with Beth, crashing through the front door singing merrily as they staggered under the weight of a whole case of French wine and, making a really big sensation, a large bottle of Spanish brandy. No one dared ask where he came by such things but there was a lot of hushed appreciation and talk of 'disposing of the evidence'. The meal went late into the evening and Johnny became quite comically drunk. At one point, he stood up flat against the wall, and spinning round he wrapped himself in the hangings! Then, striding forward, declaring himself king, he pulled them off the wall. Everyone looked on in horror; Mary had only just bought them, but she so loved Johnny she just laughed, much to everyone's relief.

'I decree! King Johnny, the first and only, of England, do declare that before any subject fart, he must face his bottom in the direction of the Privy Council!' he declared. Then he bent over and broke wind with such a funny squeaking noise I thought we would never stop laughing.

'And, special sign posts revealing the correct direction will be posted the length of England.'

Everyone shook with laughter.

'All commoners will be obliged to donate to the Privy Council one-fifth of the contents of their own garden privy to be deposited at the front door of the council chamber each month! And at Christmas, in it!'

Will and I sat at Bod's feet mesmerised by the drunken performance. Mary was in hysterics as she cuddled Gilbert on her lap. Father sat by the fire with Will's father. They held manly fixed smiles, suppressing their nonetheless infected laughter. A well-quaffed Johnny, now in full flight, added to the wall hangings a chamber pot, which he picked up and placed on his head then marched up and down issuing his royal decrees.

'King Johnny declares he is in need of a wife to become his queen. All prospective suitors must be of unsound mind and body and have their chastity verified by papal inspection!' he spouted.

Bod could hardly contain herself. She laughed so much we thought she would burst her bladder not to mention her breasts wobbling on top of our heads. In whichever direction we looked, Will and I found a source of hysterics. John Shakespeare had the foresight to cover the windows and make sure that no one outside was seeing or hearing this seditious comedy. Suddenly, Johnny leapt onto the table and pointed at all of us.

'There are spies in the court of King Johnny!' he declared.

Johnny looked around carefully, his comical squint scrutinising everyone in the room. We squirmed and giggled in the apprehension of what outrageous thing he was going to do next.

In the silent tension of this moment, a small mouse took its chance to leap onto the table and eat a piece of forgotten bread. Instantly, Johnny and the mouse caught sight each other. They froze!

'An assassin!' he screamed. 'Guards seize that mouse!'

The mouse ran and Johnny stood up sharply. He cracked his head on the low beams, the chamber pot shattered and Johnny collapsed on the table.

Everyone was in hysterics. Johnny's hand went up, signalling for silence.

'I will now write a poem, entitled The Mouse that Ended the Reign of King Johnny,' he slurred, and then fell asleep, snoring loudly.

The men helped put Johnny to bed, and then my father and Grace took me back to Ely Street. Outside, and to our great surprise, there was brilliant-white, thick fresh snow covering the ground. We had all been so taken up with Johnny's entertainment we had not even noticed it fall. As I was carried home looking over Father's shoulder, I watched the footprints they made, leaving a line all the way from the Henley Street front door. It felt like a line of attachment that only I could see and was never going to break. It was one of those Christmases that stay in the mind forever; the one that I always hoped the next one would be like. Was it different? Or was I just enjoying the freshness of life for the first time? These years were good to all of us; John's glove trade went from strength to strength, there was money, there was food, there was wine, cheer, love and, blessed of all, another baby arrived in the Shakespeare house, little Joan.

CHAPTER 3

One summer day in 1569 there was quite a fuss; some horses entered the yard – three of the finest I had seen in a while. Not tall but well groomed with cut tails, plaited manes and shiny coats. Sitting atop the middle horse was a fine gentleman of a smart stature. He wore a hat inserted with three colourful bird feathers, the finest clothes of wool with silk slashing and shiny leather riding britches. This was Sir Thomas – Lord Lucy – and, with his lordly authority, he scrutinised the yard. Lord Lucy and his men dismounted and they strode towards three of Father's men, who were washing out the dung cart.

'You, you and you,' shouted Lord Lucy pointing at them.

'Have you ever fallen foul of Her Majesty's law?' he demanded. The men looked awkward and shook their heads.

'No, they have not, My Lord,' said my father, approaching from behind.

Lord Lucy turned sharply on his heel. 'You Wickham?'

'Yes, My Lord, and if you have need of them, these men are honest as the day is long.'

'I do not need them, Wickham; however, Her Majesty does. The filthy Scots are plotting rebellion and our civilisation is under mortal threat. I need a thousand men at arms to put at Her Majesty's disposal.'

'I will gladly serve Her Majesty.'

'Your loyalty is duly noted, Wickham. However, you will best serve queen and state in your current position.'

Lord Lucy relaxed and approached my father quite closely. I hung on to my father's leg and he reassured me with a gentle stroke of my head. Lord Lucy dropped his voice and spoke to my father in a considered timbre, loosely masking his trust with fear.

'I need to know all movements, what horses go out, for how long and with whom. I need to know if anyone requests any form of cartage. And, I certainly need to know if any folk unknown in the locality turn up on tired horses, looking for rest and feed.'

Lord Lucy paused, sniffed the air and then looked directly into my father's eye.

'Consider it done, My Lord,' replied my father.

'Now, loyal Wickham,' said Lord Lucy, brightening up. In a grip of unspoken ownership, he placed his hand on Father's shoulder and gently squeezed.

'Ask those three men to report to the River Butts for archery practice today at three o'clock. After practice they will stay with me in Her Majesty's service till I discharge them.'

With that, he made a mount-up signal, prompting his men to follow, and, with a jangle and clatter, they swept out of the livery. My father sighed as he listened to them gallop off down Ely Street. He was now going to be short of much-needed labour, and the worst part was for how long?

After the men had finished washing out the dung tup, Father gave them three pennies each and sent them on their way. As it turned out, my father lost his labourers till Christmas. Cleaning the stables became almost farcical as the only available men were such an advanced age that they could neither see nor hear further than the length of their own arms, let alone lift a loaded shovel. However, they were plentiful and on reduced pay, so my father was able to see the daily work done and balance his books.

As they bumped into each other and constantly lost their bearings, it was very funny to watch these doddery old men moving dung and feed across the yard. Grace used to shout her head off at them to absolutely no avail. She had to constantly run after them and physically point them in the right direction. In the end, even Grace afforded herself a giggle.

Lord Lucy, however, failed to raise the thousand men he had bragged about; it was more like 600 or so we were told. Nevertheless, bitten by the gripe of this shortfall in numbers, he trained them up and worked them hard, patrolling the shire at all times and in all weather. They became quite grumpy and at times quite scary, stopping and interrogating all unknown folk going about their business. The intensity of the interrogations was very much based on the social standing of the person they stopped – a quick tug of the hat for high-status individuals, to a self-righteous royalty-inspired bashing for any poor vagabond unfortunate enough to be spotted.

Father kept Lord Lucy informed about horse movements as parsimoniously as he could. It has to be remembered that, as the hub of Stratford, Father and Grace pretty much knew who was moving what where, at any time. Our knowledge of the comings and goings of Stratford business was as total as it was extensive and Father's boss, Owen Trentham, knew this. However, as a pragmatist, Trentham realised that the authority of Lord Lucy was formidable and thus he lay as low as he could, letting Father take the driver's seat.

In November, all hell broke loose. Rebels were reported to be moving south and Her Majesty's army was moving north. It looked very much as if Stratford might well be a possible point of engagement. Rumours, conjecture and theories danced around like the sparks from a smithy's fire. Various known sympathisers vanished and other fence-sitters also quietly dissolved into the hedgerows.

Father, having sent the daily note of horse movements to Lord Lucy, was with Grace booking in the daily fees for the clerk when John Shakespeare came rushing into the tack-room.

'Jack, don't like the news. I want to get Mary and the children to my brother in Snitterfield for safe-keeping. I need cartage and horses,' he demanded breathlessly.

'Best calm, John. Lord Lucy is watching every movement like a hungry hawk,' said my father without looking up and placing coin in a neat pile.

'Are you not concerned for Grace and Tom's safety?' asked John.

My father said nothing and, massaging his lips with his tongue, focused his concentration on his limited writing ability. He finished entering the sums in the ledger and sprinkled some powder over to blot the ink. Then, after blowing away the residue, he closed the ledger. Grace placed the piles of coin in the strong box and locked it. Father looked up at John.

'Good morning to you, John,' he said.

'Sorry... yes ... good morning to you too, Jack,' John stammered.

My father stood up. 'What news has got you in this flurry, John?' he said, knowing full well what was going on.

'Rebels have amassed a huge army,' said John. 'They have taken Durham, celebrated Catholic Mass in the cathedral and are marching south, and royal troops are moving north as I speak.'

'And what be your allegiances, John?' my father whispered under his breath.

There was a pause.

'Your queen, my queen,' he whispered back curtly.

My father cleared his throat and changed his tone. 'The only cartage I can let you have is Heavens Gate and the dung cart. Everything else, I have to account for to His Lordship.'

'Well, that would be awkward, so it'll have to do,' said John.

'You will have to assist. We are currently very short of labour,' said Grace.

'What fee?' asked John.

My father looked at John for a moment and then, putting the ledger away, spoke. 'We'll carry the fee, but I would like you to take Grace and Tom with you.'

'So you, too, think this is serious?' said John.

'Oh yes, John, I certainly do. Rumour is, Queen of Scots is held in Coventry!' said my father, reaching for Heavens Gate's halter.

'How do you know that?'

My father looked at John and said nothing. Grace looked to John Shakespeare.

'This is a livery, John. Most folk on the move will pass through here,' she said.

'You think we could be overrun?' whispered John nervously.

'Who knows, but either way, John, there will be a lot of ...' My father paused, to choose his words with care, '... catch-up, settling of scores and taking advantage. Lie low, keep the nose clean and wait for the storm to pass, the only option. What do you think, Grace?'

'Always a careful one, my brother. I'd take heed, Mr Shakespeare,' she said quietly.

'I am going to stay,' whispered John, 'but I'd like my family to go.'

'Wise decision. In Lord Lucy's eyes, a fleeing man is a guilty man,' said Father.

There was an awkward pause and nothing was said.

'Right then. Let's get this tup hooked up,' replied John, resigned to the situation.

'I'll put some things together for the journey,' said Grace, and she climbed the stairs to our living quarters.

It did not take long, thankfully. The tup was washed out and, with a liberal distribution of straw, it was quite comfortable – just a little strong on the nose. John put me up on the cart and I sat watching as a few people came and went, bringing and taking horses. There was clearly a tension in the air. At one point, everyone froze as one of Lord Lucy's now-infamous patrols clattered past the gate.

Grace came out with bundles of clothes wrapped in some bedding and pushed them into the back of the cart to form a bolster. She went away and returned with a large basket of bread, cheese, some apples and several flasks of mead. It was quite a weight and John had to help her get it on to the cart. It was starting to get cold and Grace put a sheepskin around my feet and then climbed up and settled into the driver's seat.

'Stay calm, stay wise, and say little!' she said to Father, who tweaked her hand and then pushed a hard wood club beneath her feet. With a flick of the reins the cart rolled.

We stopped at Henley Street where Will cuddled up beside me whilst Bod made herself comfy with Gilbert and baby Joan. Mary climbed up and John loaded the last of the supplies. He kissed Mary, nervously touched his children's heads and once more Grace flicked the reins. We took a detour because my father had given Grace instructions as to where Lord Lucy had placed his patrols. Due to the current military activity, they were even more unforgiving.

It was a twelve-mile journey and we had gone just six short miles when a man working his paddock dropped his plough and ran out to wave us down.

'I wondered where thee was headed?'

'Too full for thee,' said Grace, pulling up as Bod quietly picked up the club.

'Simon Steedon,' he said, and put out his hand in greeting.

Gripping little Joan, Mary leant out to take his hand. 'Mary Shakespeare,' she said.

'Thee an Arden? Look like an Arden to me.'

'By birth I am,' she said as she shook his hand.

'Can always tell. Then I'll advise thee if you tell me where thee are headed.'

'Snitterfield. What advice would you give?'

'Thought as much. It's maybe not far but best stay in my barn tonight. There is men on the road making mischief with all who pass, foul drunken lot they are, claiming queen's authority from Lord Dudley. Little more than ruffians, if you ask me.'

Will's mother bid thanks to Mr Steedon and introduced us all. Taking Heavens Gate by the bridle, Mr Steedon led us a quarter of a mile down the road to his farm where he showed us into his barn. Steedon lead the tup directly into the barn and we all climbed down. By the time we had settled Heavens Gate, unloaded the cart and made up beds, it was dark. Grace took a bag of feed and made up a meal for our ever-faithful warrior. Bod laid out shares of bread, cheese, mead and half an apple for each of us; Mary offered some to Mr Steedon but he declined.

'I bid thee not light a candle, can't afford to lose the winter's feed, or the barn for that matter,' said Mr Steedon, the moonlight shining off his bald pate.

Mary reassured him we would not and with that he bid us goodnight. He closed the great barn doors, which released an ominous boom and scattered a cloud of squeaking bats, causing Will to flinch. Squashed between the bottoms of Bod and Grace, I lay in the straw smelling the aroma of old hay and droppings. Looking up, and gently moved by swinging tree branches outside, little beams of moonlight flickered through gaps in the roof. They momentarily illuminated rats as they scurried along the great wooden trusses. There were repetitive beats of air around our heads from bat wings, as they probed us with swoops of ever-decreasing circles. Will was uneasy. He did not like this place, and started to whine a little.

'William, please don't,' sighed Mary.

Will started to cry. 'It's scary in here. I can't sleep.'

Bod gently turned over and stroked his head. 'We have to stay quiet because Mabily needs to hear our breath to find us.'

'Who?' he snuffled.

'A special fairy queen, called Mabily.'

'Queen Mab ...?' whined Will.

'Mabily. She is a very special fairy, Will.'

'Why is she special?' he whispered, now soothed at the idea of a special fairy.

'Because ... she is no bigger than the agate-stone on your father's finger.'

'Does she fly?'

'She rides in a carriage. It is an empty hazelnut, its wheels with spokes made of spinner's legs. Her driver is a small grey-coated gnat and in this she gallops across the night to sprinkle sleep on young boys.'

'Why?' whispered Will, caressed by the flow of ethereal images from Bod's lips.

'So they can dream of love, of course,' she whispered.

Bod kissed Will gently and he turned over and fell asleep.

'Bod, what would we be without you?' said Mary, who sat upright wrapped in a thick blanket, feeding Joan. Soon Queen Mabily found us all.

Mr Steedon opened the great barn doors at first light and a massive shaft of light crashed on to my face waking me like a bucket of cold water. It woke us all.

'Thee should move. Those men got drunk as lords last night,' Mr Steedon said, as we all stirred. 'I have word from my milking maid they are all sleeping in the hedge.'

He started to get the harness sorted for Heavens Gate.

'Thee want to be away afore they thugs awake. Dunno what be worse – thugs with drink in them or thugs with the hoof mark of drink departed,' he said.

In no time we were loaded up and on our way. It was a damp day with gathering rain clouds. Grace took the reins whilst Mary fed Joan, and Bod organised feeds for the rest of us. Will and I sat on the back of the cart with our legs dangling off the edge. Soon enough we passed where one of the local militia had had their turnpike.

We heard them before anything – the snoring! Giggling infectiously, Will and I leapt up and scrambled to the front of the cart and hung on to Grace. There were about six men in various prostrate positions around the hedgerow, all snoring very loudly. Their fire had died out and their weapons lay around the road gathering rust in the morning dew. We slowly moved past, hoping they would not stir and indeed they did not, save one, who was in the paddock urinating the long night's bladder full of drink. He looked over his shoulder and tried to issue his authority whilst still peeing.

'Stop, in the name of Her Majesty,' he cried but still the urine flowed.

Bod, Mary, Will and I could not stop giggling. Dear old Grace stared blandly down the road keeping us on the straight and narrow.

'Stop,' he cried again, and then foolishly tried to stop peeing and run after us. It was no good and in running, he dropped his breeches and fell flat on his face in the paddock. His friends snored on and Bod and Mary practically wet themselves with laughter.

Breaking into a graceful trot, Heavens Gate soon put a healthy distance between the ruffians and us. The clouds broke and for the rest of the journey it rained. The road became sticky with mud and the going was slow. Several times we had to dismount and wait whilst Bod and Grace took a length of wood and levered the cart out of a deep claggy rut. Though wet and unpleasant, the advantage was that any ad hoc drunken militia stayed under cover and the road was clear of mischief.

CHAPTER 4

We finally arrived at Snitterfield by midday, somewhat wet through, where Will's Uncle Henry came out to meet us.

Will's Uncle Henry was very different to his brother. Where John was always serious, Henry had a smile permanently plastered to his face, a self-satisfied grin somewhere between conviviality and madness.

He had a modest but comfortable house. It was old, with a roof of thatched wheat straw, a large cobbled yard bordered on two sides by heavy stone animal stalls housing his beloved pigs. The pigs made a noise of constant squealing that was only surpassed in annoyance by their repugnant smell. I thought horse manure was bad but these pigs! Uncle Henry loved them and had names for every single one. In fact, he seemed to get on better with pigs than people. However, he had no qualms when it came to slaughtering them; his love of coin was as great as his brother's.

'To what do I owe this visit,' asked Henry, cordially.

'There is talk of rebels from the north colliding with Her Majesty's men near Stratford,' said Mary, as Bod helped her dismount.

'Yes, I heard. Who are the rebels? French, Scottish or Spanish? Either way, all come to force that Pope on Her Majesty.'

Mary said nothing.

'Which way is brother leaning these days,' Henry said slowly and quietly.

'I, like my husband – your brother – are devoted loyal subjects of Her Majesty Queen Elizabeth. That is all I have to say on the matter, brother-in-law,' Mary said quite emphatically.

There was another tense silence and then Henry released the tension with a snort and spat a large viscous lump on to the cobbles.

'So brother wants family out of the cut and thrust of battle!' laughed Henry.

'Just for a week or two till things settle down,' said Mary, visibly cringing at the phlegm deposited on the ground by her kin.

'Better come in then,' he replied.

We followed Henry inside the house and trudged up the rickety wooden stairs as he led us to where we assumed we would bed down.

'How is dear John? Haven't seen him in such a long time. When did I see him last?' Henry mused gaily.

'When he lent you ten shillings,' replied Mary dryly.

'Do I owe brother? Surely not,' he laughed.

'Talking of money, I will need sixpence a week lodging for each of you.'

I thought he was joking but he wasn't.

'I'll give you tuppence for each of us and you had better feed us well,' muttered Mary through gritted teeth.

Henry laughed heartily. 'Tuppence it is! But you get the harvesters quarters for that,' and he took us into the attic under the eves. It was all open and cold. However, there were plenty of bags of bedding straw and in no time Bod, Grace and Mary had made one big cosy bed into which we could all snuggle up and keep warm.

At the back of the farm there was the most delightful orchard that went up a small south-facing slope. The weather cleared in the late afternoon and we hung our damp clothes to dry in the last rays of sun that penetrated the dark leafless branches of the cherry trees. Bod took out a book and started to read as Will cuddled up to her. I could see her teaching him some words. Mary jiggled Gilbert, fed Joan and, looking in the direction of Coventry, her lips pattered in silent rhythm with her rosary as it flicked through her fingers.

I wandered around the orchard with Grace, picking up any dry bits of wood for kindling. Grace was ever practical with an innate nose

28

for survival. Soon she was wandering about the property looking for anything that may sustain us. In the eventuality, this was two turnips the pigs had failed to get, a bag full of field mushrooms and a large wedge of kale. In the house Henry sat with his feet up in front of the most measly fire. Grace and I entered with our bundles of wood, pushed it all into the fireplace and pretty soon it was roaring.

Henry was pleasantly surprised. He stood up and, with a giggle, warmed his hands. 'What's for supper?' he whispered gleefully.

Grace rolled her eyes, went outside and then returned with our basket of findings and placed them on the table.

'Golly,' smiled Henry, 'Looks like I might get a hot meal tonight?' he grinned.

'What do you eat normally?' grumbled Grace.

Henry laughed, pointing to a trencher with some stale bread and rotten cheese.

'Unless I've killed a pig, that's it,' he said, still laughing.

'Do you have any meat?' asked Grace with a tone of sardonic optimism.

Henry went to the bare cold-room and retrieved a sack, which he put on the table. He pointed to it ominously. Grace approached the sack with caution and went to open it.

'Boo!' shouted Henry, giving Grace quite a start.

I thought it was very funny but Grace just rolled her eyes as she retrieved from the sack a large and somewhat aged leg of mutton. Pushing her nose to it, she ascertained that, although there was a bit of a smell, it was not going to make us ill.

'You have a pottage pot?' she wondered out loud.

Henry comically ducked under the table and came up with a great big iron vessel, which he banged hard on the table, giving Grace another start and himself another giggle.

Grace snatched it and, sniffing it, gave it a good inspection.

'I never use it. Food always tastes of metal,' said Henry.

'Never cured it,' said Grace.

'Didn't know it was ill?' said Henry, and then laughed hysterically.

Grace rolled her eyes once more.

'Any beef fat?'

'Now as it happens I swapped a pair of broken cart wheels for a bucket of beef tallow and a sack of sprouting only two days ago.'

Henry danced off into his cold-room again and came back with a bucket of beef fat, and then still giggling, he danced off once more to return with a bag of brussel sprouts.

'Go on, cure the pot and make a pottage,' grinned Henry.

I looked to Grace and laughed but she just rolled her eyes. Taking a wooden spoon, she dug out a large wedge of beef fat and ran it all around the inside of the iron pot; she did another and another till the pot was well lined. She then took the well-greased pot and laid it in the fire on its side and with a stick she pushed embers all around it.

'Pottage!' squeaked Henry, nudging me.

At that moment, Mary came in with Joan, Gilbert, Will and Bod. Mary looked at the pot being cured in the fire.

'Oh Grace, are you going to make a pottage.'

'Try me best, mum.'

'Pottage, pottage, pottage,' squeaked Henry, dancing around in a circle.

'Maid, can you get the flour from the cart and make some bread,' said Mary.

'Yes, mum,' replied Bod and bobbing a curtsy she went out into the twilight.

Grace turned the pot around in the fire as the beef tallow smoked and glazed the inside giving it a good seal. She then casually went to the table, took the mutton leg in one hand and, with the other, deftly pulled out a long, thin and very sharp knife from under her pinny. It fair surprised Mary.

'Do you always carry that?' asked Mary, curiously.

'Yes, mum,' replied Grace, matter of fact, as she sliced the meat off the hock with the efficiency of a battlefield surgeon. Bod came back in with the flour sack, which she bumped onto the table. When the bone was cleared of meat, Grace took the axe from the wood fire and with one scary swipe she struck the bone, effortlessly severing it in two. She pushed the two bones into the pot, which was still on its side and pushing the embers up around it she left the bones to roast.

'Well?' Grace asked, looking to Henry.

'Well what?' he chuckled nervously.

'Water, Henry. Where's the well?' said Mary.

Henry thought this was hysterically funny and once more rolled back laughing.

'Well what, what well, there well, where well, what!' he laughed pointing to the corner of the kitchen.

Will and I looked up from under the table to the rollicking Henry, both of us having a good giggle at this eccentric relative.

Grace took a bucket to the well whilst Henry, still tears of laughter in his eyes, produced some lamp bowls and, with the beef tallow as fuel, organised some light around the night-fallen kitchen.

The women had everything organised. Grace had a smoked mutton, mushroom and sprout pottage under way whilst Bod kneaded great lumps of dough on the table and placed them under cloth near the fire for curing. Mary sat in the corner, close to the fire, nursing Gilbert while Joan sucked contentedly at her mother's breast. Bod asked Will and I to make bun-sized pieces from the dough to bake. Grace and Bod pulled all the rubbish out of the bread oven – it had not been used in a while. They shovelled loads of embers into it and soon it was hot enough to bake the buns and bread.

It was a pleasant evening as we sat around Henry's big, rough oak table. Tired and exhausted we dipped Bod's fresh, crispy bread into our bowls of steaming mutton, mushroom and turnip pottage bobbing with sprouts. There was no talk at all – even the giggly Henry was silent. The only noise to punctuate the air was the crackling fire and the rhythmic slurping. When we were all fed, everyone sat back bloated by the hot food. The silence was broken by Henry.

'Do you think there will be a blood-soaked reckoning in these parts?'

Mary said nothing but just gave a disapproving look in our direction. Will and I looked to each other. We knew these were things that grown-ups would not discuss in front of us. Henry rose from his chair, went to the shelf and pulled a book from it. Handing the book to Bod, he asked her to read from it.

'The one thing that brings me sadness is never having learnt to read like my dear industrious brother,' he said sitting down and becoming a shade melancholic.

Bod looked at the book. It was a Bible and the Gospel of Luke.

'Please read for me,' asked Henry gently.

So with her mellifluous voice, Bod read the scripture and caressed the grown-ups towards slumber. Grace, Henry and Mary soon fell sound asleep in their chairs. Bod put down the Bible and, quietly moving over to Mary, she picked up Joan, cuddling her in one arm. She put her other hand out for Gilbert and he put a hand out for Will and then Will for me. Our little sleepy train wended its way up the rickety stairs to the bed we had made earlier. I cuddled down next to Will under the blankets; it was a little chilly on the straw-filled bags but we moved close and warmed up. Bod settled Gilbert and Joan just behind Will for warmth, and then she went back downstairs to wake the grown-ups and get them to bed.

'Do you think there will be a battle?' whispered Will, looking me straight in the eye, nose to nose.

'If there is, Father says it could be a shambles,' I said.

'Blood everywhere, all over the fields, roads and lanes, running in the gutters, rivers of blood,' mused Will.

'Just like the shambles in Bull Street?' I asked.

'Mmmm, but people, not sheep and cattle. Do you think we will ever go home,' Will wondered aloud.

'Gosh,' I whispered.

'They might burn Stratford and execute everyone, our fathers too,' mused Will mischievously.

'Do you really think?' I said, a little scared.

We heard the grown-ups creaking their sleepy way up the stairs.

'Shhh,' said Will.

Pretty soon I had the large warm bottom of Grace on one side of me and Mary and Bod on the other side of Will. Will and I struggled to sleep amid the snoring and farting of our nearest and dearest. All I could think of were rivers of blood flowing down the streets of Stratford, the fires and the executions by rampaging soldiers. I fell asleep praying my dear father would be spared. The night was a scattering of myriad dark whispers and unfamiliar noises that preyed on my imagination without mercy. So when I heard the first birdsong of daybreak, I was tired but very relieved.

I pulled myself out of my bed of flesh and straw and tip-toed across to the stairs.

'Tom!' Will whispered his face peering up over Grace's bottom.

'What?' I replied.

'Wait for me.'

In our bare feet, we tip-toed down the stairs towards the kitchen. As we got closer we heard shouts and screams coming from the yard.

'What's that,' I asked, more than a little scared.

There were more shouts, sounds of wrenching rope sinews and screams of a horrible high-pitched nature.

'Soldiers?' gasped Will, as we ventured into the kitchen. Now the sounds were not only definite but horribly violent, indescribable and right outside the door! Will went to open the door but I stopped him.

'If they see us, we may be executed too,' I said, quivering and forcing back tears of fear.

Will looked at me and, though he hid it well, I knew he was frightened. We stood at the door and taking a firm hold, we gently pushed it open a tiny amount. On the shiny cobbles outside all we saw was a river of thick and glistening blood. We pulled the door shut sharply! There were more shouts and screams!

'They are here! They are killing everyone!' I croaked.

'It's a shambles!' cried Will.

Will looked at me as scared as I was. Suddenly the door burst open! We fell back on the floor and looking up we were confronted by the terrifying view of a naked man covered in blood. He moved towards us with the biggest, sharpest knife I had ever seen!

Will and I screamed at the top of our voices and raced back up the stairs straight into the arms of Grace. We were hysterical but she dropped to her knees and held us tight.

'Don't kill us, don't kill us!' we cried.

There was sudden raucous laughter.

'Shhh, no one's going to kill you,' giggled Grace.

Grace held us tight. She seemed to shoo the man away with comparative ease. When we heard the door bang shut, we thought it may be safe enough to look.

'What's wrong?' said Grace.

'Soldiers are executing everyone outside,' I uttered, still shaking with fear.

'What nonsense. It's Uncle Henry. He's killing the pigs.'

Will and I looked at each other with a mixture of abject relief and utter stupidity. We wiped our tears as Grace took us to the front door. Opening it she revealed quite a display of the temporary shambles. There was blood everywhere; four pigs having already been slaughtered were on a bench being cut up by some men. Four other pigs were hauled up in the air by their hind legs across a large A-frame gibbet. The hanging pigs squirmed and squealed at the end of their ropes as Uncle Henry, wearing only a loin cloth and covered in blood, sharpened his knife. Seeing Grace, Will and I standing at the door, he laughed heartily.

'Didn't mean to frighten you. Looking for a whet stone!' he shouted in the most non-reassuring act of reassurance.

'Killing now!' he called to his men.

With a great flourish of speed and accuracy he moved from dangling pig to dangling pig, cutting their throats; blood spurted in his face and then spilt everywhere, running in rivulets across the yard. The pigs soon stopped struggling and hung silent as their life drained out of them into a pail held by one of the men. Henry went to the third pig along, which was a boar, cut off its balls and threw them to his dogs which fought savagely over them.

'Great horse!' Henry shouted to Grace, pointing to Heavens Gate whose yoke was tied to the rope holding up the four pigs dangling from the gibbet.

'Pulls up four at once, no bother! Ha! I'll buy him from you!'

'Not for sale,' stated Grace.

'Fresh pork tonight?' asked Mary, coming to the door.

'No!' said Henry

'No?' exclaimed Mary.

'This all sold. Cash for my purse, not food for thee's bellies,' he replied.

Mary was furious.

'Well return the ten shillings you owe your brother,' she spat back at him and ushered Grace and I back inside. Will stayed, he sat on the doorstep stroking his mouth and watching the bloody carve for the next two hours. Sadly, the next time I saw a scene like that it was not pigs at the end of the ropes.

The weather improved and, before long, the rumours of rebellion abated, giving rise to John sending word that it was safe to return to Stratford. Leaving was sad. I was enjoying this sojourn with their eccentric relative. Also, encouraged by Grace, Bod really pressed into me with the reading and I had learnt quite a lot.

The reality of the rebellion was that as soon as the word of a royal army on the move was out, all the rebels took fright and vanished. Because there was not so much urgency, we chose a good warm day with dry roads for the journey back to Stratford and it was covered in little more than half a day, as opposed to the two days it took getting there.

John greeted Mary warmly. Plucking her off the cart like a precious fruit, he pressed his lips to hers, sucking the juice from her lips.

'How is the town?' Mary asked, struggling for breath from the shower of kisses.

'All is good, all is good,' said John.

'Did the army come to Stratford?' asked Will.

'No, my son! The word of Her Majesty's fury was enough to scare the rebels back into the holes from whence they came,' he said stroking Will's hair.

John whispered confidentially to Mary and Grace. 'The vicar, curate and schoolmaster are nowhere to be seen. Corporation had a meeting to declare them '*fugitivus*'.

'Best they stay that way for Lord Lucy will see their heads on a pike.'

After the cart was unloaded, Grace drove us back to the livery, where my father was glad to see us. Running the livery, under threat of military action and the stress of rumour and counter-rumour, had been very hard indeed.

CHAPTER 5

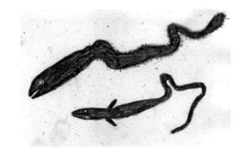

With Christmas approaching, everyone was pleased that things settled down and Father was more than relieved to get his workmen back. Once more the weather was getting cold, but unbeknownst to me, Father had struck a bargain with the Shakespeares. When I woke this one morning, instead of chores around the stables, I was taken by Grace to Henley Street. There, two days a week, in the parlour before a warm fire, I was, with Will, taught to read and write by the ever-loving Bod.

What a teacher she was. As my years went by, whenever I came across a word I found difficult, her soft words would echo in my memory helping me break it down so I could read and understand it. I never knew much about her background or where she came from, other than it was the forest of Arden and a Catholic family who lost everything that she worked for. I never learnt their name either. Mary knew her from way back, but kept that knowledge to herself. On occasion I would see Mary and Bod talk in the candid whispers of family intimacy, which has to be said was strange for one who only ever referred to her as 'Maid'.

My first day of tutelage was wonderful since it was so cold outside. The idea of being inside all day with dry feet could not have been better. Will's reading was going well but, thankfully, for my own selfishness, I was better at writing. I liked the movement of the chalk over the board and the shapes it made. My reading was slower since I had little interest in the content. I did, nonetheless, particularly like writing numbers; their shapes were satisfying and their comprehension was immediate.

Teaching us two small boys in the parlour was quite hard for Bod, since the house was a hive of activity. With the workshop at the end of the house, there were many comings and goings, noises of doors, hammering and shouting of instructions. When we became frustrated with the fractured progress of our learning, Bod's patience with us was enchanting. She convinced us that she had her fairies from the forest of Arden who, at her behest, would breathe the soft breath of patience into our ears.

One day there was an extra loud bang and a crash as three men came in the front door, evidently quite drunk. They were greeted warmly by John, who came out of his workshop and ushered them around to the correct entrance. The disturbance pulled Will to his feet and he ran out, intrigued to see who brought such cheer to his father's voice. I was not far behind, but a little reluctant as I was the receiver of educational charity.

Mary came into the corridor and stood silently with a suspicious look on her face. Bod caught up and stood patiently behind us till, purposely avoiding Mary's eye, John shut the door.

'Bludgers, plague on them,' Mary muttered and went back to the kitchen.

'Children?'

'What's a bludger?' asked Will, his eyes fixed on the workshop door.

'Not your business and, please, was it wrong to run out of class?'

Turning around we saw Bod's soft unfailing smile and hypnotic green eyes framed by her long dark hair. We melted like calm notes of music and guilt was upon us. A meek apology followed and we were taken back to the parlour.

Mary was never still; she had the gardeners to deal with outside and her kitchen maid inside. Also, Mary had a particular habit of never being satisfied with the position of furniture. If a new piece was acquired, all other furniture had to be relocated to find the best place for the new piece. If new furniture was not bought, shifting pieces could be done just on a whim. Either way, the result was much scraping, banging and thumping around rooms as the heavy elm furniture was moved.

It was times like this that Will would become particularly irritated and Bod would have to invoke the fairies. The strange thing was that Will could do writing exercises in any amount of disturbing noises and his hand was quite eloquent, too. His reading exercises, however, were different. He insisted on silence, as if a special thing was happening and he did not want to lose one moment.

I longed to know more about Bod's life and, one afternoon, she revealed a bit of it, accidentally. After quite a long morning of writing, we were tired. Will had four days tutelage but, because I was only there two days, those two days were busier, as Bod tried to cram in as much as she could for my benefit. There was a little bit more learning she wanted us to do before she finished. Even the fairies' breathing in our ears was not having much effect as we fidgeted and squirmed with word overload. Will was particularly out of sorts because he knew I was the reason for the extra work.

'Do this one last task for me and I will play you music taught to me by my favourite fairies,' she pleaded, her sweet smile now put to its greatest test.

'Who are your favourite fairies?' asked Will.

The sadness of melancholia descended over her.

'Cobweb and Pease-blossom,' she uttered so quietly, as if remembering someone of great affection long since lost.

Bod's revelation of vulnerability suddenly calmed our disparate tempers and we sat down, picked up our chalk-boards and went through the exercise with solemn perfection.

'Well done. Thank you boys,' she said, pushing back tears.

'Will you play the song for us now?' whispered Will.

Bod stood up with a rapidly snatched smile and brushed chalk dust from her hands.

'A promise is a promise and one from a fairy is a very important one, but you must wait here,' she said.

Bod left the parlour and went into the garden at the back of the house.

We waited and shortly we heard the sweetest notes coming from a small recorder. We could not wait in the parlour; it was too beautiful and beguiling. We rushed into the garden and there, under the rose arbour in the failing light, sat Bod playing the recorder. It was such a gentle sound that we were stopped dead in our steps. We crept quietly up and sat down beside her. She stopped playing and, with her voice carrying the melody she had played, she sang a heart-wrenching song about a blind boy. We sat spellbound with tears rolling down our cheeks till she stopped. There was absolute silence.

'They weren't really called Cobweb and Pease-blossom, were they?' asked Will.

'No William, they weren't,' said Bod, catching her tears.

'What were their real names?'

'Christopher and Sebastian.'

'Who were they?'

'Fine men, whom I love and I miss desperately.'

Bod stared ahead for a moment.

'Sorry,' she stuttered in a tear-filled whisper. Struggling to maintain her composure, she rushed inside.

I noticed Will look to the upstairs window. I looked, too. Mary was standing at the window looking down upon us. She, too, wiped tears from her eyes.

'Tom,' said John quietly.

I turned. Will's father was standing in the garden. 'Sir?'

'Grace is here to take you home.'

I went to the door and, bidding Mr Shakespeare goodbye, I walked home to Ely Street saying not one word, wondering what had happened to Bod that had hurt her so. Whom had she lost? Brothers, fathers, sons or husband? And how? In all my days with the Shakespeares, we could never get John or Mary to tell about it, and Bod clearly wasn't going to.

CHAPTER 6

The next few years were full of life. The Shakespeares' wealth continued to increase and they became quite a cornerstone of commerce in Stratford. John was also appointed chief beer taster, which I need not point out was a much sought-after position.

Sadly, however, they also sowed the seeds of their own financial downfall. I only know this because in adulthood I was able to understand that which I observed in childhood. Of course, with trade being good everywhere, we in the transport business did well, too. Ironically, had Father been paid by the journey, he, too, would have been a wealthy man. But there was a down-side for the livery in good times; many people who acquire wealth buy their own horses and carts, partly as a cost-cutting measure and partly due to vanity.

John Shakespeare, however, did not. He had little use for animals; the looking after, feeding and stabling of beasts in order to save a few shillings, was an anathema to him. My father heard John tell someone he was applying his mind to other things and did not want to clutter it with a team of horses and their welfare.

The glove trade was good. My father and I knew that because of the amount of leather we picked up and delivered to Henley Street. Not to mention the finished articles beautifully wrapped up in large cartons that we took to the riverside wharf. They would eventually make their way to Oxford and Birmingham, and some were sold by third-party dealers in London itself. However, the amount of coin flowing into the Shakespeare household could not be accounted for by the glove trade and rental yields from Mary's land alone. John was up to something else, but a tad on the wrong side of the law.

Partly arranged by my father, John Shakespeare took the lease on a large barn at the back of Henley Street, accessed through Guild Street. It had served as a feed store in past years, and the building was secure with only one set of doors. Windows were high up in the wall, good for ventilation and to keep out prying eyes. Since we were used as the trustworthy movers of the 'cash and notes' at the centre of this non-leather trade, we were caught in the middle. John was operating as a wool dealer.

The wool trade was strictly controlled by the state, and special licences were needed to deal in this cornerstone of the English economy. However, farmers, ever short of cash, were often predisposed to sell their entire stock of wool months before it was shorn or ready for market. The price they would get would, of course, be much less than its merchant value in June. This future buying was not legal and licensed dealers purchased in June only at shearing time. So these future traders were known as broggers and the activity known as brogging. Large amounts of wool and cash were involved. It was high risk but the gains outweighed the risk.

Sometimes, the wool was shorn, moved and stored, hence the big barn. Other times, it was done on word or notes, and then sold on with profit taken before the wool had even left the beast's backs. However, risk came in the form of nefarious freelance spies, who would spot a brogger and either dob them in to the authorities and take a cut of the fine or, more often, cut a deal with the brogger's supplier. A sharp rogue could cut a deal at both ends.

Hungry to build his family's wealth and climb the social ladder (he had even applied for a coat of arms) John took these risks with worrying confidence. Sadly, I do remember the day he was caught out.

It was a dismal day in April, one of those days you go about chores with great fortitude, blocking out the harsh rain, biting cold and bad-tempered beasts. Birds squatted under tree branches, dogs took to fireplaces if there were any or under some old cart if there weren't. The only creatures that enjoyed such a day were the frogs, and they sat around the trough singing their pleasure in loud and irritating voice.

I busied myself inside the horse boxes, prodding hiding places to flush out rats for the tikes to grab. I was also looking for chicken eggs, of which I found nearly a dozen. I was in one of the boxes on the western side when, through the horse's legs, I saw silhouetted against the rain, a figure whom I recognised as John Shakespeare.

'Young Tom, is your father about?' he asked.

I came forward with my basket of eggs and looked at him.

'Yes, Sir,' I replied.

'Be a good boy and fetch him hither,' he smiled.

I looked at the pouring rain and pursed my lips, having managed to stay out of it for most of the day. Putting down my basket of eggs, I cussed the rain and fetched my father.

'How can I be of service, Sir?' inquired my father, wiping a mixture of sweat and rainwater from his brow.

John smiled and picked up one of the eggs. Giving it a polish, he glanced awkwardly in my direction. My father took the hint.

'Can talk in front of the boy. Sharp eyes and tight lip has our Tom,' he said with a grin.

John smiled and suddenly chucked me the egg, which I caught without breaking or taking my eyes off him.

'Certainly has,' said John.

John walked a little circle and, after a small pause, he came to the point.

'I need to move two-hundred pounds and twenty, Jack,'

My father did not flinch but I was visibly taken aback. I did not know such a sum existed.

'How far?'

'Back of Snitterfield.'

'Four pound. And if we get robbed, it's nought to do with us,' my father said.

'Pretty penny!' exclaimed John.

My father said nothing.

'Think we could get robbed?' mused John aloud.

'I'll take a tup full of dung. You dress down, sit up front with me, sit the boys on the back, we'll be good.'

'Last year I did this with notes, but ...'

Father held up his hand for John to stop. 'Renting a cart for a tidy sum, that's all I need to know. The rest is your business.'

'Where'll we put the box of coin?'

'Under the dung. When?'

'Tomorrow, dawn?' said John, hesitantly.

Father nodded and John smiled. He ruffled my hair and was about to disappear back into the rain when my father cleared his throat loudly and removed his hat. 'In advance.'

John looked uneasy but putting his hand into his doublet he pulled out his purse and counted coin into my father's hat. Father placed his hat back on his head and John disappeared into the rain. No sooner had he gone, than Grace appeared.

'Mr Shakespeare?'

'Yes, sister, a trip to Snitterfield moving some goods.'

'Brogging?'

'Mmmm.'

'You seem uneasy, brother?'

'Hold out your hands, sister,' he said with a grin.

Grace obliged and, taking off his hat, he poured the coin into her hands.

'Now, what's the price for a tup of dung to Snitterfield?

'One shilling.'

'Good, enter that into the ledger. Place one shilling in the strong box and you know what to do with the rest.'

Cradling the precious coin, Grace left the stable box and went about Father's bidding.

'Come on, get those eggs washed, Tom,' my father said, merrily riffling my hair.

I realised in later years that moving cash in a brogging deal was highly risky. The returns could be high but the hazards were great – robbery or default on product being the greatest risk. So, if possible, it was best to be done with notes of promise or letters of credit. My father knew this and consequently demanded the monstrous sum to carry that much coin such a short journey.

The following day, before the sun was up, my father and the men filled the tup with horse dung. It was still cold but the rain had abated to a constant drizzle. Father took his club and placed it just behind the seat. I also saw Grace hand him a slim dagger, which he took and rolled into the folds at the top of his britches. Just as daylight began to break, I sat on the back of the foul-smelling cart and we trotted up to Henley Street. John was waiting outside, suitably dressed down. A matter of concern to my father, however, was that there was another man there, too. We pulled up and I jumped down whilst my father stayed in his seat.

'Mr Shakespeare.'

'Jack, this is my colleague, Mr Langrake.'

'Mr Langrake,' my father said, holding out his hand.

Mr Langrake was dressed in smart town clothes, save an old stable coat and yard boots. He shook Father's hand and smiled benignly; they locked eyes and read each other quite thoroughly.

'Tom,' called Father, as he stood up and jumped off the cart.

'Father?'

'Show Mr Langrake where to make a small hole in the muck.'

'I'll make a space just behind the seat,' said Mr Langrake cordially as he picked up the shovel and jumped up on to the cart.

I could see my father was not happy with this unknown aspect of the trip. Father then followed John into the house whilst I stood by the door. I listened to tense whispers as Mr Langrake made a hiding place in the muck for the coin.

'John, who is that man?'

'He's a colleague, a fine trader of wool and ... other things.'

'How long have you known him?'

'Oh, some weeks now.'

'Weeks! We are carrying two hundred pounds with someone you have known weeks!'

'Jack, tis my business and it is nought of yours.'

'Tis if we get robbed. I have my boy with me.'

'Jack, please help me with this coin.'

They both came out of the house and, with great dexterity, pushed the box of coin into the hole in the muck. Clearly, Mr Langrake knew what he was doing because he covered it in a flash and sat down.

'Mr Shakespeare, is Will coming?'

'No, Tom. He's still in bed.'

I looked up to the window where Will was sleeping and longed to be in the same bed too, warm and dry and when I woke, no work to be done.

'Come, Tom. Sit on the back with me,' said John, bringing me back down to earth.

Sitting on the driver's bench, Mr Langrake looked down, picked up father's club, gave it a twirl and smiled at my father.

'Bid you place that down, Mr Langrake.'

Mr Langrake duly complied. Father climbed on and, sitting next to the stranger, he pulled the club to within his own efficient reach.

'I don't know thee, so, we get robbed, it's your skull I'll split first,' he said with gritted teeth.

John sat on the back with me and off we trundled to Snitterfield.

John straightened my hat affectionately, trying to allay any fears I might be harbouring, but it was he who was nervous. John Shakespeare had two significant weaknesses: he was a recusant and, worse, he was a terrible judge of character.

I was nervous for the journey because I could see that my father had little use for this Mr Langrake. If the weather had been good, it would have been a simple journey, but the rain drizzled on and the ruts were full of rocks and water. We never lost a wheel, but twice we had to stop and wait whilst Father and John found wood to place in the water-filled rut so that we could get through without upsetting the cart.

Mr Langrake let them look for wood and sat holding the club, pretending to be ready to fend off any marauding thieves. To my father and I, his transparency was as clear as a millpond, but not to dear John.

When we turned into the driveway of the property we were heading for, my father leant back and called to John.

'Mr Newson – sold him a fine bay gelding last year.'

We arrived at a large house, which looked like it had been finished only recently. It was a long tall building with three floors and high lattice-patterned chimneys. There was a moat surrounding the house and box hedges that were being cut into all sorts of shapes. We stopped near the front door and Mr Newson came out – a well-attired, portly gentleman.

'I knew your father and your brother,' he said, and greeted John with a warm handshake.

'Did you?'

'Man still owes me money,' he muttered, turning to Father and me.

Father politely touched his cap, and Mr Newson nodded discreet recognition.

Father and I also noticed that, despite greeting Mr Langrake as a stranger, there was, if we weren't mistaken, a look of recognition between them. John was too busy conducting his deal to notice. Father uncovered the box of coin and John and Mr Langrake carried the box inside, followed by the gentleman.

A manservant then approached us from God knows where; neither of us had seen him creep up. He held down a large-brimmed hat with one hand and dangled a cocked pistol in the other.

'You can deposit your load over there,' he said, waving the pistol at another dung heap in the adjoining paddock.

'You can give us a hand,' said my father with a smile.

'I clean silverware, furniture and the weapons – not dung carts,' he sneered, leaving us to it.

We moved the cart into the paddock and my father threw his weight behind the shovel and unloaded the dung on to the other pile. I watched with a piece of sacking over my head as the rain thickened its penetrating descent. It was indeed a miserable day and the only consolation was the monumental profit my father was taking. When we arrived back to the front door, Mr Langrake and John came out of the house and we started the wet journey back to Stratford. Once more we had to stop to fetch wood and pack out some ruts to get the cart safely back on track. Since there was no load to guard,

Mr Langrake had no option but to help. We enjoyed a secret smirk watching his smart clothes getting soiled.

It was not till a few weeks later that we realised what Mr Langrake's game actually was. Father and I were walking down Rother Street with two fine greys, and, as we passed the courthouse, I saw Mr Langrake exit in quite a hurry. I gave a quiet whistle to Father. We watched as Langrake marched swiftly to the water trough, where he untied a chestnut mare and took off at a smart pace. Soon after, John Shakespeare came out looking incensed, and then he suddenly stamped his foot, turned around and kicked the wall of the courthouse several times.

'Good-day, Mr Shakespeare,' said my father, as we passed by.

John composed himself and replied with a grunt, whilst we carried on walking.

'Reckon Mr Langrake dobbed in our John,' my father said quietly.

Father was right. One of the horses we looked after belonged to the court clerk and that evening we heard that John had been fined twenty pounds, of which Mr Langrake received half for standing witness. This also meant that Mr Newson no longer felt an obligation to John and had refused to return the money till after shearing in June. It was an expensive day for John, but, nevertheless, Father carried out three other noted brogs for him that month. John Shakespeare may have been down, but he wasn't out.

CHAPTER 7

In childhood there are two worlds: the big one and a child's one. Occasionally events happen in the big world, which, despite not affecting one directly, do produce a profound disturbance in the child's world.

In 1570, there was one such event that reverberated through the country like a silent but strongly felt earth tremor. The damage was probably quite severe at its epicentre, and though the ripples took a while to reach us in Stratford, reach us they did. When this news came through, I was staying with Will at Henley Street whilst my father and Grace took some horses to sell at Appleby in Yorkshire. Mary, with baby Joan, was visiting Beth and Johnny in Edstone. Now High Bailiff of Stratford, John's status was ever growing and, though he never said it, he was unhappy having cousin Johnny around. Johnny was fun, but his propensity for the drink was starting to have an effect on his life. As an outspoken recusant, his drink-fuelled opinions were becoming very loose and the family feared they could catch up with him if he did not curb his ways.

It was a sombre evening. John was brooding by the fire, prodding it with the iron repeatedly, like baiting a dog that refused to bark. Will, Gilbert and I lay in a big shelf-bed that was against the chimney breast in the second room upstairs. It was February and a chilled wind swept through Stratford. Gilbert always went to sleep as soon as his head hit the sack. Will and I, like all six-year-olds, thought we were grown up and unfairly put to bed before we were tired.

However, the gentle and ever-loving Bod sat in the flickering candlelight and soothed us with yet more of the most wonderful stories about the fairy kingdom. We had started to wonder if the fairy kingdom did exist, but we hung on hoping, dreaming, wishing, longing that it did, such was the gentle magic of the stories that fluttered from her sweet smile and glorious eyes. Nonetheless, we were quite wide-awake when Mary came home from visiting.

It was about four hours before midnight when we heard Mary enter the house. We expected her to come up and see us, but only Bod came up and put Joan to bed. Will instinctively knew something was up. We could hear furtive mutterings. We slipped out of bed and trod down the stairs as far as we dared, begging Bod not to give us away.

'Did you tell Johnny?' we heard John say.

'Oh no, everyone has kept it from him', said Mary.

'Very wise,' said John.

'It takes so little to set him off,' Mary muttered, as she put some wood on the fire.

Bod went down to bring her travel belongings upstairs.

'Are the children asleep?'

'Yes, mistress,' lied Bod and scuttled back upstairs.

'I don't know what to do,' wondered Mary aloud.

'Best keep away from Edston and Orton for a while,' declared John.

'When did the news reach here?'

'This morning. It was brought by Lord Lucy and read to the council meeting,' said John, uninterested.

'What did everyone think'? probed Mary.

'No one really said anything.'

'They are all so gutless in that chamber,' Mary snapped.

'Realists,' John sighed.

The tone had changed downstairs and Bod came and sat with us.

'Realists?! The Roman catechism of Christ is real! She had it coming!' snapped Mary in a raised voice.

'Wife! Hold your tongue right there,' said John, his demeanour now changed to one of utter seriousness and authority.

We froze. John only called her wife when he was angry with her. Bod tried to get us to go to bed but Will would have none of it; the titanic charms of Bod were suddenly useless. The talk became tense and quiet. It was dangerously serious, whatever it was they were talking about.

'Why should I hold my tongue?' growled Mary.

'Because,' said John in a tense whisper, 'in walls and on streets, the ears are ever growing. Words such as those can kill us.'

'She will kill us anyway. Every papal flower is now a weed to pluck and burn!' whispered Mary angrily.

Closing his eyes, John took a deep breath and raised a hand up to Mary.

'Wife, tiredness has your spirit,' he said, with authority.

'Unlike yours, which has been sold for thirty pieces of silver.'

Mary was in no mood for compromise. Will and I craned our heads to see them both; John rubbed his forehead in desperation whilst Mary prodded the fire in anger.

'I cannot continue with this,' he groaned.

'For fear of losing your precious aldermen; bludgers, who despise you, use you, borrow money. Why? Because they know the secret Papist is a warm coat and a loose purse.'

John snapped and shouted at Mary, 'Wife! How do you think I built this trade, bought this house. We need those aldermen if I am to restore the family fortune to what your forebears once enjoyed.'

'And what of our faith?' demanded Mary.

'You cannot have both. That is the way it is. That is the way it is going to be for the rest of time. You know that!' John shouted, flinging his hands out to emphasise the two sides.

Mary simply went for her emotional weapon of choice.

'I never thought my husband would have his hand in the bucket of blood that flowed from our Catholic destruction.'

John collapsed into a chair and dropped his head into his hands.

Long before we were born, the old guild in Stratford had been suppressed and dissolved by King Henry VIII. Local merchants petitioned the king to destroy the ancient guild and create a corporation. This he did and consequently granted the local merchants full municipal power. Mary's father referred to these commercial opportunists as 'the town weasels'. Despite being twenty-five years in the past, the Ardens had long memories and little ability to adapt. John always hung on to his faith but worked with the system, which was fine, so long as he never did anything where he had to cross a line of confrontation with his beloved Mary, or the new corporation.

That was until the year just before Will was born. The aldermen found themselves given a three-dimensional test of loyalty to crown and government. There was a royal edict to remove all 'idolatrous' images from places of worship. In Stratford this required the aldermen to remove the seventy-year-old wall paintings that adorned the guild chapel. Till this time, most Stratford councillors and aldermen played lip service to the new ways and systems, but this was a royal edict. In Stratford the council looked for a 'new boy' to perform this unpalatable deed, and so they placed the sword firmly in John Shakespeare's hand.

The vibrant wall paintings inside the Guild Chapel of the Holy Cross depicted the last judgement, the crucifixion, the martyrdom of Thomas-a-Becket, the whore of Babylon and the dance of death. It was one great moving cascade to England's testament of religious history and stories. Mary loved the Guild Chapel; for her it remained an unspoiled relic of so much that had been so savagely destroyed.

John, ever a sailor of fair winds between the rocks of life, and now under pressure, opted for applying a layer of whitewash to the paintings. Thus, the images were gone to all and he could placate his wife with the hope that, if times changed and allowed, they could be recovered to their former glory with but a pale of water. It was a false hope.

Mary raged at John the rage she had raged so many times. 'I watched them burn that abbey, gripping my aunt's finger with all the might my little hand could muster. I watched tears flow from her eyes in greater quantity than the precious waters of Holywell. They threw book after book on to the fire, like cooking fuel. Books older than our great-grandparents.

'I put that pain in a dark hole and locked it there for eternity or so I thought! No! Years later I come home to find our chapel paintings vanquished and that hole unlocked. And, when I arrived home, what did I find? My very own husband is covered in the white blood of their execution!'

John had had enough. He quickly stood up and struck Mary hard across the face. Mary froze in disbelief. Will was shocked and held his mouth. Bod buried her head in her hands. I stared, breathless.

Even I knew at this tender age a child should never witness his father strike his mother, though it happened in all too many dwellings. John left the room to go into the workshop. He stopped, turned back and looked at his still-shocked spouse.

'If the Bishop of Rome sees fit to excommunicate our queen, there is nothing you or I can do. However, Elizabeth Rex is our queen and in this house we will continue to obey her laws, whether we like them or not. I will keep my faith within the vessel that was designed to hold it, my heart. You, wife, will do the same or you can expect to receive more of what you were just given.'

John left the room and shut the door.

Mary sat down by the fire. 'Maid,' she called in a teary tone.

Bod ushered us back to bed and went to attend her mistress.

'Did the Pope execute the queen?' I asked as we both crawled back into bed.

'No, he stopped her taking sacraments,' Will murmured, still trying to get over the shock of seeing his normally mild-mannered father strike his mother.

Suffice to say in the following years, Will never heard the Guild Chapel paintings mentioned again.

The following morning was tense, with Mary saying little whilst John went straight to his workshop. When I stayed over, Bod would often take us into the garden after breakfast and we would find tiny loaves of bread left for us by the fairies, but this morning I think both Will and I realised there were no fairies. We wandered in the garden after breakfast. Bod jiggled Gilbert up and down and tried to hide her tears but it was no good; the night had been a big shock to all.

'No fairy bread today, Bod?' I asked.

'Mmm, fairies must be busy somewhere else, Tom,' said Bod as she sniffed and wiped a tear in the chilly morning air.

'Do you think fairies quarrel?' asked Will.

'Oh, maybe, sometimes,' mused Bod.

'Do they hit each other?' pressed Will.

'Umm, no, I doubt it. Probably make mischief with magic tricks instead,' answered Bod, at last mustering her enchanting smile.

When we went back inside, Grace and Father were at the door whispering to Mary and John, who stood on the threshold and, to our relief, were holding hands. I never knew what they were talking about in those guarded whispers but I reckoned it was about the Pope excommunicating the queen. It was, however, reassuring for both Will and Bod to see some harmony return to Mary and John.

There must have been much remorse from both John and Mary for their conflict, since six months later she bore the swelling in her tummy that could only be a baby.

It was also at this time the real redemption came. The old cook house of Henley Street was demolished and a brand new modern kitchen was installed, complete with indoor pump. It was more than a new kitchen; they put on another floor like a house on the house, albeit a little one.

This building work gave me my first job. I was horse minder for the tradesmen, for which I was paid one farthing a day by the Shakespeare family. It was a simple enough job for a six-year-old: just sit there, watch the horses as well as keeping a keen eye for light-fingered scallywags taking the men's tools from the back of their carts.

The worst part of the job was boredom, so I amused myself watching the comings and goings of folk to and from the house. Fellow aldermen would drop in and give great admiration to the work as it progressed; some would take mead with Mary in the parlour; others would talk intently with John in and around his workshop.

I could hear the banalities about which they chatted with Mary, but more intriguing were the conversations in the workshop, because, after them, there was always tension between Mary and John. The leatherman who worked for John in the shop was as deaf as a post, so he was never a liability.

One day I decided to creep down to the workshop window and listen; what I heard was quite a revelation. It was an overcast day and quite dry but there was a fair bitter wind. John was in the workshop talking with a Mr Perkesis, I believe the name was. This is what I heard.

'John, to not trust a fellow merchant is indeed a sad affair. Especially a fellow alderman who turns his eye away from certain matters of faith, and in the face of much state legislation against … popery.'

'How much?' was all John said in reply.

'Forty pounds repayable in June. I'll give a tidy interest of one quarter.'

I listened as John said nothing but I heard the strong box being opened and coin being counted. Nothing else was said and, taking his loan, Mr Perkesis left by the door to the left of me. The window opened above my head, and John called out.

'June 18.'

Mr Perkesis momentarily turned, bowed and sardonically doffed his cap, and then carried on his way.

'You spying on me, Tom?' said John looking down.

'No Sir, keeping from the cold, Sir.'

John grunted and closed the window. I was to realise years later that this was the pattern of behaviour that was breaking poor John. I saw Mary walking down the street with Will, Bod and Gilbert. They had been in town shopping. I was curled up against the wall to reduce the wind chill.

'Tom, for goodness sake, what are you doing out in this cold?'

'Minding the horses, Mistress Shakespeare?'

'Ridiculous. What horse is going to bolt or wander in this weather? Much too cold, come inside,' she said quite authoritatively.

Bod and Will smiled at me and each put an arm around me as we went into the house. I spent the rest of the afternoon with Will by the fire in the parlour – bliss. Mary went down to the corridor to the workshop where, entering the room, I heard her say,

'What did Perkesis want?'

John put a look towards us through the door and then closed it. There were then the muffled sounds of tense and irritated discussions. Clearly, Mary knew what was going on but she seemed powerless to stop it. Eventually, she emerged from the workshop leaving the door open with no sign of John.

'I'm not selling another paddock!' she called over her shoulder, walking down the corridor as the door to the workshop closed.

'Now, Maid, I think hot food is required on a day like this.'

Bod pounded away at some dough for manchet loaves.

'The stall was empty of good meat this morning, Mistress, but I did get four woodcock.' Bod wiped her hands and placed a small wooden cage on the table with four tweeting birds inside.

'Well, it will have to do,' Mary said with a sigh.

Suddenly, the front door was flung open!

'Stoke the fire! I bring fish to fry and wine to drink!'

There stood Johnny, triumphant, a sack in one hand and a wine bladder in the other!

Mary screamed; Bod laughed; Will ran forward and leapt up into Johnny's arms.

'Good morrow, Cuz!' Will yelled, hugging him tight.

'Gosh, the neck, the neck. Wonderful to see you, too. Don't spill me goods.'

'What brings you, Johnny?' grinned Mary.

'Passing through on my journey of life, have to see my favourite cousins!' he stated, struggling to place his booty on the table.

He grabbed Mary, who screeched as he gave her a great kiss whilst still hanging on to Will.

'And, foresooth, another child!' he exclaimed, standing back and seeing Mary's protruding belly.

'And works going on! A great kitchen! Another floor! Life is good,' declared Johnny looking around.

'Mr Somerville, your sack is trying to get off the table?' said Bod, pointing.

Sure enough, the sack was squirming its way towards the cage of woodcock.

'The sack, yes! Now! Did have two bladders of wine but me horse lost a shoe. A kind chap put a new shoe on him. Having no coin, gave him a sack of wine for payment but he thought that too much, so gave me these as well!

56

Johnny grabbed the squirming sack, undid it and, upending it on to the table, five live angry eels shot out like loose cannon shot. Convulsing like crazed lunatics, they knocked the cage on to the floor which broke, sending the scared birds into the air.

Everyone squealed and birds flew around the room banging into pots and pans like frenzied drummers. The eels squirmed around the floor, tripping everyone up. Will and I tried to grab them but the strong slippery creatures were hard to get a handle on. Mary slipped on one but luckily fell into a chair, laughing hysterically. Johnny joined us in pursuit of the eels but he was in fits of laughter under the table as he tried to corner them.

Bod snatched the birds from the air, cracking their necks each time and laying them dead on the table. Then, efficiently, she helped us trap the eels and killed them too, banging their necks hard on the counter. Silence and stillness returned as, exhausted, we all sat catching our breath between giggles.

'I'll stoke the fire,' said Johnny, getting himself to his feet.

'I'll skin and bone this lot,' said Bod, wiping her brow.

The workshop door opened and John wandered slowly down the corridor; he was partially engrossed, giving a piece of fine kid leather experienced tugs, this way and that.

In the kitchen he stopped and looked at the table with the woodcock and eels all laid out.

'What a commotion? Johnny! How are you?' he said with a tolerant smile.

'Well, dear Cuz, well. Excuse the noise, brought some eels for to eat, but the slippery beggars made a bolt for freedom.'

John looked to the table.

'They were unsuccessful?'

'Indeed, John Shakespeare, my old chum! The fecundity in this household is astounding!' he declared, gesticulating to Mary's swollen figure, young Will and the building works.

'What brings you to Stratford?' said John.

'Wife said such same thing! Love and a fair wind, old cuz!'

Not believing him, John sighed and raised an eyebrow.

'Very well,' Johnny groaned. 'Punched a bloke in a public house in Warwick.'

'You drunk?'

'Why else would I punch someone? Come, give a gent some standards. Turns out the chap I laid out was son of a judge.'

'Why did you punch him, John?' laughed Mary.

'Sadly, that memory has gone the way of the brandy, down the old privy,' he cackled. 'Just thought I'd lay low for a couple of weeks.'

John Shakespeare looked concerned.

'Here?' he said.

'No, no, no. Calm yourself, Cuz. Me kipped down with old John Frith at Temple Grafton.'

'How do you know him?'

'He was me tutor at Oxford, damn fine one too, one of life's great men of God, unlike this canker-blossomed family that's gripped the Crown! But no more of that talk, don't wanna get chucked out before fish is fried and birds roasted, eh what?' he said, throwing a sweet wink at Bod as she put the eels into a bowl.

In minutes, Mary had the woodcock feathered, gutted and on a spit pasted with plums and fat. Bod brought in eel fillets and put them onto some spikes to toast over the fire. I was still sitting by the window checking the horses, when the artisans came in and begged their leave of Mr Shakespeare. I went to help stoke the fire and turn the spits. Bod pushed the bread into the oven and then filled an iron pot with a mixture of onions, cloves, bay leaves, carrots, turnips and some Virginian potatoes that Mary had bought on a whim. Johnny poured the wine into glasses.

'Where did this come from?' asked John.

'What care you, unless it's sour?' muttered Johnny.

'Cuz, I like its taste. I care not to quarrel.'

Johnny looked to John as Bod put out the marvellous-smelling roast birds and the succulent eel fillets with the spicy vegetables and some fine pale bread.

'It comes from a country we fear,' said Johnny, 'but with whom I have contact for one reason only, that which is in this glass. None other. Your health, Cuz!'

He toasted them in silence. They all toasted back in silence and sat to table.

'Now, John! Is boy at school yet?' said Johnny.

Bod cut the birds in two and served them around, Johnny dished out the sweet-smelling eel fillets and Mary did the same with bread and vegetables.

'September,' replied John.

'Well, young Will, when you get there, you will be introduced to this man, Mr Ovid,' he said, waving a book in the air, as everyone relished the delicious food.

'Should you have a decent Catholic schoolmaster, of course. If not, you'll just get a stick across your arse for not knowing *amo amas amat amamus amatis amant*. Learn it now.'

'*Amo amas amat amamus amatis amant*,' smiled Will.

'You know it?' asked Johnny, taking Will on to his knee.

'No, you just said it,' giggled Will.

Johnny turned and addressed John.

'This boy has recall, John. Get him into school this instant.'

'September,' said John, quite firmly.

'Well meantime, listen to this,' he said, turning back to Will.

We all sat as Johnny started to read Narcissus and Echo from his precious book of *Metamorphoses* by Publius Ovidius Naso. He read the Latin and translated as he went. As he read, he disappeared into another world, tears slipped down his cheeks and passion quivered a melancholic tune in his voice. Tears also fell from Mary and Bod's eyes as the sweet poetry flowed effortlessly from Johnny's lips. Will lay across his cousin's lap with his forefinger on his upper lip. In respectful attention, John leant against the stone fireplace and gently massaged his own head in contemplation of the poetry.

When Johnny finally finished, he closed the book with great reverence, and there was a hushed silence. After a few moments John spoke.

'Thank you Johnny. That was really most affecting,' whispered John, trying to maintain his composure as head of the house, but also wishing to honour the great talent for reading his fair cousin had.

Johnny rose and placed Will on the floor, and looked him in the eye.

'This, Will, is my most prized possession. When I die, it will be yours. It holds all you will ever need in life.'

Will nodded a smile.

'But I ain't going to die just yet. So methinks I'll hang on to it. Now, mistress of this glorious house!' he said, by way of bringing up the tone and he, taking Mary's face in both hands, kissed her on her lips.

'Thanking you for the victuals, fair Cuz, I must leave thee for to Temple Grafton I take myself, a gentle walk on me old horse before nightfall.'

He turned, bowed to all and let himself out of the front door. I have to say his horse was a frightful old nag and walking was surely all it could deliver. Nevertheless, he mounted it with all the aplomb of a great general at the head of a mighty army. He blew a kiss to us all, waved and wandered off down Henley Street in the direction of Temple Grafton. Everyone went inside except Will and I. Watching him go, and, with a gentle clarity, Will whispered:

Do not any longer time thus lingering fondly stand.
Shall I then leave brother, sister, father, kith and kin,
And household Gods, and native soil, and all that is therein,
And sail I know not whither with a stranger? Yea: why not?
My father surely cruel is, my country rude God wot:
My brother yet a very babe: my sister I dare say
Contented is with all her heart that I should go away.

Will looked to me and smiled.

CHAPTER 8

In September, 1571, despite being only four feet, six inches tall and the grand age of seven and a half years old, as far as I was concerned, I was a man. I could file a palfrey's hoof, wield a shovel, start a smithy fire, repair tack with good accuracy, and carry two pails of water on a yoke, albeit with a bit of a struggle and spilling most of it. Height was my problem, not strength.

Will had enjoyed a less arduous childhood but when time allowed he was there for me. He was my only respite from the rigours of life at the livery. This was all about to change. He was enrolled at the King Edward School in the High Street. Like the tutelage, my exclusivity was gone; he would meet new friends. I also knew that we would both change: he would become a man of education and I simply a working servant of Equus.

One of the first responsibilities I ever had was around this time. Horse owners liked to pick up their steeds from the trough in Rother Street or the trough outside King Edward School. So my father and I would lead them there and he would leave me to mind them, pick up the fees from the owner and return with the coin. I had already been sent to Rother Street with Heavens Gate, where I had collected the fee from Mr Sandells for a day's hire. Father trusted me with Heavens Gate because he was such a calm beast and always responded to me. There was never any fuss. Other horses could be flighty and too much to control for one as young as I. There was nothing more dangerous in the street than a horse in a wild passion. It would spread to other horses and, sure as death follows life, disaster would happen.

I arrived at the trough outside King Edward School where my father had left three beasts. I was minding the three horses on this day, the first of the school year and the first day Will attended King Edward.

It was easy to spot the new pupils; they clung to their parents like young yearlings. In turn, the parents walked with the confidence of a trader at auction, proud to display their magnificent progeny to the world, but equally glad to be free of the constant attention they required.

Someone flipped my hat off! I turned. It was Will standing there with a very proud Mary and John.

'What say, Tom?' he grinned.

John was beaming with delight as Mary glowed, about to burst with the impending child she carried in her womb. Will looked a picture: new hose, britches, boots and vest, and he carried a small chalk-board with a bundle of quills bound in twine and a sheet of paper.

'Hey, Will,' I said picking up my hat and flicking hair from my eyes.

'Good morning, Tom,' said Mary.

'Tom,' said Mr Shakespeare, rather formally.

'Lovely fresh morning,' I said by way of cordiality.

'Fresh morning for a fresh start on a new part of life,' said Mary with great glee.

The gatekeeper walked into the street and, taking his nod from the headmaster, rang his handbell with hollow authority. I knew two of my horses would flinch at the sound of the bell, so I was there and ready to soothe them when it rang. The headmaster greeted the new pupils and we all breathed in, slightly nervous as we watched the students file into school. The headmaster caught John's eye and gestured to him to speak with another man standing at the gate – a man holding a ledger, the bursar.

'What's he want, John?' said Mary under her breath.

'I'll see,' muttered John, and he hurried over to the bursar, fondling for his purse.

Mary took Will's hand and, with a matriarch command under-pinned with a waddle, she led Will to the school gate. She acknowledged the headmaster, and then proudly waved Will goodbye as he entered the school.

I noticed John Shakespeare hand over some coin, which the bursar took, but then there was further discussion and the bursar pointed to a page in the ledger. John patted his clothes, then there was more conversation, followed by consternation on John's part. Eventually, after looking to me for an awkward moment, he walked smartly back to where I stood.

'I don't suppose you have sixpence, Tom?'

I could not believe this. Yes, I had sixpence but it was not mine. It was the fee I had collected this morning and had to be booked by three o'clock. Here was I, too poor to attend school, yet I found myself contributing coin for my friend's tutelage. I thought it was free on account of his father being an alderman.

'Yes, Mr Shakespeare, but this is livery coin and must be entered in the box and ledger by three o'clock,' I uttered awkwardly, taking the six pennies from my purse.

'Without fail, I will send Bod with it before midday,' he stated.

Whilst John paid the bursar the full amount, Mary waddled back, looked to me and then to her approaching husband.

'What gives, Tom?' she asked curtly.

'Mr Shakespeare was sixpence short.'

Mary looked surprised. She said nothing. She simply raised one eyebrow and stroked her tummy with both hands.

'Short for what? Husband, please explain why we are in debt to a seven-year-old?'

'Not me, Mrs Shakespeare, the livery,' I said.

'Thank you, Tom,' she snapped, firmly waiting for the explanation.

John rubbed his temple awkwardly and sighed. Then, as if making a quote, he spoke.

'As known recusants our progeny are not allowed to attend school. So to be unentered in the register, it was one shilling and sixpence, which, I did not have in totality on my person, but I do in the workshop. I will send it by our maid upon our return.'

'Could the bursar not wait one hour?'

John sighed in desperation. 'Apparently, not.'

Mary was irritated beyond belief. She looked to me and paused for a moment, went to speak, then restrained herself, momentarily closing her eyes for self-control.

'Tom, we are grateful to you,' she said cordially, and with that she departed.

'Come, husband,' she called, walking away like a heavily laden lighter on the river.

'Upon my return,' John reassured me, before complying with his wife's order.

As I watched them go, the owners of the horses I was minding came up, paid me and took their horses. Save the odd pail of waste being called and thrown out of windows, the street was now empty, the world having gone about its morning business. I looked to the school and heard the chanting of Latin phrases by the pupils. I looked to Mary and John as they rounded the corner and disappeared up Henley Street, imagining the grief John would get as soon as the door of Henley Street closed. I was alone, and strangely I liked it. I felt a sense of control in my destiny, which was attractive to me, though I did not fully understand it at that young age.

Indeed, true to his word, no sooner had I returned to the livery than did Bod turn up with the six pennies as promised.

'Here, Sir, is the debt Mr Shakespeare owes,' she said sweetly as she handed the money to my father. She seemed a little embarrassed by the situation and spoke with me briefly on leaving the livery.

'All well, Tom?'

'Aye, Bod,' I nodded, placing my bucket down.

'Mr Shakespeare asked me to say if I saw you, he is in your debt for helping him.'

'Debt cleared, Bod.'

She looked to one side and looking back she spoke again.

'Quite a passion erupted in the house, frightened all the fairies away,' she whispered discreetly.

My father was none too pleased with the situation. Had we not been able to reconcile the coin with the clerk at three we may well have found ourselves on the street that very night. However, he saw my dilemma and, knowing Mr Shakespeare to be a man of honour, he understood my situation. Nonetheless, he made me swear on the soul of my mother to never make livery fees available to anyone ever again, no matter what the circumstance.

'If a man cannot manage his coin, that is his problem. Never a lender or borrower be, my son,' was his parting comment.

At three o'clock, like every day, the clerk arrived, counted all the fees, reconciled the ledger, signed it and took the coin away. In later years, when I witnessed the untold success of my friend's plays, the fact that I could have put an end to his education on its first day was an irony that was not lost on me. Amid the great applause, it always brought a smile to my face.

Later in the month, Mary went into labour. Grace took charge, as Bod did not have the kind of experience of birthing that she had. I meanwhile, ran up and down, taking towels and jugs back to the kitchen where Bod replenished them all, steaming hot. God knows what they did with them. I certainly was not allowed in the room. This was strictly women's stuff but there was constant moaning, screaming and soothing.

John kept Gilbert occupied in the workshop and dear Joan, bless her, slept through the whole affair quite peacefully. Every so often, John would sneak out of the workshop and ask me what was going on but, inevitably, before I could say anything, he was distracted by a crying Gilbert. The afternoon wore on; Will returned from school and eventually, just as the sun started to set behind the late birdsong, a sound that is different to all others was heard – the first cry of a newborn baby. Even John heard it through the workshop door and, as soon as it cut the air, he was through the door, down the corridor and up the stairs. Will and I rushed to the bottom of the stairs just in time to hear.

'A girl!'

'You have a sister, Will,' called John from the bed chamber. We both gave each other a hug and Bod came out of the scullery and we all hugged together.

'Anne, her name is Anne,' said John, descending the stairs.

'Will, you can go up and see your new sister. Where's Gilbert?'

Wee Gilbert was standing in the corridor, a might confused by all the commotion. As Bod and Will ascended the stairs, John put out his hand.

'Come on, Gilbert. Let's go and see your new sister,' he said.

Gilbert took his hand and slowly they went upstairs.

'You too, Tom,' called John over his shoulder as he turned the corner of the stairs.

I climbed the stairs. This time the door was open and all was quiet, save the gentle hum of cooing. Tentatively, I put my head round the door and saw a womb within a womb. Surrounded by wall hangings, the cosy candle-lit chamber cradled everyone at Mary's bed as they all smiled at the now suckling Anne. By the window, Grace busied herself clearing up the debris of childbirth. The lovely atmosphere was disturbed by Joan waking and wailing. Bod brought her up to the family fold. I was sitting watching the whole Shakespeare family cuddled up together, when I received a tap on my shoulder. It was Grace.

'Come on, Tom. Leave them to themselves,' she whispered in my ear.

Grace and I crept downstairs and we were just about to slip into the night when Bod caught up with us.

'John asked me to give you this,' she said, pushing a shilling into Grace's hand.

'But from me, thank you for all your help,' she said, strangely losing her balance.

'Ooh? You all right?' asked Grace.

'Tired, bit of a headache; long day and a long night to come,' said Bod, looking a touch out of sorts.

'Chew a willow stick, love,' said Grace.

Grace always reckoned a good chew on a willow stick sorted a headache. Bod nodded with appreciation.

'Bye, Bod,' I said.

'Tom, goodbye and thank you, too, for all your help. Maybe one day I'll come and do the same for your wife,' she said and kissed me on my forehead.

Bod leant on the door-post and smiled as we left. I looked back and she really looked quite pale. In fact, when we arrived back to the livery and I was put to bed, I overheard my father discussing it with Grace at the bottom of the stairs.

'She don't look well; seen that before,' whispered Grace.

'Like George's cousin, David?' whispered Father back to her.

'Mmm,' Grace conceded.

Father took an inward whistle. I sensed they were worried about Bod, so in bed, I said a prayer, hoping the fairies would look after our dear sweet maid.

I was woken by the sound of Will hammering at our gate. In fact, it was so early the sun was only just peeking through the trees and Grace and my father were still sound asleep.

'Tom, Tom!' Will cried, as he hammered on the old gate.

'Will?' I replied, rubbing my gritty, sleep-ridden eyes and pulling off the bar.

'Get Grace! It's Bod!' he shouted as he burst in.

I ran to get Grace, but she was already stirring.

'I heard. I'll be right there,' she murmured, as I pulled on my clothes.

'What's wrong with her, Will?' I asked.

I looked at Will's face. It was sad and teary. I feared the worst as Will simply turned and went back downstairs.

Still pulling on clothes, I ran down the street and caught up with him. We both ran all the way to Henley Street, leaping the turgid rank drains that were particularly bad at this time. At Henley Street we ran through the parlour, upstairs through the bedchambers, past Mary, who lay in bed feeding Anne, her tears flowing onto the little mite's head.

At the end of the house, Bod had a bed in a small alcove above the workshop. We rushed in and stopped dead, gripping each other hard. There she lay on her bedding, dressed in nightshift and bonnet, her eyes open wide staring to the heavens, her face as pale as the finest porcelain and a smile as sweet as a fresh gardenia.

'Is she dead?' I whispered pointlessly.

'I came to get into bed with her this morning and she was like this already,' Will whispered back.

I knew she was dead. Though it looked like Bod, there was something missing. She was not there; an empty shell with a smiling face, the spirit departed. It was like an empty house; the possessions remained, but the owner departed.

We both stole forward and gently knelt beside her. Will reverently took her hands and, clasping them together, placed them on her chest. I closed her eyes with a gentle stroke of my hand, noticing her skin was as cold as iron. It sprang a well of ice-cold sadness in my heart. I had seen dead people at burials; that was part of the business of the livery – cartage of the dead. But this was different, I had never looked upon the cold dead body of someone I so loved and it was such a strange feeling – a mixture of pain and incomprehension.

'What happened?' I wondered out loud.

'Fairies took her in the night,' sighed Will as he wiped his tears.

We became aware of the sound of more than one pair of footsteps approaching, but we ignored them and continued to kneel with our heads resting on our dear departed Bod. The footsteps came to a halt at the doorway.

'Boys,' came the sombre words of Will's father.

Will looked up to his father and I turned, too. There at the doorway was John with the vicar and the physician.

'Better let those who know what to do take charge, mmm?'

Will stood up and went and hugged his father. I stayed clinging to Bod's cold hand, and then John beckoned me and I acquiesced. John hugged us both and led us out as the vicar and the physician closed the door and went about their ritual of preparing Bod for her last journey.

When we passed through Mary's bedchamber, Grace was comforting Mary with Joan and Anne. Downstairs we found Father comforting Gilbert. Nothing was said that morning and we all, except Will, who was nowhere to be seen, sat around listening to the comings and goings of John, the vicar, the physician and, ultimately, the grave men.

The physician had little explanation other than a night expiration on account of bad blood humours, undetectable or preventable. The vicar briefly explained that God had taken her in the night to place her in the bosom of Abraham on account of her good service to God and her masters. It was times like this I never believed grown-ups; they would always pretend they had the answers to it all but I knew they didn't. It was only people like Bod who were truthful enough to tell us they did not know what it all meant. Fed up with the grown-ups' pathetic attempts at comfort and understanding, I went in search of Will.

I found him sitting out in the garden, intently watching a bee take nectar from a rose. His face was worn with tears. I put my arm around him and rested my head on his shoulder and we sat there for what seemed like an hour, saying nothing, just listening to the bees buzzing and each other's breath.

Dear Bod had no family and few possessions; her Bible and clothes were sold to help pay for her burial. Thankfully, John and Mary contributed enough money to enable her to be interred in Trinity Churchyard, rather than suffer the ignominy of the paupers' yard out of the town.

Grace arrived at Henley Street driving the best cart we had at the livery. Father had placed a board covered with a piece of purple cloth and flowers. Grace massaged the reins in her hand and stared straight ahead with not a tear on her face but, for those who knew, the pain in her heart was plain to see. Some school friends of Will's turned up having heard the news from the headmaster. They had a group hug with Will, but not me. Strangely, Will seemed to forget I was there.

At three o'clock the Trinity bell rang once. First to emerge from the house was the vicar in plain vestments that fluttered gently in the wind. Mary stayed in bed, feeding little Anne, still unable to move after giving birth. The vicar took position beside the horse and cart and John, Father, Mr Quiney and two other leather workers emerged from the house carrying Bod's body tightly wrapped in a white shroud. They placed her on the cart and we all formed a procession behind, except for the vicar, who walked in front.

Our solemn procession moved down Henley Street to the High Street. From there it was a straight run down Chapel Street and Church Street past the school and left on to Mill Lane for the last bit to Holy Trinity. Along the way men stopped, took off their hats and bowed, and women made deep and long curtsies, lowering their heads. Whispers ricocheted around the onlookers to find the identity of whom we took to their grave. When Miss Bodicome's name was mentioned, there were some gasps, some sudden tears. Quite a few people, particularly the shop merchants, stopped what they were doing and joined the procession, so much so, that by the time we arrived at Holy Trinity, there must have been fifty people behind us.

She was simply 'Maid' to Mary, Bod to Will and I, and Miss Bodicome to everyone else, but she was well-loved and touched all who came across her. No one knew her without a smile for the world or good words for any person, no matter how ill-humoured they might have been.

We stood and watched for what seemed an eternity as the vicar rambled on and on about life, love, death and dust. This was followed by psalm after psalm, but it all came to a sharp shivering climax when she was finally lowered into her grave. Disappearing from view as the earth was piled upon her, there was no going back. She was gone. My heart was heavy, sinking to my feet. From that moment on, in times of great pain, sadness or confusion, it was always Bod I wanted to talk to.

When the final shovel of earth landed on the grave, the diggers patted the pile with their spades in some vain attempt at comfort for the dead. Will looked across to me with great sadness. At that moment the sun came out from behind a cloud and shone on us all. We looked to each other and both laughed. We knew whatever, wherever, our dear Bod was there.

With Bod gone, Mary needed a maid. There was a succession of women who really did not suit, on account of a contrary Mary, two babies, one toddler and a recalcitrant William. The work was as demanding as it was hard. Mary pleaded with Grace to take the position but she was devoted to her brother and could not be swayed, thank goodness. I worked on, hard and harder and I grew stronger and stronger. I would see Will now and again but his schooling took much of his time. After Sunday Mass we would sometimes visit Bod's grave and take time to catch up.

'You miss her?' I asked one Sunday as we stared blankly over Bod's grave.

Will simply shrugged, and then walked away and wandered round the side of the yard, dragging his hand through the edge of the yew tree that grew in the corner. I sat on a gravestone and watched Will wander the yard in his thoughts. After a couple of circuits, he came back and sat beside me.

Suddenly a voice rang out over the churchyard.

'William Shakespeare, what are you doing sitting in the dirt in your Sunday best consorting with peasants?'

Will stared at the ground.

'Mother's new maid, a trollop from Birmingham. More voice than a live goose and less brain than a dead one,' he said in total deadpan.

I choked on my laughter as Will stood up and dusted the dirt from his backside as the buxom maid strode up to us, barely containing her bosom in her bodice. I stayed seated.

'Really, what would your mother say? Look at you.'

She looked at me and forced a smile to her face. 'With due respect, William's a gentleman. He shouldn't be seen holding talk with your sort,' she stated, with all the superficial politeness she could muster, before dragging him away by the scruff of the neck. As it happened, she didn't last long – too outspoken she was, so Mary gave her marching orders.

CHAPTER 9

The following months were damp and dark. I saw nothing of my friend. School ran most of the waking day, six days a week and so did the livery, except it went for seven days. Will had new friends, and important friends, too, it seemed. I knew who some of them were, as their fathers were customers but that was about all. Occasionally, I would see him on his way to school, when I had a horse to deliver. I was generally walking in the opposite direction. We would wave at each other, but the waves started to get weaker and less meaningful.

Christmas came and went. We barely noticed it; work was so busy. Then three weeks into the New Year, just as the chill was gripping, I was taking a horse to Rother Street and saw Will with friends. He was so engaged he did not see me, so I ran with my horse and called out loud, 'Will, Will, Will!'

Will and his friends kept walking, but one turned and saw me running and calling.

'William, there is a ragamuffin with a nag beseeching you,' I heard him laugh.

Will turned around and, still walking in a skipping stride, he looked me straight in the eye and turned back to his friends.

'A servant's son. We used to play in the garden as children,' he shouted haughtily, and carried on with his friends.

I stopped and watched them laugh their way up the street. Further along, two of the boys threw momentary glances at me, as if Will was saying unkind words about me. I stood and watched them walk into the distance, their receding vision replaced by a thousand ants scurrying and tingling over my heart. I walked slowly back to the livery. My feet could barely feel the road beneath – even the horse limped with my heartfelt pain. Whilst tying up the horse, Father came over.

'All good, Son?'

'Yes, Father.'

Father looked the horse up and down, and then picked up a hoof and flicked out a stone.

'Not notice he had a stone?' he asked. He looked at me. He could see red in my eyes, which we often had from hay and tiredness, but he knew this was from welling tears.

'No, Father, sorry.'

'Thee all right, Son?'

'Father ... when something ... hurts you deep inside, what do you do?'

He took my chin with his finger, and though as rough as an old hoof rasp, it was still gentle. 'If you are rich and educated, you take time, let tears flow and maybe write a poem about it.'

He then turned my chin towards the yard. 'But if you are poor and uneducated, you put a cold poultice on it, and get on. Time of the poor is owned by others.'

I nodded.

'What gives, Son?' he vaguely inquired.

I just sniffed, and wiped my nose. '... I have to get on, Father.'

January went to February and the days turned from chilly to as cold as a dead mare's lips. I would try to busy myself cleaning tack, for no other reason than being close to the warmth of the smithy fire. It was late one evening and I had been cleaning tack since midday. I thought it was all done, but my father had asked apologetically if I could do two bridles and saddles for the dean of St Mary's visitors. I knew Father would be taken up grooming the beasts so it was not as if he was putting upon me.

I had done the saddles and, by candlelight, was myopically cleaning the intricate brass-work of the bridles. They were classy pieces of work and must have cost a pretty penny. I was just about finished when a familiar voice floated across the room.

'Hello, Tom,' said the voice, a touch awkwardly.

I looked up and in the flickering light saw my friend leaning casually on one of the saddles. Despite being wary of him, I noticed he looked freshly handsome. It was a new Will. In the glow he looked as if he were posing for a great portrait to adorn the wall of a great house. His hair was cut in a different dash; he had grown quite a bit and had some fine new clothes. I, on the other hand, was covered in the grime of leather oil and brass polish, looking the picture of a 'ragamuffin', as his friend had so kindly put it. I said nothing but, placing down the bridle, I grabbed a cloth and started to wipe my hands.

Will did not wait and, taking me quite by surprise, grabbed me in an all-enveloping bear hug. '*Meus frater in lacte*,' he whispered.

'Been a while, friend,' I replied.

I almost became overcome with emotion but I held it back. I sat down on a stack of sacks. Will grabbed an old stool and, sitting down, looked me in the eye and grinned.

'How's the school?' I asked, by way of trying to break the ice.

'Good, my friend, good,' he said, and started to look at the floor.

'What's up, Will?' I asked,

'I've been a cur, Tom – a canker-ridden cur,' he admitted and looked up.

'Nuh, not to me,' I said with a forced smiled.

'Last month in Rother Street,' he admitted.

'So what?' I said, feebly hiding my pain.

'I heard you call me and I cast you aside, the act of a cur,' Will said apologetically.

'You've come to see me now. That's not the act of a cur.'

'On account of my new schooling, I had become too high and mighty; so I want to make reparation and share with you my new friends.'

I said nothing but nodded in silent agreement. At that moment, three young boys slid silently into the tack-room and their remorseful faces caught the flickering light. One boy was tall and blond, good-looking but skinny. One was dark, touch of the gypsy tar brush maybe, sharp dark hair with a pointed chin and blue eyes, whilst the other was a freckled red-head. They stood awkwardly waiting for someone to say something.

'They are the three Dicks!' said Will.

'Richard Field; call me Fieldy,' said the red-headed boy as he put out his hand, which I took and shook.

'Richard Quiney; call me Quiney,' said the dark-haired boy as we, too, shook.

'Richard Tyler, known as simply Tyler,' said the blond boy.

'My friends, your friends. We are all friends and I will never behave like that again,' said Will.

We both gave each other another great hug, accompanied by applause from the other boys.

'So who's top of the class?' I asked.

'Me,' said Will, as the other boys all pointed at him in unison.

'Our master, Owen Trentham. His son, Godfrey, goes there, does he not?' I asked, which seemed to light up Tyler.

'And, is his sister not the prettiest maid you ever saw?' Tyler laughed. 'Juliet! Fourteen with breasts like roses and lips like sweet peas! Everyone wants to be Godfrey's friend, but such an ugly boy, with less brains than a pile of horse shit.'

'Are you his friend?' I quipped, suddenly pointing at Will.

'Tom, there are limits.'

'Limits? In the pursuit of pretty girls?'

'Juliet is a picture, I'll grant you that. But she is too aloof. She has eyes for the university boys that come to assist the teacher. See her outrageous glances to their eyes, when she comes to pick up her brother after school.'

'What's the master like?' I asked, smiling wryly as I forgave the silly arrogant schoolboy and savoured this new and confident William.

'Bent old man, smelling of tallow smoke, stale wine and aged cheese,' said Quiney.

'Do 'Creaky'!' demanded Tyler.

Will then held us in hysterics as he started to imitate the Latin teacher who taught him.

'Remember when he said he would put anyone top of the class who could conjugate eight Latin verbs by the morrow,' said Fieldy.

'Will leapt on my desk and told Creaky he would go better. He would know them afore the third hour post midday,' chipped in Quiney.

'Did you get in trouble for leaping on the desk?'

'Swear an oath he did. Creaky danced like a full moon madman!' said Fieldy.

Will gave an impression of the old Latin master losing his temper.

'What happened?' I asked through my giggles.

'He said, for my cheek and arrogance, if I did not know them by three o'clock he would thrash my arse till it bled!'

'Did you learn them?'

'I knew them already; he forgot he had written them on the blackboard the previous day.'

We all laughed hysterically at Will outwitting the old fool. And then went strangely silent as we acknowledged it was actually quite a feat of the intellect that Will had performed.

'And you remembered them without writing them down?' I asked, incredulously.

Will became pensive.

'Yes, Tom, I did. I just seem to be able to remember things I like, with really, very ... great ease.'

It was not the first time I had witnessed this but, as the others nodded their acknowledgment, it was clear Will was starting to create an impression around him.

'Do you like Latin then? You good at it?'

'Not really, it's boring. I like the poetry though.'

Grace came into the tack-room.

'Time you bedded down, Tom. That tack all finished?'

'Yes, Aunt,' I replied.

'Hello, Grace,' said Will with a gentle smile.

'Mr William. What brings you here this time of night?' she said,

'Only time I could steal to see my good friend.'

'And apologise?' said Grace with hint of sarcasm.

'Oh, you heard,' said Will, throwing a look my way.

'Don't go looking to he for telling,' she snapped. 'He never said nought, nor showed the pain. I saw you that day. I was coming out the grocer.'

'Tis all well, Grace,' I begged.

'No, Grace is right. I wronged you, and, Grace, that is why I came here tonight, with my friends, with no other intention other than righting that wrong and sharing my newest friends with my oldest.'

There was a silence.

Grace then did something quite extraordinary, something I had never seen her do before or since. She went forward and, taking Will's head firmly in her hands, she kissed him on both cheeks. I was totally stunned.

'Takes a big man to do what you just did, and you being just a boy. Sure makes you set for a great man,' she said, and then looked to the other boys, 'Master Quiney, Master Field, Master Tyler, I bid thee all good night.'

'Good night,' they all said in unison.

Grace left the tack-room.

'She knew our names?' said Tyler.

'Grace is like that,' I said.

'Like what?' asked Fieldy.

'If it's there, she will see it,' I said.

'We had better go,' said Will.

'See you soon enough, my friend.'

Will ushered his friends out but hung back a moment. 'Do you wish you could go to school, Tom?'

Of course I did, and Will knew it, but what could I say? 'My place is here, Will,' I said quietly.

Will nodded in silence. He put one soft punch on the doorpost, and then, stroking his upper lip, departed and, with his friends, walked into the night.

I blew out the candles and stood for a moment in the light from the dying fire. I looked around to what the 'here' was that I had told my friend I belonged to. The truth was that I longed to escape from this 'here'.

CHAPTER 10

Spring arrived and brightened our spirits. One day in March Johnny Somerville turned up at the livery alone, just before the onset of Lent. I had been slushing the central courtyard with pails of water when I looked up and, in the light of the glistening cobbles, there he stood – Johnny Somerville. His clothes had always been in whatever hue of yellow or, 'gold' as he referred to it, he could find with the cloth merchants. He stood there, posing in his yellow hose, fawn leather breeches, boots, doublet, cloak and hat. Hand on sword, he stroked his moustache and surveyed the skyline as if waiting to be greeted by a thousand admirers.

'Mr Somerville. Good day to you, Sir,' I said, placing my pail down.

'Why, it's young Tom! How the devil are you?'

'I am well, Sir,' I replied.

'That's good. Now young Sir, it is my birthday in a few days. There will be a celebration, so I need to talk with your old man. Is he about?'

Johnny was always in good humour and, drunk or hung over, he only ever talked with the confidence of royalty. He never forgot a name, a person or a good deed and addressed everyone with a degree of equality and affection that just demanded you love him.

'I shall fetch him, Sir,' I said with a smile.

'Good man,' he replied and admired himself in a non-existent reflection.

I fetched my father who was mending tack in the tack-room.

'Jack, how the devil are you? Trade good?'

'Can't complain, Mr Somerville. My master, Mr Trentham, is happy with the monthly takings,' my father returned, cordially.

'Good, good. Now look, my dear friend, tis my birthday in two days and I thought a trip with me cousins to Coventry for the mystery plays would be a right Catholic way to celebrate it,' he declared.

'Most agreeable, Sir,' my father replied.

'Excellent. So for an equally agreeable sum, you can supply cart and beasts to convey myself and the Shakespeare family to and from said event?'

'Certainly, sir,' said my father. 'Four shillings.'

Johnny did one of his comic double takes. 'Gosh, seems an awful lot.'

He patted in his doublet for coin, expressing further comical surprise.

'Carriage costs must have passed me by. No mind. I have here a crown of the rose, so there is sixpence in it for you. Bring young Tom, too. Now do we have a contract?' he asked.

'A contract, indeed, Sir,' grinned my father happily.

Classic Johnny, protest with nothing more than generosity. He pulled out the coin and paid my father forthwith.

'You residing at Henley Street, Mr Somerville?'

'Jack, for God's sake call me Johnny. I ain't one of them. No, no, I am not. Old John's gone up in the world and finds me a little outspoken for his humble home. Beth and I are staying with an old university tutor, Father John Frith at Temple Grafton – most charming fellow.'

'Shall I pick you up there?' my father inquired.

'Let's all meet at Henley Street and set forth to the car of Thespis from there.'

'Car of Thespis?'

'Place of the play, in this case Coventry.'

'Getting you now, Mr Johnny,' replied Father in a wry smile.

Johnny bid us both a good afternoon and left the livery. I picked up the pail and went back about my work. Grace came out, drying her hands on her apron.

'Mr Somerville?' she asked my father.

'Taking the family to Coventry for the plays.'

'Fine. Let's hope he don't get drunk,' groaned Grace.

'Four shillings and sixpence, though.'

'Sixpence over the price? Where he gets it from, I just don't know.'

'Do the work, take the profit and don't ask,' said my father.

'Never truer word spoke,' sighed Grace.

I threw another bucket of water across the cobbles.

'Two more buckets Tom, then come and get some bread,' she said.

'Yes, Aunt,' I called, pushing the pail into the trough.

The wretched pail was made of oak staves and as heavy empty as it was full. I had just returned to the trough and was plunging it in again, when the almighty clatter of hooves heralded the arrival of Lord Lucy and his stewards. Father had heard the horses and came out into the yard.

Lord Lucy leapt off his horse with a fine fit swing of his body.

'Boy,' he called.

My father ushered me to respond. I ran over and took the reins of his horse. The other two men stayed mounted.

'Your Lordship,' my father said, holding his cap in hand and lowering his head.

'Wickham?' said Lord Lucy.

'Your Lordship,' my father replied.

'Tell me about this livery, Wickham,' he asked, looking around the tidy yard.

My father told him it was owned by Mr Owen Trentham and that he had been foreman for eleven years. He told him they held horses for the headmaster of King Edward School, several tradesmen and many merchants of Stratford. He pointed out that all dues were met on time and the clerk never reported a loss in the eleven years he had been there.

'I know. I have seen the ledgers,' replied Lord Lucy.

He gave himself a tour of the livery, looking at all the stables in turn, stroking the horses in a way that made me realise he not only understood Equus, but probably had a greater affection for them than for man. He looked the horses in the eye, but not one of us did he look in the eye. They then went into the tack-room and small smithy stable. Lord Lucy inspected all the tack hanging neatly inside. It was clean and beautiful. I knew that; I spent enough time cleaning it.

'You a farrier?' asked Lord Lucy, looking at the various tools.

'No, My Lord, but I can clip hooves and repair a loose shoe. We have a farrier who comes from Tredington the first of the month,' replied Father.

We exited back into the yard where Grace was waiting with a tray on which was placed a cup of mead for Lord Lucy. He took it without a glance in her direction, drank it and placed the empty cup back on the tray. Grace curtsied and went back inside.

'Wife?' asked Lord Lucy.

'Sister, My Lord,' said my father.

Lord Lucy beckoned to me and I took his horse to him. He grabbed the saddle pommel, raised his left leg and, without further prompting, my father grabbed it and helped him up on to his steed.

'This is a good establishment. I have made Trentham a fine offer. As from tomorrow, you will be working for me. Keep it up as you have and I will treat you fairly,' he stated in that clear crisp voice of nobility.

With that Lord Lucy brought his horse about and, with a charge, galloped out of the yard followed by the other two men, whoever they were. As soon as they left, Grace came back out into the yard.

'Don't trust a man who never looks one in the eye,' she murmured.

'Trentham has sold on to Lord Lucy, so you button your lip and we keep our communion records good,' advised my father, tapping Grace's nose kindly.

'Why communion, Father?' I asked.

My father looked at me. Nine years old I was; my father knew I had had to grow up fast. Nonetheless he crouched to my level. 'Young Tom, there are those who still fear Rome's bishop. It is said His Lordship keeps a note of all of unsound folk. It is said, he calls it his map of loyalty.

'We never want to fall off that map,' he added with quiet gravity.

I thought for a moment. I was about to speak but my father placed his weathered finger on my lips. 'What the ear doesn't hear, the head doesn't know,' he said.

Grace gave me a look of profound agreement. I looked back to my father.

'Two ways to survive in this life: with money or with wit. You have no money, nor do I or Grace.'

He patted me on the back and sent me with Grace to get some bread.

I never questioned or commented on anything political or religious again.

It was a fine dawn the day of the plays, and Grace had bought me a bright-red fitted felt cap to wear. I grinned and placed it on my head and showed it off to her. I thought it may raise a smile but she simply acknowledged my gratitude and bid me to get on with my chores as we had an early start. The one thing I was desperate to do in life was see a smile on dear Grace's face, but it was not to be today.

Granby Jacobson arrived to work early as arranged so we could set out and get a good start, for the plays began at midday. I brought out the two cobs we used for the cart. They were strong beasts with plenty of stamina for the nineteen-mile journey to Coventry, which would take about four and a half hours. That could stretch to a day if it was wet but fortunately the weather had been good, the road was dry and it was a full moon, so coming back in the darkness would be benefited by a cloudless sky.

Father and Grace wheeled the cart into position and, with a gentle tapping and clicking of my tongue, I edged the two cobs into the shafts. Father strapped them in and did up all the harness. Grace came out with a cloth containing some bread and a gourd of mead, and she pushed it under the driver's seat. My father took the club and placed that, too, under the seat. There were robbers on the road so he always took some form of weapon. I was not worried about robbers. They notoriously went for frail or lonesome victims. We would be three fit men, two feisty boys and a woman whom the devil himself would think twice before attacking.

For the outward journey, the sack of oats served as an excellent seat for father. We arrived at Henley Street and the Shakespeares were all waiting ready for us in family formation, with a very proud Johnny in

83

the middle. Of course not enough to surprise the family with this trip, Johnny had also put together a great basket of food for the day, on which he had placed one victorious foot.

'Hi, Will,' I called to Will, jumping down from the cart.

'Good-day, Tom,' said Will, and we greeted each other with a hug.

'Dear Cousin, when are you going to tell us where we are off to?' cried an excited Mary, jumping up and down.

'Come on, Johnny,' urged John.

'Tell them, John,' said Beth.

As Will stared up into the eyes of his favourite cousin, Johnny let forth his speech. 'My dear young Will, I hear from the talk of school folk that you have the gift of Thespis, so this day I wish to pour a fertilising tincture upon it. Beth and I, at great expense, will convey you to a stage of players, who will perform such a delight of play-acting that it never ceases to move me to tears.

'If I had my way, all plays would be not in streets, but in houses and played every day all over the country for all to enjoy. So from Henley Street to Coventry, the good Jack Wickham will convey us. Load up and lead on, my good Jack.'

I could see Will was in absolute raptures. He had heard lots of tales of the mystery plays but never seen them. This was certainly going to be a day to remember. We all clapped our hands for Johnny, and Mary gave him a huge embrace.

'You are such a good man, Johnny,' I heard her whisper in his ear.

We loaded up the basket of food and some extra blankets for the return journey. In the basket, Beth spied two bottles of wine and, gently removing them, she quietly passed them to Mary, who took them inside the house. Johnny didn't notice, because he, too, was also being underhand. Rather furtively he pushed a box under the driver's seat. It took my father's attention. Johnny silently hushed my father, who gently lifted the lid. I just caught sight of the polished metal of a pair of pistols.

'Never know, Jack. Bad sorts on the road between here and Coventry,' he said quietly.

'You have a sword. Is that not weapon enough?' whispered my father.

Johnny quietly pulled his sword from its scabbard. There was only four inches of blade; the rest had been snapped off. 'Broke it cutting the necks off wine bottles last week!'

He placed it back in its scabbard and comically demonstrated how it was still useful. With irrepressible optimism, he feigned grabbing his sword and pausing before actually drawing it.

'If there's some bother, you go to draw it, hoping the other fellow backs down before you have to actually pull it out,' said Johnny.

'If he doesn't?' wondered my father aloud, his tongue firmly in his cheek.

'Could be awkward,' Johnny replied dryly and jumped up on the cart.

My father said nothing more, and, mounting the cart, took up the reins. Everyone climbed aboard. Father moved the cart forward and I took the small shovel, picked up the horses' soil and placed it in the pail hanging beneath the cart. John Shakespeare put down a hand, which I grabbed and, pulling me up, we were off on our journey.

The journey would take us straight past the ruins of Wroxall Abbey, where Mary's aunt had been prioress. It was about two hours to Wroxall. The road was good and Mary sat in the back feeding both Joan and little Anne. As we approached the farm at Wilmcote, where she was brought up, Mary pointed out the orchards and paddocks left her in her father's will that brought in fine rents. Passing the actual farm Mary revealed it was Bod's grandfather who had built the very impressive dovecote. When we pressed Mary about Bod's family, she would not be drawn to tell anything further.

We stopped at Wroxall Abbey to rest. The overgrown and looted remains were a sight. In the main they were pitiful but, in the flickering sunlight, a touch poetic. There was not much left. Locals repairing their houses had taken much of the stone and in the remaining masonry, trees and shrubs had established root. Mary stepped down from the cart and walked into the old ruin with Johnny and Beth. Mr Shakespeare stayed on the cart.

I followed with Will and, catching up with Mary, Will noticed she was shedding tears, so he took her hand. The various bits of wildlife that had made it their home took off on our approach. Under one of the half-collapsed arches, a deer stopped its feeding, briefly twitched an ear in our direction, and then looked straight at us, chewing slowly as it wondered what to do. In an instant it took flight.

Beth held on to Gilbert and then I noticed that she, too, was crying. What was it they were crying about? The abbey had been destroyed years ago. I was really quite confused. To Will and I, the destruction of this abbey, King Henry and all that was not a fresh memory; it may as well have been a thousand years ago. A fresh memory to us was our sore bottoms from the bumpy cart. Nonetheless, I still picked up on the eerie atmosphere that leached out of the place.

'No fairies here?' I asked Will.

'No, Tom. No fairies here.'

We followed behind Mary and Will as she picked her way through the undergrowth deep into the ruins. Mary stroked the stone-work, like she knew every stone intimately, as if they were the gravestones of her own children. 'They burnt six hundred books, right there, see,' she said, pointing at an area outside the main door.

'Who did?' asked Will.

'The king's men.'

'Why?'

'The king feared the words within those books,' she sighed and started to cry again.

Johnny looked about and kicked the earth.

'The burning of books is the greatest crime that does not shed blood, Will,' he said.

Will squeezed his mother's hand, which seemed to offer some comfort.

'Only fools fear words, Will,' said Johnny kicking the soil again. 'But fools wield much power in our green and pleasant land and there is nothing more deadly than a powerful fool.'

We wandered around the ruin, Mary feeding her memory, her anger, her fear, her passion, her loss, and all the time comforted by her young son who seemed to constantly rub his lip.

This was the start of Will's signature mannerism. If something took his attention, he would stroke the area between his upper lip and nose, known in equine circles as the philtrum. I came to realise this action indicated, that whatever it was he was noticing, was being stored deep in his memory.

'Were you there, too?' I asked Beth, wandering back to the cart.

'No, Tom. Too young. Mistress Shakespeare was; she was only five, though.'

'Why is she still upset?' I asked in childish naivety.

'Tom, sometimes things happen which upset us, and they never leave our hearts.'

The rest of the journey to Coventry was pleasant enough. The wheels stayed on the cart and there was no chance of robbers, since there were a lot of folk on their way to see the plays. Just before midday we spied the large city walls a few miles off. Inside the walls, my father and I found somewhere to tether the horses, not too far from a clean trough where the water was fresh. Times were hard for this once-wealthy city and many of the buildings were in a bad state of repair. Father took a bucket of pig fat to grease the cart wheels and I watched as the Shakespeare family set off for the cathedral where scaffolds had been set up for the plays.

As the jolly family wended its way through the dilapidated streets, I so wished I could join them.

'Well go on, Tom,' my father said.

'Thanks, Father!' I replied with a gasp of surprise.

I ran and caught up with them in no time. The crowds were as thick as winter barley and, unlike the wide streets of Stratford, the streets of Coventry were narrow and wound around in a higgledy-piggledy way. Mary, Beth and Grace gracefully held their dresses high to avoid the dog excrement, spittle and the claggy gutters. As skinny-legged boys, Will and me, well, we ran on, as free as the smelly dogs yapping at our ankles.

Soon the cathedral started to tower over us. When we arrived, the street opened up revealing the biggest building I had ever seen in my life: the great cathedral of St Mary. It was more awe-inspiring than a herd of horses at full gallop.

Outside the main cathedral doors a series of scaffold platforms had been erected, each furnished with curtains and painted cloths.

On the biggest one there were lots of things happening. Someone said it was a play of the creation of the world with one of the local butchers playing God. He was suspended in a massive cauldron above the stage, a huge beast of a man with an enormous hairy stomach and long white beard.

God shouted for light. People rushed around the stage below with great flaming torches. Then he yelled for the oceans to be made and all these other people rushed around in flowing robes painted in blue colours. After a bit they all came together and formed an ocean swaying together. And, all the time, other people rolled barrels of rocks, banged metal and blew horns to make the loudest sounds I have ever heard. It was just like being there, at the beginning of the world.

God called for land and, out of the ocean, came people dressed in green and brown. They climbed up over the people dressed as the ocean and soon the mound of people looked like an island in the ocean. It was so clever.

I looked around for Will. He was not with Johnny or Mary or John. Then I saw him, he was up the front and, having climbed the scaffold, was practically sitting amongst the players. His eyes and smile were as wide as the sky; he could not take his attention off what was going on.

I went on my hands and knees and crawled through all the feet, legs and muck to the front of the crowd. Then, clambering under the splintery wooden scaffold, I pulled myself up to where Will was perched. Will did not even see me. I tugged his vest, and he simply put his hand out to help me up without taking his eyes off the spectacle before him.

'Did you ever see anything like this, Tom?' whispered Will, his eyes still locked to the players.

'No,' I answered, just as two bakers came on in their bakers work clothes. The first was wearing one big leaf over his trousers and the other had three leaves – two on his shirt and one on his trousers. A roar of laughter went up from the crowd.

'Who are they?' I whispered.

'Adam and Eve,' whispered Will, taking care not to avert his eyes from the scene.

God roared on again and people wheeled in a great tree made from old sticks which had huge brightly painted apples hanging from it.

'What's that?' I whispered.

'Shhh! Tree of knowledge,' said Will.

Then the devil came in as a great long snake carried by lots of people. It was all really funny. I wanted Will to explain more but he kept shushing me so I just kept watching until the end. When they finished, everyone who was in the play came on to the scaffold and stood in a line. There was clapping of hands and cheering the like of which I had never heard. It went on and on and on.

I saw Will watch in utter amazement. He, too, was clapping and cheering but he would look to the players, then look to the cheering crowd and then back again. He was sucking it all in, like the air up the chimney of a roaring fire. I was in absolutely no doubt something had entered his spirit and it was never ever going to leave.

After the applause subsided, people drifted off and the players started setting up other stuff on the scaffold.

The crowds separated and went to the many stalls to buy refreshments. There were people selling roast pig and bread; there were oysters, fresh oranges, baked peascod on bread, bowls of pottage and fish. Also, there were some sweet things that were just so expensive. I had never seen so many traders selling so much food. I wandered around with Will, in a daze looking at it all.

I saw Mary and she called out, 'Will, Tom. We are going to the cart. Johnny has a lunch for us.'

We all trundled back to the cart where Johnny opened the basket of food. Mary and Beth laid it out and shared it with my father and I.

'Where's me wine?' said Johnny looking in the basket.

'Wine, what wine?' asked Mary, in an appalling imitation of innocence.

'Two fine bottles of moselle' he pondered, delving to the bottom of the basket.

'Don't know, love,' said Beth.

Johnny looked in further.

'Well, either left 'em behind or they bin purloined by persons unknown ... to keep old Johnny sober,' he groaned quietly. 'Hey ho, pass me a slice of that fine pork and spinach pie and a cup of that unpalatable warm mead.'

He smiled in good humour and set about enjoying his lunch.

I was given two plates of food and, turning to hand one to Will, I realised he was not there.

'Mistress Shakespeare, Will's not here.'

'He'll show up. Give it to me,' she answered.

'Do you think he's all right?' queried Beth, but Johnny wasn't worried.

'Surely, exploring the car of Thespis. Did you see him? Pushed himself straight to the front, practically on the platform in the action. Never seen a duck take to water with greater ease. Boy's a thespian, mark my words.'

'Just who is this Thespis, thespian, what?' queried a puzzled John.

'Thespis, Greek fellow, was the first man to act in a play. At Oxford the wits call all such fellows thespians, and the places of such plays the car of Thespis,' said Johnny, in his usual learned tone, and then he downed his cup of mead in one.

'By God that was horrible,' he said looking at the empty cup.

He then turned away and quietly took a flask from his doublet and poured what smelled like French brandy into his cup.

We finished the splendid fare from the basket and were just about to set off for the next big play, the Passion of the Christ, when a highly excited Will came rushing up at a pace matched only by a horse in flames.

'Oh! You should have seen it! There was the story of Noah on the back of a cart by the fish traders' guild and on another cart I saw the story of of, of ... the fall of Lucifer by the blacksmiths. It was incredible and another had ...'

Will was stuttering and stammering with excitement as Mary tried to give him some food. Will grabbed fistfuls of bread and pie and, stuffing them into his mouth, he spat lumps everywhere as he told us how the devil caught fire on the back of the cart whilst performing the fall of Lucifer, and it was Noah from the other cart who threw a pail of water over him to put him out. Will not only described the scene in such colour, he acted it and danced it, too.

'The tailors too! They did a play about the massacre of holy innocents!'

Will reflected for a moment, and then he quoted as though he had known the words all his life:

King Herod in his raging charged he hath this day, his men of might, in his own sight, all young children to slay. Then woe is me poor child, for thee and ever mourn and deep of sigh; for thy parting, neither say nor sing by-by lulla-lullay. By-by, lulla, lullay, ye little tiny child. By-by, lulla, lullay.

Will went on and on and on. He had memorised the entire text. Eventually he stopped, breathing heavily and flushed pink with enthusiasm. He had quite taken everyone's breath away. I still remember the sight of his teary grin, his mouth laden with bread, eyes wide open and chest heaving to feed much-needed air to the over-excited spirit.

'The boy's a genius, John,' declared Johnny, breaking the silence. He patted John Shakespeare heartily on the back.

'A genius glover will pay a way in life but I fear a genius poet or play actor will not,' stated John quite firmly.

'Pish,' quipped Johnny and, reaching into his doublet, he pulled out his book and waved it at John.

'Publius Ovidius Naso, 1600 years old and we are still reading him, eh? Where'll your bloody gloves be in ten years, let alone 1500! Our Will is a poet; I can smell it. And, he'll be like this man, still read by all in a thousand years.'

Johnny popped the book back in his doublet and poured another cup of mead for himself, quietly lacing it with more brandy. Indeed, something in Will was there that no one could describe or name, but unequivocally, something everyone could see.

'And, and, and! They are ending this day with *The Passion*!' Will blurted, like a vital message suddenly remembered.

'And incredible it is! Enjoy it. Chance be you'll never see it again,' said Johnny downing his cup once more.

'Why not?' asked a puzzled Will.

'The State banned these plays these last four years. Only matter of time before it's enforced with all the rigour State can muster,' he sighed.

'Why do they want to ban poetry and play acting?' asked Will innocently.

Beth became unsettled. Her eyes darted to John, and then back to her husband, worried about him launching into one of his diatribes.

'Because, young Will, rather than a scaffold flowing with the tears of poets and players, the State prefers to see it flow with blood! The blood of Papists. Remember young Will, Catholics create, Protestants destroy.'

'What do you mean?' asked Will.

John become distinctly nervous and dragged Johnny away, and Mary skillfully interjected.

'And soon to start. It's on the biggest platform near the cathedral!' she said nervously. 'We must hurry to get a good place. Go to. Go to, Will.'

Distracted by the thought of the biggest play to come, Will ran off down the street, beckoning us all to follow.

'Will, wait!' I called and ran after him.

Looking back, I saw Will's father pull the flask of brandy from Johnny's doublet and try to empty it on to the ground but Johnny successfully wrestled it back. Beth left them to it and, with Mary, she sauntered after us. I found it difficult to keep up with Will. He headed straight for the front, where they were all preparing for the big play of the night, *Christ's Passion*.

Will completely vanished under the scaffolding. I went back to the place from where I had watched the creation play but there was no sign of Will. Pretty soon the play was under way and I watched with considerable awe. It was such a spectacle, the like I had never seen. They went through the whole story. Then suddenly, there! At the trial of Christ by Pontius Pilot, a boy brought the man playing Pontius Pilot a bowl of water in which to wash his hands; the boy was none other than our Will! Here before me, this was the first public performance on stage of William Shakespeare. Of course, at the time I had no idea of the significance of what I was witnessing, but it did excite me.

They had timed the crucifixion to coincide with the setting sun and, at the moment the Christ died, all went to darkness. There was a hush in the crowd that was strange. You could've heard a seamstress drop her pin. Then, a baby cried and women started to shed tears. Suddenly Will appeared at my side and he held on to me like a brother, saying nothing, just watching the moving scene with hawk-like intensity.

In an instant, there were crashes, booms and flashes of gunpowder. Huge pieces of hanging cloth were ripped in two; it was like there was an army attacking us in a storm. Everyone held each other tight as they watched flash after flash throwing light around the platform. Then all the players put out every torch at once, the flashes stopped and again we were plunged into darkness. An eerie hush again came over the crowd.

Two players playing Mary Magdalene and Holy Mary wandered across the platform with torches. The crosses had gone and they revealed the scene of the empty tomb of Christ. A gasp went up as, high above them, lit by torches, dressed in white from head to toe, appeared the risen Christ. He held a crook in one hand and a lamb cradled in his other arm; unexpectedly, the lamb bleated and at once everyone cheered, clapped and cried. I did not realise I was witnessing the power of the theatre. Will certainly did, and he wanted it.

I sat with my father, drifting in and out of sleep, as he drove the cart home. The Shakespeares lay across each other, sleeping as newborns and we creaked our way back through the moonlit night to Stratford. Will was not asleep, though. He sat on the back of the cart dangling his feet, looking to where he had seen this incredible event. It was like he was re-living it in his head over and over again, so as to savour every little morsel for eternity.

When Father and I finally dropped off the Shakespeare family, a now-sober Johnny picked up a sleepy Will.

'Do you require conveying back to Temple Grafton, Sir,' asked my father.

Johnny shook his head.

'You have more than earned your fee,' he said drowsily and, bowing gently, he carried a sleeping Will into the house.

Father and I got back to the livery at about the second hour after midnight. In the smithy stable we found Lord Lucy's second steward

Mr Cornall asleep across the oat sacks. Obviously he wanted something on behalf of His Lordship and, being that he was not a man to be kept waiting, we thought best not to wake him. We tried to creep around, putting away the harness but ill-fate struck and he awoke. Cornall was a young stocky brute of a man, well-toned, very fit but unfortunately, when intelligence failed him, he routinely communicated with his fists. Since he was a man of low wit, this was quite often.

'Where in the devil's name have you been?' he barked, sitting up all bleary eyed.

'Working. Took a party to Coventry,' said Father calmly.

'What do you charge for that?' he grunted.

'Cart and pair of cobs, one day, four shillings,' replied Father ushering me to the door.

'Good price. In advance?'

'In advance, paid in and booked. You can see the clerk. He'll be by at three the morrow,' said Father as he ushered me to bed.

'Where are you going?' said Cornall.

'Mr Cornall, we are unslept these last twenty hours. We are going to bed.

'Verily, be up in two hours,'

'For why?' asked father.

Mr Cornall jumped off the feed sacks and became quite curt.

'Your master has need of the entire livery tomorrow for three days. Her Majesty, Queen Elizabeth, is to stay at Charlecote House and her retinue will require more livery than is available at Charlecote. This livery will be cleared by midday and made available for horses of the royal retinue and staff.'

My jaw was on the ground. We had nine hours to find somewhere to place, not only the livery horses but also the beasts of a dozen fee-paying owners, who were not likely to be at all pleased. My father's face was a masterpiece of composure, which was where I eventually learnt the art from. He did not bat an eyelid or wince a muscle.

'Inform His Lordship his bidding will be done. Now, Sir, I, my son and my sister bid you a goodnight.'

And, with that, my father turned his back on Mr Cornall and ushered us out of the stable.

CHAPTER II

Indeed, the following morning I awoke but not at the sixth hour as I thought; it was past the eighth hour. My dear father and Grace, up at the sixth, had started preparing the livery and, bless their hearts, they had left me to sleep. When I came into the yard, all the horses were milling around – a technique my father created and had taught me. We would leave them for about a half-hour or so, watching to see which would be the lead horse. Sure enough, they all settled and were soon licking their lips and cocking legs, eyes calm and ears soothed. My father then looked around the herd. This was a job of patience. I watched intently, and then I nudged Father. Mr Harding's bay mare was being touched and bowed to by the others. Father smiled and shook my hand in respect as the mare moved casually around the herd establishing her authority.

'You take them to Jennifer Grayson's paddock on Kissing Tree Lane,' he said.

'Yes, Father.'

'After, to Charlecote and inform Mr Cornall the livery is at Her Majesty's service'.

'Yes, Father,' I replied.

Grace quickly shoved some mead and bread into my hands.

'Heavens Gate is outside,' said Father, getting ready to saunter into the melee and pull out Harding's mare.

I quietly made my exit into the street where the ever-dependable Heavens Gate stood. Supported by his still majestic legs, slightly leaning forwards, head in the air and great hairy hoofs the size of pottage bowls, I could not help but love him. Riding him bareback with just a bridle, I had Grace help me up. I sat with my legs virtually horizontal to my body. I was quite a comical speck of a thing on such a massive beast. It was testament to my father's faith in me that he would entrust his nine-year-old son with forty horses, none of which he owned. It made me proud to be his son.

I pulled the magnificent Heavens Gate around and Grace opened the gates of the livery. My father tossed me the lead rein on Mr Harding's mare. I caught it and started off down the street. Like well-behaved school children on their first day, the thirty-nine horses all followed.

It was a drizzly wet Sunday morning and, as I closed on Clopton's Bridge, there I saw Will with Mary. They were up and walking early. I waved for him to follow. I could not stop; you cannot do that with a herd of horses. It is important to keep them moving.

'Come on!' I yelled.

'Wait,' called Will.

'I cannot! If you want to ride with me, you must run!'

I stood on Heavens Gates back and faced Will, the horse's back was so big and flat a class of twelve children could have stood with no bother. At first, Will did not understand but then, with a prompt from Mary, he got the message. He ran and ran and soon was alongside. I put my hand down, he grabbed it and I pulled him up.

'Take care of our Will, Tom,' called Mary.

'I will,' I called back.

We made such a fine noise crossing Cloptons Bridge heading for the paddock. We felt like a pair of generals at the head of a great army. Will stood up and raised his fist in the air.

'To France to France! Calais shall be ours once more!'

He sat down. 'Why are you moving all the horses?'

'Lord Lucy has need of the livery stalls. Her Majesty comes to Charlecote this day.'

'Her Majesty at Charlecote?'

In Stratford, up till this moment, only my father, Grace and I held this news. Will was rightly stunned. This was a big event to which only he so far was privy.

Kissing Tree Lane was quite close and, when we arrived, Will jumped off and opened the gate. I then cantered in and led the herd in a big circle around the paddock. It was a wonderful feeling cantering round on that wonderful old war-horse. I felt like a great knight leading the charge.

'Agincourt! England and St George!' shouted Will standing high on the gate.

I laughed and raised a fist, and then, pulling the lead horse close, I pulled off her halter. She immediately ran free, kicked and bucked. I galloped out of the paddock and Will closed the gate behind, as if we had been working as a team for eternity.

I leapt off Heavens Gate and Will and I watched as the horses settled down. 'What's Aginccc …?'

'Agincourt. A battle we won against the French.'

I looked at Will out of the corner of my eye.

'It proved us English to be the greatest archers of all time,' said Will.

'We have to go to Charlecote and tell Mr Cornall the livery is at his disposal,' I said.

As we trotted to Charlecote Park, I listened to his story of the great Prince Hal who, when he became king of England, led his loyal Catholic subjects to take back from the foul-breathed French what was rightfully ours.

We arrived at the gates of Charlecote and were about to ride down the drive when, suddenly, a clod of earth hit me on the back of the head. This was followed by the most billowing voice.

'If you ride that pox-ridden thing down my drive, you will be dog meat!'

Seeing a freshly raked driveway, I pulled up Heavens Gate sharp. All the way down the drive was a flurry of activity. The source of the clod and the bellowing approached; he was a tough and weathered groundsman in no mood for two boys on an oversize horse messing up his hard toil.

'State your business, you scrawny bastards, or feel my fist.'

'I have a message for Mr Cornall,' I said, hoping the steward's name would calm his passion.

'Down the road, cross the second paddock. He's in the stable yard.'

We duly took the instruction, crossed the paddock that was the temporary service entrance and arrived at the back of the park stables. Will and I stared agog at the activity. Carts were being unloaded with more produce than I had seen at a Christmas fair. There were whole pigs on poles gutted and ready to roast, baskets of game birds, baskets of fresh oranges, grapes, figs and apples. I saw barrels of oysters, fresh fish and enough wine casks to float a galleon – never mind enough bread to feed the five thousand.

The servants were running hither and thither, fetching and carrying; people were shouting, calling, ordering, demanding. Looking up at the windows, the maids could be seen billowing bedding, while men cleaned and polished glass. Gardens and paths were being raked and trimmed in all directions. I saw Lord Lucy cross the yard. He was not his usual haughty self and was as agitated as the rest of them.

'Wickham!' called a sharp voice.

I turned. There stood Mr Cornall, arms akimbo with customary aggression lurking in the creases of his scowl.

'Sir, my father sends word the Ely Livery is at Her Majesty's disposal,'

The stable bell struck and rang out the hour.

'The ninth hour! Just in time. Tell your father to expect the retinue of the queen's outriders, twenty-three beasts and men. Now! Go!'

'Sir!' I replied.

Pulling Heavens Gate about, I galloped out of the yard, with Will hanging on tight but still frenetically looking around and taking in all the activity.

'Did you ever see so much food!' cried Will, as we galloped across the paddock.

'Never,' I called back.

Halfway across the paddock in the distance, heading towards the main gates I saw a score of riders flying the royal standard.

'Outriders. She's here!' I shouted.

Distant shouts went up and travelled in sequence across the park. I pulled up and watched as suddenly all the frantic activity ceased. Everyone hid themselves, diving behind bushes, jumping into ditches and stashing tools. In an instant, Charlecote looked the essence of a silent palace of perfection, elegantly awaiting its monarch. Will nudged me and pointed to the rooftop where the royal standard was being hastily raised.

The outriders fell out of their canter and, in military precision, they lined up along the driveway either side in a guard of honour and might.

'Come on! Let's see her,' said Will.

I squeezed my heels and made for the road. We galloped to the front gates but were suddenly greeted by the sharp ends of four pike-men. I pulled up Heavens Gate quickly. A man dressed in black rushed forward and, with a gesture, ordered us from our horse. The man beckoned us over. We obliged and he made us stand either side of him beside the gates. The pike-men stood to attention either side of the front gates.

'Very small men for such a large horse,' the man commented.

There was suddenly the thunder of hooves along the road and Her Majesty's cortege approached. Will and I both wanted to see what our queen looked like. Which would be her carriage, we wondered, peering down the road. Suddenly a wave of royal standard-bearing horsemen rounded the bend, the flags cutting a chattering flutter to the rhythmical thud of their hooves. The man beside us removed his hat and bowed long and deep. We carried on watching, more interested in catching a glimpse of our queen than doing her any honour. Still in his bowing position, the man grabbed the hair on our necks and forced us down into a bow.

'Feet! Hands!' he snapped.

Will looked across to me and copied the gesture of the bowing submission the man was making, I suddenly understood the idea and I copied, too. In the next instant, in a cloud of road dust and horse sweat, Her Majesty's retinue and carriage swept by. It was very disappointing. We saw nothing but hooves and wagon wheels. However, we felt everything! The power of this retinue was utterly unlike anything we had ever witnessed.

That was our first contact with Her Majesty, Queen Elizabeth. Little did we know it would not be Will's last. Once the cortege had passed, we stood up.

'You must be young Wickham,' the man in black said.

'Yes, Sir,' I replied, a little perplexed.

He walked over to Heavens Gate who was enjoying a meal of Lord Lucy's hedgerow. He took the rein and walked him back to us.

'Good to see the old boy is still around,' he quipped.

'You know him, Sir?'

'Heavens Gate?! Brought him into the world and trained him, sold him to Lord Lucy,' he stated with a happy grin. 'I am Lord Gregory of Aylesbury. So my outriders are billeted at the livery your father runs for Lord Lucy.'

'Your Lordship.'

Lord Gregory clicked his fingers and the groundsman, who had so foully abused us, appeared from behind a hedge and meekly brought over His Lordship's horse.

Lord Gregory bent his leg and waited for the groundsman to assist.

'Come on, man,' he snapped.

Will and I giggled as the grumpy old pig helped Lord Gregory on to his horse. Will provocatively held his own leg for a lift on to Heavens Gate and, biting his lip in a grin, he looked cheekily in the direction of the grumpy man.

The old groundsman clenched his fist and quivered as he contemplated whacking Will.

'Go on,' ordered Lord Gregory.

Oh, did he seethe as he helped both Will and I on to Heavens Gate. He was spewing by the time we were mounted. Then, if insult wasn't enough, the ever-sharp Will had to add injury. Will looked down the destroyed driveway and snorted laughter.

'Better get the rakes out ... again,' he yelled.

Will and I rode beside Lord Gregory as we directed him to the Ely Street livery. Of course, by the time we crossed Clopton's Bridge, word of the royal visit was out. A lot of Stratford folk were lining the bridge and, when they saw us approach, they cheered, thinking we were the royal cortege. Needless to say, Will made a series of royal gestures to the folk lining the road.

When we arrived at the livery, Father and the others, hearing the approach, had the gates already open. The livery was a picture of perfection. He and Grace and the other stable hands stood in a line in welcome. I pulled up outside and allowed Lord Gregory to ride into the yard with his outriders. I gently slid off Heavens Gate but Will dismounted with a confident flourish and smile of grandeur across his face. I could see him thinking. Mystery plays yesterday and royalty today! Where would it all end?

'I ... umm, duty calls, Will,' I said, bringing him back to earth.

Will looked into the yard where the horseman were dismounting and removing tack from their horses. Our stable boys were fetching water for rub-downs and bringing feed bags. Will realised he lived in a different world and felt a touch awkward.

'Thanks, friend. See you soon,' he said shyly squeezing my shoulder. He turned and ran off.

I got stuck into the next lot of work: Twenty-three rub downs, twenty-three feeds and twenty-three sets of harnesses to be serviced. Thankfully, Lord Gregory was a congenial man and he and all the horsemen pitched in to cover the work. Nevertheless, it was nearer the fourth hour after midday that we finished with a final slushing of the yard. When all was done, everyone lay down in the hayloft and fell sound asleep.

It was darkness when we woke. A sweet smell permeated the air. Rising from my rest and going out into the yard, there in the middle was a huge fire with a large pig roasting on a spit. Tables had been put out with bread, wine, small beer, cheeses and pies.

'Army marches on its stomach,' said Lord Gregory.

He seemed to be in charge of this stunning array of victuals. I was astounded. Lord Gregory pulled out his sword, cut a slice off the pig and offered it to me. I hesitated.

'Go on, plenty for all,' he smiled.

I took the sweet meat. It was delicious. I had never eaten it before.

'Could get used to this, Lordship,' I grinned.

'Work for me and you can,' he said casually.

'Father needs me here,' I replied awkwardly.

Lord Gregory nodded understandingly; for goodness sake, I was only nine years old.

Soon everyone woke from their rest and that night we ate like I had never eaten before. It seemed quite normal to the horsemen; they were all in the pay of Lord Gregory who, in turn, whenever the queen travelled the country, was paid by the royal purse.

'We are paid to look good rather than be cavalry. More horseman than swordsmen,' said Lord Gregory, sitting by the fire prodding the dying embers with a stick.

'Does the queen have mounted swordsmen,' I asked naively.

'Oh yes, some fine cavalry.'

He pondered for some moments. I could see he was under the drink.

'She has some right mounted savages too, under Topcliffe. You never want to cross paths with him ... believe me.'

Lord Gregory looked at me and took my hand. I pushed my hair to one side. He smiled awkwardly.

'You have a talent with horses, don't you?' he said.

'I believe so, Lordship,' I replied, as he inspected my hand, squeezing it gently.

'You do, you do,' he muttered. I saw his eyes well up. I felt awkward but, at that moment, Grace came and took me by the shoulders.

'Lordship, pray allow me put my nephew to bed. He has worked hard all day for all of us.'

'Please, please, by all means.'

He came out of his melancholy and smiled softly as he wiped his eyes.

'The smoke, I think,' he muttered, feeling a little embarrassed.

Grace took me to my bed and tucked me up, something she never normally did.

'I'm not really tired, Aunt.'

'Best go for bed. Lord Gregory has a liking for boy.'

'Yes, I can see that. He seemed very nice but something seemed to upset him.'

'He's unmarried.'

'He must be lonely.'

'Yes, dear. You must sleep now. This lot are off in the morning and all the horses have to come back.'

Grace blew out my candle and I soon fell asleep, to the wonderings of what was troubling Lord Gregory. It took me another three years to work that one out.

Thank you, Grace.

CHAPTER 12

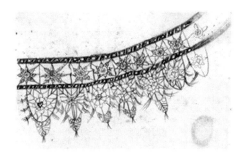

In Shottery, there was a young maiden whose delicate hands and singular focus not only knitted the finest silk stockings but also made the most perfect bone lace. John Shakespeare had been shown her work by a fellow alderman. He had been so impressed he placed an order for lace pieces with which to cuff his finest gloves.

The first time I met this young girl was a warm autumn day in 1574. Will was near the end of his first year of big school and it was just after the birth of Richard, Will's new brother. It was a Friday, about the third hour after midday. The descending sun flickered through trees, flushed with dying leaves, and the smell of freshly scythed lawn grasses filled the air. I was minding a horse on the corner of Scholars Lane and Church Street. It belonged to the headmaster of King Edward School, who wished to take early evening exercise after the finish of school.

At the end of Church Street, I saw a young girl flitting silently along the cobbles. In one hand, with great daintiness, she held a small neatly tied linen package. The other hand delicately raised her dress, enough to clear the dirt but not so far as to reveal her ankles. She sweetly pitter-pattered towards me with the dexterous precision of a young filly keeping up with its mother.

Suddenly, the school windows released roar after roar of hilarity and applause. The pupils were performing the school signature play for the staff and parents. As the young girl approached, the sun revealed a face hidden in the shadow of a bonnet and I realised this diminutive creature was not a girl but a young woman and one of the prettiest young maids I had ever seen in Stratford. I was only ten years old but most women I came across worked so hard that by the time they reached twenty years their backs ached, their faces were weathered and their hands hoary. It was a delight to see a pretty maid whose beauty had not been worn down, and nor was it on account of the fortune of nobility. She probably had been brought up a spinner; spinners kept their youth for some reason. My aunt said it was the oil in the wool that kept them looking young; they constantly rubbed it into their hands and faces.

I watched her in quite a trance as she approached. Just as she arrived at the school, the audience hushed and the distinctive sound of Will's voice took her attention instantly. Time seemed to freeze. She stopped, turned and listened acutely; Will let fly his prose with such a charismatic flourish that a glow appeared on her face. Her ears were captivated; surely the heart and body would follow. Will finished his speech and was greeted with an explosion of applause from the building.

She crossed the road and entered the school. What would she think when she found the source of her beguilement was but a ten-year-old boy like myself? I tied the horse to the bollard and quietly followed the young woman into the schoolroom. I pressed through to see where she had gone. She had pushed her way straight to the front and, with a smile as sweet as honey, she sat enraptured by Will as he led the play to its riotous climax.

I, however, suddenly found my ear in sharp pain. Some bony thumb and forefinger gripped it and was twisting it in a direction it was not used to.

'Livery boy can wait outside with his charge,' said a toothless voice, lubricated with road stones.

Using my ear as a useful handle, I was dragged out into the street and released by the school gate-keeper – as he titled himself. I knew he was just Pete, the privy washer. Either way, he was bigger than me and had it in for anyone of lower social standing than himself, which covered about four people in Stratford of which I was one.

Eventually the play finished, school finished and all the pupils and parents spilt out on to the street. Mary had been watching, too, and she came out with Will, crossing to where I was standing with the headmaster's horse.

'Good afternoon, Mrs Shakespeare. Will raised the roof, eh?' I inquired cordially.

'And good afternoon to you, Thomas. He certainly did. How's your father and your aunt?'

'They are well. Father is in Coventry selling horses and Grace is at the livery.'

'Excuse me, are you Mrs Shakespeare?'

Mary turned and there she stood, still holding her package, still glowing. I saw Will look at her and he turned a rose shade of red.

'I am,' Mary replied with a smile.

'I am Anne, Miss Anne Hathaway, from Shottery, I have some ...'

'The lace, yes of course. My husband said your work was of the highest quality, is that it? Shall I take it to him?'

'Thank you, and, oh, thank you, yes.'

Mary was quite sharp, she knew if she took it, John could get a few days before payment had to be made. 'I can't pay you of, course. My husband will have to do that.'

'Of course, of course. I will be by next Tuesday.'

'Wednesday is better. I am sure he will order more.'

'Surely, Wednesday.'

Anne handed the package to Mary. 'Have you met our son, William?'

'I just saw his performance. It was truly magical, Mrs Shakespeare.'

'I wrote some of it myself,' whispered Will.

'That must have been the bit that so touched my heart.'

They looked at each other. Will went even redder, and then Anne, too, blushed, quite fully, surely down to her bosom.

'Mr Hunt says he has quite a gift,' interjected Mary proudly.

'Well, Mr Hunt is certainly right there. A gift of words is a gift indeed,' said Anne, still with eyes only for my fine friend.

'This is our friend, Thomas – Thomas Wickham,' said Mary.

'You can call me Tom, Miss Hathaway.'

'Pleased to meet you, Tom. I must be on my way Mistress Shakespeare.'

'Good afternoon to you, Miss Hathaway,' said Mary.

We all stood and watched as Anne floated off, carried by a summer breeze and her little feet.

'Well, she has turned pretty as a picture,' mused Mary.

'You know her, Mrs Shakespeare?' I asked.

'As a child. She must be eighteen now, they farm a hundred acres at Shottery, not far from my father's old farm; pretty place with two chimneys, called Hewlands. Her father grows the finest herb garden I have ever seen and he knows more about their uses than anyone I have ever met. Noisy house though – two wives, eight children,' mused Mary as we watched Anne walk into the distance.

'Why is he allowed to have two wives?' I asked.

'His first wife died. He married again. He still owes my John money,' said Mary.

'What for,' I asked innocently.

Unsurprisingly, Mary ignored the question. Noticing Will was still absorbed with watching Anne departing, Mary ruffled his hair. 'Come along, William, can't stand around all day looking at pretty girls.'

I was thankful for the bit of reading and writing Bod had taught me. She also taught me to work with what you have, not what you wish you had. There's plenty to make one content without the trappings of wealth, she would say. I think it was a brave face on a hard life, but it made me practical and observant for opportunity. I never did have much time for envy. But if I did ever wish for anything, it would have been what went on in that school room and the universities of Oxford. It all seemed to be a great water trough of fresh and luscious knowledge that only very few could drink at. A farthing pinged on to to the cobblestones at my feet.

'Thank you, boy,' a voice said.

By the time I picked up the coin, the headmaster had mounted his horse and was away.

Anne made lace for John Shakespeare on quite a regular basis and she always came by the school, even though there was a quicker way to Henley Street. She was so enchanted by young Will from the moment she first heard his voice, she never passed an opportunity to hear or see him.

There was a lot of activity emanating from Henley Street. As well as moving gloves to the wharf and the brogging, Father was providing haulage horses for moving timber and other building materials for John. Their destination confirmed the rumour that the Shakespeares were building a country house in Wilmcote, aback the family paddocks that Mary had inherited from her father. One morning I saw it.

Father woke me up early. He was in a jovial mood, tacking up his favourite horse, Zeus. Zeus was a fine black gelding. It did not belong to him but its owner never minded Father riding him. We gave him a good feed and a rub down, and then Father saddled him, mounted up and pulled me up, too. It was a bit of a squeeze as I was not so small anymore.

'Father, why can I not ride another horse?' I asked.

'You will see, my son,' he said with a cheeky smile and trotted out on to Ely Street.

We made our way to Wilmcote through the Rother Street Market, which was busy with early customers, eager for the best produce. It was a bright morning and a breezy ride. When we turned up, I could see John Shakespeare presiding over Henry Burbage and his men. They were fine carpenters and starting to cut up timber for the main trusses.

'Jack! Good to see you!' Mr Shakeseare shouted.

My father just raised a hand above my shoulder. We pulled up, dismounted and stood watching the activity going on. This was the start of what was going to be a big house. There was constant hammering and sawing, with the carpenters working in expert unison. The unceasing noise was augmented by shouts and struggle as wood was cut, chiselled and pushed this way and that. The workmen looked like ants rushing all over the structure, as beams and sections were pushed vertical. Standing in front was a very pleased-looking John Shakespeare.

'Right, settle up. Then I must back to town to meet Mary,' said John, taking out his purse.

He pulled out coin and counted it out into my father's welcoming hand. My father tugged his cap, and bid him thank you and farewell.

He remounted Zeus, helped me up and we took off as swift as the wind. I looked over my shoulder to see John, who had already turned back to the carpenters. His hands on hips, he had a bit of a swagger in his gait.

Father gave a whoop and a yell as we galloped down the road towards Temple Grafton, the hedgerows whipping past my ears like wasps on a hot summer's day. Eventually Father pulled up at a very neat farm on the south side of Temple Grafton. He trotted smartly down the drive and up to the stables. The stables were very busy with a lot of workmen cleaning what seemed to me to be already spotless.

Father dropped me off and dismounted, and the foreman of the work force came over.

'Good day to you, Jack,' he said, his hand outstretched.

'Good day to you too, Peter. This is my boy, Tom.'

'Tom,' said Peter and there was a lot of good hand-shaking. Father took out his purse and tossed it to Peter with a great grin.

Peter caught the purse and, after feeling its weight, he turned to one of the boys.

'Bring him out,' he called.

The boy put down his shovel and went into the stables. I watched and waited in great anticipation for what was going to appear from the blackness of the stable entry. Whatever it was, it had to be something impressive judging by the size of the grin on Father's face. First, I heard the shoes on the stable cobbles, and then I saw a white face with a black star appear out of the darkness. The most beautiful grey stallion with a stunning long white mane strode out into the yard. It was a magnificent beast, standing about sixteen-two hands tall.

'Oberon,' said my father, looking to me with a terrific grin of self-satisfaction.

The boy holding the horse gave him a flick and, on cue, Oberon reared up in the air and beat his hooves. I was wonder-struck by the beauty of this horse; the way he stood and held his head. It was superior poetry in the extreme.

'What do you think, Tom?'

'How much?' I asked.

Peter laughed out loud.

'Boy's a trader!' he said to my father.

'Five pounds,' replied Father.

'Wow,' I replied, moving closer to Oberon.

I approached him, leant my face towards his, lightly breathed into his nostrils and Oberon soothed, allowing me to stroke his philtrum very gently. We just stood there breathing each other for a minute or so.

'Boy has the touch, too,' Peter whispered to my father, who nodded in approval.

This was the first stallion my father had bought and he was a good choice. Though the five pounds was really expensive, I was sure Father reckoned he would soon make it back on service fees. Peter walked over with a bridle and put it on Oberon.

'Bring it back next week. Don't want to see you fined your profit for not having a bridle.'

'Obliged to you, Peter,' said my father.

The illegal activity of riding a horse without a bridle was strictly enforced in Stratford and could incur quite a fine if caught. The magistrates always took a poor view because nothing was more dangerous in the street than an out-of-control horse.

I waited with both horses while father went into the stable and signed the bill of sale. Oberon was now one hundred percent legally his. He held the document up in triumph when he came out. I rode Zeus back to town following my very proud father astride his Oberon.

As we approached the Guild Hall Chapel, there was a lot of screaming and shouting. Some men were hurling things into the street and other men were pounding things with a hammer. As we closed in, we could see a hysterical Mary Shakespeare being restrained and pulled away by John. The last statues of the Guild Hall Chapel were being pulled out of the church and systematically smashed, right there in the road. It was like a massacre of the already dead, a desecration of any remaining holy memories of the old faith. As an embarrassed John led his wife away, she howled again and again into the distance.

'Assassins! Assassins!'

The government thugs kept smashing the statues. We pulled up our horses, which became skittish at the violence. A head rolled towards me

III

and spun to a halt on the cobbles in front of Oberon. A thug rushed to the forlorn head with a large hammer, and Oberon reared.

'Stop,' my father shouted, pulling back on Oberon to restrain and calm him.

The thug stopped, his big hammer still raised. Father leapt off Oberon and handing me his rein he approached the thug, who simply placed his hammer on the ground and stood legs apart all arrogant, like an executioner waiting for his next subject.

'I have the warrant of Lord Lucy, direct from Her Majesty, the Queen, to remove all idolatrous statues,' he stated with self-important authority.

'That you may, but it doesn't include scaring horses and creating havoc! I am the steward of the Ely Street livery owned by His Lordship. Should any grief come to his horses, I will inform His Lordship, how, why and by whom!'

This possibility worried the thug and thankfully the tension relaxed. I looked at the ground and, there at the feet of the thug, lay a broken piece of statue, a pair of hands in prayer; the image was not lost on my father, either. He remounted and we picked our way through the smashed statues. Needless to say, as soon as we were at a good distance, the smashing started again. Father tried to ignore the impact of the desecration as best he could. He was not for one side or another. Live and let live was his constant prayer.

I think this was the one day that I saw my father truly happy. He understood horses well, though I would not say he loved them. He realised this horse, despite having its keep deducted by His Lordship's ever-sharp clerk, was a high-quality stud and would earn good money over his wage.

Oberon did do Father well, covering his cost in the first season. However, he did really well when the first yearlings were shown around. Those in the know realised what a fine stud Oberon was, enabling Father to double the service fee. Over the next three years, Father made nearly forty pounds in service fees.

That evening, after we settled Oberon, I went round to the back of Henley Street. There was little sound from the house and I was about to throw a pebble at the upper window to get Will's attention.

'Don't!' whispered Will.

He was sitting underneath the workshop window with little Annie on his knee. Her eyes locked on to me as she sat sucking her thumb whilst Will comforted her.

'Did you see what they did?' I whispered.

'No, but I heard it and we have been collecting mother's tears for the last five hours,' he said, beckoning me over. 'Did you see it?'

I nodded and told him about the horse Father had just bought.

'Mother went off her head at them,' he groaned. 'Father had to take her away before they arrested them both.'

'I saw your father leading her away,' I said with a sigh of commiseration.

Will rubbed his face with pain and desperation and looked up at me all dog-eyed.

'She's right, though. How can you fear a statue, Tom? A motionless statue, a threat to our queen. For why?' he asked looking up to the sky.

I knew not what to say. I cared not for this kind of talk. That was the indulgence of those with wealth and education, not the working man – or boy, as was my case. So we both sat, Will looking to the sky and I the ground. I did, however, want to bring my friend out of his solemn mood.

'How is the schooling going?' I asked, sounding chipper, trying to make little Annie smile too.

'Mr Hunt is a dream, Tom,' he said with a smile.

'That's good news.'

'We are studying Ovid, quite a master poet,' he declared dreamily to the sky.

'Tell one,' slurped Annie through her thumb.

Will not only obliged, but he proceeded to recite stanza after stanza of Ovid's work. It was quite magical. Annie sucked her thumb and listened intently. I so enjoyed it – not just hearing such a fine rendition of Ovid, but also witnessing my friend's rapidly burgeoning gift.

For the next two years, John Shakespeare proceeded to work, deal and wheel like there was no tomorrow. I can't remember a week going by when he did not come into the livery for either cartage or a horse for himself. John was moving so much wool, we had to hand business on to the Fleming family, who had two big cartage teams in Tredington.

I did not see so much of the Shakespeare family during this time. Mary was busy with the affairs of the house and Will was at school. He spent a lot of his free time with Fieldy, Quiney and Tyler. It was not personal because I was kept busy working.

CHAPTER 13

In the late spring of 1577, Father was offered a good price for Zeus, so he sold him. He had allowed me a progeny of Zeus from one of Lord Lucy's mares, but of course I'd had to pay the brood fee of four shillings. Nevertheless, he was a beauty. I had him gelded and called him Orlando.

It was about this time I first remember things becoming less stable for the Shakespeares. I was just shy of thirteen years old. At work we had a horse called Daggard, a chestnut standard bred who had been lame with a bad abscess. Now recovered, I tacked him up and took him out for exercise. I was riding the quieter, less stony, road towards Temple Grafton and there, sitting beneath a great elm tree, reading a book and scribbling notes, was Will. It was a fine day, the sun was warm and everything was green and beautiful in the late flush of spring. I casually waved as I approached.

Will looked up and then stood. 'Tom!' he called, and then gave me a big smile followed by a deep and formal bow.

I raised my hat to him and came to a halt. 'Good day to you, Will,' I said.

'Indeed it is, Tom,' he said, approaching and stroking Daggard.

'No school?'

'Mr Hunt has a fever, and home is overrun with the noise of little kin,' he said, looking at Daggard with great intensity and continuing to stroke him gently.

'Teach me to ride, Tom?' he asked, looking at me with a smile.

I nodded and jumped down. Daggard's hoof was now good and actually he was not fresh at all, so this was an opportune moment. Will picked up his notes and book and put them into a linen bag.

'Before you do anything, you have to know how to inspect a horse's hooves and pick them out,' I said. 'A lame horse may just have a stone stuck in an uncomfortable place.'

Will nodded with a smile as I showed him how to stand, run his hand down the leg and raise Daggard's hoof. Taking a pick from my belt I showed him the hoof, where the frog was and how to avoid it when picking out. Will nodded observantly and, placing Daggard's hoof back down, I took Will's bag from him and told him to do what I had done. Now, I am no teacher and an uneducated boy, but Will did exactly as I had shown him, move for move. He was a natural learner.

I showed him how to mount without assistance and, when in the saddle, how to sit and place his feet in the stirrups properly. I led Daggard gently down the road.

'How's the new house coming on?' I asked.

'Mother wants to move there end of the summer but Father thinks we will still be too busy.'

'Your father is a very busy man,' I replied.

'Mother wants him to make sure we have enough to school all of us.'

'That is a lot of work,' I said.

'Mother says money is made with brains not hands.'

'Your father is out at all hours.'

'Mother says we have to improve our position.'

'Mother has a lot to say,' I quipped.

'She does. Can we go faster, Tom?'

I stopped and looked up at Will.

'Yes, we can, but speed is nothing without control.'

I was not a gossip but I did listen to Will's comments and was aware of what was going on around me. Things were getting tight for recusants. The old faith was rapidly becoming a luxury that fewer and fewer could afford.

'Give me your right hand,' I told Will, standing on the left side, 'now, hold me and grip hard with your knees.'

Will obliged and with a quick jerk and a pull, I mounted Daggard, sitting just behind Will. The saddle was an adult one so, still being boys, we were able to sit with reasonable comfort.

'Right, you have the stirrups. I'll take the reins but you take my hands, too,' I instructed.

I told Will to give a gentle kick with his heels and soon we were trotting down the road. I instructed Will how to rise with the trot. I told him how to steer and pull up. He was pretty quick at picking it up.

'I want to gallop!' Will demanded.

There was a paddock coming up on the left which I knew to be a good shortcut to Shottery and, knowing it belonged to Mr Fulks of whom we were good stock feed customers, I felt confident enough to cut across it at full tilt.

'Hold on. You ready for this?' I said as the open gateway approached.

'Indeed!'

With that, I pulled Daggard left into the paddock and Will heeled him hard. Daggard was a strong horse with a good reach so he flew off at one hell of a pace. As we galloped across that paddock, I held the reins with Will. I gripped my thighs hard and, squeezing Will tight with my elbows, I let our middle bodies float with the rhythm of Daggard's motion. Will's head was raised, his nostrils flared and he sucked in the wind, the speed, the passing summer grasses, and scent of flowers. We went on and on. It was a long paddock with a slight downward slant that came to a brook on the western side of Shottery – close to an unused flour mill.

I knew the brook was coming up and started to ease Daggard up and slow him down. In fact, I only just pulled us up in time.

'Wow!' declared Will, as I jumped off.

We were all dripping in sweat. We must have covered a fair few furlongs.

'That was pretty good for a first ride,' I said.

Will sat for a moment feeling the reins and saddle, clearly pleased with his lesson.

'Make a circle,' I said, and using my crop, I signalled him to ride a circle with me at the centre.

I spent about an hour schooling Will. It would have been easier with a rein but I did not have one at hand; nevertheless, Will soon had good control of Daggard.

Still wet with sweat from the ride and dirty from a morning of chores, I told Will I was going to the millpond for a wash down. As we walked along the bank towards the pond Will sat very comfortably on Daggard, surveying the land around him.

'What is it like to be a gentleman?' Will mused.

'Comfortable?' I said.

'Mother wants Father to retire and to be a gentleman.'

'When?' I asked, but Will said nothing by way of reply.

We arrived to the millpond and Will dismounted. I took Daggard to the water's edge where he gave himself a good long drink, and then, securing the reins to the saddle, I left him loose to graze.

'Why not take his tack off,' asked Will.

'If I do, he will think he is done for the day and take off over the paddock. So long as he is tacked up, he knows there is work to do so he'll stay close,' I explained and took off my clothes.

Will took off his clothes too and walked over to the millpond edge.

'We're growing up,' said Will, looking at my freshly toned muscles and newly grown body hair.

'We are,' I smiled as I took a large lump of mud from the bank and whacked it on my chest with a splat.

Mud was good to wash with. It was more pleasant than vinegar and washed you cleaner than well water. We both had a good coating of the mud and rubbed it over ourselves, helping each other when it came to our backs. For a while we stood at the bank letting it dry, I suppose we looked like the black men from the African lands that we had heard of. We dived into the crystal-clear water and, thrashing around, we washed the mud from our bodies. Stepping out of the pond, with glistening lily-white bodies all fresh and clean, I became aware we were being watched.

Turning around, I saw a maid standing on the roadside of the upper reach. It was Anne Hathaway. We stood ankle deep in water so immediately covered our genitals. She placed her hand to her lips and smiling, she flushed. I waved to her with one hand. She laughed and then blowing a kiss, she ran away.

'One kiss for whom?' said Will.

'For me, of course,' I declared with my tongue in my cheek.

I suddenly stretched my arms out to the heat of sun.

'For me, for her kiss is as warm as the breath of the sun,' I declared to the sky.

Will laughed at my terrible poetry but then he thought a moment. Looking to the sky, on a breath that could stop an angel, he said:

Of course for thee! Take her! But; when she shall die, cut her out in little stars, And she will make the face of Heaven so fine that all the world will be in love with night, and pay no worship to the garish sun.

Will looked to me; there was a stillness in his smile.

'Is that Ovid?' I asked curiously.

'No.'

'Who then?'

The world went silent for a second or two. 'Me,' he said softly, as if confessing to something over which he had no control.

'When did you make that up?'

'Just now,' said Will, looking to where Anne had been standing.

We dressed and I was just letting down Daggard's stirrups for the ride home when Will asked me something I was not expecting. 'You know Father was rejected for a coat of arms?'

'I heard that, yes.'

'It is said it was because he is a usurer.'

Now that was quite an unpleasant and scurrilous thing to be. I really did not quite know what to say or how to react.

'Tom, have you heard the talk that Father is a usurer?'

The thing was I had not. At the livery we hear most town gossip but Father always says gossip is useful to know, but dangerous to trade in.

'No, Will. I have not.'

'He was fined for it last year.'

'I never knew.'

'They kept it quiet. My bed is above the workshop and the boards are thin so I hear everything.'

Will thought a moment and became quite bitter. 'Tom, it's not right. Men come and plead Father for loans and they offer to return him great interest sums. Then they renege on their payments and claim his usury over excessive interest – sums they themselves offered.'

'That's not right. I'm sorry, Will.'

'The price of staying with your faith.'

Will stroked Daggard's withers and, about to pick up his hoof, asked quite pointedly, 'Do you believe in God, Tom?'

I was quite taken aback.

'Yes,' I said, 'yes, I mean, I want to, I need to … but then … I suppose I wish I didn't have to. Do you, Will?'

Will looked to the ground and gently pushed a dead beetle with his foot. 'To believe or not to believe, there's a question. If you die, do you sleep, do you dream? In the sleep of death, what dreams follow?'

He looked up with a stare as empty as a deserted ship.

'In the still of night I would have to whisper, "I don't know", Tom.'

Will said little else and we both mounted Daggard and rode back to Stratford at a walk, soaking up the afternoon sun.

CHAPTER 14

One day in August I walked into the yard and found Anne Hathaway there, which was a little unusual since she walked everywhere and so never had need of a horse. I had not seen her since the time she saw Will and I bathing in the old millpond.

'Mr Wickham?' she said gently.

'Father's not here,' I said, washing my hands in the trough.

'No, it's you, Mr Wickham, I wish to talk to,' she uttered nervously.

I dried my hands on my britches. 'You can see I am in need of another bath,' I said in jest.

Looking down, Anne blushed and placed her hand on her chest.

'Umm ... please call me Tom. How can I be of service?'

'Tom, I know you to be a boy of great discretion and close friend of young William Shakespeare.'

I nodded reassuringly.

'Mr John Shakespeare owes me money and I have no experience in these matters. I am at a loss. What would you suggest I do?'

That question hit me like a horse-tail flick against the glaring sun. I had to think for a moment.

'Depending on the gravity of the sum, my father accepts the loss but refuses further trade till the debt is paid,' I told her. 'But indeed, Mr Shakespeare has never owed us money.'

Anne pondered this for a moment and then took my hand gently and squeezed it.

'Thank you, Tom,' she whispered and, releasing my hand, she left the yard.

I have to say her hand was the softest touch I ever felt. That inquiry was the first sign that things were starting to really stack up against John Shakespeare. The following week there was an evening that I shall never forget. It was one of those nights where you wished your ears did not work, or longed that one's memory would suffer total collapse. It also showed how right Will was about what he told me of his father that day we washed at the millpond.

I was sitting on the ground in an empty stall mending some tack when two men entered the opposite stall and started to whisper about something quite earnestly. Shortly, they were joined by a third and the whispering became quite tense. I froze, unable to move. I knew if I were discovered they would never believe I had not heard their talk. However, the only word that I can use to describe them is one taught to me by Johnny Somerville; they were conspiratorial. The thick vein of arrogance increased their volume for a moment, and I heard clear words that needed little interpretation.

'If we have to sign the oath, who cares! But I'll be damned if I pay debts to those that don't,' said a voice.

'Good time to borrow from a Papist then,' said another.

Despite shushing their friend, they sniggered in agreement. One of them, relaxing in his pomposity, leant back and, placing his hands on the wooden stall, revealed to me the distinct agate stone ring of an alderman.

After a few more minutes of further protracted discussion they left. I sat tight till I knew they were out of the yard. God knows who they were, for when I broke my cover the two stable boys said they had seen them but not recognised them.

'They just said they wanted to inspect our horses,' one said.

'All aldermen?' I asked.

The boys simply shrugged, still too young to realise that keeping an eye on what's around you is one of the more important aspects of life. The sad facts of Will's story were coming to pass and set to get worse; however, I did not know what this 'oath' was.

Father rode into the yard and, taking his horse for him and with feigned naivety, I asked, 'Father, are you signing the oath?'

'Why would I? I'm not in public office.'

'What is the oath?' I said, taking off the bridle.

Father removed his saddle and looked at me suspiciously. 'Son, why are you asking me about something of which you are uninformed, as if you are, indeed, informed?'

I told him the story of the men in the stall.

'Aldermen using my stalls as their conspiracy rooms. Plague on the bloody wretches!'

I followed father into the tack-room, he threw his saddle on the rack, turned and snatched the bridle from me.

'Oath of supremacy! A royal act that makes everyone recognise the queen as head of the church, not the Pope. Anyone in public office must sign. It would seem aldermen that have signed are ready to take advantage of those who have not.'

Now I knew the Shakespeares were in trouble. Mary would never let John sign that act. John was going to find himself between hard withers and a stall wall. This was going to cost him dearly.

We carried on trading with Mr Shakespeare but payment was getting slower. Twice Father booked in his own coin to cover the lacking of payment, and this really upset Grace.

'Can't have what you can't pay for,' she would always say.

Lord Lucy's head steward was most meticulous and any non-payers were never given a second chance, so, being an old friend, my father did cover him.

The movement of timber to Wilmcote became slower and slower as did the work. Father soon found deliveries difficult because the carpenters thought he was bringing their money, so there were some harsh words.

Once again, Anne appeared in the yard but this time with a fine-looking man of middle years. I was up to my arms in muck; I looked like a chimney sweep and smelt like a tannery.

'Good afternoon, Tom, and, yes, you are ready for a bath,' she said with light-hearted cheek.

Well, this showed her in better humour, for which I was pleased. 'Good afternoon, Miss Anne.'

I turned to the gentleman. 'You, too, Sir,' I said, tugging my cap.

'This is a friend of John Frith, of whom I am a friend,' said Anne awkwardly.

He dipped a bow with a small smile.

'He wishes to meet Will.'

'Indeed, the school or Henley Street after the sixth hour,' I suggested, somewhat perplexed.

Anne stepped close to me and spoke quietly into my ear.

'He is John Cottom. He used to teach at the school. His brother is a Papist most hunted and he is unwelcome at the school nor does he wish to bring suspicion upon the Shakespeare house, so it is better he does not visit.'

I pulled back and looked at the man. He seemed benign. The Cottom name was not known to me. Frith was, a funny old priest at Temple Grafton and friend of John Somerville, so really I saw no harm.

'What would you like me to do?'

'Take us to meet him?'

'Where?'

'A trip to the mystery plays. He so loves them,' said Anne.

'Yes, he does. I remember, a few years ago now.'

There was a quiet tension, and then John Cottom approached the trough and sitting on its edge, beckoned to me. I walked over accordingly and stood, arms folded like the man I believed myself to be, not the fourteen-year-old boy I, in fact, was.

'I hear from my good friend and colleague, John Hunt, that William is a most-gifted pupil. I also hear that his father is in debt and not attending the aldermen meetings.'

He looked to me for a reaction but I gave none.

'Things could get difficult for the family and I may be in a position to help.'

'Money?' I asked.

'Other ways,' said Mr Cottom quietly, as if I had totally missed the point, which I think I had. Nevertheless I nodded.

'Arrange that trip,' he said and, bidding goodbye to Anne with a pleasant bow, he left the yard. Anne then walked over to me.

'Did you get paid?' I asked.

She shook her head, but then nodded.

'You seem unsure?'

'He told me he would not pay me till I re-supplied him. I told him I would not re-supply him till he paid what he owed,' she said, flushing as she did.

'And?'

'Mary escorted me out of the workshop and slammed the door. Three days later, I was paid and sent a message that further lace would not be ordered.'

Anne started crying. 'It was quite an unpleasant affair, but your counsel was good. I wish to be my own woman and not attendant on the whim of anyone.'

I was not sure what to do. I could not comfort her as I was a tad filthy, and, looking up, she laughed when I made a gesture to suggest that.

There was a silence as she tried to wipe her tears.

'I know he is but a boy, but I think I love him, Tom,' she blurted out through her tears and dribbling nose.

'I … um, really need to wash,' I said, suffering an instant bout of emotional cowardice.

Anne did not hear; she just carried on. 'I spoke with John Frith and he told me that in twenty-five years in a schoolroom Mr Hunt had never met a pupil like Will. They say he has a great destiny before him. Of course I knew that already; the first time I heard him read a poem.'

Anne looked to the sky for a moment. 'Mr Cottom and Father Frith want him go to university and study with the best, but he needs to go to school and they fear that on account of his father's increasing ... problems ... that will not be possible.'

She was really quite distracted and more tears flowed. 'Help me, young Tom. I am shy but not foolish; I am gentle but not weak; I understand the heart. I seek only to love, not possess.'

This was most disconcerting. I had never seen a young woman so out of sorts. I asked myself if this is what love reduces a person to. Was it something best avoided?

'I will arrange a cart for Coventry and we shall all see the mystery plays together,' I said, nervously trying to bring peace to her troubled soul.

Her tears were as relentless as autumn rain, so in desperation I offered my shirt's only clean edge, which she grabbed and into it she blew the entire the contents of her nasal passages. Then, picking up the hem of her dress, she ran out of the yard.

I was in a bit of a spot, quite not sure what to do.

Grace came out of the smithy. 'What did Miss Hathaway want?'

I pondered the tears and mucus in my shirt. 'She has booked a cart to Coventry to see the plays,' I said.

'Five shillings.'

'Used to be four?'

'Tom, times are changing. Prices are going up.'

'Five it is, Auntie. I'll tell her,' I lied.

I had six shillings of savings, so I would carry the fee myself.

'How many?' she asked

'Not sure yet, Aunt.'

'Any more than three grown-ups and three children, then it will be six shillings.'

I nodded compliance, shielding the afternoon sun from my eyes. Grace went back inside. Picking up my shovel, I finished the job I had been doing. Father rode in and I helped him unsaddle and settle his horse.

Grace came out and greeted him, too. 'There is some fine peascod for supper.'

'I certainly have a hunger, Sister,' he smiled.

'Miss Hathaway just booked a cart for the plays in Coventry,' said Grace.

'Oh?' said my father, with a worrying tone of disbelief.

He carried his saddle and bridle into the tack-room without saying a word, which only served to reinforce the notion. Upon his return, he doused his face in the water trough. Grace handed him a cloth and he wiped his face. 'I just met with Miss Hathaway. We spoke briefly. She made no mention of booking a cart and … she had been crying.'

Grace and my father both looked at me. I was caught out.

'A lie is a lie, even if it is wrapped in an act of generosity,' said Grace.

I hung my head for a second. 'Sorry, Grace,' I said, raising my head to look her in the eye.

'Son, please tell?' inquired my father.

I told them about the visit from John Cottom, what he had said about Will and the state of his father's affairs. My father nodded in agreement. He knew full well what was going on but had said little, neither he nor Grace being ones for tittle-tattle.

'You have only six shillings to your name, and rather than keep it for your own benefit, you seek to benefit a friend?'

'Yes, Father.'

'How were you going to work this? You lied to Grace. What were you going to tell Anne? Who were you going to take? What were John and Mary to make of this? What lie were you going to tell them?'

'I had not thought that far ahead, Father.'

There was a difficult silence, and I felt awful.

'Tom,' said Grace, 'lies beget lies. They breed like rabbits and feeding them takes a memory as deep as a well, with a conscience as cold as the water in it.'

She looked at me, struggling between anger and sympathy.

'Sorry, Aunt.'

My father was not angry. He put his arm around me and gripped me tight.

'Son, get cleaned up and we will speak of this over some of your aunt's most hot and crispy peascod fritters!' he stated warmly.

By the time I washed, cleaned myself up and put on some fresh clothes, I could smell the sweet smell of Grace's crispy pea, parsnip and cod fritters fried in pork fat. These were a bit of a treat because it was not often that cod was on the fish stall but if it was be sure if there was more than thruppence in the kitty, Grace would buy some.

When I came to the table, the sun was setting. Father lit a candle and we sat for a moment whilst he said grace.

'Lord, thank you for these foods, fruits of thy bounty.'

We all said 'Amen' and Grace dished up.

'Son, your reasons were good and pure, so I have decided that I will carry the fee. And, as a mark of the enduring friendship and good humour of our two families, I shall take you, Will and your friends to the plays in Coventry. Also, from what I hear, I am pretty sure they will be the last ones for a few years.'

There was a rare smile from Grace. I stood and embraced my father. 'Thank you, Father,' I whispered.

'However, never let there be anything other than truth between us all,' he said rhetorically.

I nodded with great humility, and then took a whole fritter and stuffed it into my mouth!

The following morning being a Sunday, we attended church and were duly noted there. The Shakespeares snuck in late at the back, and then out again before the end. I hated the whole affair. Under the cloak of clerical respectability we were preached to that it was God's will that 'we' worked our fingers to the bone every day for bread and pittance whilst, 'they' kept the enemy from the door. Even as an uneducated fourteen-year-old, I was truly sceptical as to whether we would receive any harsher life under the Spanish, French, the Papery, Jews or whatever demon 'they' happened to drag to the scaffold next.

CHAPTER 15

It was so beautiful the following day, so I took the opportunity to walk the pleasant path through the hedgerows to Shottery, where I would find Miss Hathaway. I arrived at Hewlands farm where I saw a gentleman working in what was probably the most meticulous and beautiful garden I have ever seen. Combined with a constant chorus of birds flitting from shrub to shrub, the smells and scents that emanated from it were a sensation.

'Good day, Sir,' I called from the road.

The gentleman looked up and, placing his hoe against a trellis, wandered over. 'Good day to you, Sir,' he said.

'You have a fine garden, Sir,' I replied.

'Why thank you, young man. It's rare that a garden is appreciated by one so young. Now, what service can I be?'

'I am Tom Wickham and I am looking for Miss Anne Hathaway.'

'Of the livery at Ely Street? Jack's boy?'

'Correct, Sir.'

'Well, I am Richard Hathaway, so you are looking for my daughter.'

He put out his hand, which I took and, though his hands were rough and gnarled, he took mine with warmth and shook it kindly.

'Pleased to meet you, Sir.'

'Call me Richard, please.'

A woman came out of the house, to whose skirt two children clung for safety. It was a big house with two chimneys and an upstairs the full length.

'This is my wife, Joan,' said Richard, as she curtsied to me. 'And my son, John, and daughter Margaret.'

The children briefly put their heads around their mother's dress and smiled. Joan was quite tall with cropped brown hair and an elfin face with pretty freckles.

'Not Anne's mother; she is no longer with us, God rest her soul,' Richard added.

'It's very peaceful here, Mistress Hathaway,' I said, by way of politeness.

They both laughed and gave each other wicked smiles.

'We have two other boys,' said Joan. 'They are working in the paddocks, and when Anne's brother and sister visit, well! Come the sixth hour, this house is as busy as Rother Street on market day.'

'Will Anne be back at the sixth?' I asked.

Richard took Joan's hand. 'Anne is currently engaged in service for the Whateley family at Temple Grafton but we will tell her any message you care to trust us with.'

'If you could tell her I have made an arrangement to see the plays she wished to see.'

'Coventry, yes. She expressed a desire. I fear she has a sweetness for the Shakespeare boy. Will he be going, too?'

'I believe so, Sir,'

He looked into Joan's eyes. 'Too young, that boy, but chance may favour them.'

'How so, Sir?' I said, with loose-shoed innocence.

They both looked to me and smiled.

'Because love is timeless,' said Joan, resting her head on Richard's shoulder and cuddling her little daughter as she peeped round once more.

Without another word, they saluted me and he went back to his hoeing and she inside the house. I took my route back via Henley Street to call on Will. I went around to the garden door at the back, as I was used to, and there, under the arbour where Will and I had played so much as boys, I found Gilbert, Joan and little Anne being directed by Will in a play. They did not notice me at all, so I decided to sit and watch. Will was really animated as he placed them here and there on the make-believe stage.

'But I don't want to be a wall,' declared Anne.

'Why not?' asked Will with kindly patience.

'Wall is not important.'

'No, Annie, wall is not important; wall is *the* most important!'

He picked her up and, sitting her on his knee, beckoned Gilbert and Joan to stand either side. Then he showed Anne how he wanted her to be a wall.

'Between the houses a common wall.'

'I'm not common!' stated an indignant Anne.

'Between the houses a pretty wall,' Will emphasised.

Anne smiled and, with a tiny prompt from Will, she thought of her lines.

'A narrow chink ...' she looked to Will.

'To give ...' he prompted.

'A narrow chink to give their kisses room,' Anne stated.

'We are grateful we owe to you,' declared Gilbert, holding a stick for his sword.

'A pathway for ... sweet words of ... lovers true,' said Joan, staggering through the lines.

Will put little Anne down between Gilbert and Joan, and stood back.

'Glorious,' he smiled. 'Now again without me.'

They charmingly staggered through this sweet and much-shortened version of one of the poems that Will had plucked from his memory of the Ovid poetry. At the end I applauded. They were quite surprised.

As soon as little Anne saw me, she beckoned Will to pick her up, for a shy little creature she was, but oh so pretty. She looked at me from the safety of Will's arms.

'I'm going to be a player!' she declared wistfully.

'You certainly are,' I smiled.

'What news, Tom?' asked Will.

'I have an invitation.'

'An invitation?'

'By way of celebrating our families' long-standing kith, my father and I wish to take you and whoever you wish to the plays.'

'That is an invitation, eh little Annie? Would you like to see the plays?'

Mary came out into the garden with young Richard in her arms.

'Good afternoon to you, Thomas. William, little ones must in.'

Will put Anne down and she immediately ran to mother's skirt, keeping a firm eye on me.

'Gilbert, please go with our mother and take your sisters,' said Will, instructing his brother.

I wondered why she had not sent out the maid.

'Mother, Tom and his father have invited us see the plays.'

'That is a kind invitation and most generous, Thomas. William is free to decide but my husband and I are simply too busy to take the time. This year, trade is quite … tight,' she said with a slightly prosaic grin.

'Brother and sisters, they should see the plays,' said Will enthusiastically.

Mary was silent before turning to me. 'Bidding you goodbye,' she said as she took the little ones back into the house.

Will looked to the ground and pushed a seed pod with his foot.

'Everything all right?' I asked quietly.

Will put his arm around me and we walked out of the garden into the back lane. 'No,' he whispered quite emphatically.

We headed out to the paddocks at the rear of town in the direction of Wilmcote. 'Father sold more of mother's paddocks,' sighed Will.

'Holy brethren!'

'Indeed,' said Will, plucking a long stem of grass.

He told me how his father had let the workshop tradesman go and the maid, too. 'His determination to replace family fortune is indeed noble but at times he stares fortune's fool in the face,' he said.

'For why?' I asked.

'As I told you before,' Will said with a desperate heart.

We wandered for a while, saying little, just enjoying the air. 'John Cottom wishes to meet you,' I said.

Will was truly surprised.

'Do you know who he is?' he said.

'I have been told.'

'Does that fear you?'

'I cannot say really, but you know my discretion.'

'So, he will be at the plays?'

'I believe.'

'His brother is a most-hunted man. He takes great care with whom he consorts.'

'Is it unwise?' I asked, a touch concerned.

'Discretion be the greater part of valour.'

'Should I ask Anne?' I said with jest to lighten the mood.

Will looked a tad perplexed. 'Anne Hathaway?'

'Yes.'

'Think you I am sweet on her?' he mused.

'No.'

'You!'

'She blew me a kiss!' said I, indifferently.

'Oh, you she blew that kiss to you, did she?' he laughed.

'I was pretty sure,' I declared, all cocksure.

Will sighed and looked away.

'Mother finds her an irritant since she held her ground over coin owed,' said Will solemnly.

'Nothing comes of nothing and one who faces your mother is certainly not nothing!' I said, and Will laughed.

'Indeed, yes, But she did blow that kiss at me,' he grinned with self-satisfaction.

I shrugged and grinned defeat.

'She arranged this, did she not?' asked Will, casually chewing his grass.

'Umm.' Oh, I felt awkward. I am such an appalling conspirator.

Will laughed at my predicament.

'It will be a fun day. I will bring the little ones. I do, however, think this will be the last year these wretched plays play.'

Will threw his arm around me and hugged me hard.

'*Meus frater in lacte*,' he smiled with a whisper.

I arrived back at Ely Street just as the sun was falling and there was my father, standing in the yard with an equally fallen face.

'His Lordship's steward has been by,' he declared.

Well the books were straight, the stables were in fine form and turning good profits for His Lordship so that could not be the call of the long face.

'What did he say, Father?' I asked.

'No horse or cart is to be hired to anyone who wants to visit the abomination of the holy word that is illicitly presented in the city of Coventry,' he said.

I simply shrugged. 'His Lordship's will, will be done,' I muttered under my breath.

'Blasphemy is blasphemy, no matter how quietly spoke,' growled my father as he walked away.

The following week, a young newlywed couple took over Handly's bakery at Henley Street and Will brought them to the yard. They pulled up outside on a fine strong cart pulled by two very sturdy cobs.

'Tom, these are our new neighbours, Mr Hamnet Sadler and his good wife, Judith,' said Will, by way of introduction as he jumped off the cart. 'They have taken the old bakery on Henley Street. They will turn it into a much finer establishment.'

It took me a wisp of horse-hair to spot the rosary adorning Judith's neck, and indeed it took her less time to notice that I had noticed, and she to cover it. They were Catholics.

'Pleased to meet you. How can I be of service?' I answered cordially.

'They need some supplies moved from the wharf,' said Will.

'Those are fine beasts and that a good cart?' I asked somewhat perplexed.

'We have a sled of fire bricks to repair the bread oven,' said Hamnet.

'I told them you had a horse that could pull a house across a marsh,' said Will.

'Heavens Gate. He will pull your sled for half a crown.'

'Half a crown!' exclaimed Will.

He approached me and, putting his arm around me, treated me like his closest friend and brother.

'These are family, Tom. They are modest people for whom work is a prayer,' he said, trying to get my price down.

Judith was overcome with giggles as was Hamnet.

'Half a crown is fine,' said Hamnet eventually.

These two were clearly taken by Will and, if I were honest, I felt a slight touch of the sticky brush of jealousy.

'I can be at the wharf at noon,' I told them.

'That's fine. We are off to Tredington to buy timber for benches and make an account with the miller there,' said Judith sweetly.

'The miller is a Mister Ward and his wife, Sally,' I said. 'He's a quiet man of few words but kind as he is honest.'

They thanked me and left. Will turned to me with a smile that I knew to be as genuine as French brandy in a pottery jar.

'When did they arrive?' I asked

'Yesterday at noon,' said Will.

'You got to know them pretty quick, for one who is at school all day,' I said, being purposely provocative.

Will looked at me, smiled, placed a playful punch on my shoulder and walked off, but then he turned back, talking to me as he trotted away in reverse.

'Oh, I heard Lord Lucy's edict, so Judith and Hamnet are going to take me to Coventry. Nevertheless, thank you for what you did, Tom.'

He walked away with a whistle in his step. Something was not right. What was he hiding? I had a suspicion what it might be.

I told my father I had booked Heavens Gate for a sled towage for half a crown and he was pleased. I went and gave the old boy a good feed of oats to get his energy up. After cleaning his hooves, I oiled up the yoke, as it had not been used for a month or two. I turned up at the wharf just as the noon bells rang, and there by the wharf steps was the biggest sled of fire bricks. I did just wonder if Heavens Gate would manage it, but I yoked him to the sled and, with his great understanding of a load and without a hint from me, he leant into the yoke pushing his powerful legs against the ground. There was a slight crunch as the sled started to shift and sure enough the sled moved across the dirt. From the wharf to Henley Street was quite a long uphill journey but, one sturdy step at a time, the silent, ever-strong Heavens Gate pulled that sled. By the time I arrived, I realised the old beast was probably getting beyond this kind of load.

Hamnet was waiting at the door and directed me where to place the sled.

'We are obliged to you, Master Wickham,' said Judith as she held out a single half-crown piece for me.

'Thanking you, Mrs Sadler,' I said, taking the coin and tipping my cap.

I don't know how old they were but they looked very young for a newlywed couple, probably only eighteen years old or so. I walked Heavens Gate back to Ely Street via the Rother Street trough, where I paused for quite a while as he practically emptied it.

The next morning something that I had suspected was confirmed. It was the first Thursday of the month and the tannery delivered leather to Henley Street every first Thursday of the month. Under the auspices of exercising horses, I woke at the fifth hour and walked two horses down Henley Street. Sure enough, there at the workshop door was the tannery cart. It had finished unloading and the first light was just peeping between the houses. I stopped in the middle of the road and, as the tannery cart moved off, it revealed Will standing in work clothes and leather apron. Upon seeing me, he instantly looked embarrassed. I wandered over.

'You up early, Tom,' he said.

'You not at school?'

'I am. Just helping Father before school starts,' he lied.

I nodded and went on my way. So, Will was out of school; things must have been really bad to be barred from school. Had Mr Shakespeare been sacked from the City Guild? I passed the bakery where the Sadlers were already up and hard at work building bread ovens. Carpenters had also just arrived to build their benches. By the time I had done my route, Will was waiting there at our gate.

'Shame pushed me to lie, Tom.'

'No harm done,' I said.

He nodded at me, quite despondent.

'Nothing is forever, Will,' I said by way of encouragement.

'Father is facing ruin. Mother has sold much of her property. He needs me in the shop,' he said, and looked at me with a stiff and lifeless smile.

It was hard to see my friend and his family staring down the gun barrel of such hardship. One might think I would feel a bit of 'welcome to the world we all endure', but I did not; my life may have been hard but I never begrudged anyone fortunate enough not to endure it – even the wretched gentry to whom I owed the very roof under which I ate and slept.

'You are going to Coventry to see the plays tomorrow,' I said cheerfully, but there was little reaction.

'Who knows what you will see.'

'Yes, indeed, Tom. I must be back to the shop.' Will smiled.

'And I to the stalls.'

He held his hand out straight to me, his fingers splayed open. I returned with my hand, our fingers touched and he turned and ran.

In the yard, Father was waiting for me.

'Cornall was here. His Lordship needs you at Charlecote stables,' he sighed.

'I'll go anon, Father,' I said, looking at the tiredness in his face.

Father simply shook his head, rubbed his face and waved me away.

'Go now, please.'

'As you command, Father.'

I saddled up Orlando and took off to Charlecote. I was there lunging his rotten two-year-olds for four days without any let-up. His standard breeds really were pretty useless beasts; they were slow with little life and no character. Even their loyalty was strictly feed-based. Thirty-eight of the wretched animals I lunged, once they had been broken by Cornall, and a hard breaker he was. The best horses capitulated quickly to him, realising the sooner they gave in, the quicker the easy life would return. Still these poor things had little use other than for slow local transport. I would never take one to London. It would probably be dead before reaching High Wycombe.

It was the fourth day and the sun was going down when I finished the last of them. I had not seen Father or Grace in that time. I had been fed the absolute minimum and was given raw straw for a bed. I was in the yard stripped to my waist washing myself down hoping to get away before darkness set in.

'Good job, boy,' cut His Lordship's voice behind me.

'I thank Your Lordship.'

Lord Lucy looked around and pondered what to say; I had, in fact, turned his cheap nags into serviceable creatures and I knew he knew I had, but he sure as hell was not was not going to admit it.

'I think my stock needs new blood.'

'It is my humble opinion Your Lordship is most correct.'

He sniffed and muttered inconsequential words that I took to be thanks.

'Well, good. That's it, well done. Wash-up and get back to your duties in Ely Street. Your father needs you.'

I bowed dutifully.

'Thanking Your Lordship.'

He walked back to the house without giving me a second look. Cornall walked over and, stroking Orlando, checked him over without any shame, and then – looking to me with disdain – he left. Alone in the yard, I dressed and took off on Orlando as quick as I could. Arriving back at Ely Street, I found Grace slushing one final bucket across the yard, which glistened across the cobbles in the final light of the setting sun. Aching with tiredness I dismounted and started to remove my precious steed's tack.

'The help is all gone, love, and your father is mending tack.'

'All good, Aunt. I can manage.'

'There were some good fat rabbits on Rother Street.'

'I'm starved.'

'I heard His Lordship's food is not so good for visiting servants,' said Grace as she pushed the gates of the livery shut.

I rolled my eyes with a smile and took the saddle and bridle into the tack-room and greeted my father who pulled at the stiff leather needle with his sore fingers.

'Lordship happy?'

'Indeed.'

'Never crossed my mind otherwise, my son.'

'Smell that rabbit, Father?'

'She made that just for you, Son,' he whispered.

Dear Grace always kept the greater part of her generosity secret. After I gave my dear Orlando a good rub down, a feed and a fresh stall, the three of us sat down and ate Grace's most delicious stewed rabbit and bread. I ate myself to a standstill, and then dropped on to my bed and fell into the deepest sleep.

It was a beautiful morning. I crossed the yard, the cobbles still slippery with morning dew, and opened the gates ready for the first customers and the arrival of the help.

As I pulled open the gates, there stood Will with little Anne holding his hand and young Joan holding the other.

'Will, Annie, Joan! Good morning to you,' I said, locking back the gates.

'Tom, Annie has decided she likes you and wanted to ask why you did not come to the plays?' said Will.

I crouched down and held her little hand. She was such a sweet girl, soft round face with auburn hair, thick freckles and the prettiest red lips God could give a child. 'I had to work for His Lordship, Annie. Did you enjoy the plays?'

Annie nodded shyly.

'How were they?'

'Diminished,' said Will.

'Diminished?' I asked curiously.

'Many people did not take part. There was an atmosphere of … fear. Sadly, the last we shall see of those plays.

'John Cottom?'

Will shook his head. 'I fear Coventry was thick with government spies. But little Annie loved what plays she saw, eh?'

Annie did a little jump with joy.

'Righteousness will we make!' said Will, by way of prompting Anne.

Annie looked up into Will's eyes and pushing her sweet little memory, she became shy and could not say a word, but she fought and thought a bit, and suddenly chirped up:

I will that my son be man;
For reason will that there be he,
A man, a maiden, and a child:
Man for man, Maiden for maiden,
Child for thee, thus by your God shall he be.

'Wow, that's beautiful, Annie,' I said.

'I'm going to be a player.' She smiled and looked to her brother so adoringly.

'Wanting to be is now going to be!' I said with a grin.

'We saw the nativity by the weavers,' said Will.

'Did Miss Hathaway go, too?' I asked tentatively.'

'I gather she was kept in service by the Whatley family.'

'She has worked there since …'

'Since Father no longer has need of lace,' sighed Will.

'You taking the apprenticeship, Will?' I asked in a worried whisper, trying not to let the girls hear.

Will looked to me with a cold depression.

'What else? I have to take my place in the working world, and Father needs me.'

'Is that the working world you want?'

Will looked to the ground and Annie gripped his hand and Joan looked to my eyes.

'In the morning of my life, the day looked long and full of prizes. But, by the end of the day, it would seem my choices are little greater than yours, Tom.'

I did not know what to say, maybe because of my own lack of education. I wanted to say so much but I could not find the words. Here was my friend with a gift that I, and many others, knew to be no ordinary gift, yet here his parents sought to keep him for their own purposes. I knew the Shakespeare family had money troubles but they would ride them and bring them to heel; they surely need not exploit their own gifted son.

'Come, my little lamb. Breakfast time, then to play for thee and work for me,' said Will, picking up Annie.

'Take care, my friend,' I said.

'*Et tu, meus frater in lacte*,' said Will.

I watched him sweetly jiggle Annie and chat to Joan as they wandered back to Henley Street.

Two men arrived wanting horses for the day. My usual day had begun. However, gnawing inside me was a feeling that I could not let lie; I could not bear the idea of Will spending the rest of his life in a glove shop. After setting the two customers up with horses and booking their fees, I saddled a recent purchase that was in need of exercise, a fat horse called Moot.

'Where thee to?' asked Grace

'Can you give me two hours, Aunt? Tell Father I am exercising this fat old Moot here.'

'Will do, Tom. Mind to share with me?'

I sighed a heavy sigh. 'Aunt, I want to help my friend. He is not for our world; his life is for a pen not a leather needle'.

'Can't see how thee can help.'

'True, but maybe Annie Hathaway knows what should be done, for she so loves him.'

'Verily, go Tom, but you shall see fate is our master and choice the indulgence of the wealthy.'

Wise words I knew, but I was young and determined to prove her wrong.

When I arrived at Temple Grafton, I actually had no idea which was the Whately house. As I passed the church, I noticed an elderly man in ecclesiastical clothes walking to a small bothy at the rear of the church. I dismounted, tied Moot to a tree on the verge and followed the man. The old bothy was slab built in oak with pretty garden borders that were a profusion of sweet-smelling herbs. I knocked on the most ancient door I had ever seen. The door opened and an elderly but kindly looking man greeted me with a smile and piercing blue eyes.

'Father Frith? John Frith?'

'Tis I, unless you are claiming to be he,' he said with a mischievous grin.

'Tom Wickham,' I said.

He put out his hand and I gently shook his soft ageing paw.

'Please come in, Tom, and speak. Excuse me whilst I tend this poor creature.'

In the small wooden bothy were some little timber cages housing various ailing animals to which he was tending. Around my head dangled bunches of dried herbs and on shelves there were rows and rows of terracotta pots of tinctures and ointments, all with

Latin inscriptions. I looked around, somewhat impressed by this extraordinary little den.

'Be free to speak whilst I work,' he said, as he opened a cage and took out a blackbird, all bandaged up with what I assumed to be a broken wing. With great tenderness, he proceeded to feed the bird from a pot of grubs.

'I was looking for the house of Whatley?' I asked.

'Do you mind if I ask why?'

'I seek Miss Hathaway.'

'Richard's daughter, a fine young lady with deep soul and great heart,' he declared, turning around to face me.

He smiled and stroked the injured bird with great affection and said nothing, which made me feel awkward.

'I would speak with her … about a friend,' I said tentatively.

'I apologise. I was not meaning to pry. Whately family are, let me say, the private sort. They have dogs, angry dogs.'

He raised his eyebrows and lifted the little bird knowingly, and then turned around and placed it lightly back in its wooden cage.

'I would hate to find myself doing the same as this for you.'

Father Frith picked up a wooden stool, which he handed to me. He then rummaged around for a second or two and, picking up a hammer and some small wedges of wood, gave me a broad smile.

'Come, I need a nice strong man.'

He ushered me out and I followed him back to the church. The church was very old with some heavily rotted timber and a lot of crumbling stonework.

'Built by the Saxons,' he declared.

Father Frith scraped open the large door across the stone floor. It had dropped on its two great iron hinges due to the stonework rotting around them. I could see at once what he wanted: me to lift the whole thing whilst he hammered some timber wedges under the hinges.

He put the stool in position and, gripping my shoulder for stability, he stood on it, found his balance, and then waited with hammer and wedges in hand. I gingerly let go of him, went to the door, found some good hand positions, and then – with a one, two, three – I lifted the great heavy piece of iron-studded oak. It took every bit of strength I could muster! Father Frith was thankfully quick. He rammed in a wedge and, with several sharp accurate clouts, whacked it home.

'The Lord provides,' he smiled.

We took the rest of the wedges and hammered them in, too, for a good solid job. He stood on the stool delighted, as I swung the door freely with a great sense of satisfaction.

'I have been waiting a long time to do that, for sadly most of my flock are older than I.'

'John Somerville?' I asked.

'You know him? Literary man; never works with his hands,' he grumbled.

I laughed to myself. I could indeed picture it being a lost cause – Johnny Somerville doing any form of manual work.

Getting off the stool, Father Frith dipped his hand into a holy water stoop and crossed himself, and then he crossed me too.

'Do your congregation use that,' I wondered out loud.

He looked at me and said nothing but grinned the smile of a man whose freedom lay in his heart. So, beneath the guise of an old and decrepit church, this was a little corner of Catholic derring-do.

'Now, you seek young Miss Hathaway?'

'I do, Father.'

'Take the lane to the end and then take the left road. It is rough but leads to Shottery. You will find her walking there about this time; she leaves the Whatley house for her father's house where she resides.'

'I'm obliged to you, Father,' I said. I was about to walk back to my horse, when he spoke again. 'You have concern for your friend,' he said.

I stopped, and looked at the ground thoughtfully. 'Young William,' he added.

I looked up.

'There are a few people who have noticed what you have noticed,' he stated.

'What think you, Father?'

'I think God's will, will be done, with a little help from Will's friends. Now, please take this message to Miss Anne. I have sent word to John Cottom's brother, Thomas, that there is a young man, of pure heart and fresh spirit, in need of a position that will carry his scholastic soul forward.'

I nodded.

'You have that?'

'Yes, Father,' I said and repeated it to him.

'Good. Go to ... before you miss her.'

I thanked him and walked smartly down the church path to where Moot was tied up. At a brisk trot to the end of the lane, we turned right on to the poorly maintained Shottery Road and, sure enough, caught up with Miss Hathaway.

'Tom, good-day to you,' she said upon looking up and realising it was me.

I dismounted and walked with her at a leisurely pace.

'Father Frith asked me to give you this message.'

I passed on the message. She said nothing but thought for a few minutes as we walked.

'Tom, I thank you for your concern of, my – nay, our – friend. It is good to know you feel as we all feel.'

'That Will is not a glove-maker?'

'Indeed.'

'What is he then?' I asked provocatively.

'I know not, Tom, but unlike you and me, he is destiny's child, is he not?'

'Without any shadow of doubt,' I said and re-mounted. 'Miss Anne, I must be back to work.'

'You are a true friend, Tom,' she said with a smile.

I tipped my cap and galloped off back to Stratford.

Naively, I expected the world to kick in and things to happen. I imagined, spurred on by good words from the faithful, the wealthy and powerful friends of the Shakespeares would come to the rescue. I assumed Will would find a patron, be offered a place to study at Oxford and his great path of destiny would begin. But, wretchedly, little happened. In fact, in the coming months I became depressed as the world set in around us all.

Work at the livery was relentless, and Will worked long hours in his father's shop. Even Gilbert was fetching and carrying. Sadly, after selling much of Mary's inheritance, this was all the means the Shakespeares had left to pull themselves out of the mire they were in.

CHAPTER 16

It was March, 1579, and certainly the word was that Coventry plays would not be a part of Easter this year. However, something did descend on Stratford that put us all back on the cart of joy after such a dismal year.

I was cleaning the cobbles when horsemen, accompanied by two carts full of every sort of baggage, clattered their way in and completely filled the yard. The men leapt off their horses with the confidence of a conquering army. They exuded the air of gentry but gentry who had not been able to buy new clothes in a while. What they wore was flamboyant, and once upon a time of the highest quality, but now it was old, battered and worn.

'I seek Mr Thomas Wickham?' declared a young but swarthy and well-dressed young man, complete with neat beard and moustache.

'I am Thomas Wickham,' I said, removing my hat and bowing.

'Excellent! I have it on good authority from my friend John Somerville that this be the best livery in town.'

'Good Sir, you are indeed correct. This livery is owned by His Lordship Sir Thomas Lucy, to whom we answer,' I said.

Any friend of John Somerville had better be aware of whose allegiances this stable was under.

'Good, tell His Lordship that Lord Strange's men wish to take use of his livery's services whilst we spend a few days making our mark on this town with our considerable talent as play actors!'

Play actors in our town! Real play actors! I could not wait to tell Will. I told Lord Strange that we were quite full. Nevertheless, I informed him of our fees and services.

'Thank you, young Tom. We are booked to play in the inn on the high street for four nights at two pennies a head. Tell all your friends.'

'I will, Sir. If you desire the empty stalls we have, you will need to book and settle with my father,' I told him. 'You will find him in the tack-room yonder.'

'Anon,' said Lord Strange and he went smartly to the tack-room.

A motley lot were these players. They did not stand or relax; they sort of posed, as if some great artist unseen was painting their portrait, or as if they were awaiting a retinue of servants who were yet to show up.

One of them swaggered towards me; he had a great hat full of plumage, dark features and a heavy moustache. His shirt and jerkin were open, baring a chest of thick, black curly hair festooned with what looked like expensive gold jewellery but, as he drew closer, it was plainly brass and copper. Spurs on his well-worn thigh-length boots jangled provocatively as he approached. Placing his hands akimbo, he looked at me, presenting his right side.

'We wish to take lodgings with food and bed, for two shillings. Know thee of anywhere that is warm and dry?'

'You can take the best lodgings in town if you want to pay that kind of sum,' I told him.

He displayed a look of confusion.

'Two shillings, for all of us?' he said, rotating his finger in an inclusive gesture.

There were twelve of them! That was tuppence each. They would get an empty piggery for that!

'Including victuals,' said a voice from the back.

I knew players worked in the land of make-believe but they had to eat and sleep in the real world, did they not? Lord Strange came out of the tack-room.

'Don't listen to them, Tom. They have enough to pay. Their purses are tighter than an alter boy's arse. James, we can leave horses here, but the carts and pulling beasts we need to find elsewhere.'

'Ferdi!' replied James with a salute of compliance.

'Ferdi? Who is Ferdi?' I asked but was ignored.

'Now, Tom, know you where we can place our carts and pulling beasts?'

We were the best biggest and most central livery in Stratford but I did know of an empty barn currently leased by a man who was very short of coin.

'I may be able to help, Sir, but I need to run an errand first,' I told him.

'Good show, Tom. Right, James, get the horses settled here. Robert, get these wagons turned around and everyone else up to the high street. Oh, James? Glue and bills.'

Everyone started to organise themselves. James handed some paper bills and a bucket to Lord Strange, which he took and placed on the ground. The medallion man smiled at me, gave a wink of his eye and, with equine poise and smooth motion, he leapt on to one of the carts. He stood proud like the captain of a galleon, and, pointing at the gates, he delivered a speech with great passion:

Princes of France, the sparkling light of fame,
Whose glory's brighter than the burnish'd gates
From whence Latona's lordly son doth march,
When, mounted on his coach tinsell'd with flames,
He triumphs in the beauty of the heavens;
This is the place where Rodomont lies hid:
Here lies he, like the thief of Thessaly,
Which scuds abroad and searcheth for his prey,
And, being gotten, straight he gallops home,
As one that dares not break a spear in field.
But trust me, princes. I have girt his fort,
And I will sack it, or on this castle-wall
I'll write my resolution with my blood:–
Therefore, drum, sound a parle!

James rolled his eyes, and clicked the team. The cart thus moved, jerking this player, but he firmly held his pose. This man brought such a grin to my face! Will was going to love this, and did I have an idea!

'Now, Tom!' said Lord Strange.

'Your Lordship,' I replied, turning to give him my full attention.

'First, I am Ferdinando Stanley, Lord Strange. To some I am Your Lordship, others call me Ferdi, you will call me Sir. Now you said you have somewhere for our carts but you need to run an errand?'

'Indeed, Sir.'

'Good. Run your errand and meet me at the inn where we will set up our baggage but, on the way, paste these play bills where you can.'

So saying, he handed me a pot of foul-smelling horse glue and some play-bills.

I looked at the play-bill: *The History of Mad Orlando* by Robert Greene. It looked exciting. It was a short walk to High Street so I took a long way round – Sheep Street, Waterside Bridge Street and up to Henley Street – and found a few well-placed positions for the playbills which I duly pasted up. The doors of empty buildings were the best positions. I knocked on the Shakespeare workshop door at Henley Street, which was opened by John with scissors and pattern in hand. I could also see Will in the background pulling leather; he neither looked up nor paused his work.

'Tom, good-day to you,' John said cordially but clearly busy.

'Sir, do you still have a lease on the Guild Street barn?'

'Empty and three months to run, curse's yes I do!' he grumbled.

'I can get you four nights at two shillings a night, eight shillings in all?'

'Make it ten shillings and you have a deal. Who wants it?'

'Lord Strange's men. The players are in Stratford playing at the inn on the high street,' I said purposely loud for Will to hear, and hear he did.

'Lord Strange's men, here in Stratford?' he said, dropping his leather and running to the door.

'Hello, Will. Yes, they are on tonight,' I said and handed him one of the playbills which Will seized with irrepressible enthusiasm.

'Only a tuppence a head. Father. Can we see them?' he uttered without looking up from the text.

'There is much work to be done … and tuppence a head is a fair sum,' he exclaimed.

I felt Will's heart sink. 'I will pay for Will … and I will get His Lordship to take the barn, Sir.'

John Shakespeare relented. 'Will has been hard at work of late. Obliged to you, Tom.'

'See you later, Will,' I said, but he was still scrutinising the playbill. 'I'm coming, too,' he said.

'Will, these patterns must be cut and stretched today!' demanded his father

'It'll be done, Father,' he said, throwing off his apron.

We left and took off for the high street as his father, resigned to his situation, closed the workshop door. Outside the inn we found the two carts now unloaded and standing in the street.

In the courtyard, Ferdinando Stanley was organising a stage and working out how many spectators he could fit into the surroundings. Will was in raptures as he watched the activity. There were baskets of brightly coloured costumes being emptied and organised.

There were all sorts of chattels, swords and things the players referred to as properties. On a platform that looked like it might be the stage, three players practised a sword fight; it was really fast and exciting. Up in the gallery the medallion man was posed on the balustrade, spouting lines. Ferdinando carried on directing players, ordering staff and conducting business. Upon realising I was there, he called out to me but still carried on ordering the inn staff about.

'I don't want anyone sneaking in the gallery without paying, so where does that door go? Tom! What news?'

'Nowhere, sir,' said the maid.

'A barn in Guild Street big enough to take the horses' carts and bed down twelve players, Sir.'

'Price?'

'Four nights, twelve and six, Sir,' I said giving a guilty glance to Will but he simply smiled back. I did not know whether or not he had noticed my profit-taking.

'We'll take it. James, pay this boy.'

James came over and, taking out the coin, handed it to me.

'Tom, know thee a cook? Food here is poor and pricey,' whispered James.

'What do you want?'

'Pottage and bread for twelve, after the performance back at the barn,' he said.

'What are you paying?'

'A crown for four nights?'

'Done. My Aunt Grace and I will bring it over.'

James put his hand back into his purse and flipped me a silver crown which I caught with a smile. Putting an arm around Will, I pulled him away.

'Gotta go, Will.'

'Who's your friend, Tom?' asked Ferdinando.

'William, Sir; William Shakespeare,' I said and turning the still-dazed Will around, I presented him to Lord Strange.

'John Somerville's good cuz?' said Ferdinando, putting his hand out.

'Indeed, Sir,' said Will, shaking it.

'Heard much about you. We shall speak. Jenny!' he shouted.

Jenny put her head round a curtain hung on the gallery.

'Sir?'

'See these boys. Tonight they get in free!'

'Sir.'

'But no one else!'

Will went to thank Lord Strange, but he was already on to something else.

Will and I walked back to Henley Street.

'That's what I want, Tom! That, that's me. It's in my heart, my soul. I know it!'

I said little, besides Will would not have heard me. In his head he was still with the players.

Back at the workshop, I paid John his ten shillings for the barn, which pleased him greatly. Bidding to meet him for the performance later, I left Will catching up with his work and went back to Ely Street. Grace was very pleased to cook bread and pottage for a shilling a night for the next four nights. So, I took some profit for myself, but modest it was and, besides, what makes the world happy anyway? I was chuffed, everyone received what they wanted and I earned three shillings and sixpence for arranging it.

The play-bills I had posted had been somewhat pointless since, other than the public flogging of some poor fool, little ever happened in Stratford by way of excitement; and word that the players were here spread like wildfire.

The inn was besieged by five o'clock for a performance that was not due to start till seven. Will turned up carrying little Annie and both their faces were lit up with the impending excitement. We all struggled to the front and I tipped Jenny the wink so we squeezed in, much to the annoyance of all those waiting in line. The performance was now going to be after dark and there must have been a hundred candles and lanterns put around the stage. The dear old inn-keeper, Mr Christopher Blackwell, was chewing his jerkin sleeve in abject fear of a fire, so much so that he stood with a jug of water in each hand at all times.

Ferdinando gave the word and Stratford was given entry, each person dropping two pennies into the box that Jenny was holding, as well as deftly spotting any smart arses trying to creep in without paying. We took our places in the best seats we could find, with Will keeping his very excited sister on his lap. We watched as the courtyard filled up with all of Stratford's finest, mightiest, strangest and poorest. Richard Field was one of the first to get in as the throng massed its way across the yard. He came and sat with us.

'What say, Will, Tom?'

'Didn't see you outside,' said Will.

'Only just arrived, but Tyler and I launched ourselves at the throng!'

'Did, um, er … you see Miss Hathaway,' asked Will quietly, trying not to let his sister hear.

'You sweet on Hathaway?'

'Yes,' said Annie squelching her thumb as she sucked it.

Will blushed as Fieldy and I both prodded Will in jest.

'No, Will,' said Fieldy. 'A lot of people did not get in.'

'What about Tyler?' laughed Will.

We all looked for Tyler, and sure enough there he was in the gallery, with a pretty girl on his arm, waving frantically to us.

'Tyler!' I snorted with a laugh.

'Where did she come from?' asked Will, waving to his scurrilous friend.

'Haven't seen her before,' I whispered.

'Never misses a filly, does young Tyler' said Will.

There was suddenly a hush as the main lanterns were extinguished, leaving only candles to light the stage. Suddenly, six men appeared on the platform and two others in the gallery. They were dressed in incredibly rich and sumptuous costumes. There was a hushed silence of reverence and we all watched the players. Their faces were made up with a heavy paint, to accentuate their eyes, cheeks and lips. Against the flickering light, it was a spectacle to the eyes. The vision was held aloft by the smell of candles, lanterns, sweating bodies, beer and scented face paint. It evoked an atmosphere somewhere between that of a church and a brothel. I kept that observation to myself, for we hadn't paid to get in and we were there to enjoy ourselves – not be thrown out for blasphemy.

A man came to the centre of the platform and absorbed the taut anticipation of the crowd assembled. He first gave a great grin of self-satisfaction, then, snatching a pose fit to defy the sky itself, he delivered his speech with the energy of a stampede in full flight:

Victorious princes, summon'd to appear within the continent of Africa;
From seven-fold Nilus to Taprobany,
Where fair Apollo darting forth his light Plays on the seas;
From Gades' islands, where stout Hercules Emblaz'd
his trophies on two posts of brass,
To Tanais, whose swift-declining floods Environ rich Europa to the north;
All fetch'd From out your courts by beauty to this coast,
To seek and sue for fair Angelica;
Sith none but one must have this happy prize,
At which you all have levell'd long your thoughts,
Set each man forth his passions how he can,
And let her censure make the happiest man.

A massive applause went up before the next actor could even begin his lines; they had to pause a good while.

I was not sure who was who in this spectacle but, after a bit, it did all start to make sense. Orlando, it seemed, was supposed to look after some king but had fallen in love and gone off with a maid called

Angelica. But then she had gone off with someone else, one of the king's enemies. She left Orlando distraught and as mad as a stallion on a hot summer night, so he had gone and trashed all in his path to find her. Orlando's friend travels to the moon to find a cure for Orlando's madness, which he brings back in a bottle and cures Orlando, who goes back to his king and leads the army victorious over the king's enemy. I think that was what the story was.

There were some great speeches and even the boy playing Angelica was pretty enough to wed and romp. And the sword fights! With real swords! Heavens above! In one, it was so fast and furious we really thought they were going to kill each other.

At one point in the play I nudged Fieldy and pointed Will out to him. Will's eyes were alight with the magic and as he cuddled a beaming Annie, his lips pattered rapidly, silently following the words. Fieldy, nodded to me in recognition.

What applause at the end, as all the actors came on the platform and bowed to us! We must have clapped our hands and cheered for an aeon! My hands were sore and ringing like a thousand bees had stung them. Nevertheless, Will out-cheered and out-clapped us all. Even Mr Blackwell put down his jugs of water and joined the appreciation.

I have never seen so many people leave a building with such smiles upon their faces! When not sleeping or working this was indeed the most delightful way to pass the little time we had. In the mêlée of the exiting crowd, I lost Will and little Annie but Fieldy and Tyler caught up with me in the street.

'No Quiney?' I asked them.

'Don't know what happened to him?' declared Fieldy.

Tyler's little bint fluffed up to him. 'I want to go home,' she whined.

Tyler looked at me with a naughty grin. 'Her parents are away and the servants take the chance to drink themselves to sleep,' he whispered.

'We'll go anon,' he said turning to her and stroking her cheek.

Will came out of the inn with his sister and they skipped over to us.

'Annie told them she wanted to be a player but they said no women allowed on the stage,' smiled Will.

'Not fair,' whined Annie in her own sweet protest.

'One day, darling sister, one day,' Will reassured her giving her hands a squeeze.

Leaning forward to me in a player like aside, he whispered excitedly, 'I am invited by the players to sup with them in Father's barn!'

'Well I must go and help my aunt carry that supper to them,' I said, taking my leave.

'I'll take little sis home first,' he added discretely.

As I walked away, the players came out of the inn and shook hands with those who had hung around to offer a personal appreciation of their spectacle.

Back at the livery, trussed up in a hay-box all piping hot, Grace had a huge pot of pottage. Next to which was a large basket of bread and a dozen spoons and bowls. We loaded it on to a small cart and off we trotted to Guild Street.

If the inn courtyard had resembled a cross between a church and a brothel, then the barn simply resembled a brothel.

All the players had made themselves comfortable, their bedding all unpacked from the cart and laid on the gallery. There were a bunch of Stratford women with them, some known to be whores, others not but, nonetheless, with loose morals. The wine was flowing and the laughter was at full gallop.

A great cheer went up when Grace and I brought in the food. The players all set upon it like hungry wolves. Grace and I served it as fast as we could and it was demolished in a few minutes, players clearly like their food, and their wine, and their women, it would seem. I saw Fieldy had come along, too, and was getting one of the actors to show him his sword-fighting tricks. The noise of merriment was intense and at the centre was medallion man, whom I later found out was called Lucus. He was in direct quoting competition with Will. Lucus was able to finish a poem that Will had started and Will had not finished three poems Lucus had started but did well enough to really impress him.

'Damn it, this boy is a vessel!' cried Lucus.

A big grin came over Will's face.

'Ferdi, Ferdi. This boy's a vessel. We should have him in the troupe!

Ferdinando wandered over, a little worse for wear with sagging eyes, glazed and bloodshot by a mixture of stress, exhilaration, tiredness and drink.

'This boy is a thespian?' slurred Lucus. 'Join him to the troupe! Now! Thish inshtant!'

Will's face lit up and his breath stopped.

Ferdinando looked to Will.

'Can't. Too young, not enough room, we're a tight ship, not enough coin,' he said in a slurred way, as if someone were stretching his tongue sideways.

I did wonder about the age bit, as Ferdinando was only a few years older than Will and me. Will took it all well. He knew they were all under the drink, but for Will this night had been what it was all about. What he had seen had left the Coventry plays for dead. This was not a brief distraction from the toil of hard lives; to these players, this was life.

I helped Grace gather all the empty bowls and we stacked them with the pot back on the cart.

'Stay and enjoy some cheer,' she said, mounting the cart.

I stayed on and watched all these noisy players sparring, joking, swapping tales and quotes. Gradually, about the first hour of the morning, they started to slow down. One by one they retired to bed – some alone, some with company, and to Will and my surprise, not all of the opposite sex. We all went back by Will's house, then Fieldy and I chummed each other down the rest of Henley Street and went our separate ways at Bridge Street.

On the second night, Anne Hathaway turned up with her father and step-mother to see the troupe. They took a seat on the gallery and, even though Will's attention was near impossible to take off the players, I did see that they threw the odd glance at each other during the performance. Richard and Joan Hathaway stopped with Anne after the performance. Briefly they spoke with Will before they whisked her away. I don't know what was said. Will was quiet about the encounter.

Fieldy, Will and I saw all the other performances, afterwards spending the evenings with the players in the barn at Guild Street.

On the last night, Quiney turned up with Tyler and we Stratford boys made a night of it, but still we were no match for the players when it came to making merry. They were such a raucous lot. I did, however, notice they slept for a lot of the day. Will, I noticed was getting on well with Ferdinando and some of the other players. I dearly hoped they could give him a job. Ferdinando had crammed in about 300 people into the yard and, at tuppence a head, that was ten pounds for the four nights. This play-acting could certainly create some good coin.

It was a silent day when the players moved on and we all went back to our lives – Fieldy, Tyler and Quiney off to school, Will to the glove shop and I to the livery. I wondered if Will felt as I did. I'd wager good coin that he did. The drudgery of repetition was so excruciating. I looked to adults and wondered how they put up with it, without so much as a flinch. I knew there was little alternative but, for pity's sake, was I, too, eventually going to be as numbed by life as a January frost. Something inside urged me to not give in and to find a way out, to make my own world, be my own master, but what? I threw yet another bucket of water across the yard and once more picked up my broom, and once more, tried not to notice the stench of horse urine.

CHAPTER 17

It was the third day of April, 1579, at some unearthly hour, when there was frantic banging on the yard gates. I jumped up and pulled on my britches and boots. Grace woke, too. We ran down the treads and across the yard.

'Who's there?' I called, letting loose the dogs who ran to the gates barking.

'We are armed!' cried Grace, wielding the crossbow that hung in the tack-room that she had grabbed but failed to cock.

'William!' cried Will, desperate and gasping for breath.

I threw off the cross beam, which thudded to the ground just missing the dogs. We pulled open the gate and were immediately confronted by a distressed Will.

'Anne! Grace, please come quick,' he blurted.

Grace thrust me the crossbow.

'Get my cloak.'

I ran back to the tack-room, threw down the crossbow, ran up the treads, grabbed Grace's cloak as well as my jerkin and ran back out as quick as I could. Will and Grace were already on their way. Catching up, I threw the cloak around a chilly and grateful Grace.

'What is it?' I asked.

'Annie is coughing and not breathing,' panted Will.

We ran all the way to Henley Street and straight in the door, held open by an ashen-faced John. Grace ran upstairs to where Mary was tearfully holding little Annie's hand and mopping her brow. Grace pushed forward and made the little mite sit up. She was soaking wet with fever and her little eyes looked straight into mine. I could see her lips were blue and, as she rubbed her eyes, I could see her fingertips were as well. I knew this was not good but at least there were no boils, so it wasn't the plague. Grace picked her up and moved her to sit near the window where she jiggled her on her knee.

'Will, get a bowl and a jug of boiling water.'

Will ran off down stairs.

'Mary, get me another blanket. Tom, open all the windows.'

Mary grabbed a blanket. I opened the window next to Grace and the wind rushed in and Grace held Annie to the rush of air. Taking the blanket she wrapped Annie tight and held her but still offered her face to the draught.

'Where's the doctor?' snapped Grace.

'Playing tennis in Oxford,' said Mary, tears running down her face.

'Come on, darling. Get the fresh air. How long has she been like this?'

'All of yesterday,' sobbed Mary.

'Should have called me sooner,' sighed Grace quietly.

Suddenly, Annie vomited all over the floor.

'I'll get a swab and bucket,' I said and ran downstairs.

Will had some boiling water in a jug and he went smartly back upstairs with it. I filled a bucket with water from the kitchen pump but, as I came to the stairs, I heard Grace call me.

'Coming,' I called back.

I put down my pail. Will and Grace were turning Annie upside down.

'Help William.'

I grabbed Annie from Grace as she took the jug of steaming water and poured it into the big basin.

'Put the cloth over us, near the window!'

We held Annie upside down by the window with the steaming water near her. Mary held the blanket over us as Grace started banging little Annie's chest with her hand. She coughed and coughed as yellowy pussy stuff came out of her mouth. We turned her back up rested and tried again, more stuff came out but she was still blue and getting weaker.

Grace tried and tried. Still more stuff came out. But, as the night went on and despite fresh infusions of hot water, Annie became bluer. The coughs became weak and her breath shallow, and soon we, too, were all exhausted.

Eventually Grace looked at Will and whispered, 'It's no good. Lay her down, hold her hands, and let her die in peace and love.'

I helped Will carry his poor little player to her bed. She shivered as small tears fell from her sad eyes. Mary collapsed, sliding down the wall to the floor where she sat frozen. As I gripped my own tears, I watched Annie's chest pulse pathetically as she grabbed air with little gasps; her eyes fixed on a non-existent sky. Grace collapsed by the windowsill, she, too, taking in much-needed fresh air.

It was only now that I noticed a terrified Gilbert and Joan hanging on to the doorpost, their faces red and wet with tears.

We made Annie comfortable in her bed; she relaxed a little and, though there was still a stare in her eyes, strangely a smile came across her face. Will sat on the floor holding her hand to his cheek, and Mary crawled across the room to be beside her, too.

I swabbed up the vomit and sputum as Grace pulled herself together and we left the Shakespeares to spend their last moments with Annie alone. Grace and I sat downstairs awaiting the inevitable. John sat outside in the street, staring at the dawning sky and, just as the first ray of sun hit the street, the inevitable arrived. Mary screamed, a scream as long as it was loud, and fearsome enough to fill a thousand buckets with tears. In all the world, there is no sound like the scream of a mother for her dead child.

Will came downstairs looking like death itself. I stood up and he grabbed me so tight his chest pulsed with sobs into mine and a river of his tears flowed down my back.

'Why her? Why not me,' he grimaced, through his tears. Will let go of me and ran out of the door. I went to follow but John stood up and went after him, so I left them.

A few minutes later, my father rode by and, stopping by the door, I told him what had happened.

'Heaven preserve them. I'll get Haycroft,' he said and rode off towards Trinity to get the vicar.

Judith and Hamnet turned up, too.

'We just saw Will and John,' said Judith.

'Is there no hope?' said Hamnet.

I shook my head. They both went inside and upstairs to be with Mary.

Grace came out into the daylight, wrapped in her cloak. She was pale and exhausted.

'We are done here, Tom,' she sighed.

We wandered back to the livery saying nothing, the silence only broken by morning bird song and the elm tree leaves gently fluttering in the breeze. Grace went to wash herself and change out of her nightshift. I took out the small cart, the elm boards and black palls to make ready for a funeral.

Having picked up a coffin, we turned up at the Shakespeares with it on the cart and took it into the house. Judith Sadler had purchased a shroud and bonnet for Annie and, with Grace and Mary, she assisted in washing and dressing the dead child. Will and I tried to take the coffin up the stairs but they were narrow and it was too long to fit around the corner.

'Will, would you take Tom upstairs and bring your sister down,' asked John with the gentlest dignity he could muster.

The women came down the stairs and Will and I went up. Will and I stood looking at little Annie for a few minutes on our own. Dead children strangely do not look dead, not like adults whose flesh sinks to their bones and their features become sharper, making them look different. A dead child lies quietly with puffy little cheeks and you almost expect a smile to appear and eyes to open. Then you touch them and their flesh is as cold as an anvil on the harshest January night. Will and I gently picked up her cold body, dressed in pretty white shroud and bonnet. Will alone carried her down the stairs and placed her in the coffin that was attendant on the table.

I need not tell you this funeral was a tragic affair for everyone – a sweet little girl, shy but so beguiling. She loved her brother and, indeed, was very proud of him. Eight sweet and beautiful years she gave the world.

The news was already all around Stratford. Annie's little girlfriends were soon there, waiting in the street, all dressed in white and carrying little posies of May and cherry blossom with white daffodils, their tears glistening on their rosy cheeks. Fieldy and Quiney turned up with their parents and so did Tyler.

Inside, doing all the legal things required, was Vicar Haycroft with the bailiff and a somewhat sheepish doctor. We were waiting outside in attendance on the coffin when, in language I cannot repeat, there came the most appalling cacophony of shouting and screams from Mary. Vicar Haycroft, the physician and bailiff all swiftly walked out into the street, their faces as red as fresh rhubarb.

'In the name of sweet Jesus, she was a child!' screamed Mary after them, and then sobbed relentlessly.

We all stood bewildered as John came out and spoke briefly with Vicar Haycroft.

'I cannot do such a thing,' the vicar remonstrated with John in a terse whisper.

John rubbed his temples and pleaded with him, 'I crave your forgiveness. She is very upset.'

Vicar Haycroft's fingers gripped his Bible in some attempt for spiritual authority, but he looked more like an angry dog clenching its dead quarry.

'Of course, indeed, but I cannot acquiesce to her request,' he said, eyes closed and breathing deeply to calm himself.

Will came out and beckoned his father back inside, and we all waited as things calmed down. Eventually, Will and Judith Sadler came out. Will spoke with the men, and Judith with the children. All was almost ready, and then I caught Will's eye.

'Mother wanted the prayers for the dead but it's popery and Vicar would not have it,' he whispered.

For the love of God, the State is fearful of its grip on power in the face of a small child's death; where will it end, I thought to myself.

We all took great breath. Father and Grace were to drive the cart. Will, Fieldy, Quiney, Tyler, Gilbert and I carried out Anne's coffin. Poor Gilbert was not quite tall enough and had to tip-toe to keep carrying. We placed the coffin on to the cart and everyone fell into line as the wind gently flapped the black palls. In front of the cart, Vicar Haycroft, Mary and John. Behind the cart, all the young maidens clutching their white posies. Behind them, Will, Gilbert and Joan and finally myself and all other family and friends. It was the most sombre walk up the high street to Trinity, and when the bells rang, they cut the air like a blunt butcher's knife.

Will, the boys and I carried Annie's coffin to her grave and, as she was lowered, the maidens threw in their posies. The vicar read a funeral rite whilst Will, Gilbert, Joan and John did their best to support Mary as tears and wails poured from her like a storm drain in flood.

After the burial, everyone wandered back to Henley Street dazed and desolate. Hamnet, Judith and Grace laid out cups of mead and cold-meat pastries from their bakery. Little was said as we all milled around, taking the food and drink for nothing more than fuel to sustain us through this wretchedness.

Father, Grace and I took our leave first. When we returned to the livery, the help had thankfully covered the work well, so Father rewarded them with an extra penny.

Since death waits for no one and Stratford was busy, with our numb hearts and sore hands the following weeks were hard. Our own horses were in much demand, as well the ones we kept for their owners. There was a lot of other work; we had a new pair of horses to train, then there were several bogged carts for Heavens Gate to free, not to mention two more funerals.

I did not see Will at all during his family's time of grief. Eventually, one night he turned up, just as I was about to close the gates.

'Can I stay tonight?' was all he asked.

'Of course,' I replied.

Poor Will. He looked terrible. Tired, worn, with hands darkened by tanning stains and blistered from working leather. He came and supped with us. He said nothing, just ate. You would have thought he had not eaten in a week, which as it turned out he hadn't. He fell into my bed and there he slept, not just the night, but the whole of the following day, too, and into the following night! He did not move.

It was a whole two days later when he not only quietly rose from my bed, but the strangest event happened, and, as it turned out, the most fortunate.

It was the fifth hour in the morning and, as usual before opening the gates, I was washing down the yard. The weather had been warm. It had rained in the night and there was a mist. I opened the gates, pushed them back and locked them in place.

The river mist rolled into the yard, a diaphanous wave of luminous moisture. Pushing it gently aside, in walked a fine-looking man leading a splendid horse. He wore exquisite clothes with a wide hat sporting magnificent feathers. From his great silver buckled belt, an ornate sword hung at his side. His horse was a bay with socks as dark as night and tall too, maybe seventeen hands. I had never seen one but I suspected this beast to be one of the sought-after Holsteiners.

'Sir Richard de Hoghton,' he declared as I took his horse from him.

'Your Lordship, how can we be of service?'

'Feed and water my steed for starters,' he said breezily as he looked about the yard.

'At once, Your Lordship,' I replied.

I took his horse over to the trough and tied him to one of the rings whilst he took a drink.

'I am looking for William Shakespeare. A friend said if he were not at home, I should find him here, so I came here first,' said Sir Richard.

'I am William Shakespeare,' said Will, standing in the yard.

It was the first time Will had risen in two days.

'Sir Richard de Hoghton,' he said, removing his glove and holding out his hand.

Will shook his hand with some trepidation.

'May we talk somewhere?' asked Sir Richard.

Will looked to me, and I nodded to the tack-room.

'Indeed, Your Lordship,' said Will, offering direction with his open hand.

I went to the feed bin and pulled out a nose-bag for the horse.

Well, whatever they spoke about, when they re-emerged into the yard, Will had the first smile on his face I had seen in months. Sir Richard walked over and untied his horse as I removed the nose-bag.

'May I ask what breed, Your Lordship?' I asked.

'Holsteiner, from Saxony,' he said, inspecting in his hand the feed that I had given his horse.

'A friend tells me you are a fine boy of Equus?'

'I believe I have an affinity, Your Lordship.'

'Good, next season I want you to match our mares,' he said and mounted up.

'Where?' I asked.

'Hoghton Tower.'

'Where is Hoghton Tower? Lordship, I am engaged here. I need my lord and master's consent.'

'I'm told you are also resourceful; you will get it,' he said with a smile.

'But, but, but, how,' I faltered.

'No buts! "How" is your concern not mine. And that feed, it's good quality. I like that – means you are honest,' he said and, tossing me a whole shilling, he turned his horse about and took off.

'Next season, be there!' he cried on exit.

I turned around and Will was standing there, grinning from ear to ear.

'What in heaven's name …?'

'I am now children's tutor to his brother's family, Alexander de Hoghton,' smiled Will.

'What?'

'And paid a month in advance,' declared Will, tossing a purse of coin into the air.

Will looked at me and, smiling through his tired and tear-worn face, he walked over and embraced me tight.

'Friend, one day with my pen, I will make plays and poetry so fine! And they will all be about the same thing.'

'What's that?' I asked, as he released me.

'True love and true friendship,' he whispered looking into my eyes.

Grace came into the yard, and then the help showed up and Father kicked open the hayloft doors with a bang.

I smiled. It was suddenly a new dawn and we both felt it. Will went to Grace and, to her surprise, he thanked her with a great embrace.

'Jack, I will need a horse in two days,' he called to my father.

'Anything for you, Will.'

Will bowed deeply to all of us and skipped, yes skipped, out of the yard.

Two days later with a saddled Moot, I turned up at Henley Street. His parting was done in classic Will style, no fanfare or celebration, a gentle morning mist into which Will would quietly dissolve. I waited, holding Moot. The front door of Henley Street was ajar, but no Will.

Sir Richard arrived, greeted me and looked at the horse I had brought for Will. Seeing Sir Richard wince, I sought to reassure him.

'Slow but strong, My Lord, and as the weight comes off I am sure his pace will improve. Besides, it won't create strife if we don't get him back in a hurry. We haven't listed him yet.'

Sir Richard laughed and thrust me a folded paper.

'I understand you can read,' he said.

I unfolded the paper; it was instructions on how to reach Hoghton Tower.

'Be there.'

'I will do my best, Your Lordship.'

'Where is the boy? We need to ride.'

Sir Richard was displaying a touch of impatience so I went inside to find Will. He was standing in the parlour, holding his bundle of belongings. His brothers and sister were gathered around; a teary Mary sat at the table, pouting. Will's father was seated in the chair at the head of the table in posture reminiscent of a king missing his crown.

'Your mind is made up, my son?'

'It is, Father.'

'I think you are making an error. A life of position can only be built on trade.'

'Your father needs you. I need you,' wept Mary.

'Don't go,' whispered Joan.

Will turned and, seeing me, gave me one of his tiny nuances of expression, telling me exactly what he needed. I took his bundle from him and waited. Will went over to the little ones and kissed them.

'I have to go,' he said.

He kissed his mother.

'Mother, do not weep. I will see thee anon.'

She gripped him hard, and then released him. Will faced his father.

'You must do what you must do,' he said, without looking at Will.

Will went down on one knee and kissed his father's hand. Still John would not look at him, and so Will left.

I followed him into the street and was just helping him to load his belongings when a slightly breathless Anne Hathaway pitter-pattered her gentle way towards us. Will's face lit up at once. Beaming her smile directly at Will, she handed him a small bundle of bread, cheese and apples.

'Take care, my fair friend,' Anne stammered sweetly. Will nodded, his eyes caressing her pretty face.

Sir Richard beckoned me listen and quietly he spoke.

'Present the publican with a farthing, queen's head towards him, and say, "small beer for a large journey". He will serve you, you will drink, and after, he will see you safely across the marshes.'

'Sir?' I said confused.

'The instructions. The only bit I left out.'

'Verily, Sir,' I replied, clutching the paper he had given me.

'Tom!' shouted Will, slapping my back and mounting up. I think he was even shedding a tear.

Off they rode, probably for the next three days or so. I was so jealous about Will's adventure that, there and then, I resolved to get to Hoghton Tower for the next breeding season. Anne and I, alone in the street, looked at each other slightly awkwardly.

'How did that prospect come to will?' I asked.

'Walk with me to the lanes,' replied Anne.

As we walked, she told me how she had spoken with John Frith of Will's plight. He had then spoken with John Cottom, and he with his brother Thomas. And in turn, he spoke with Alexander de Hoghton.

I told her of my invitation and showed her the instruction paper.

'How will you get release from Lord Lucy?' she asked as we wandered along the road.

'Oh, a few bits of choice rumour and gossip, dropped in the right places, should do the trick,' I said with a cheeky grin.

'Indeed, I think you know man as well as horse,' said Anne and, giving me the sweetest smile, she took her leave to walk the last mile alone.

CHAPTER 18

It was 1580, my seventeenth year and my first real ride in the open paddocks of life, which, as it happened, turned into quite a gallop!

I was called into the stewards quarters at Charlecote. There I found not Cornall waiting for me, but Lord Lucy.

'I understand de Hoghton wants you to look at his horses and match them.'

My ruse worked but, having been careful where I sowed the seed, I had to be impressed. He was indeed well informed. 'That is correct, My Lord.'

'Mmm, what did you tell him?'

'You are my lord and master, Sir, and I can do nothing without your word, My Lord.'

Lord Lucy stood looking at me, thinking and nodding to himself. 'A man who can be trusted in small things can be trusted in greater things, or so they say.'

'My Lord.'

He threw me a bag of coin, which I caught, and by its weight alone it had to be gold.

'A dozen sovereigns.'

'My Lord?'

'Go to the de Hoghton's. Serve them as they request, but buy me a stallion of exception.'

'As you wish. My Lord, if I cannot source such a beast?'

'I want a good stallion. Our stock is heavy and slow. We need to move on with the times. If you can't find anything there, go elsewhere and, if need be, use that coin to trade and increase the sum. Find me a good stallion – light of hoof, nimble gait and solid temperament.'

'As you command, My Lord.'

'What do I require?' he demanded condescendingly.

'A good stallion, light of hoof, nimble gait and solid temperament, My Lord.'

'Good. Now,' he said, holding up a document, 'this is my letter of instruction. Anyone who requests your business, show them this and, should they detain you without cause, they will answer to me.'

'My Lord,' I said as I took the letter with its impressive seal.

'One other thing. Do you know this man?'

Lord Lucy held up a printed portrait of a kindly looking man.

'No, My Lord,' I said.

'I cannot give you this because it is the only one I have. He is Jesuit Edmund Campion and the greatest threat to our Crown and State.'

'Indeed, My Lord.'

Lord Lucy looked me in the eyes with dark severity.

'If you see him or become aware of his whereabouts, you will immediately report back to me; if need be, ride all night.'

'As you command, My Lord.'

'Indeed, I do,' he said, smirking his right of birth and walked out.

A tall order, I thought to myself as I emptied the coin into my hand. I counted it. I had never seen so much coin. The coin I had moved for John Shakespeare's brogging deals had always been in a locked box. My attention was moved by the thud of a large leather ledger on the table; it was Cornall.

'Make your mark here!' he snapped, holding out a quill pen.

I pushed the letter of instruction into my doublet and looked at the book and against my name there was a note for the provision of twelve sovereigns, two shillings and sixpence. Now, I did not trust Cornall to give me that extra coin after I signed.

'I only have twelve sovereigns, Sir,' I queried.

Cornall sighed and, putting down the quill, opened his purse and took out two shillings and six pennies, which he placed on the table. I picked up the coin and, taking the quill pen, signed my name.

'Who taught you to write?' asked the indignant Cornall.

'And read and count. My aunt did,' I lied.

I did not need him to be too closely aware of my association with Will's family.

'Well, the two and six is lodgings and food for yourself and horse. The rest is for trading. When you return, all coin must be accounted for,' he said. 'And since you can write, record all coin in this.'

He handed me a small bound ledger.

'Why coin? Could he not give me a promissory note?' I asked.

'Our Lord and Master does not use promissory notes with suspected Papists.'

'But business is business, so the secret coin it is,' I replied half-smart and regretting it as the words left my mouth.

'May well be, clever boy!' he snapped, and then stepped closer.

'But lose it and I'll call it theft; then you'll be as good as on the gallows.'

Cornall closed the ledger with a grin that revealed a distinct desire for my failure.

What to do with this coin? How to stow it and not lose? What if I had the misfortune to be robbed? With some sacking, a bone needle and thread, I took the coins and sewed them tight into one thing that could not be taken by stealth or by force without a fight. The twelve sovereigns I stitched into the waist-band of my britches.

It was mid-June and it seemed we were being bestowed a good summer. The days were certainly heating up. For me, this was a fine opportunity to get out of Stratford and experience the wider country. Also very exciting was the prospect of catching up with my dear friend. It had been eleven months. I longed to see how he was faring as the tutor of the de Hoghton children.

It was a hard ride up there – three days and two nights. To save money, I did not stop at any inn after dark. I would find a paddock full of cattle and slip in amongst them. This way I saved myself sixpence. It was a risk, as the law could have come down on me for grazing theft. During the day, I would stop for rest and feed at a public house; there I found adequate sustenance for Orlando and I could be had for tuppence-halfpenny.

There were a lot of government officials at points along the way. I lost count of the number of times I was asked to look at Campion's image. I was also glad for the letter of instruction – the sight of that seal never failed to clear my way.

I approached Hoghton Tower from the south and, through Chorley with Great Hill on my left, there stretched out in front of me I could see the great marshes in Sir Richard's instructions. A magnificent sight; it was dawn and the rising sun brought a pink glow to a gossamer mist. It protected Houghton Tower like a thin veil that no sword could penetrate on account of its softness. As instructed, I followed Great Hill around to the village of Withnell, where I quickly found the public house. I entered and, approaching the bar, held my farthing in the way I had been instructed.

'Small beer for a large journey,' I said.

Sure enough, I was guided across the marshes and left at the bottom of the imposing hill upon which the house was seated. Unless you were local or had the assistance from the publican, navigating the wetlands would be time-consuming, so warnings of approaching strangers were always available.

When I arrived at the house, it was very busy; other than Charlecote, it was the only large estate I had been to. It was more relaxed and friendly than Charlecote and, though I was simply a servant, I never felt so. There was a great atmosphere of conviviality among the staff – and even the family. Will, having used the vantage point of the recently completed gate-house, had seen my approach and greeted me on the driveway outside the rear stables. Indeed, the mist now cleared, looking out I could see there was a view all the way to the sea in the west.

'Come to the well house,' said Will, ushering a groom to take my horse. I was covered in dirt and sweat from the ride.

'It's the feast of Corpus Christi on Thursday,' declared Will, as if I should know.

I shrugged with ignorance and took off my shirt. Will pulled a bucket of water from the well.

'Old Catholic feast, very important to the un-reformed,' said Will.

I looked to Will, a little shocked.

'Of which there are more here making more noise than is prudent,' I whispered.

Will snorted a laugh of agreement.

'They love a holy day – a good excuse to indulge the belly and the liver.'

I laughed.

'Wow!' I shouted as Will sloshed me down with the water. Despite being as cold an executioner's heart, it was welcome.

He explained there was going to be a great banquet and dressing up in characters of animals and fantasy. He also told me he had been requested to prepare the children to perform a short play of Pyrimus and Thesbe. I could see by his enthusiasm and smile there was new fire in his soul.

'The family butler, Roger Anderson, is desperate to be a player and every second moment he gets on my back to cast him a role.'

The door creaked open and there, on the threshold, stood said butler with one of the stable grooms.

'I have been given orders to instruct this groom to bring Mr Wickham to the mares' paddock, if it pleases you, Master Wickham?'

'Certainly it pleases me,' I replied, pulling back on my shirt. It was certainly a change from the grumpy bark of Cornall's orders.

'Mr Anderson,' said Will, by way of introduction.

I stretched out my hand to him and we shook.

'Roger Anderson. In sole company, Roger; otherwise Mr Anderson. Pleased to meet you, Mr Wickham. We have heard a lot about you.'

'Indeed,' I answered politely.

'I have arranged a bed for you in the kitchen to the left of the hearth. You will find it both quiet and warm.'

'I'm obliged,' I said, thanking him.

Mr Anderson changed his focus to Will, quite forgetting his position, let alone my existence.

'Mr William, if I may petition, please, please may I have a role? You know well it is my earnest desire to be a player?'

Will laughed and rolled his eyes.

'Stuck in this tragic role for the sole purpose of feeding my kin, I do play it as honestly as life demands, but just a chance to show this world what a vessel of concentrated talent they have missed!'

'Tis a play by the children, Roger.'

'Just a small insignificant role?' he begged. 'I will play it to the hilt with such passion and awe. It would be such a heart-given thrill.

'If I did ...?'

'Yes, yes, a role? What shall it be?' he squeaked jumping excitedly.

'If I did ... may it be that you would not appreciate the role I give you.'

'Not a chance, Mr William. I, a humble servant, a poet's beggar, who cannot choose anything in his life, therefore any role assigned me would be a privilege – a trust born in love from your generous self,' he pleaded.

'Wall!' stated Will.

'Marvellous, what a perceptive choice. "Wall", wall of passion, his life thrusting poetry across the stage to a hushed gathering, that we shall call ... audience ... um, what kind of character is Wall?'

'Stone! Now, Roger, duty calls,' said Will and, patting him on the back, went about his business.

'Stone? Stone ... wall, stone?' muttered Mr Anderson to himself, genuinely confused but trying to appear optimistic.

Laughing awkwardly, the groom and I left the well house through the busy kitchen, where we were accosted by a kitchen maid very full of life.

'Oh, Mr Wickham, I have heard so much about you. Here is where you be sleeping,' she said, leading me to a shelf bed beside the enormous kitchen hearth. In fact, the kitchen was as big as a cathedral crypt. There were many shelves and great long elm tables at which servants busied themselves pounding dough and cutting meat.

'Come meet my brother and I this evening. We will show all around the estate,' she said seductively, patting the rough bed as I placed my saddle bag upon it.

'I feel I will be otherwise engaged,' I said. 'Groom, first let us see what male seed our lordship can provide.'

'Master Wickham?' he queried.

'Stallions; first show me the stallions.'

'Of course,' laughed the groom.

The maid pursued us across the floor and stopped me briefly at the kitchen door. She looked me straight in the eye with the hot breath of a mare in season and, placing her hand on my chest, spoke with a hushed voice.

'Mid-summer is upon us, the nights are warm and the moon is clear. I know a way to open us up and let the stars flood in to occupy every sensation in our being!'

I swallowed. In truth this maid put quite a flutter in my chest, but I endeavored not to show it.

'To be sure, and how? Miss … umm?' I answered, slightly clearing my throat.

'Susannah, a woman of purity and virtue from the Book of Daniel, so I am told,' she said, her eyes flitting around my face. 'You can call me Susie. My brother Robin, Robin Goodfellow, we shall meet him.'

'So, you are Susie Goodfellow?'

'If it pleases you?' she replied, licking her lips wetly.

'You be careful of them two, Sir – right pair of scallywags,' said the groom as he dragged me away.

Looking over my shoulder I locked eyes with Susie and she blew me a kiss. I had not been here two hours and the wildest intrigue was lighting a fire beneath me.

The groom and I saddled up and rode over to Lea Hall where, in a old Saxon barn, I saw four stallions, and very strong winter haulers they were. However, at the end of the barn in separate stalls stood two of the finest stallions I had seen in a few years. They were excellent: a grey with spotted flecks of bay standing a good sixteen hands and the other, as black as night and standing as tall as the sky at seventeen hands. Both held their heads back and high.

'Where did Sir Richard find these beauties?' I asked, marvelling at them as they sniffed the air for the smell of a mate and scraped their stall in coital frustration.

'He acquired them from Appleby. I believe they may have come from across the sea and, having a fondness of Greek, he named them Demetrius and Lysander.'

175

'Demetrius and Lysander,' I murmured as I inspected these fine beasts with my breath, my touch, my head and occasionally leaning on their withers.

I ruminated on their bloodline. They were fine animals, and whoever picked them either knew Equus well, or was plain lucky. I silently wondered if they might part with one for a good price. Lord Lucy would be delighted.

We rode back towards Hoghton and to nearby paddocks where the herd of mares was held. There were some good animals but a few old dogs. I picked the four best – solid broodmares with good straight legs and temperaments both strong and protective. Two more I wanted and, as fortune would have, it in a small paddock under an oak tree and standing alone, nose to tail, I saw two mares whose posture was quite striking. I walked slowly towards them as they stood flicking their long tails with soft swishes to disperse the summer flies. They certainly had a gentle temperament. Even when I touched them, they stayed as calm as a millpond.

'Their names?' I whispered.

'Thomas de Hoghton purchased them as yearlings and, continuing his cousin's fancy for the Greek, they are Hermia and Helena and they are maiden,' he said pointing to them respectively.

'Maiden indeed. Do you know anything of their bloodline? I inquired, looking into Hermia's mouth.

'They keep the bloodlines tightly held, but I know they hail from the Hesketh stable,' he answered.

According to Will, the Hesketh family stood for all things lavish, so they probably possessed a fine bloodline. We took the mares to the main stables, which, as it turned out, were absolutely filthy.

'A good matching and the consequential covering is all about smell,' I said to the groom.

'Enough of that here,' he said.

'All the wrong kind! In this yard I want the smell of mares in season and fresh straw only! It must overawe the arriving stallions. We won't get any good interest with the stables in this state.'

'We'll need some extra labour, Sir.'

'Certainly will.'

I looked at the groom. He looked at me stroking a horse.

'Go to! Find labour. I am but an outsider of no authority. Petition the steward!' I snapped.

The groom buckled to and ran off in the direction of the house. I was sent five boys to wash out the stables – young fresh-faced things with mops of foppish hair, looking about fifteen years of age.

One of the boys arrived a while after the others and seemed particularly shy and winsome; nevertheless, I put him to work with the others. I watched on as the young Catholic boys, with the enthusiasm of the suppressed but not beaten, went about their work. We dug, scraped, pushed and shovelled bushel after bushel of dung – all barrowed by hand to the back of the eastern gardens, where no doubt the gardeners would find it excellent for the roses. In order to flush out the stalls, we formed a chain to the well-head and, with six buckets, we started the first of a thousand quarts of cleansing water.

I noticed the shy boy, though eager in his work, was not quite as physically productive as the rest. There was something different about him. Most of all, one thing bothered me: a stable is an itchy place at the best of times and this boy did not scratch his balls once.

After about three hours, the sixth hour was approaching and thankfully the stables were now fit for a queen. I sent one of the boys to tell the groom that the mares could be brought in. Shy boy was leaning casually against the wall in the stable half-light when Will walked in. I saw their eyes lock for an instant.

'Tom,' said Will.

'Will,' I replied.

'More labour than Ely Street,' he stated casually.

'Mmm indeed,' I replied.

'Kitchen asked me to tell you we eat in one hour.'

'Obliged to you, Will.'

Will grinned to himself and left the stable.

'Groom!'

'Master Wickham?'

'Fetch those two stallions but hold them back till we have stalled the mares, and then bring them into the yard.'

The groom acknowledged me and went about my request. I told the boys to go and help fetch the mares but asked 'shy boy' to stay back. Clearly uncomfortable, there was titter from the others as they left.

I looked at the boy; he seemed worried and tried to stand tough as I approached. I smiled. I knew what was going on. Mostly the hands of nobility were white and un-scarred but these were particularly so.

'Good work, boy,' I said with a skip and a smile. Suddenly I clapped my hands and feigned a kick at his groin. There was no reaction to guard the all too sensitive part of the male body. I laughed.

I flipped off his cap, revealing a head of shiny auburn hair cropped for a wig revealing him to be a her.

'I have lost my wager, it would seem,' 'shy boy' muttered.

'And what wager was that?' I asked, failing to cover the fact I was quite beguiled.

'That I could pass myself off as a boy.'

I smiled. She was very beautiful, a petite girl of probably about seventeen years with large, smiling turquoise eyes. She looked straight into my eyes with her pretty grin and then, with a cheeky laugh, she betrayed the fact she knew full well it to be the most ridiculous wager. She reached under her shirt and unravelled a long strip of linen she had used to hold her breasts down. Her back was towards the open stable door and unbeknownst to her, the low evening light was rendering her shirt transparent. I tried to suppress palpitations, as I watched her soft breasts fall loose within her shirt. There was a new kind of heat in my heart and on my breath, a feeling to me as fresh and as pristine as an hour-old foal.

There was a clatter of hoof irons as the boys brought the mares into the stables.

'What's your name?' I asked, closing the door of the stable and following her into the yard. The groom and his fellows turned up with the two stallions. She skipped over to the trough and stood on it, well out of the way.

I took control of the stallions for this could be a dangerous situation but I wanted to see how best to match these horses. I put a twitch on Demetrius, and bid the groom hold him. For those not familiar, a twitch is the only way to control a hot stallion. A lead-studded twine around the top lip, it is only painful to the horse if pulled.

Lysander I took myself. On a long rein and with a lunging line, I led him around the yard. The smell of the mares was too much for both of them and Lysander reared calling to them, bellowing with loud neighs.

'Bring Helena to the door!' I called.

Groom brought Helena to the stable door and instantly there was rearing, stamping and hot calls; it was quite a job to keep control of the situation. Out of the corner of my eye, I could see my 'shy boy' was quite taken by the show.

Suddenly, there was a colossal crash and shouting within the stable. Hermia, with flying hooves burst through the stable door and skidded into the yard prancing with incredible provocation. Her tail risen and loins offered, Lysander went wild. It was all I could do to control him.

'Get a line on her!' I screamed as my arms came close to being torn from their sockets.

The grooms were fast and decisive; they caught Hermia and succeeded in pulling her back into her stall, enabling me to tie off Lysander.

In the commotion we had not noticed that Helena had calmly walked over to Demetrius held in a twitch. She stood facing him in silence, her head lowered in amorous submission.

'Think we have our matches, Master Wickham,' said the groom.

'We do, we definitely do,' I replied.

Whilst putting the stallions into pens adjoining the yard and settling the mares, I had forgotten about the beguiling 'shy boy' who had stood the entire time on the water trough. I was rinsing my face in it when she jumped down.

'Teach me to ride?' she uttered breathlessly.

'I have a long day's work tomorrow,' I uttered.

She looked into my eyes with all the amorous heat of the mares.

'Be here before dawn, absolute. I can give you one hour,' I answered, not taking my eyes from hers, nor she mine.

'Dawn it will be,' she whispered with a smile.

Lysander called loud from his pen and instantly Hermia answered. Without warning 'shy boy' placed a soft kiss on my lips of such sweetness, and then she ran away before I could even gasp, let alone once more ask her name.

By the time I entered to the kitchen, the mixture of the 'shy boy' and the rampant horses had fired up my heart and had my loins rearing like Lysander. When Will saw me, he fell apart in laughter.

'Who is she, Will?' I demanded with enough breath to barely form the words.

Will became evasive and pretended not to know of what I spoke. I chased him around the kitchen so hard we were thrown out by the head cook.

I carried on pursuing Will around the rear yard asking him who this enchanting creature was. Will thrust his face into the horse trough and, pulling his head out sharply, the water from his hair shot up an impressive fountain of spray.

'Lady Sophia de Caron,' said Will, removing his shirt and using it to wipe his face. The fun and enthusiasm instantly dropped from mine.

'You look despondent, friend?' he asked gently.

'Nobility, Will?'

Will hit me with his shirt.

'All pretty girls are nobility, because all pretty girls have never done a day's work! That's why they remain pretty!' he said.

'Anne Hathaway?'

Will flinched.

'Exception! Grant you, though less of a girl these days,' Will mused.

'How is she?' he asked coyly.

'Well, she is well' I muttered, still distracted.

I looked at him with a sigh and, at that moment, Will looked into my soul with unnerving penetration.

'My God, you've been struck!' he murmured, approaching me as one might a skittish yearling. 'A trifle – a pretty plaything, to tickle your humours, or so I thought?'

I looked to the ground. Will did not understand that no girl had ever looked at me like that; in fact, no girl or woman had looked at me at all! Damn it! It was the first time I had been kissed! I struggled inside and continued to stare at the ground.

Will crouched and looked into my lowered eyes.

'Beelzebub be damned; there's love in your heart!'

Will threw his arm around me and walked me away towards the house.

'The kitchen! We will sup and we shall eat this foolishness away,' he declared pompously.

Then, gripping me tight, he launched me into the horse trough. Damn it! I did not see that coming! It was as cold as winter ice and washed all thought of love from my head in one heavy splash! As I thrashed my way out, all I could hear was Will's laugh receding into the distance. However, as I stood alone and the water drained from me, thoughts of Lady Sophia de Caron trickled back into my head.

After supper, Will was required to read poetry to the family. I made myself a bed on a shelf at the back of the kitchen as was customary for visiting servants. I had just finished this when Susie approached me.

'Master Wickham, if it pleases you, you are asked for in the withdrawing room,' she said, bobbed a courtesy and, with a cheeky chuckle, she scuttled away.

Availing myself of a candle I made my way down the many dark corridors up to the withdrawing room. Outside, and now playing the role of austere family retainer and barely recognising me, Mr Anderson took my candle. He opened the door and ushered me in. The room was astounding: large, with a fireplace big enough to roast a pig, great wall hangings, not of painted cloth but embroidered scenes of hunting and great hours in the family history. It was warm and comfortable, a thousand furlongs from the Shakespeare house and another world from the tack-room in Ely Street.

The de Hoghtons were gathered around the fire. They were dyed-in-the-wool Catholics with lineage as extensive as it was confusing. Sitting relaxed were brothers Alexander and Thomas de Hoghton. Their cousin, Richard, stood by the fireplace. It was he I dealt with. He resided at Lea Hall and was the horse trader in the family. Their wives sat dutifully by the fireplace pulling needle point. 'Shy boy' had swapped her britches for a dress and cap for a wig. The Lady Sophia de Caron looked ravishing against the candlelight. She tugged gently at her tapestry and, despite her not putting a single glance in my direction, my heart raced. Another woman, tall and very striking, stood next to Will, who stood at a table scattered with a variety of poetry books from which he had been reading. She leant quite close to Will and was clearly under his spell or he under hers; I could not rightly tell. As I entered the room everyone, except Lady Sophia, stopped their occupation and turned their gaze towards me.

'My dear Mr Wickham, have you found some good mares amongst our wide and varied stock?' asked Alexander, as the door was shut behind me.

'Indeed, Sir, you have some fine brood mares, but I am particularly interested in the young mares, Helena and Hermia.'

'You are? And the stallions?' asked Thomas.

'Of the four, without doubt Demetrius and Lysander are exceptional and, despite having them perfectly matched already, I still crave to know their bloodline.'

'Do you, Mr Wickham? Do you? Demetrius and Lysander will be sired with Hermia and Helena, respectively.

'With respect, Sir, I believe that would be incorrect … Sir.'

Suddenly there was a deathly silence, and I realised I may be standing up to a family member who was not used to such opposition. Thomas de Hoghton rose from his position and, after flicking an icy stare in my direction, walked towards the sideboard.

Briefly pausing at Richard, he put out his hand. Richard pulled a key from his doublet and passed it to his cousin. On the sideboard, Thomas unlocked a large inlaid walnut box, the content of which I took to be the bloodline trees of their best horses. Holding a large book and a folder of other velum papers, he made a declaration that I can only describe as at best, regal, or worst, despotic.

'By the law that is in this book, this law of blood and all that is virtuous to the heritage of these maidens I will have done as I demand with what is my property, Mr Wickham.'

Concerned there was chance to miss an opportunity to produce some magnificent offspring, I had to strap myself tight as fully as I could in order to make a reply.

'Sir ... horses, much like humans, find their own affection ... Sir, and your maidens are both affected by both Lysander and Demetrius indeed, but in a manner that defies your wishes ... Sir,' I replied in gloomy trepidation.

Will stood quietly, his eyes darting from person to person and all the time stroking his philtrum; he was truly fascinated by this conversation.

'I will be obliged by my servant to carry out my orders. If not, I will have the maidens put to death, as is my prerogative with property that I own,' declared Thomas, with quite casual authority over the life and death of the poor horses.

Alexander de Hoghton rose and, standing at the fireplace filling his Madeira glass, he made effort to calm the troubled waters.

'Brother, Master Wickham is in fact my servant. T'was I who asked cousin Richard to find and engage a good man of Equus so that we might improve our stock and, henceforth, the family financial position.'

'Reform is the only way to improve that particular position, brother,' snapped Thomas.

'Sir, gracious Lord, if I may be so bold,' I uttered as obsequiously as I could.

Whilst he stared down his brother I cautiously approached Thomas. I looked through the book of papers that he held and ran my fingers over the trees of Helena and Hermia. Flipping through loose and heavy velum pages I found a tree for Demetrius.

'Aha! Sir, see! The sweet maidens know what we knew not at the time, 'I said. 'Here! Lysander's forefather, two generations back. This is why there are the spots of bay in Demetrius. Lysander shares a great-grandmother with Hermia. This will result, at best, a bad temperament or at worst, body defect. But, coupled with Helena, their colouring and the fine lines from which they have derived, will produce offspring ...' momentarily I looked to Thomas, '... of the finest colour, strength and composure,' I said, my voice falling off in the face of his frozen stare.

There was an awkward silence. Alexander sipped his Madeira with imperceptible self-satisfaction, after which he spoke.

'And given that Demetrius and Lysander have my heart; they thus obey my command?'

Thomas said nothing and, pulling the papers from me, he replaced them in the box, which he locked, and then pointedly left the key on top of it. Alexander turned to his brother and we all waited with breath bated.

'Would you follow the wish of a servant against the wish of your brother?' Thomas challenged.

Alexander sighed in desperation and attempted to embrace his brother with open arms.

'The path of family love is not smooth, is it, brother?'

Thomas turned to me.

'Prepare to sire the maidens as I wish or prepare to make their burial,' he demanded with great turpitude and then, turning to the room, he bid all goodnight and departed.

I stood awkwardly for a moment.

'Thank you, Mr Wickham,' said Alexander with an authoritative smile.

I bowed and with a heavy heart, I graciously took my leave. At least I knew purchasing one of these beasts was quite out of the question. No sooner had Mr Anderson shut the doors behind me, once more the room came alive with chatter. Mr Anderson touched his nose and, with a wink, he handed me a candle and ushered me on my way.

In the darkness of the corridor approaching the kitchen I was aware of someone in the shadows. Thomas de Hoghton stepped out of the shadow and into the light of my candle; he was close enough for his breath to cause it to flicker.

'I have had a moment to reflect. Boy, you have a command of Equus that would be an abomination to ignore. Therefore, I bid you do as you see best for my sweet maidens, and subsequently the succour of my family, whose foolish ways I can only see leading to the Tower.'

And with that, he retreated into the darkness and was gone.

In the kitchen, all was cleared and scrubbed with cutlery laid out ready for the making of breakfast. I went to my shelf and, sitting on it, pulled off my boots and lay down. I was very tired.

'Interesting first day at the tower of de Hoghton' said Will.

I sat up and banged my head on the shelf above.

'Sorry, friend. Just came to bid you goodnight,' he said sitting at the end of my little bed.

We sat and laughed about the day's events but when I mentioned the evening situation, Will became less forthcoming – even when I told him of the postscript event with Thomas de Hoghton.

'Mmm, understood. There is some struggle within the family over reform and … other things,' said Will in an evasive statement of loyalty.

'Where do you bed?' I said to change the subject.

Will stood up with a tired yawn and pointed vaguely upwards.

'Sleep well, Tom,' he said and took himself off into the darkness.

CHAPTER 19

I thought I had been asleep only a short while when I found myself being gently shaken by Susie's hand. 'The Lady Sophia. She awaits you in the stable yard, Mr Wickham.'

'What hour is it?'

'Little before dawn,' she replied, playing with my hair and looking around my face.

'Damnation, I forgot!' I snapped and pulled myself out of bed.

Susie wore nothing but a shift and, holding a candle, she smiled to herself at my being late. To her delight and with her assistance I pulled on my britches, shirt and jerkin. Passing through the well house she pulled a bucket for me, into which I doused my face and washed the sleep away.

'Tom?'

I looked to her.

'She's promised in marriage, Tom.'

'Meaning?'

'Meaning, anything you need to know, you ask young Susie here.'

'Why you?'

'You never served in a big house, have you?'

I shrugged indifferently.

'Ladies maids hear everything,' she whispered.

'We are the well you draw from, Tom,' she added seductively, and dropped the bucket back into the well, where it made a distant splash.

'Meet me with my brother tonight. Bring your friend.'

She giggled and then scuttled out the door.

In the stable yard Lady Sophia was waiting ready and dressed in fine lady's riding clothes. She had had the groom tack up two horses, Demetrius and Helena.

'You are ahead of me, My Lady,' I said, still straightening my attire.

'You made a promise.'

'I did.'

'There is little time and I want my lesson,' she smiled.

To my absolute horror, she had the groom leg her up on to Demetrius. With a knowledgeable pull on the reins and an experienced flourish of her crop, she pulled his seventeen hand jet-black frame about and took off at break-neck speed! Plainly it was I who was going to get the lesson.

'Holy … !'

I ran over instantly loosing Helena. I leapt on her back and took off after Lady Sophia. I was more concerned for the horses than Her Ladyship. If either of these horses came to grief, I may as well castrate myself and hand the severed articles on a plate to the de Hoghton family. I followed her down the hill, into the open meadows and the rising sun. This girl could really ride. Her Ladyship set an incredible pace; she cleared a five-bar gate with hideous ease. I had to stop and open it. It was too tall for Helena and, besides, I was not going to risk a fall, self or horse. By the time I caught up, she had made it to the river and was standing triumphantly by a weeping willow at the water's edge, Demetrius having been tied up to a good and heavy branch.

I pulled up fast, relieved to see both rider and horse were safe.

'Exactly what lesson of horsemanship did you require, My Lady?' I asked breathlessly, leaning on my pommel.

'Don't call me "My Lady".'

I leapt down, leg over front in my signature attempt to impress.

'Your Ladyship?'

I tied Helena to a tree a good distance from Demetrius.

'Not that either,' she said, calmly walking towards me.

'Madam?'

'Please, you are not my servant,' she said, getting closer.

'What then, Sophia or Sophie?'

Standing face to face she smiled so sweetly, looking up at me, deep into my eyes.

'Finch.'

'Finch?'

'A little bird whose capacity for love and flight is very great,' she whispered, smiling ever deeper into my eyes.

'What lesson, Finch?' I smiled.

'Love?'

'I am not well versed in that subject,' I stammered.

'Would that you kiss me?' she asked, looking about my face.

'Yes,' I answered nervously.

Before I could move, she placed a kiss on my lips.

'Tonight, would that you lie with me?' she whispered.

'Tonight, tomorrow and ever after,' I gasped.

She kissed me once more, soft and deeply. Her tongue very slightly entered my mouth, caressing and lifting my heart into a place it had never been, and would surely never wish to return from. Releasing me, she walked back to Demetrius.

She untied him and, holding his reins ready to mount, she turned and looked to me with her leg raised. I rushed over and, taking her leg, went to help her up but she slipped a little while twisting around. My hand slid up the smoothest silkiest thigh, landing in her soft nest of woman, of which I had heard but never before touched. She made a sweet gasp. Opening and turning my hand, I clasped her gently and softly placed her into the saddle whilst my face promptly turned the colour of a freshly boiled beetroot.

To hide my embarrassment I moved to Demetrius's head, held his bridle and stroked his philtrum.

'Tom?'

'Yes?'

'Are you a kind man, Tom?'

'Not really for me to say, but I like to think so.'

She laughed sweetly. 'Your hand tells me you are.'

I laughed and hid my face. I knew where this was going but I had no idea how to deal with it. I was still but a green colt. Was a girl ever as sweet as Finch? All those things foolish men do over women, I was ready to do them all, and more.

'Finch?'

'Tom?'

'Where did you learn to ride like that?' I asked, standing back to look her in the eye, trying to cool the mood.

'My father, in France …' she said with a fond yet painful smile.

Then, before I could reply, she looked far into the distance and her mood hardened.

'Before the king had his head cut off,' she added.

Finch flicked the reins and took off once more. Wow, I thought, there was I imagining she was a spoilt and privileged young girl with not a care in the world. In reality the nobility were as vulnerable to the whims of the Crown and State as any common servant.

I re-mounted Helena but dear little Finch took off homeward faster than the rundown. When I arrived back to the yard, there was no sign of her and the grooms already had the tack off and were rubbing down.

The rest of the day was spent managing servicing the mares. At one point, all the maids and Will, too, came out to watch as Demetrius took and covered Helena. Having patently matched themselves, the subsequent passion coming from both beasts aroused all those who looked on. From a distant window, I saw Finch stealing a look, and she saw me catch her.

The 26th of May, the morning of Corpus Christi, I woke just as the sun rose but there was the strangest atmosphere in the house. It was as silent as an empty stable. I got out of my bed and quickly rolled it away but noticed there was no kitchen activity. Pulling on hose, britches and a shirt, I listened and looked around, trying to sharpen my senses. I took myself around the house but there was no one anywhere.

Walking through the great hall, I could see breakfast was laid out for a great many. I became aware of the murmurings of crowds of people down the hall. I moved quietly along the great stone passage towards a large door leading to the personal rooms of Alexander. It soon became clear the murmurings were in Latin and emanating from this room, or thereabouts. There was silence, and then the most beautiful plainsong I ever heard floated into the air. It was magical, radiating a soft intensity that gripped my whole being.

Someone behind me cleared their throat. I turned around.

'Roger?'

He looked at me and whispered with purposeful reverence, 'In this instance, Mr Anderson. Mr Wickham, may I suggest this be an opportune time for some stable work?'

At that moment, the sound of the plainsong increased. The great oak door had opened a fraction. I saw the face of John Shakespeare looking right at me. The door was then closed with an ominous and private boom and a secure click.

Roger Anderson cleared his throat once more and gestured to the corridor. I took his direction and left for the stables. Stripped to the waist, I threw myself into the work and set about mucking out. During my exertion, the house came to life and I heard a loud and hearty breakfast being consumed in the great hall.

At the eighth hour Will appeared in the stable with a basket.

'Breakfast, Tom?'

'Obliged, Will. Were you hearing Mass, too?'

Holding very clear thoughts in his head, Will carefully placed the basket down on a buckle of straw with which I was about to litter a clean stall. 'Tom, I, um, only just woke up.'

'I saw your father.'

Will pulled the cloth off the basket. 'Look – bread, ham bits, and, oh, this is the sweetest small beer for miles around.'

I cleaned my hands in the trough, took the flask of small beer and drank from it. Indeed it was good, clear, sharp, cold and very refreshing. 'I said, I saw your father, Will.'

Will looked at me with a smile of deaf denial.

'Bring the basket back to the kitchen when you have finished.'

He left the stables without another word. I picked at some food and watched him cross the yard. This was the first time he had stonewalled me since school.

I spent the morning with the grooms, exercising horses and looking after the welfare of Helena and Hermia. I was eager to know if they were in foal. I had little doubt but I would have to wait a few more days before I could be sure, using my own invented test that, though I say it myself, never failed.

In the afternoon, Will was busy rehearsing the play for the evening celebrations. I helped the gardeners and kitchen staff move great tables on to the lawn of the rose garden at the back of the house. The gardeners had built a small stage in one corner and enclosed it in a pretty wrought-iron arbour. They wove into it the most beautiful garlands of freshly cut daffodils. Carefully placed white buds of magnolia were intermingled with rosemary, thyme and sage, and festooned with fennel plumes. It was not just a visual delight but the most seductive sensation to the nose as well.

The tables looked majestic, with white cloths fluttering gently in the breeze. Servants came and went, carrying bowls stacked with towers of glazed fruits of all kinds and colours. Yet more flowers were brought out, accompanied by skyward-reaching silver candelabras. Finally, the food was brought to the tables and kitchen staff tottered across the lawn with precariously balanced terrines. They delicately inverted them on to sumptuous platters revealing great vistas of sparkling fish suspended in aspic among a flotilla of eggs and vegetables. Two large glazed hogs heads surrounded by a king's robe of carved vegetables made a dramatic centerpiece. Roasted pheasants, woodcock and pigeon were poised and arranged to create an apparition of frozen flight.

Cheer suddenly erupted in one corner of the garden, and I saw the arrival of some old friends. Will rushed over to greet his cousin, Johnny, who crossed the lawn with Beth and another man; and it looked like Lord Strange behind them.

'Tom,' Will called.

I trotted over to greet them.

'Tom Wickham, good to see you!' called Beth, as Johnny and Will embraced.

'Cousin Edward,' exclaimed Will as he greeted the other gentleman, whom I took to be Edward Arden.

'Tom, this is my cousin, Edward.'

I shook hands cordially with Mr Arden, who seemed a quiet man with little to say but with a gentle touch to his hand.

Johnny suddenly cut in.

'Now, Lord Strange, the inimitable Ferdinando Stanley, I believe you have met my fair cuz?' said Johnny, his arm still firmly around Will and presenting Ferdinando.

'Indeed, I have, sir.'

'Ferdi, please, and how are things here Master William?'

'Very good. They have a library second only to a university. When not tutoring the children, I cannot pull myself from it.'

'Good, good,' smiled Ferdinando.

'Never knew you were here, Tom?' called Johnny.

'The horse trade moves far and wide, Mr Somerville.'

'Indeed, Tom. Call me Johnny, please.'

He smiled and, turning back to Will, lowered his voice. 'Now, Will, I believe Father has continued on,' whispered Johnny under his breath.

Others looked to me with the subtle smile of exclusion, so I took my leave and left the family to exchange private news with each other. Besides, there were still things to be done and the gardeners were a little over-stretched.

As the sun set, I assisted in placing candles in the candelabras, whilst other staff placed small lanterns around the garden and the stage. Before the festivity was under way, Johnny was already comically under the drink. I saw him pick up an ass's head – a costume prop lying in a basket – and putting it on, he went on one knee and recited Ovid to his dearest giggling Beth.

'Crazy man he is. She does love him so,' said Will quietly in my ear. Both he and Ferdinando had also been watching the comical act. I wandered the garden as guests arrived in small gatherings. It was a magical sight, the garden lighting up with love, life and celebration.

'Pssst!' I heard behind me. It was Susie behind a rose bush.

'Come to the place where the wild thyme and oxlips grow,' she whispered.

I was caught by surprise and stuttered.

'When?'

193

'Now! Will knows, and Finch, bring her, too.'

Roger Anderson crossed the lawn. 'Wonderful. *Trop joli*, everyone,' he called.

I turned to Roger. 'Where is Maid Goodfellow?' he asked.

I turned back to Susie, but she was gone.

I shrugged with a smile, which distracted him. I saw Will across the lawn with Ferdinando still issuing last-minute instructions for the stage. I looked around for Finch. I could not see her anywhere. I went over to Will. Again I was called by Roger Anderson. I called back some excuse of prior pressing need, which he accepted and turned his attention to something else.

'Will, do you know the place where the wild thyme and oxlips grow?'

'I do,' he said, his mind still engaged on the stage.

'Susie bids us meet her there now.'

Will turned to me and, with Ferdinando leaning on his shoulder, they both smiled.

'Good, we shall meet her! But first, Tom, some housekeeping, mmm? said Will cryptically.

'As you wish,' I replied, a tad confused.

He and Ferdinando looked at me, eyeball to eyeball. 'You never saw my father here today,' said Will.

They both looked long and deep into my eyes.

'What music was played?' I asked with a touch of benign sarcasm, intended to reveal an internal strength they knew not to be trifled with.

There was quiet.

'Thomas Tallis?' said Will.

'The queen's composer?' said Ferdinando.

'A Papist?' I answered rhetorically.

Ferdinando spoke with hushed gravitas.

'Tallis is inviolate. He has total protection of the queen. Music, love's own food, is the only common ground that remains. Tom, nothing in this world is what it seems.'

Will looked at me more deeply. 'I ask again, you never saw ...'

'As you wish, my friend,' I cut in.

They both smiled and, grabbing my shoulders, Will turned me around. There stood Finch, in an exquisite soft-silk gown of purple and summer green. Her eyes shone like the sun and she had a smile on her face that could dismount a thousand horsemen.

Will stepped up on to the stage and put his hand out for Ferdinando, and he his for me, and I put mine out for Finch. She placed her soft little hand into mine. We all connected and, with the sun scattering its setting rays through the trees, we walked under the arbour of flowers and out the back of the little stage. It was as if Will was leading us into an enchanted world.

Through the bushes, there was an old, crumbling stone gate-post with rusty iron gates that had dropped on their hinges. Still holding hands we ran through the woods to a grassy bank bedecked with wild thyme and oxlips, and there Susie was waiting for us.

She sat on a low-slung branch of a chestnut tree, swinging her legs as she smiled her saucy smile. On the bank, among the thyme and oxlips at the base of a giant elm tree, lay a barefooted man stripped to the waist, his arms outstretched and with a hat on his face.

Susie leapt off her branch, rushed over to Will and she must have jumped five feet or so in the air to be caught by him. Will laughed hysterically and twirled her around before she planted a massive kiss on his lips. I looked to Finch, who smiled and raised one eyebrow. Will put Susie down.

'Who's he?' she said, looking at Ferdinando.

'Like us, a soul-bred artist who seeks the universe,' replied Will.

Susie was suspicious. 'Then come on this journey with us or leave now and betray me not,' she stated emphatically. 'I do not want to end my life on a ducking stool.'

'Journeys are the fruit of life: pluck, eat and swallow,' replied Ferdinando, with a twist of an eyebrow and an engaging smile. 'Forget the fearsome fool who leaves such fruit to wither and die upon the branch.'

Susie grinned and called to her brother. 'Rob!'

Rob sprang to his feet and, with his hat in hand, he honoured us with a long deep bow. 'Friends, Robin Goodfellow at your service. You may call me Puca!'

'Like the woodland elf. Good evening to you, Puca,' said Will.

Puca danced from side to side and then turned two somersaults. He landed near a small knapsack. Reaching into it, he pulled out a stack of horn cups, which he deftly threw to each of us. He then took out a glass flask of a darkly gold tincture. Pulling the cork from the flask, Puca came over and, with the same saucy smile of his sister, poured us each a cup full to the brim. He then looked at the remaining tincture in the fading light.

'Drink, and within one hour an entire new universe of heart, soul, vision, touch, and even smell, will be revealed to you,' he declared.

I was a bit nervous. Was this … was it, witchcraft?

'Is this sorcery?' I asked, sounding a little frightened.

The others giggled. Puca, with only a movement of his eyes, lifted his gaze from the tincture to me. 'An infusion from certain fungi that grow in these paddocks. The question is, which fungi? And how are they prepared? Not many know this; however … I do.'

'But that is sorcery?' I asked, trying to be responsible.

Puca sighed, and looked to Susie with concern. It was, however, the deep knowledgeable tone of Ferdinando's voice that came to the rescue. 'Sorcery is the invention of those who wish to control you by the fear of things they themselves can never explain,' he said.

'So drink and see those things that "they" will only ever fear,' said Puca, with the grin of a scary elf.

Puca drank from the flask. Ferdinando, Will and Susie drained their cups. Finch smiled, stroked me gently and, following her lead, I too drained my cup of the bitter-tasting tincture.

'Shall we understand those things?' I asked Puca.

'No.' He laughed and swigged more tincture.

'But you will see them,' he whispered, putting the cork back into his flask.

I'm not sure when the tincture kicked in, but it was slow and gradual. I was first aware of enhanced sounds of the trees around me. Then, incredibly, their leaves seemed to shimmer with the brightest colours I have ever seen. Finch suddenly leapt into my arms in what seemed like slow motion. She left the ground and seemed to take an aeon to travel through the air into my outstretched arms. Immediately placing her lips on mine, the sensation was as deep as it was massive. Charging through my head, her lips felt as big as a horse's, as did mine. Her tongue felt like it was going to reach all the way down to my thumping heart.

There was a thud on my back. Finch and I released each other. It was Will. He had an extraordinary ring of gold and silver sparkles all around him.

'We must go,' he said. 'The play is soon to start. Try to look and be normal.'

All I could think was why he was telling us in such a low, long drawn-out voice.

When we arrived in the garden, we saw the feast in full swing. The candles and lanterns had all been lit, and the kitchen servants were serving food to the de Hoghtons and their guests. Various people waved welcome to us but I could barely recognise them as my vision fractured, flickered and sparkled. I could not tell what was real and what was the effect of the tincture. I would swear that Will was floating across the lawn not walking.

As I walked, I felt it was I who was stationary and, beneath my feet, it was the world that was moving. The colours were the most incredible I ever saw. Bright indeed, they seemed charged with some kind of supernatural power. It was as if lightning had become stationary and gave its power to any colour my eyes fell on.

As I wandered around, I saw, at the bottom of one of the great elm trees, Johnny lay sleeping. Still with the ass's head in place and with Beth beside him, holding the hand of the drunken fool she so loved. Beth looked up to me; she had tears in her eyes, but spoke words in a language I did not understand. There was fluttering sound, and then by her side were Finch and Will. They had wings of dragonflies and held glasses of water and plates of fruit, which they gave to Beth. She sat with Johnny, stroking his chest as Will and Finch gently removed the silly ass's head from him and lay his head down on the tree root. Whilst shedding tears, Beth tenderly fed him fruit and water.

Will and Finch each took one of my arms and led me away. Will walked on whilst Finch paused and, with her kisses, gently drank the tears from my eyes. I did not even know I was crying. Indeed the universe was opening up around me in a way that moved me from one elemental place to another, all upon the softest cloud of fairy breath.

I heard crashing next, a rhythmical, soft crashing sound, a thousand hands with echoes to match. I flinched; it was applause. The children, led by Roger Anderson wearing an absurd wall costume, came on stage to perform Pyrimus and Thesbie. Finch led me over to the stage where Will was already waiting for his young thespians. They all bowed to Will and he to them; he then turned to a small orchestra and also bowed to them. The music and the play began.

Finch and I sat on the ground and watched as Roger became almost consumed by the wall. Around the flowers of the arbour I was suddenly aware of dozens of sparkling little fairies hovering and flitting around and across the stage. I could not see Bod; I could not feel her presence, but she came to mind. She had to be here, she had to. All things she had alluded to in her tales were swimming around me. It was as if they were real after all!

I sat and watched the play. It went on for an eternity – the colour, the beauty, the motion and light; it was utterly intoxicating. The music was heaven sent, as if a thousand-piece orchestra were moving through echo chambers of a hundred caverns. The poetry delivered by the children floated around the stage in dreamy words that caressed my ears. Roger actually became a wall – bigger, stonier and heavier than anything you might imagine. At the end, the applause was long and loud enough to bring the animals running. Will took endless bows with the children and Roger, the blessed man, looked like happiness personified.

I don't remember a lot of what happened next. I walked around the feast, looking, touching and whispering to all and sundry. I had conversations with friendly servants who seemed to comment on my smile quite a lot. I remember seeing Alexander de Hoghton gazing around with huge diamond eyes, smiling upon his people like a great spiritual king absorbing his empire. I saw the tall striking woman who had been so interested in Will the night when there were arguments over the pairing of Demetrius and Lysander. She listened intently and with great interest to a highly animated Ferdinando. He not only spoke constantly; his hands danced and gestured with great passion. What he said I could not tell. I for one could hardly get my tongue and mouth to synchronise.

Running! Next I was running. That's it – through the meadows, peeling off my clothes, feeling the wind and tall grasses against my near-naked body. The sky was clear, the moon full and the stars spinning like a majestic maypole of the universe! Finch was in front of me doing the same thing, and soon she, too, was naked save her stockings; she stopped and turned, our flesh colliding as I ran into her. She pulled my shirt from me and, pushing me to the ground, she pulled my aroused member into her velvet entrance. She proceeded to ride me like a horse at a most gentle canter. It was wonderful; I sat up, held her tight and we rolled in the soft warm grass as my body surged to a full gallop. Her legs locked round me tight, one hand round my back the other entering my bottom, when suddenly, seizing our bodies, a thunder strike of fizzing fire sent ream after ream of my love pulsing into her. Gasping, pulling and sweating, her clenching passion squeezed every last drop from me.

We lay still as the moon, just gently kissing, touching and smelling each other's young bodies. Our souls were sensuously soothed. But the sun rose, pushing the sad motion of time over the hill and from Finch's cheek I licked the irrepressible tears of inevitability.

We fell asleep in the grass for what seemed like a few hours but from the position of the sun it was only a few minutes. Asleep in each other's arms, I was woken by someone on a horse crossing between the sun and us. We both sat up sharply and shaded the sun from our eyes. I wondered if trouble and punishment were upon us. It was the tall striking woman again. Not ten yards from us, a naked Will and Susie also sat up in the grass and grabbed her attention.

'William, the house is risen and about to take a ride,' she said calmly. 'You should all take appropriate action. Then, pulling her horse about, she rode off across the paddock.

'Who was that?' I asked.

'Lady Montague. She has an eye for Will,' said Finch.

'Bit old?'

'His gift, not his body,' declared Finch in a serious tone.

'Shirt!' yelled Will tossing me my shirt as we all looked around for our clothing. Suddenly my heart pounded! Where had I discarded my britches? We all wandered around picking up our clothes. Finch found my britches and brought them to me.

'Don't think you want to lose those?' she chuckled as she threw them over. The relief on my face was palpable. If I had lost those, I was as good as dead.

'A ride on a hot summer dream, was that not?' I said, to move my mind from what might have happened.

'You all right?' I asked Finch, since she seemed a tad sombre.

She simply smiled and nodded and, with the help of Susie, picked up her scattered clothing and put it back on.

We walked back towards the woods, tired but smiling, Finch resting her warm head on my shoulder and Susie on Will's. At the gate, Puca sat atop the gate-post, an ear of wheat in his mouth.

'Good morning, friends. Was your revelation satisfactory?'

'Indeed it was,' said Will.

'How do you make that tincture, my friend?' I asked.

'I am not your friend. I am Puca. That tincture is my secret which you should never try to copy, for many fungi will bring you nil but death.'

He leapt down from the post and, in a long deep bow, bid us goodbye and skipped off into the woods. I never did see the funny Puca again. Until of course, he became immortalised as one of my friend's greatest creations.

'How did he learn to make that tincture?' I wondered.

'He was in the navy,' said Susie. 'He picked it up in the new world and brought it here.'

CHAPTER 20

Ferdinando, Somervilles and Ardens, I did not even see them depart. After our sublime but exhausting flight across the universe, there followed a morning of cleaning stables and feeding stock. Come the afternoon, I took food in the kitchen and fell sound asleep on my shelf. So much so, I woke at about the second hour after midnight unable to sleep further. I sat up and, in the distance of the vast kitchen, noticed three figures deep in discussion at the end of the biggest kitchen table. One of the figures was Will but the other two I did not recognise. However, the fact one of them froze and became agitated when I stirred, gave me inkling to his possible identity.

'It's my good friend, Tom. Fear not,' whispered Will to the others and beckoned me over.

The men visibly relaxed. I stood up and walked the length of the kitchen to where they were sitting. Will had a series of books and some pamphlets around him. The men smiled at me and then carried on talking to Will. One of them ate from a bowl of pottage; he was of a diminutive stature with soft wavy hair, a kind face of gentle features with a trimmed beard and moustache. I knew exactly who he was. My memory took the image of his face and at once seamlessly merged it with the picture on the pamphlet that Lord Lucy had thrust in my face, and it was also all over England.

The words of Lord Lucy echoed in my head. 'If you see this man, I want to know! Ride all night if necessary.'

I picked up one of the pamphlets. It was entitled, 'Contract and Testament of Faith'. It was undiluted Catholicism. There was copy that was also handwritten in what I thought looked like John Shakespeare's hand. I briefly read some of the literature but, seeing Will was a little uneasy with my reading these papers, I placed them back down. If ever pieces of paper could get you executed, these were they.

So, this was Father Edmund Campion, meaning the other man was either Robert Pearson or William Hartley. Either way, this was dangerous company to be in. I sat down and pulled off a piece of bread from the loaf that lay there.

'Tom, I have been engaged in the most fascinating intercourse with this gentleman,' said Will, introducing me to the men with gesture only. I toasted their presence with my bread, letting them know I knew exactly in whose presence I was.

'Dominius vobiscum,' I whispered and dipped my bread in his pottage. Will gave me a glance of surprise. Campion smiled in a mixture of flattery and relief.

Will looked to Campion. 'If there be no mercy left, from whence does mercy come? For it is there, we should surely look,' he said, getting back to what appeared to be the height of a protracted discussion.

Campion turned back to Will and looked at him for a few moments. He took some bread and he began to talk, dipping his bread into his pottage and eating as he spoke. 'My friend, there are figures in this land whom have forgotten certain things. Let me quote.'

He sat back, looked to the ceiling and spoke from memory.

Omnipotence is specially manifested in God's sparing and having mercy, for that he forgives sins freely, declares his supreme power. He, who is bound by the law of a superior, is not free to forgive offences against it. By sparing and having pity on men, he brings them to share the infinite good, this is the crowning of God's mercy. Thus, the carrying out of God's divine mercy is at the root of all God's works. We are entitled to nothing, except on the basis of what has come from God in the first place as a sheer gift. Here above all things, omnipotence is discovered, for it lays the foundation of all good things.

Will was quite stunned at this eloquent testament. I was, too, for that matter. Will sat thinking, trying to formulate words, whilst Campion carried on eating.

'You said "quote". Did you write that?' Will asked.

'Thomas Aquinas, 300 years ago.'

Will thought again. 'I must read Aquinas,' he said.

'Sadly, books of his that resided in this green and pleasant land were burnt many years ago,' Campion sighed.

There was a quiet pause of solemnity.

'Will it end?' Will whispered gravely.

Campion took a napkin, wiped his mouth and looked Will in the eye with great intensity. 'Where can anything end when two monarchs fight over the possession of a small child,' he stated somberly.

Will became quite despondent at the truth and gravity in what Campion had said. Sensing this, Campion picked up one of Will's journals and flipped through it. He read a bit, then more and some more. It appeared he was unimpressed because, finally, he tossed the book on to the table with unexpected disdain. Will and I looked at each other perplexed.

Campion finished his food with a precise scrape of his wooden spoon, then tapped Will's notebook with it. 'Young man, if those are your words, God has decided unequivocally you should serve mankind with your pen. My thought is, be careful how you do or you will find yourself joining a long and fast-moving line to the scaffold.'

'I am honoured, but you ... what will you do?'

'Continue my journey.'

'Where to and who for?'

'My lord and master. I have no love for anyone but he, and journeys only end when lovers meet.'

He smiled both the sweetest and the saddest smile I ever saw. I sat and listened as Campion seduced us with words of spiritual poetry fluttering around us like butterflies among summer grasses. With Will, he discussed the books, cross-referenced them with the philosophers and, though it was a joy, they lost me quite quickly among a herd of names and titles. Campion even made annotations in one of the books, which slightly horrified Will, but he was too taken with him to make any protest.

Eventually, Campion took the book of Ovid and read it out loud to us. He went on until we both fell asleep. I know this because at daybreak we were awoken by kitchen staff and, as I lifted my head off the table, I saw Campion and his friend were gone. The books and pamphlets remained but I mischievously appropriated the hand-written 'Contract and Testament of Faith'.

Will lifted his head and looked about bleary-eyed. 'I have never been so struck by the interior of such a human being,' he stated, still in a haze of amazement.

'Better off forgetting you ever saw him,' I replied, assisting the staff to clear the table. Will stood and grabbed my arm with some certain aggression.

'How do you forget the unforgettable?'

I looked to his grip, then to him. He released me. 'Sorry, Tom,' he said, and dusted my sleeve.

I leant to his ear and whispered, 'Campion is the most hunted man in England. Remember your life and forget his.'

I walked away as Will casually picked up the books and papers. He picked up the spoon Campion had eaten with and contemplated it like some holy relic till a scullery maid took it from his hand.

In the stables, I organised the welfare of Helena and Hermia and went to see if their coupling had been successful. Normally one would have to wait a goodly time to know. I, however, had a little trick up my sleeve that I had happened upon myself.

Having removed my shirt, I approached Helena very quietly and, after standing with her and sharing breath for a few minutes, I ran my hand very quietly along her back. I continued this in one long slow and sensuous movement down her warm soft coat towards her teats and there, on the soft, almost hairless bit of skin beside, I stopped. I stood still; Helena softly flicked her tail. I gently lay my head on her, keeping my hand as still as a millpond. I breathed gently, and she relaxed and stopped flicking her tail. After she and I had been motionless for a minute or so, I simply made one tap with my ring-finger. With my hand just above her womb, I could feel the unmistakable reverberation of fluid, as opposed to the normal dull reflection of flesh. Helena was in foal.

I kissed Helena and whispered congratulations. She flicked her tail in appreciation. She turned her head away to reveal Finch, standing in the stall looking at me.

'How long have you been there,' I smiled.

'Long enough,' she whispered with an imperceptible but definitely coy smile.

She was a little aloof. I almost wondered if I should be calling her 'ladyship' once more. I picked up my shirt and started to put it on as she flitted those sensuous turquoise eyes over my body.

'Is she?' she asked, breathlessly looking straight into my eyes.

'Yes, but only you and I know.'

Finch picked up the hem of her gown and, turning around, she walked away and left the stables. This was so painful, to have such love ignited in your heart, yet know it would never be anything that could be other than a dreamy vision momentarily crossing like a cloud reflected on the glassy surface of a water trough. I soothed my aching heart with knowledge that my work here was done. However, I still had a fine stallion to buy for my lord and master and the only two contenders I had seen so far could not be parted from their owner for any sum. I turned my attention to Hermia's womb, which in the event took a little longer, but indeed it was welcome news.

'Tom.'

I turned around and saluted the morning to Sir Richard.

'Your time is done here, is it not?'

'Indeed, Your Lordship,' I said bowing.

'Fee,' he said throwing me a bag of coin, the ten shillings we agreed I assumed. I put it under my belt.

'Thank you, My Lord.'

'You seem unsatisfied?' A sharp reader of men was Sir Richard.

'My master, Lord Lucy, sent me on a mission to secure a fine stallion. All else is satisfaction indeed.'

Sir Richard thought for a moment, chewing a fingernail. I put on my jerkin. 'Well, Demetrius and Lysander will be staying here.'

He pondered some more. 'Tom, you have served us well and we should show you better appreciation.'

Biting his lip he looked about and gathered an idea. 'Close to London, there is the Royal Shire of Chiswick, which indeed has one of the best auction rings in England,' he said. 'Great stock, great prices but also great rogues – so care is needed.'

He clasped his hands as if in prayer and rested his fingers on his nose for a moment. 'I will sell you one dozen beasts of your choice which, if you take to Chiswick, should fetch three times the price. And there, you certainly will find the stallion that your master craves.'

Taking a dozen horses to Chiswick? Now that was a challenge. 'How much?' I asked.

'Ten guineas.'

'Six.'

'Ha!' laughed Sir Richard, but seeing my face without expression, he stopped.

'Eight,' he replied.

I put out my hand and he slapped it.

'Good! Lea Hall this afternoon,' he said and departed.

What had I done? Taking a herd of a dozen horses to London! I must have been mad, but the lure of three times the price was too much to turn down.

That afternoon I mounted up and started the ride to Lea Hall. I stopped for a moment and looked back across the lawn to the upper floor of the house, where, with all the windows open, Will was teaching in the school-room. I do not know what he was teaching but he was reading and moving around with great animation, enthusiasm and endless fountains of delight and encouragement. I could see this was how, when and where he came alive. Will came to the window and suddenly yelled some lines of poetry to the garden and all the children followed suit. Unaware of me, they went back inside. I could see Will's relentless drive bourgeoning forth as the little heads of the children became ever more captivated by his spell.

At Lea Hall, I separated off a dozen very handsome beasts: four two-year-olds and eight three-year-olds, a mixture of geldings and mares. So, with coin entrusted to me by Lord Lucy, I purchased a dozen beasts of which one of the mares was a fine lead horse, so, hopefully, I would not have too much fuss moving them. I unpicked the waistband of my britches and settled up with the fastidious estate clerk. And he not only gave me very good instructions as to how to make my way to Chiswick, but also advised me that negotiations could best be prevented from backtracking by producing the agreed sum in exact amounts. Thus he changed my other sovereigns into pennies, florins and crowns.

One day for preparation of the journey, then off the following day. With four sovereigns left, the cheapest way to move the herd would be to buy a couple of asses and carry enough feed, but I wanted to make time to get to Chiswick a day before the auction and with the horses in good condition. This meant short days and a quick pace with both fresh feed as well as dry; so I opted to buy feed along the journey.

Will came and joined me for supper that night. We ate together at the lowest end of the long table with all the other servants. There was something melancholy about that meal. What it was I knew not, maybe the last of our childhood or the first of our adult life. Either way, we were suddenly independent souls whose lives were separating but with hearts inseparably joined.

'I hear you have bought some horses,' said Will as he ate.

'Yes, I will sell them in Chiswick. I am told it is a good auction ring.'

'Will the tutor; Tom the horse trader. We are now men, Tom,' he mused.

'I watched you in the classroom. You are a great teacher.'

Will snorted a laugh of embarrassment. 'We were performing parts from King Edward's School plays. They loved it.'

'So, one day, will the world, my friend,' I said, but he ignored the prophetic compliment.

'London. Will you go to London? I would so love to go there.'

'If I have time, but my lord and master is not a man to keep waiting.'

'Indeed. Now, speaking of which, I have to go and read for my lord and masters,' he said finishing his mouthful. 'Walk with me,' he whispered.

Wiping his mouth and bidding thanks to the cook and Mr Anderson, he led me out of the kitchen and across the main hall where he stopped by the stairs, looked me in the eye and spoke very quietly.

'Lady de Caron wants you in her bed chamber tonight.'

'But, Will, we can never be,' I whispered, my stomach and heart churning inside me.

Will looked at me with such a gentle smile. 'Oh, Tom, the strongest hearts are always worn on the sleeve,' he leant forward, whispering. 'Better to have loved and lost, than never to have loved at all.'

I contemplated for a moment. 'One thing though, Will.'

'What is that?'

I pulled the pamphlet, 'Contract and Testament of Faith', out of my doublet and handed it to him. 'Careful where you leave this.'

With a half-smile, Will took it from me and wandered off to the withdrawing room.

A light appeared halfway up the staircase. It was a candle held by Susie. Whilst my friend held the family at bay with fine poetry, I was led to the bed chamber of Lady de Caron.

Susie did not say a word as she escorted me up the stairs, opening the door without looking in my or Finch's direction. She ushered me in then, closing the door, took a chair outside to keep watch. There was no candle in the room. The soft moonlight from a summer night cut a single path across the chamber and, settling on the bed, it illuminated the pale, naked body of Finch. Slowly, I took off my clothes as she smiled that soul-melting smile of hers. She held out her hand for me and the love that night was exceptional. No extra-sensory sensations from the tincture of young Puca, not even loose inebriation from wine. Just silky young flesh on silky young flesh, lain out on a soft down mattress and flax linen sheets.

That was a night of love I have never forgotten. In times of great loneliness, I would lie down in some dark space and, to caress my wounded soul, I'd conjure up the memory of that night.

I was brought from my delicious slumber of spent love with a shake on my shoulder from Susie. I sat up and looked about. Finch was not beside me, and the dawn was just starting to break.

'Where's Finch?'

'Master Tom, you must be gone. If you are found here, there will be trouble,'

'Finch, where is she?' I demanded, grabbing Susie's wrist.

'Her Ladyship is gone,' she said pulling her hand free.

'Where?' I demanded, leaping up and pulling on my clothes.

I received no answer and, with my shoes on and in a state of love-struck panic, I headed for the door. Susie reached it first and, blocking my way, she grabbed my shoulders and looked me in the eye.

'Tom, Tom, look at me. Get about your business and put this under the dream pillow.'

I felt a wrench inside, a wrench that made me want to scream, but I stayed silent and calmed myself. Nonetheless, a single tear escaped my eye and, with her finger, Susie gently took it, placed it on her tongue and then held me warmly.

She released me and went out to see if the house was yet to stir. 'Come, Tom,' she whispered. 'Go to the stables not the kitchen.'

'You are a good man, Tom,' she said, placing a kiss on my cheek.

I scurried off towards the stairs to make my way through the well house and over to the stables.

I paced around the stables, desperate to saddle up Demetrius and take after Finch wherever she was. I struggled with the knowledge that it was pointless and could only end in blood and tears. Eventually, after placing a few punches on the wall, I washed the tears from my face, pulled my broken heart together and prepared myself for the journey to Chiswick.

Just as I was gathering a small physician's kit of bandages, honey, rosemary, a sharp blade and some twine and needles, Lady Montague's butler came in.

'Master Wickham, Her Ladyship will require her carriage and horses tomorrow at the eighth hour.'

'I have nothing to do with them. They are at Lea Hall,' I replied curtly, without looking up. 'It's their task, not mine.'

'But I wish you to do it,' said Lady Montague, appearing behind her manservant.

'Ladyship,' I said, immediately changing my tone and bowing.

Lady Montague signalled her butler to leave. She walked over to me, a tall stately woman, who knew the world. She knew its ways, its foibles, its traps, its pitfalls and ladders, and she knew them well. She inspected my polished saddle.

'Master Wickham, have you known Master Shakespeare long?'

'My mother died in childbirth and I shared his mother's breast.'

'*Fratres in lacte.*'

'Indeed, Your Ladyship.'

'You know Latin?'

'Little.'

'Greek?'

'Less.'

She pondered, still inspecting my saddle. 'Are you both close?'

'I like to think so,' I answered. 'Friendship is a beating heart, not a passing of years.'

She turned her head to me, clearly impressed.

'Have you noticed anything about him?' I asked, looking at her directly.

'Do you mean him or his gift?' she smiled.

I said nothing. In front of a woman with such sharp and incisive wisdom I was a fool.

'Tom, he does not realise it yet, but William is destined for great things. He will need friends, the right kind of friends, at both the upper and lower ends of life's table.

'There are those who despise the gifted. I can see he is protected at the upper end. You must stay close to him. He will need you in the coming years.'

I nodded. I knew she told the truth.

'I leave for Chiswick the morrow, before dawn.'

'Then, please. Tom, beseech the grooms to see my carriage and horses are brought over for the eighth hour.'

It is done, Your Ladyship,' I replied.

'You are wise to leave this place, Tom. The eye-glass of the state is pulling ever closer. If they do not …' she looked about, choosing her word '… adapt …' and she looked me in the eye once more, 'there will be tears in the Tower of Hoghton, if not blood.'

'I thank Your Ladyship's counsel.'

She smiled and turned to leave. However, my torment took me and I could not hold it any longer. I had to know. 'Where did she go?' I stuttered pathetically.

Lady Montague stopped and sighed heavily. She turned around and looked at me sternly. 'Of whom do you ask, Master Wickham?'

I knew I had stepped outside my warrant. I dropped my gaze to the ground in shame and held my cap tightly. 'No one, Your Ladyship,' I muttered.

There was silence. Neither of us breathed. Then, a touch irritated with my foolishness but with a sympathetic intake of breath, she told me.

'The Lady de Caron left at the fourth hour to make a Liverpool boat bound for La Rochelle in France. She is to be married to her betrothed, the Count Nathan Bonnie, a notary in the king's court. And, if I speak my mind, a man whose lust for women is as wide as it is active. A foolish marriage for love, but a wise one for income.'

I gripped my cap, clenching my teeth, and hoped no tear would escape, but one did and it dropped to the ground like a porcelain vase crashing to a cold stone floor. There was a second tear that Her Ladyship caught in her gloved hand. She rubbed it between her fingers and looked upon me.

'Master William truly has a most valuable friend. Love is a wild animal with a harsh master and neither will ever be tamed,' she said. 'A flighty little thing, hence her *nom d'affection*. Thomas, she will only ever bring you pain.'

I could not move. I muttered my thanks to Her Ladyship without looking up.

'I have sons, and one slightly older than you, so I understand these things, to a degree.'

I heard the rustle of her dress as she walked away. I slowly raised my head and stared at the empty doorway. In the hayloft the grooms started to stir.

'I need three of you to round up my dozen and bring them to the holding paddock, and who wants to ride with me on my first day?' I shouted, still looking at the empty doorway.

There was no answer. I looked up and saw all six of the grooms gathered around the hayloft door. Two of them quietly raised their hands.

'Good, thank you,' I said and went to the water trough to wash my face.

It would seem my baptism of love and subsequent romantic branding was the full knowledge of all.

I was making some minor repairs to my bridle when Will came into the stable. He picked up my riding gloves that lay by my sewing kit. He pulled them this way and that and inspected them as only a glover would.

'Father's.'

'Two years old and still good,' I mused, as we stared at each other.

'Father always makes good gloves. That's one of his pair, not the apprentice's.'

'I go tomorrow before dawn,' I told him.

He nodded, and then hugged me closely.

I spent the rest of the day getting my horses and provisions ready for the long journey to Chiswick.

CHAPTER 21

Iwoke at the third hour and rolled my bedding. Susie
brought me some bread, cheese and mead. Mark and Harry,
two of the grooms, came into the kitchen and said they were
ready to ride.

'Susie, I want to bid goodbye to Will. Where does he bed?'

'Don't you know?'

I shook my head.

'You? ... um.'

She rolled her eyes.

'Not Lady ...'

'For pity's sake! Either the library or the school-room, dependent
on his reading,' said Susie dismissively. 'You still have much to learn
about your friend.'

I felt stupid, but this morning I was vulnerable. I apologised and,
putting a hand out, I touched her.

'What?' she sighed.

'Finch? You always said to ask you.'

'What do you want to know?'

'Did she ... love me?'

Susie heaved a generous sigh of sorrow and affection. 'As much as
she loves anyone in the hour. But I think your hour may have lasted
longer than others.'

I nodded knowingly, appreciating her frankness, and made my way along the passage to find Will. The door of the library was ajar and a flickering light emanated from the room. Surrounded by a dozen or so books, an ink-well, sheets of paper and a spluttering candle, there at the table slept my dear friend, his head pillowed on a large book. I walked over and blew out the dying candle. Will's hand was stuck in another large book. I pulled it free and closed Holinshed's *Chronicle of English History*. Not wishing to wake him, I stroked his head and walked away.

I was about to leave the house through the kitchen when I was stopped by Lady Montague's butler in his nightshirt.

'Her Ladyship was insistent that you receive this,' he said, handing me a folded paper.

I opened it – a letter of introduction from Lady Montague stating I was conducting her private business and that she enjoyed the favour of Her Majesty the Queen, complete with seal. I was a little astonished.

'Her Ladyship trusts you to use this wisely, only in extreme circumstances and, above all, you must guard it carefully.'

'Thank Your Ladyship. I am at her disposal any time,' I replied.

Her butler bowed by way of acknowledgment and shuffled back down the passage.

I rode with Mark and Harry as the first smidgen of dawn lit the horizon. As I looked back to the house I saw a light in the school-room moving around. It came close to the window and I could see it was Will with a candle in one hand and book in the other. I waved, but he did not see me. I smiled to myself and rode on, savouring the fact that in six short days I had been shown visions of the universe; I had fallen in love, discarded my virginity, felt the mortal wound of Cupid, become a horse trader, a steward of men and had had the favour of nobility bestowed up on me. In short, I had become a man of the world in less time than it took God to create it.

The ride was long and hard but, with my Lord Lucy's letter of instruction, it was trouble free. I moved the herd un-shod, at a brisk pace on a short day, after which the grooms and I would wash them down with water soaked in rosemary. I took on fresh grooms for each section of the journey, paying and letting them go after each day. I used good money to feed the horses well. By the time I reached Chiswick, they had fine coats and were in good form from the exercise.

I booked some stalls and had a glance at the great ring where the auction would take place. A few other early arrivals took stalls and wandered over checking out my stock. There was a good farrier doing the rounds so I asked him to clip and shoe my herd. He cut back the worn feet to the new shining growth and shoed them a treat. Following that came meticulous grooming. I brought a shine to them like Apollo's own steeds. I slept with my horses, but all night was a continuous stream of arriving stock. Normally, with that much noise I could not sleep but I was so tired that I had no trouble.

In the morning I registered my stock. But, being a newcomer, I was placed far down the list and it looked like it would be afternoon before my lots came up. I watched the first sales, and when the bidding started it was fast and frantic. This was my first time in a big ring and, try as I did watching the buyers, could I spot who was making bids? Could I hell. From what I saw, I was convinced my animals were fine lots. Although being late in the sale, I felt there was still a chance of a good price.

The time before my sale I spent on the lookout for a good stallion but there really was nothing that I would have happily presented my lord and master. If I wanted to make Lord Lucy a happy man and enjoy his consequential favour and trust, I needed something exceptional.

At about the third hour, my lots came up and I led them around the arena. Prospective buyers leant over to smell my horses' noses to see if I had given their nostrils a garlic wipe – a common trick to put spring in their gait. Upon seeing they were genuine beasts, they then rushed over to the nail to be sure to get a bid in.

When the bidding started, it was even faster than the morning. I reckoned I probably had the best beasts there that day. I was utterly astounded as my prices went higher and higher. I sold those horses for an incredible five times what I had paid. Another horse trader tried to come over and punch me when he found out they were mine. Fortunately, other traders held him back, as well as their laughter.

'Wretched little upstart! Who are you?' he screamed as his good-humoured friends dragged him away.

Even after costs, Lord Lucy was seeing the coin he entrusted to me tripled in as many months, but I still had to find the stallion I was instructed to return with. It was two hours from sundown when settlement was finished and all my horses were on their way to their new homes. I was back at the stalls having settled up. Making sure no one was watching, I packed my forty sovereigns into a leather purse, which I then sewed into my saddle under the pommel. I had just finished and was saddled up when a deep voice in a husky foreign accent cut the stable air.

'Well, you certainly put Mr Trembow's nose out!'

I turned around; there stood a man of dark skin colour, swarthy and bearded. He wore a long gown and around his head, looking like laundry, he had a cloth wrapped.

'The ... um ... oh! Yes, is that his name?' I said, shielding the sun from my eyes.

'Mmm, you are new to these parts,' he stated.

'Yes, I always heard that this was a good auction.'

'Where are you from?'

'Stratford upon the Avon,'

The gentleman looked confused. It appeared his knowledge of England was not great.

'And you?' I asked.

'Jerusalem.'

Well, I knew where Jerusalem was! Of course I had never been there. 'But you are not a Jew?' I asked tentatively.

I knew Jews from Stratford. They were good traders, drove hard prices and could produce the best merchandise from seemingly nowhere. No small wonder there was animosity towards them, but I for one could not care.

'You don't like Jews?' he asked with a smile.

'A man is as good as his honesty. No land, family or religion can make a dishonest man honest,' I told him.

The man laughed heartily. 'Arab,' he answered.

I had heard of Arabs but little else. 'You Christian?' I asked with caution.

He smiled, flicking the flies from his face with a long-handled soft and fancy brush. 'Muslim, Allah.'

I hadn't a clue what he was talking about.

'Abraham,' he said.

Abraham of the Old Testament, I realised.

'Yes, Abraham,' I agreed, vaguely understanding.

The Arab nodded with a smile. 'What do you call yourself?'

'Tom, Tom Wickham.'

'Salim, Muqaddim.'

I could not quite get the name. His accent was hard to distinguish and his voice quite guttural.

'Just call me Sa-lim,' he said, rolling his eyes, clearly used to this problem. 'I see you look at all the stallions. You need one?'

'Yes, my master needs a good one for his breeding stock.'

'Today, only dog meat here,' Salim declared disdainfully, gesticulating in the direction of the dealing ring with his fly brush. 'But you sell good horses. You shake my hand, you are a good man. Come, I show you good stallion.'

We shook hands. I was, however, a touch nervous. 'Ride?' I asked nervously.

He nodded and left the stalls. I followed leading my horse. Was I being lured into a trap? I had forty sovereigns that were not mine. If I was robbed, I was finished. Outside, Salim untied a donkey and mounted it.

'Following,' he stated. He rode off on this beast at a slow pace but nevertheless with an air of royalty.

Well, at least I knew that if he robbed me there was no chance of him making a quick getaway. We rode for about half an hour when he turned into the gateway of a recently built and substantial two-storey manor house made of beautiful red bricks with tall patterned chimneys. The gates closed behind us and young dark-skinned boys ran across the courtyard to take our mounts. Salim dismounted and his donkey was taken away.

I gazed up in amazement at the beautiful building. Three women looked from the windows and I have to say they were the most beautiful pictures of woman I had ever seen. Yes, even Finch. These women had the brownest skin, the darkest eyes and longest blackest hair. As I looked straight at them, they slowly pulled veils up to their noses.

'Do not look upon what is not yours to look on,' said Salim, patting my leg kindly.

The windows closed and I felt embarrassed.

I dismounted but became nervous as the boy tried to take my horse away. After all, it had a very expensive saddle on it. Salim saw my anxiety and speaking rapidly in what I assume was an Arab language, the boy stopped and stood in the middle of the courtyard holding my horse.

'You Christian?' Salim asked.

I nodded.

'Good. Now, my brother in Abraham, for you, waiting,' he said.

Salim and the boy took off at a smart pace to the stables, the Arab's gown billowing as he walked.

I stood and waited. After a few minutes he returned leading a black stallion the like of which I had never seen. This horse was as black as night, not big, maybe fifteen hands or so but the proportions, the neck, the muscle tone – they were exquisite. His head was something I had also never seen. It had a sort of gentle scoop down the nose, giving it a feminine, almost-ethereal, look.

Salim led him around the courtyard with great pride. 'Rafsaan!' he declared as the horse reared and beat his hooves.

'What breed?' I asked.

'Arabian,' called Salim.

I had never heard of Arabians let alone seen one, so I had not a clue what attributes this type of horse would have. Salim shouted in Arabic and at once two boys came out of the stable, one with a saddle and one with a bridle. In seconds flat, Rafsaan was saddled and ready to go.

'Tom, you! Riding!'

Salim gestured me to get on Rafsaan so I duly obliged and, as I did, the boys opened the gates and offered me the road.

'Yallah!' shouted Salim!

Yallah. I didn't know what it meant but Rafsaan was off faster than a bride's nightshift! We galloped on to the road and took off down the lane towards the river meadows. His pace was remarkable for one so small and sure-footed in a way that I had never experienced. In front of me, there was a line of young willow trees and so I pushed him in and out of them. His maneuverability was magnificent. After about two furlongs, I really let him go – a great smooth reach and such speed. Seeing a fence coming up, I imagined an obstacle in my path and pulled him up as quickly as I could. I can honestly say, I never managed to pull up a horse as quick and as safely as Rafsaan. Looking at the fence, I had an urge to jump him but, since I was already very impressed, I decided to not push my luck.

This was quite a horse and quite a breed. Crossed with our standards we could well produce a lighter horse that was not only strong but nimble and sure and fast, too. I was excited. I walked him back at a gentle pace for a horse needs to be as responsive at a slow pace as a quick one. I re-entered the courtyard and once more the doors were closed behind me. I dismounted with a big grin on my face.

'You like? Fine Arabian, yes?' laughed Salim

I knew he was the future. English mounts needed some fresh blood in the stock and, without doubt, this was it. However, convincing Lord Lucy that this diminutive horse was what he really needed to make a mark on his stock was going to be tricky.

'How much?' I asked

'These horses are loyal. They will follow you round like a lost lover for all your life. They are as surefooted as mountain goat and will carry you all night and all day without tiring.'

'How much?

'I ride him from Jerusalem to here in twenty-three days, no rest.'

'How much?'

'His seed will carry all these magnificent things into your mares and give you a herd of majesty that even our Abraham would smile upon.'

'How much?' I grinned once more; we were both openly enjoying the negotiation.

Salim spoke to the boys and they took Rafsaan away, and the boy holding my horse removed my saddle and stood beside me. Salim put his arm around me and smiled.

'How much,' I whispered.

'You are merchant. I like that. Now you stay in my house and eat with my family,' he said, leading me towards the house.

At the front door, Salim stopped and turned to me. 'In my country you never trade in a man's home so, now I know you want the horse so much, forty sovereigns!'

The exact sum I held, with no coin to ride home, the horse and I would be practically dead on arrival and Lord Lucy would surely finish us off if he realised I had spent such a sum on one horse! I had to think fast. 'You are a merchant, too! I also like that. Ten,' I stated with a smile pushing my tongue into my cheek.

'My friend, my brother in Abraham, I am Muslim and unlike Christians, I do not have one wife. I have many wives to care for. A good horse needs a good price and great horse needs a great price! Thirty.'

I smiled but became sombre for I knew even ten was a great price for this horse. So to pay fifteen would still rile both His Lordship and that mutton-headed steward Cornall. However, if I did spend that, yet return with the original twelve sovereigns intact and twelve more, I would be able to pour oil on any troubled waters. I looked to the ground and drew a line with my foot. Raising my gaze, I looked straight into Salim's eyes.

'I am a humble servant, who holds the coin of a master who would not understand a man such as you and to him I must answer. Fifteen.'

Salim understood and, smiling, he nodded and then guided me into his home.

'You are a good merchant. I like that,' he said as I crossed the threshold.

'Shoes, custom,' he said, allowing a boy to remove his sandals. I removed my boots, placed them with all the other shoes and followed him up the hall, somewhat embarrassed by my well-ventilated hose. I was led through this just-finished house into the main hall with hammer beams big enough to be a ship. I wished Will was with me.

It was decorated with long runs of fine cloth gathering at a point and hanging from the central beam. There were woollen carpets covering the floor that were as thick as Lord Lucy's lawns. Dozens of cushions of all shapes and sizes and colours surrounded a great brass tray, supported by an intricate and geometrically carved trellis.

Upon the cushions were three boys. Maybe twelve to fourteen years of age, they lay around like the lords of some sumptuous palace of untold power and wealth.

'My sons,' declared Salim.

At once the boys leapt to their feet, their demeanour changing from arrogance to submission in an instant.

'Salim, Abdullah and George.'

'George?' I asked in shock.

'Making fun! Afshin,' smiled Salim, clearly enjoying his little cultural joke.

All three boys bowed to me. This was actually quite a moment for me because, to this day, no one in my life had ever bowed to me.

'Tom, our friend,' Salim declared to his boys with open arms. I bowed long, deep and low in great appreciation of this hospitality.

Afshin came to me and offered me his place to sit and, as I sat, the women came in with trays of small cups and steaming jugs. On other tray there were plates of glistening dried fruits which I did not recognise. I do say women, because it needed a degree of assumption since they were covered from head to toe in black with only the narrowest slit for their eyes to peer through. Peer through they did, with the most penetrating gaze I have ever received from a woman. They poured me a small cup of the blackest and most aromatic hot liquid.

Salim gestured me to try it, and I'll say it had a punch but I liked it.

'Ka'hwah. You like? It's good, strong?' laughed Salim and gestured the women to hand me one of the dried fruit.

'Tamarah,' said Salim.

The little brown tamarahs were sweet, very sticky and delicious. I liked them and although not sure how many to eat to be polite, I still ate three or four. As I finished my ka'hwah, I took one more of the fruits, and the boys, with their father, laughed and applauded; even the women allowed themselves a coy titter behind their veils.

After this refreshment, Salim and his sons took me out to the rear garden of the house. It stretched down to the banks of the River Thames and was still under construction, with lawns, rose beds and box hedges being pushed into the ground by a team of gardeners. Salim took little notice of the work as we stood and watched the river-boats make their way up and down stream.

'You have a lot of gardeners' I said casually.

Salim looked over his shoulder, disinterested. 'They are not mine. This is not my house I make ... um ... how do you say?'

'Rent?'

'Yes, rent. We go back to Jerusalem in one week.'

'You just come to trade?'

Salim rocked his head from side to side searching for his answer. 'To see the world, which grows in breadth with every sunrise. It is a good thing to see all of God's creation and show it to my sons.'

He then spoke to them in a stream of smiling Arabic and they hugged their father and he them. Clearly elated, Salim held his sons as though he had the biggest, most-aromatic bunch of flowers in his arms. 'God's greatest gift?' he declared, and they all smiled.

I, too, smiled and nodded. Whatever someone's nationality or religion, I could not argue with that one.

He spoke again in Arabic and at once the boys released their father, bowed to me and ran back to the house. Salim and I walked along the bank of the river and watched the sun as it started to dip. He looked at me before he spoke.

'Come with me to my country. Teach my sons to speak English. I will pay you well.'

'Were I a free man, Salim.'

'Freedom? As precious here as water in my country.'

'Is water scarce?'

Salim laughed at the great chasm between us. 'So! My friend you have bought a fine horse. This night you eat with my family and we make your bed here. At dawn, we will settle our sale and ask God to give you a swift and safe journey to your master.'

'I am in your debt, Salim.'

Salim looked at me with great seriousness. 'No, my friend. I am in yours. When you first looked at me, you could see I was different. I noticed that, but you never let it come between us. You are a good man and you deserve to be a free man. If you were mine, I would give you your freedom. To hold such a man as you to service is against the will of Allah. I fear for our cultures. The three great families of Abraham should be reconciled as one but I fear we never will.'

'Who's the third? I asked innocently.

'Jews.'

This was all quite a lesson for me. That night we ate like I have never eaten before. Instead of sitting at a table, we sat on the cushions around the big brass tray. Roasted lamb was served in the centre with a wheaten kind of grain, couscous I think he said it was called. It was mixed with some vegetation and mint, and was quite delicious. There were also breads with some kind of savoury-tasting fruit in them – olives, Salim said they were. I dipped this divine bread in a thick white sauce that was made from the milk of goats. It was like a sour milk, yet did not taste so; that too was delicious.

Afterwards, there were honey pastries with a nutty paste that were delectable. I am slightly embarrassed to admit I did eat three. With the meal, we drank a frothy milky drink. It, too, was like sour milk, but did not taste so and was very refreshing with food. They did not seem to take wine or small beer of any kind.

After we had supped, Ashfin showed me a bed in one of the rooms. It lay under long hanging drapes like a tent within the room. It was sumptuous – a soft-down mattress, silk cushions, woollen rugs and flaxen sheets, like the ones upon which I had lain with Finch. With a belly full to bursting, I lay down in what I can only describe as God's cradling hands. So soothing was it, that that night I made a promise to myself. If ever I were to become a man of wealth, to hell with big houses, fine clothes, wine, food and servants. First and foremost, I was going to have a fine comfortable bed; I then fell into a deep slumber.

I was awake when Salim's youngest son, Abdullah, entered my room with a large bowl of water with rose petals floating on it. It smelt so good, I thought I was supposed to drink it, which caused great hilarity, before I realised it was to wash in. Abdullah handed me a towel and I dried my face, but when I looked for my clothes I could not see them; they were gone. A moment later one of the young serving boys entered with a neatly folded pile of my not only freshly laundered clothes, but repaired and darned too. Once I was dressed, Abdullah clapped his hands and two serving boys came in: one with a tray of breads, pastries and dishes of smooth, thick soupy stuff, the other with a pot of a sweet minty tincture and little glasses. The boy with the pot poured a glass of the minty tincture whilst the other made a gesture to the tray of food.

Abdullah pointed to the foods and told me what they were and, smiling in appreciation, I was none the wiser. But I had some of each dish and it was a most delicious breakfast. With a glass of the sweet hot mint drink, I felt quite ready to take on the day.

Salim's eldest son (also Salim), escorted me to the stables where Salim stood waiting with my horse all groomed, bridled and tied up. Nearby was Rafsaan, haltered and also tied up; and then there was the boy, still holding my saddle.

Salim walked forward with some papers.

'Bloodline – useful in my country. Not so here,' he declared ironically.

I looked to the boy with my saddle and beckoned him. He duly brought over the saddle and, pulling my secreted knife from the spine, I slowly cut free the purse of coin and counted fifteen sovereigns into Salim's hand. He took the coins without taking his eyes from mine and handed them to his eldest son.

The sale was done, I took some five shillings and placed them in my jerkin pocket and sewed the remaining sum back into the pommel. It took a few minutes but, when finished, the boy took the saddle and mounted it on my horse.

'Salim, has that boy been keeper of my saddle since I arrived?'

Salim nodded.

I put my hand into my jerkin and pulled out one shiny shilling, which I gave to the boy when he finished tightening the girth.

Salim smiled with great appreciation as the boy grinned from ear to ear.

I mounted my horse and the gates were opened for me.

'Allah smile upon you, my friend,' declared Salim.

I gripped his hand firmly and said nothing, for I had tears in my eyes. Ashfin handed me the rein of Rafsaan and out into the world I rode.

I rode back to Chiswick because, near the auction ring, I had noticed a stone on the road showing the direction to Oxford. It was a cloudy day with intermittent rain but the ride was pleasant enough. The weather had been dry the last few weeks, so the roads were still quite firm. I met up with the London to Oxford road near a village called Harrow. The road was good and quite busy, so I felt comfortable there would be little threat of robbery.

Aware of the failing light, at a town called Beaconsfield, I stopped at the trough to water Rafsaan and Orlando. I spoke in passing with a man who recommended an inn called the Old Mother Redcap, at a village called Loudwater not four miles on.

He was right. Loudwater was a pretty little village, one of a series across an expansive water meadow. I found the small but pleasant inn. To the rear there was access to one of the biggest vales of common land I have seen. I was able to let both horses have a good rest and graze.

The next day was very wet so I opted to stay another night, hoping that the following day would be dry. In fact, it was three days before the weather improved. I stayed on. The innkeeper made good food and the common land by the meadows was a rich pasture. So, despite the wet, my two horses took good feed and rest.

Finally on the Friday, the morning was clear so I set off for Oxford – a good ride at a smart pace. I took a break at one point to change over to Rafsaan. My saddle was a little on the large size for him but nonetheless this horse was an excellent seat. I trepidatiously hoped Lord Lucy would be pleased with my choice.

CHAPTER 22

I made Oxford about the sixth hour. It was very pretty, riding in with the setting sun and all the bells ringing to mark the hour. It's a grand town with the universities standing imperiously amongst the great green foliage of elm trees and willow-lined rivers trickling into the Thames. It was busy, too with many well-clothed people moving hither and thither clutching books and scrolls. Oh, my dear Will would so love this; it was really his kind of town: the learning, fountains of knowledge exuding from every stone.

Thinking that I would start early and make a hard push to Stratford the following day, I looked for an inn on the other side of the town. I duly found one strangely called The Ship. As I rode through to the livery I noticed two well-dressed foppish men sitting outside, drinking. They took an unusual interest in me and my horses. Not only that, when I booked a stall, they took off without finishing their drinks.

Concerned that I may be the subject of a night-time robbery, and on the pretext of wanting to get an early start, I asked the livery keeper if there was an inn on the Stratford road that he could recommend. He told me there was one two mile down the road, so I bid him thanks and set off in its direction. Once on the Stratford road, I found another inn, not the one I had been directed to. The horses and I were going to stay together tonight, so I took two stalls at the back of the livery for a penny. After feeding and rubbing down Orlando, I made myself comfortable in the other stall with Rafsaan and the tack. For a farthing, they gave me a plate of pretty dry peascods with some stale bread, but it was food.

I bedded down on some straw next to Rafsaan with my head resting on my saddle. I put my hand in my jerkin and pulled out Lady Montague's letter. I hadn't forgotten about it, but I knew I was going to be back in Stratford tomorrow. In the right situation it was indeed useful, but if Lord Lucy knew I had such a letter, that was a dangerous liability. Whilst pondering what do with it, I read it again and, though unconnected, it took me back to that breathtaking night – the universe alight, Will's play, and above all, the beautiful Finch. I decided to secrete the letter in the lining of the pouch that held my horse doctor's kit. A dozen stitches later it was concealed.

It was about the fourth hour and one away from dawn, when I became aware there were people in my stall. There was movement and scuffing of straw, not made by Rafsaan. My heart started to beat hard and fast but I kept my composure and feigned deep sleep. My arms around my saddle, I slowly moved for my knife, an easy unseen grasp. I readied myself to snap to my feet. Trying to get a sight on my intruder, I noticed not one but three pairs of boots. Taking on three in a fit of violence may be a foolish move, so I released my grip on the knife. Suddenly, they grabbed my feet and in one quick move they pulled me out of the stall and on to the gallery cobbles.

'It's him.' said a voice in a sharp, confident brogue.

Dizzy with darkness and sleep I tried to get to my feet and see my assailants only to receive a boot in my face and back to the ground I fell. I decided to stay there and, looking up, I saw the two fops from the previous inn holding lanterns and between them stood a man who, by his attire, I suspected was gentry.

'Tried to outsmart us, didn't you?'

'Sir, I am at a loss, a simple traveller on an errand …'

'Shut up, prigger! Do not take me for a fool.'

'Indeed, Sir, I do not, but I have not stolen any horse.'

'Where did you steal that horse from, prigger?'

'Purchased from an Arabian gentleman four days since.'

The man picked me up and pulled me so we were face to face.

'The only thing I despise more than a prigger is a liar. You are a thief and will hang for this.'

He thrust me away, banging my head against the hard oak stall.

It seemed this man was going to need some persuasion. I was not unduly worried as I had Salim's bill of sale and Lord Lucy's letter of introduction, but my head was a tad sore.

I put my hand into my jerkin.

'In my jerkin, Sir, I have …'

But in a flash the man pulled out his sword and instantly I found a rapier poised at my throat.

'A thief, a smart thief. May he hold a weapon in his jerkin?'

'No weapon, just paper, Sir,' I reassured him nervously. Gently, I took the papers from my jerkin and held them between my thumb and forefinger in hope they would not only persuade him to drop his blade but also, that upon reading them, he would see I was neither vagabond nor thief. No, he simply used his sword to knock the papers to the ground and, worryingly, ignored their existence.

'I care not for whatever forgeries you may carry. You, boy, are a vagabond and a thief. Tomorrow morning you will face court for swift and punitive justice.'

The man dropped his sword.

'Bind him and bring him to the watch house.'

The two fops grabbed my arms, but then the door of the livery opened and, silhouetted by the dawn light, a gentleman walked up the gallery.

'You found him, Edward?' said the man, also clearly gentry.

'Indeed, Robert, we did. The bloody vagabond had twice double-turned on us,' he answered.

'But we found him!' he added triumphantly.

When the man came to look at me I recognised him, even in the half light. It was Lord Robert Gregory, the man in charge of the queen's outriders, whom Father and I had stabled when the queen stayed at Charlecote. However, that was nine years ago; I was a boy then and a man now. Would he recognise me?

'You kept us up all bloody night looking for you?' he said, as he chewed on an apple.

'Lordship … Lord Gregory?' I asked hesitantly.

'You know me?' he replied, genuinely surprised.

'Yes, Sir. I am …'

'No, no, don't tell … Hang on, you … yes, you are Jack Wickham's boy, Ely Street livery, Stratford upon Avon,' he declared with a grin, as the other man sheathed his blade.

'Robert, you know this vagabond?'

'Yes,' he said with a smile as if he had won a wager and took another bite of his apple.

'Is he one of your …?'

'No, Edward. He is not.'

One of his what? I wondered, though I could fashion a guess. I went to say my name but Lord Gregory made a shush motion with his finger to his lips and pondered a moment.

'Thomas, Tom!'

'Lordship.'

'See, Edward. I never forget a name or a face, even when they have grown up.'

I was truly relieved.

'So, Tom. Where and why did you steal this horse?'

Relief short-lived! Please not.

'Lordship, if you examine those papers you will see I have the favour of Lord Lucy. On his behalf I purchased this Arabian stallion from the gentleman from Jerusalem, Salim Muqaddim.'

'You purchased that horse! From that foul-smelling Arab!' snapped the man, whom I now knew was called Edward.

Lord Gregory made another shush motion, this time to Edward and he picked up the papers. He also indicated the fops should unhand me, which they did.

Lord Gregory went through the papers, clearly impressed, and then he pushed past us all to see Rafsaan who had been remarkably calm during this set-to. After a protracted inspection of Rafsaan, and much to the consternation of his friends, he came out of the stall grinning at me.

'Tom, how the hell did you come to buy this horse?' he asked with impressed disbelief.

I told them the story of buying twelve horses from a family in Lancashire and then the story about selling them at the Chiswick ring and finally the story about being approached by Salim.

'Prince Salim,' said Lord Gregory, casually correcting me.

I was dumbfounded. I knew Salim to be evidently a man of wealth but I did not realise he was royalty. I went on and told Lord Gregory about staying the night with Salim and eating with his family. Everyone was quite enthralled by my extraordinary tale.

When I finished, Lord Gregory narrowed his eyes inquisitively.

'You have absolutely no idea that this has been one of the most sought-after horses in the kingdom this last month?' he asked, with a big knowing smile.

'I did not, Your Lordship.'

'Prince Salim was offered fifty sovereigns for this beast but he would not sell. I offered to buy him, as did my good friend here, His Lordship Edward de Vere, Earl of Oxford.'

Edward made a polite bow to me with his eyes only, which I accepted, but then realised it was actually a cue for my submission.

'Lordship,' I said, and bowed to him, long and deep, which seemed to get the brain-dead fop's pleasure.

'So how did a simple livery boy persuade that ignorant prince to part with this magnificent beast for a mere fifteen sovereigns?'

'I have no explanation, Your Lordship,' I said though, given the way they had referred to Salim, I had a pretty good idea.

'Well, the fortune is with Lord Lucy not us. So! Edward, what about some breakfast at your house?'

'Indeed, I am quite tired and fair famished,' he replied.

'Excellent. Tom get your things.'

'Not the boy,' declared Edward with affront.

'Yes, Edward, the boy. Damn it, you have ruined his sleep, put fear in his heart, falsely accused him of thievery and subsequently threatened him with the gallows. Least you can do is give him breakfast.'

'He's a peasant!' protested Edward.

'Peasants have to eat, too,' said Lord Gregory. 'Where will they get the strength to clean your wretched boots!'

He ignored Edward and walked out into the daylight.

'Well, you can eat in the kitchen,' Edward spat and, gesticulating to his two fops, he followed Lord Gregory.

Alone once more, I started to gather my things and saddle up Orlando. That was one strange incident which I cared not to repeat, but breakfast was a welcome recompense.

I rode out on to the road leading Rafsaan, where they all waited on their mounts.

'No one on a mare, are they?' I called.

'Thankfully not,' replied Lord Gregory.

'I have to settle,' I told them.

''Tis done! Damn it!' raged Edward, and with that he took off down the road, followed by his two fops.

Lord Gregory laughed at the ignominy being suffered by his friend and rode beside Rafsaan and I as we headed off to the earl's family seat.

The family seat was, I have to say, as impressive as it was large. Then I discovered it was not the family seat; it was 'a trifle', 'a cottage for respite'. It had the most extensive array of topiary box hedges, which had a small army of men meticulously scything them.

At the stables, my horses were taken from me and the groom led me to the kitchen where the kitchen maid served me a never-ending supply of food. There was smoked fish, bread, ham, apples and oranges, cheese and pies. It was quite incredible, really – more than I could eat in a week, let alone breakfast.

After breakfast, Lord Gregory came into the kitchen with Edward de Vere.

'Now, Tom, in two days Edward and I were headed to Shipton Under Wytchwood to see a chum. It's on your route so we have elected to journey early and ride with you.'

'Honour is mine, Your Lordships,' I said and bowed.

'No hard feelings, Master Wickham?' said Edward, a tad reluctant.

'None, Your Lordship,' I declared.

We all smiled, and then Edward reached into his purse and pulled out a folded pamphlet.

'Master Wickham, my favour with Her Majesty is currently at a low ebb. If I could have presented her with that horse, my favour would have indeed been reinstated.'

He unfolded what I knew was a Campion pamphlet. 'Never saw this man on your travels, did you?'

Raising an eyebrow, I took a cursory glance at the pamphlet. 'No, Lordship, I have not.'

'You barely looked at it,' said Lord Gregory.

'These are all over the country, Lordship,' I replied.

If they could have felt my heart, they certainly would not have believed me. In fact, the way Lord Gregory looked at me, I do not think he did.

'What's his crime?' I asked.

'Just some seditious priest who if anyone turned in, they would be in favour with both Her Majesty and the Privy Council, too. Never mind,' said Lord Gregory taking the pamphlet folding it up and returning it to Edward de Vere.

'Spies and state intrigue. Keep clear of it. I would. Write her a play, Edward! She loves a good play does Her Majesty.'

'I did, and she hated it!' snapped de Vere, clearly wounded.

'Write her a poem under another name?'

Edward breathed in and pursed his lips. 'I did,' he said.

'Well! Looks like your best bet's a shot at the New World. Come on, let's ride!'

A little before noon, and at leisurely pace, we set off for Shipton Under Wytchwood, a gentle walk listening to birdsong and farmers chatter as we sauntered along the road. At the turnpikes we never had a problem. The ever-confident Earl of Oxford would simply declare his and Lord Gregory's titles and that they enjoyed the favour of Her Majesty.

It was about an hour before nightfall when we arrived at Prebendal House, home of their friend. A bed was clearly not going to be offered by the owner, their 'chum'. I took my leave and pushed on to Stratford, which, with any luck, I could make by midnight.

I was a little concerned at this last stretch, since darkness was the choice of thieves. So, to give myself the best chance of outwitting any robbery attempt, I opted to change horses. At a suitable gateway, I stopped and whilst I fed the horses the last bit of oats, I changed over the tack. I knew Orlando well and, if separated, he would follow. If separated from Rafsaan, he may not and he was, of course, the more valuable of the two beasts.

There was one other thing: Rafsaan was faster off the mark and more sure-footed than Orlando, so out-running or out-manoeuvring thieves would be easier. As one last safeguard, I took some light branches from a bush and wrapped them up in my blankets and hung them across Orlando. The parcel looked like booty to any thief, but was nonetheless light enough for Orlando to flee. As it happened, my precautions were wise.

It was late. I do not know how late, but I had been riding some hours. I had seen a stone for Tredington reading ten miles; Charlecote was five on from there and Stratford another five. The section of road was long, slightly downhill but with steep banks on either side. It was a cloudy night with some light rain but not too much. Every so often the moon peeped out from behind a cloud and gave light.

At this moment, it did so with great fortune for it briefly illuminated two men standing at the end of this stretch of road. I looked behind me and in the distance, sure enough, there were two others blocking any retreat. The banks either side were too steep for even this sure-footed Arabian. These thieves had picked their spot well. My hand on the rear of my saddle looking relaxed, I sauntered on. The reality was different, however. My hand was firmly on my knife; my heart beat fast; and I could just arrest the gulping in my throat.

As I drew closer I saw the man on the left had a club whilst the other had a sword. This was tricky. Blunt or blade it was no contest. I figured I should take off fast, run down the man on the left and stay wide of the man with the sword. I waited till the last possible moment, I quietly released Orlando, pulled my knife, gripped the reins and …

'Yallah!' I shouted, spurring on Rafsaan.

Rafsaan loosed like an arrow! I charged the swordsman, and then suddenly slung left away from his whipping blade as Rafsaan's withers slammed into the man with the club. But, damn it, he clung to my boot! I dished out a slash with my knife; where I caught him I don't know, but he released his grip with quite a scream. Rafsaan and I took off at an unmatched pace. Over my shoulder I saw, thankfully, Orlando had also made his escape.

We galloped for what must have been two miles before I finally stopped to catch our breath and wait for our hearts to stop racing. I checked Rafsaan and Orlando to see if they had taken any wound from the sword, which fortunately they had not. It had all gone so fast, I could not believe what had happened. I looked to my hand; it shook like a leaf. I looked at my knife and there was blood and matted hair on it. Goodness knows where I struck the bastard, but I would wager it left a good wound to lie about. I cleaned my knife with some wet grass and replaced it in its saddle sheath. Looking at the moon as it came from behind a cloud, I sighed, put my hands together and gave praise to Jesus – and the Allah chap – for my survival.

Thankfully, the rest of the ride was trouble free and I reached Ely Street at the first hour. As I entered the yard, all was strangely silent. There was an emptiness I could not place. I saw a light move in the smithy and out came Grace, holding a lantern to meet me. She gave me one very short and equally rare embrace.

'Your father ... and my dear brother, is dead this last week,' she uttered into my ear.

I froze. I dropped the reins of Orlando and Rafsaan; everything spun around. I felt dizzy. A boy came out into the yard.

'Mr Nym, this is Tom Wickham, your late master's son,' said Grace.

'Truly sorry, Master Wickham. I only knew him three days, were it a lifetime, though. He was a kind man.

I nodded thanks, struggling to breathe, to hold back tears and stay strong.

'How?' I asked Grace.

'Took a fever. He was gone in four days.'

'Not plague?'

'Thank the Lord, not,' said Grace.

'That His Lordship's stallion?' she sniffed, wiping her nose with a handkerchief.

'Indeed, whilst he may be small, he is a remarkable horse,' I stammered, in a daze, still flattened by the devastating news.

'Never believe those words from anyone else,' said Grace, forcing a smile.

Nym took Orlando and Rafsaan from me and led them to the stables.

'Where does he lie?' I asked.

'South of the river in St Margaret's yard.'

A burial ground for the poor but not a mass grave for the destitute, thankfully. However, I knew father had some six pounds in coin hid behind the smithy fire.

'He had enough saved for Trinity, surely?' I asked.

'And Lord Lucy would have thought him shorting the clerk, so it would have been seized, with you and I turned out into the street. No, I thought it best to leave that in its place. It's yours now.'

She never missed a trick, did dear Grace; nevertheless, I declared we would share it. Exhausted and still lightheaded, I staggered up the treads and I stood looking around the loft. I half expected my father to climb the stairs, or turn over in his bed. No, my father was gone at forty-three years of age. Within these walls, he had worked hard all his life and was now in Abraham's bosom. Was that a good thing or bad? I could not tell. But in the last six weeks I had seen more of this land and what it had to offer than my father ever glimpsed in his entire existence. I looked at the straw-filled sack that was my bed. I longed for Finch's bed or the bed given me by Salim. Thinking of my father's life, I made myself a pledge that I would go wherever life took me, but if it took me nowhere I would bloody well find somewhere to drag it myself.

I woke early, still in shock at the news of my father's death. I rose and went down to the trough to wash my face. I looked around at the livery yard, noticing it was in exceptional order considering its steward had departed. Nym and another boy were up and going about the early duties of feeding and rotating horses.

'Master Nym, keep any mares in and bring out those two I brought with me and wash them, would you?'

'Indeed, Sir.'

Grace came to the door and called me for breakfast. I went to sit at the table where I always sat but Grace offered me my father's chair. 'You are the master now, Tom,' she said.

I nodded thoughtfully, still trying to get into my head that Father was gone.

There was some fine cheese, bread and cured ham – more than we could normally afford.

'A gift from Mr Kyteon, in remembrance,' stated Grace.

'Kind of him,' I murmured as I started to pick at the food.

'Do you want to hear of my travels?' I asked Grace.

Grace looked at me and shook her head.

'Why not?' I asked.

Grace poured me a cup of mead from the jug and, placing it in front of me, be damned she shed a tear.

'I do not want to hear what I was never brave enough to do, or fool enough to take. And besides, one look at that stallion tells a greater tale than any man could ever tell.'

I stood to hug my dear aunt, but she kept me at arm's length.

'You must go to Charlecote this morning. A runner is sent every day at noon to see if you are returned.'

Out into the yard I went and the boys had brushed up Orlando and Rafsaan a treat. I oiled Rafsaan's hooves and then trimmed and plaited his mane and tail.

We walked slowly to Charlecote; I did not want Rafsaan to break sweat. He shone majestically in the summer sun and, as we walked, I thought of my dear father and how he would have loved to hear of my journey.

We took a light canter down the driveway and all the mares in the paddock followed us down the fence line. It was quite an effort to keep Rafsaan's attention as they all kept calling to him. This triumphant arrival, of course, roused the house and there in the stable yard, stumpy hands on hips, stood Cornall.

I leapt off Orlando, leg over front and cocksure, I threw Orlando's rein to a stable boy. I led Rafsaan around the yard at a trot, snatching a whip from one of the boys as I passed. Out of the corner of my eye, I saw Lord Lucy standing in the arch with the estate clerk. I made a figure of eight and doubled back on myself then, with a flick of the whip at Rafsaan's ankles, he reared and beat his hooves in the air, right in front of His Lordship.

I, too, bowed to His Lordship, and then tied Rafsaan to one of the wall rings.

'My Lord, I have returned.'

'So I see,' he muttered, wandering over to Rafsaan, where he inspected him quite meticulously.

'I am sorry about your father,' he stated quite formally.

'Thanking, Your Lordship,' I replied.

'Strange-looking breed this, bit small. What makes you think he will make good stud?'

'He is Arabian, fast, nimble, sure-footed, great stamina and with exceptional loyalty. He is exactly what our heavy standards need.'

'Mine – my standard breds; they are not yours.'

'Lordship.'

'How much did you pay for him?'

'Fifteen sovereigns, My Lord,'

'Fifteen sovereigns! I can buy an entire herd for that, with tack! Explain!'

'The Earl of Oxford offered me fifty for him.'

'Why didn't you sell to him?'

'I had bought him for Your Lordship. He was not mine to sell.'

He calmed and nodded approval at my honesty. 'I only gave you a dozen sovereigns. Where did you get the other three?'

I told him of my trades at the Chiswick ring and how I came to buy Rafsaan. He listened intently showing little emotion.

'So, where did you meet the Earl of Oxford?'

'Oxford, Lordship,' I said nervously.

'Don't be clever.'

'Lordship, truly,'

'Was he with that sodomite Gregory?'

'He was with Lord Gregory, Your Lordship.'

'And, Hoghton Tower, did you see that Papist Campion?'

Before I could answer, he answered for me. 'Course you didn't. You would have ridden all day and all night to tell me if you had, wouldn't you?'

'Indeed, Your Lordship,' I stated, bowing deeply to hide my guilty face.

'He'll be found,' Lord Lucy sneered and, stroking Rafsaan, he thought a moment.

'So! I gave you one dozen sovereigns and you return with an Arabian stallion and twenty-five sovereigns, if my calculations are correct.

'Twenty four. I had inn and livery costs on the way back.'

Lord Lucy nodded in agreement. 'You have done well. Settle up with the clerk and get back to Ely Street. You have my livery to run and it's two shillings and sixpence a week.'

Without another look in my direction, His Lordship walked back to the house.

I followed the clerk to his office where he meticulously counted my coin, placed it in a strong box and entered it into the ledger. He logged the bill of sale and took back the letter of instruction. He inspected my ledger of expenses, added them up, set them off against all monies received and traded. Satisfied, he drew a line under them, signed them off and paid me my wages.

When I returned to the yard, Cornall was holding my horse. 'This a livery horse?'

'No, he's mine,'

'A son of Zeus?'

'Yes.'

'Sell him to me?'

'No.'

'Why not?'

'Because I don't want to.'

'What kind of reason is that?

'Mine.'

Cornall hoiked up a lump of phlegm and spat it on the ground, and then threw me the reins and walked off. I rode back to Stratford, now manager of the livery on a wage of two shillings and sixpence for the week. When I arrived back to the livery, there to greet me was the ever-gentle Anne Hathaway.

'I am so sorry about the loss of your father, Tom.'

'Me too ... and thank you, Anne.'

'It was a shock,' she said.

'Yes, stranger for me. There when I left; gone when I return,' I sighed.

'Yes, yes, indeed.'

'You want to hear of Will?'

Her eyes lit up at the sound of his name. 'It would thrill my heart to hear of him,' she said.

We sat down at the table and Grace gave us some lunch as I told her of my time at Hoghton Tower. I did omit the tale of Puca's tincture and any mention of Susie or, indeed, Campion. It was funny, these two cryptic sweethearts. They never professed any love for each other. Yet, whenever they were mentioned to the other, they would be overcome with soft smiles and bright eyes. Whatever happened, they were destined to be together.

'I will go to his mother and father and give news this afternoon,' I said.

Anne looked to Grace.

'He does not know,' said Grace.

I looked to them both.

'There has been trouble in the Shakespeare house,' said Anne.

There was silence and I looked to Anne's troubled eyes, which darted back and forth from Grace to me.

'His Lordship made a list of suspected recusants in Stratford, which he presented to the Privy Council,' said Grace quietly.

Anne looked over her shoulder and then drew close to me. 'Mr Shakespeare was on that list and called to present himself at Her Majesty's bench in Westminster,' continued Anne.

Well, I knew that was serious.

'But he did not go,' said Grace.

'On account of his late daughter, Mr Shakespeare went to St Winifreds at Holywell, to offer prayers for her soul,' said Anne.

I had heard that St Winifreds was a Papist stronghold and also on the route from here was Hoghton Tower. So that was what he was doing, arriving and leaving without a word or whisper. Knowledge that was best kept to myself, even though Grace and Anne were trustworthy beyond reproach. A floating thread is all authority needs to take in its fingers; then gently pull to make an unravelling of even the most perfectly sewn garment.

'He has been fined forty pounds!' whispered Anne.

That was a shock; forty pounds!

'Does His Lordship know Will is at Hoghton Tower?' I queried.

'He is not familiar with the Shakespeare family,' Anne assured me.

'Poor things. Life was good to them,' I said, genuinely sorry for their plight.

'And there's more,' said Anne.

'More?' said I, as if it could be worse.

'They have sold everything except their own house to pay their debts, and Mary is with child again.'

'The house they were building?'

'Sold before completion.'

'I do not know what to say.'

I sighed.

'Say nought. Tis not our business,' said Grace clearing the table.

Grace was right. It was time to make work a plenty and keep our heads down. Lady Montague's letter was safe in my medical pouch so I kept it on my person with good and honest reason.

In the coming months, I worked as hard as I could. I did not even clap eyes on Quiney, Tyler or Fieldy, though I did hear Fieldy had taken up a printer's apprenticeship in London.

Summer passed and autumn closed in; Christmas went and, with Grace holding good charge of the livery, I was able to make good coin from local horse trades. They always profited my lord and master greater than me but, as I steadily become known, some customers were trustworthy enough to let me cream off a little extra for myself. It was never a lot; the trust I required was total. If found out, Grace and I would be without home or work overnight.

Later in the year, Mary, gave birth to a baby boy whose choice of name was not lost on me. They named him Edmund.

CHAPTER 23

It was late April of 1581. Rather than concerning myself with the day-to-day running of the livery, I moved quite freely around the country, buying and selling horses on Lord Lucy's behalf. A lot of traders used promissory notes, so my lord's love of the solid coin I brought him, made it easier for him to avoid the attention of treasury. This, in turn, meant he asked little about where I had been or with whom I traded. However, his clerk meticulously noted all transactions and rigorously controlled the use of Lord Lucy's letter of instruction. Campion was still the most-hunted man, so the letter of instruction from my lord and master was utterly essential.

I travelled north and arrived at Hoghton Tower three days before Hermia and Helena were due to foal. I rode into the stables at the rear entrance and, sitting on my horse, I could see over the east garden wall. I glimpsed Will in the window of the school-room with his back to me. A quick tweak with my spurs and a pull on the bit told Orlando to rear and whinny, scraping the cobbles with his hooves. The result was instant; Will turned and saw it was me.

'Hermia and Helena are due any day, Master Wickham,' said Harry the stable boy as he led my horse away.

'Thomas, Mr Wickham,' a voice called from behind.

I turned and was greeted by Roger Anderson.

'Roger, are you well?' I asked, removing my gloves and holding out my hand, which he took and shook warmly.

'I am, young Tom, I am,' he replied.

'I hear you lost your father?' he said, dropping his tone to extend sympathy.

'Yes.'

'God rest his soul.'

Will came through the garden gate. We locked hands, gripped and hugged.

'A song of home and a sight for sore eyes, indeed,' he quipped with a smile. 'Sorry about your father – fine man and fine father, Tom.'

'Indeed he was. Thank you, Will.'

'And, if the library ever burns down,' said Roger, 'the de Hoghtons will have to keep this young man! For he has read all the books not once but thrice and can quote texts verbatim.'

Suddenly, the air was penetrated by a squeal of delight. I turned around just in time to see Susie launch herself through the air at me. I did indeed move quick to catch her, but there was an odd glaze in her eyes, which troubled me. I did notice Roger and Will slightly uneasy at her arrival.

'And the mares are due to foal any moment,' said Roger.

'Verily,' I said, placing the giggling Susie back on the ground.

'It's been a ride, so I'd like to rest and then look upon the mares tomorrow.'

'Susie will make up a bed,' said Roger. He ushered the still-giggling Susie into the house.

'She takes too much of her brother's tincture,' whispered Will.

I said nothing.

'Looking good, friend?' he stated with a smile and put his arm around me.

I, too, smiled. We were surely growing up, faster than I fancied but that was life.

'What news, Tom?' he asked in slightly more sombre tone.

I told him of his father's problems, which made him sigh heavily.

'Plague upon the wretched Lord Lousy,' he cursed through gritted teeth.

'As well you know, that group of Papists are still sought and I fear the longer they are at large, the greater the rage of those who hunt them,' I said.

'And the less their reason,' sighed Will.

'Have they been back here?' I whispered anxiously.

Will shook his head.

I was relieved, for things were quite dangerous these recent months. Suspicion was as rife as pox on a Coventry whore. I was quite surprised the de Hoghtons had not been visited by the state.

'But Anne is well, in good health,' I said to lighten the spirits. 'She makes good coin malting these last few months.'

Will nodded. 'Malting?'

'Yes, the Whateley steward taught her.'

'Always coin for good malt,' Will mused.

I spent a pleasant enough night on the customary bed made up in the kitchens. As usual, they fed me well; good food and wine was always plentiful at Hoghton. I'll give Catholics one thing; they know how to eat and drink.

The morning seemed straightforward enough. I rose late and washed my face in the laundry. Will was up and teaching the children in the school-room. I thought it was going to be an uneventful day spent quietly choosing yearlings and preparing birthing stalls for Helena and Hermia. I was wrong. A stable boy suddenly rushed through the laundry calling for his master. I pulled on my shirt and dashed up the stairs out into the main courtyard. I could hear the heavy rhythmical pounding of horse hooves – a lot of hooves.

I went to the drive and, in the dip, all I could see was a cloud of dust. Only I, the stable boy and two large hounds seemed to be about. I turned and looked to the school-room where, out of the window, Will was observing whatever it was.

'Cannot find our master any place, Master Wickham,' pleaded the troubled stable boy.

'Don't fret, boy,' I said, watching the drive.

Suddenly, led by one man on an impressive black horse, a retinue of horsemen flying the royal standard appeared in the middle of the drive and cantered towards the gate-house. The stable boy rushed to close the gates but I signalled him to stop. Will was suddenly there beside me.

'Where are the children?' I asked.

'In the school-room. Nurse is there,' he replied as the horses approached.

'Where is everyone?' Will whispered anxiously.

'Lea Hall, rounding up yearlings,' I said.

The retinue of some thirty or so mounted soldiers charged into the courtyard and surrounded the three of us. Jostling for position they pounded the cobbles and enveloped our faces with a viscous mist of horse breath. They stopped and waited. Their leader sat on top of his horse, staring down at us dauntingly.

I will never ever forget him. A thin hoary man with a lined face looking like it had been hewn from ancient granite – a homage to the personification of evil. He had a broken hand that he waved like a claw. His face, with sharp blue eyes at its core, locked with mine and, in that moment, he instilled a totality of dread. His stare was colder than anything I had seen in my life. This man feared nothing and enjoyed power beyond anything I could imagine. Unbeknownst to me, this was the feared Richard Topcliffe.

He dismounted, leg over front, impressive for a man of his years. He had grimy blackened leather leggings, boots and jerkin, under which he wore a brown silk shirt. His clothes smelled of fear, old dungeons' rotten sweat and putrid blood. Even the two normally fearless hounds skulked around, giving him a wide berth as he walked casually towards us. He did not swagger; he did not need to. This man's power was such he moved where he wished, at a pace he wished.

Though thin, he was all sinew and muscle with a strange gait.

I would speculate he had had a riding accident somewhere in his life. The right side of his body did not function as well as the left. His right hand had a crooked forefinger clearly broken and subsequently frozen in a hook-like position. I had seen this before; a man falls from a bolting horse but the finger gets stuck in the reins. The subsequent injuries, though not life-threatening, result in fractured bones setting in a debilitating shape.

He walked past me and, standing in front of Will, surveyed the situation.

A bruised and very-bloodied man with hands bound and a rope around his neck was thrown into the centre of the courtyard. He looked like he had been dragged up most of the driveway on his knees. He fell down and, choking, grasped at the knot to loosen the rope around his neck.

'Small beer for a large journey,' scoffed Topcliffe.

It was the publican from the Withnell Inn. Topcliffe, setting his sights on Will, stepped over the publican.

'Are you a Hoghton, boy?' he asked, with a sharp metallic ring to his voice.

'I am the family tutor,' replied Will.

'Really,' he sneered. 'Look too young to teach. What do you teach?' he asked, circling around Will.

'Latin, poetry, literature and play acting,' Will answered, as softly as he could.

'Oh God, you're a poet. The only thing I loathe more than Papists are poets and play actors. God, would I love our queen to allow them on my rack.'

Again Topcliffe looked Will up and down, sighed and then smiled malevolently at him.

Will cordially smiled back.

'Name?' Topcliffe demanded.

'Shakespeare, Sir. William Shakespeare.'

'Bit long for a poet, unwieldy. Stick to teaching.'

Topcliffe paused, said nothing and breathed the air. Suddenly he turned to the sky and shouted with an intensity and projection that sent a shaft of winter ice straight up our spines.

'It has been a winter of utter discontent but I will make glorious this summer by finding and hanging that Jesuit!'

Will's finger froze to his lip.

Topcliffe paused, waited, breathed in and, snapping round to look directly at Will, once more cut the air with his penetrating vocal chords.

'Are there any Jesuits in this house?'

Will dropped his hand from his lip and I knew he had me in the edge of his vision. With my thumbs in my belt, I gave a small sideswipe of my hand, imperceptible to anyone but Will.

'I am not aware of any, Sir,' he replied.

Topcliffe reached into his shirt, pulled out a document and flicked it open.

'Edmund Campion, Robert Persons, Thomas Cottom, Ralph Sherwin, William Hartley. Have any, or all, of these men been to this house or are they concealed in this house,' he demanded, his sharp, staccato voice cutting yet more fear into our already tingling skin.

Will muttered denial of any such knowledge. At that moment, Alexander de Hoghton and his steward entered the courtyard. Alexander marched straight up to Topcliffe.

'I demand to know who you are,' he called mid-stride.

Topcliffe relaxed and, turning slowly, placed the document back in his jerkin. He said nothing, just smirked.

'Who are you, mmm?' demanded Alexander, standing right in front of Topcliffe, who casually adjusted his glove and looked to the fluttering standard held by one of his horsemen.

Topcliffe twisted fast! He punched Alexander in the face, sending him to the ground like a shot bird, and once again his penetrating voice cut the air with poisonous speed.

'All you need to know is that I ride with a retinue of Her Majesty's military and carry her standard,' he yelled, 'thus conferring on me the authority to protect Crown and the State in any way I see fit!'

He walked away from the now profusely bleeding Alexander lying on the ground.

'Search this house!' he shouted.

With impressive military unity all the soldiers dismounted at speed and swept into every available entrance. Topcliffe used his broken finger to hook Will and pull him face to face.

'If I find anyone I am looking for, I will gouge out your left eye and violate the remaining socket with the penis of a dead donkey!' he growled, and cast Will aside in my direction.

'Man's a poet,' Will muttered, which thankfully was not heard.

The stable boy assisted Alexander to his feet and we all stood frozen in fear as we listened. It seemed an eternity: the screams, shouts, crashes, kicks, thumps and breaking glassware.

Eventually the soldiers returned, two of them dragging the six children and the old nurse. They were launched at Alexander and Will, to whom they clung.

Some of Topcliffe's men marched out with armfuls of documents and pamphlets, which they flung down in the middle of the cobblestones. Most of the soldiers could not have told the difference between a book and a trencher. However, one man did look slightly educated, and he proceeded to rummage through the papers looking for incriminating text. However, like all recusants, the de Hoghtons were meticulously efficient at destroying any remotely seditious papers. I hoped Will had his copies of *Deciem Rationes* and that copy of 'contract of the soul' well hidden. God help us, this would not be a good moment for them to turn up.

The man took various papers to Topcliffe, who inspected them with little interest, flinging them down when they turned out to be benign. Suddenly, a scrappy torn piece of paper took his attention and he read it studiously. There was a quick conference with the other man and two more such pieces were recovered from the pile; there was more study of the papers. Judging by Will's face, I surmised that he knew what they were.

Topcliffe turned to Alexander de Hoghton. 'Is this your autograph?' he demanded, shaking the papers in a very nervous Alexander's face.

'No, Sir. Tis mine I believe,' said Will.

Topcliffe turned to Will with a particularly severe expression on his face. 'Yours, boy?'

'Sir,' said Will.

'Your very hand wrote these words?'

'Yes, Sir.'

Will was frightened; he was riding an unbroken horse.

'This is sedition!' hissed Topcliffe, like a viper about to strike.

'A short play in one act, concerning a great monarch, Richard II. Tis a trifle,' Will answered softly, concealing his abject fear.

'A plan to seize the crown! A trifle! Tis sedition! I see it here before me!'

'Tis but a plan for a play, Sir – not a plan for intent,' stuttered Will.

'I am not convinced.'

Topcliffe studied the sheets.

'Sir, you have but three of five pages,' Will stammered, his eyes darting around nervously. 'The top paper and first page should convince, if they can be located.'

The man who had been inspecting the papers had another rummage and, to our relief, located the two missing pages. He approached Topcliffe and pointed out that it was indeed a plan of play-writing and of little consequence. Topcliffe took all the papers to Will and thrust them at his chest.

'There is no confession so damning as the sweet flow of ink driven by a guilty hand. I have hanged more men for what they have written than for what they have done.'

The air was taut as Will swallowed deeply and cautiously took the papers in his grasp. The tension was broken by the scream of a young woman. Susie was suddenly flung out of a door from the west wing and a worrying delight appeared on the face of Topcliffe.

'A maid,' he exclaimed, turning around with a sick smile.

'All clear, Sir,' shouted one of the last soldiers to exit.

Topcliffe beckoned to Susie, and a soldier pushed her to him. Our hearts were in our mouths. Poor Susie's saucy bravado was vanished. She was confused, terrified and also under the effects of her brother's tincture.

'The interrogation of a woman is a more subtle affair and I use a method that never fails,' he declared, as if tutoring a school-room.

What happened next I shall remember with a sombre sickness till the day I die. Topcliffe took Susie into an upstairs chamber overlooking the courtyard. After opening the window so all sound would be clearly heard, this man, who flew the royal standard, proceeded to force himself upon her with the most unrelenting cruelty. Staring at the ground, we all waited and waited and waited. Eventually, the screaming stopped only to be replaced by whimpering as Topcliffe re-entered the courtyard adjusting his cuffs.

'She knows nothing,' he stated with self-satisfied confidence.

He walked to his horse and, passing Will without looking at him, said, 'Never cross my path again Mr Shakespeare. You will not last a second round.'

Topcliffe mounted his horse. All the soldiers followed suit. He pulled his horse around and faced Alexander.

'Don't bother explaining what happened. Just say Richard Topcliffe searched this house. That will be enough.'

With that declaration, he and his retinue departed. Poor Susie staggered out and slumped to the ground in her torn and bloody smock, utterly inconsolable. Will and Alexander's clothes were wet with the children's tears. All at Hoghton Tower were in shock for a good while. I spent the rest of the day in the paddocks choosing yearlings, and, by way of desperation to squeeze the event from my memory, I concentrated so hard on the horses, that ironically, I picked the best fillies I ever bought. Even today, some seventy years later, if I hear a woman scream I still think of young Susie.

For the next two days Will sat in the school-room reading and refusing to speak. He had to be ordered back to work by Sir Richard or told he would have to leave. Will and I did meet Richard Topcliffe two more times in our lives. The second when he had just had the joy of racking a real poet, but the irony was that the poet turned out to be a tougher man than he. More of that later. Besides, I have to add, from that day forth, my Stratford friend guarded his manuscripts with a meticulous awareness that was neither noticed nor apparent to anyone other than myself.

Three days later, by the light of a lantern, I was sat with Sir Richard watching Hermia and Helena. At around the fourth hour, two of the sweetest little foals made their entrance into the world. The sight was a soothing solace after the previous violent drama. They were up standing and suckling well in under a half-hour, so that showed good strength and character. As the proud mothers washed off their offspring, the equally gratified fathers whinnied from the paddocks. I was cleaning up in the trough just as Will came into the stable.

'There is noise. Do we have parents?' he asked.

'We do, Will. Two colts,' I said, drying myself.

'How is Susie?' Sir Richard asked.

'Fair; she sleeps. She slept with cook last night,' said Will.

He sighed; I sighed. It was a wretched affair of which little could be said.

Sir Richard patted my back, and shook Will's hand.

'I will away to bed,' he said and took his leave.

It was daybreak, so I blew out the lantern and Will and I sat alone and allowed ourselves to be relaxed by watching the world of fresh equine motherhood accompanied by the gentle dawn bird song.

'Will you stay a day or so longer?' Will asked.

I shook my head. 'I will sleep today and leave tonight. The less time I am here, the fewer questions His Lordship will ask. And he is quite a burrower when he gets going,'

'Understood.'

'You?' I asked.

'Sir Thomas de Hoghton is thinking of going to France. Alexander may follow. If they do, I am without employment.'

'What about Ferdinando?'

'Maybe.'

Will eventually went back to the house, whilst I found a good dark spot with some soft fresh hay, and there I slept the entire day. In the evening I rose, packed my things, loaded some bags of good oats and malt on the fillies and tagged them together. Once more, Richard had given me a good price of ten shillings each. I reckoned Charlecote would take at least two for two sovereigns a beast and the others I could move for about three in the surrounding locality.

I went to the kitchen where I bid goodbye to Cook. A boy fetched Will and we gathered in the yard at the sixth hour. Cook gave me some bread and cheese in a cloth and a flask of small beer. The de Hoghtons stayed within the house but Roger came out and shook my hand. Will gave me a hug; it was hard. The last time I was here, there had been such joy but this was all so sad. Our hearts all sank as Susie staggered in from the east garden. Her hair was wild, her eyes wide and glazed. She wore no shoes and dressed only in a night shift, she clutched a bunch of weeds and grasses in her hand. Laughing, she proceeded to give each of us standing there a weed, making out it was a flower.

We all froze, holding back our tears, not knowing what to do, till Cook approached her and gently cuddled her close. Roger took the tragic posy from Susie and silently ushered me on my way.

The weather on the journey back home was cold and ugly but the fillies were young and fit so, carrying enough feed with me, I decided to push on as hard as possible. The first night I was fresh and the day was good, fuelled by Cook's thoughtful gift. The following two nights were tougher, taking only cat-naps here and there but I made it to Stratford in a record two and a half days.

It was good to see Grace and, bless her, did she produce a stack of good hot food within an hour of my arrival!

'I can see when a man has ridden all night without food,' she said, filling the table with peascod, roast chicken, bread and cheese.

'Thought I was a boy?' I said with a cheeky grin, for I was still short of eighteen, but recent adventures had left me stick thin.

Grace sat down and looked me straight in the eyes with great depth of feeling.

'You ceased to be a boy a long time ago.'

'I love you, Grace,' I said silently.

Grace stood up sharply, picked up her pinny and wiped non-existent tears from her face.

'I was never loved by any man, so never had a child, but it has been God's blessing to see you grow from child to boy and now to a man,' she said.

As she left to go into the yard, Grace called over her shoulder,

'Get some sleep, and then get those beasts to His Lordship. He wants them.'

After the usual routine of settling up and handing back the letter of introduction, Lord Lucy asked only a few cursory questions about my trip, for which I was relieved. I only had to omit, not lie, the one thing Lord Lucy had a nose for. He took all five fillies for two sovereigns each, depriving me of a better profit but nonetheless putting some much-needed coin in my purse. His Lordship actually sold them on himself to a friend in Oxford for four pounds each the very next month. Rafsaan he held on to and he had covered half a dozen mares in the Charlecote herd. The anticipated progeny, if good, would mean Rafsaan's service fees would be fine income for years to come.

The months came and went, and indeed Topcliffe did make glorious his summer. News came to us in late July that Campion had been arrested and taken to the Tower of London for interrogation. Just the idea of being chained to a wall and being interrogated by that Richard Topcliffe was terrifying enough.

August and September went by with little news and most recusants, sensibly, kept their heads well below the parapet. Some even started showing up at Trinity for communion. It was late October; Grace and I were cleaning the yard when Lord Lucy rode in with his clerk, both looking quite formal. I put down my pail and bowed whilst Grace curtseyed.

'Wickham, I hear Thomas de Hoghton is in France?'

'I was unaware, Your Lordship.'

'How the guilty flee,' he said, leaning forward on his pommel.

'And Alexander de Hoghton is dead,' he said slowly, teasing my anxious curiosity.

That was news to me, too, but I was concerned where this was leading.

'God rest his soul, Your Lordship,' I answered in simple acquiescence.

'Yes … mmm. It seems I know something you do not, Wickham.'

'My Lord?'

He looked at me with sustained severity, and then, to my relief, he laughed. 'They are short of money! They're clearing their herd!'

'I was not aware, My Lord,' I said.

He took a purse of coin and threw it to me. 'Go on! Get me some bargains!' he said, as I caught the weighty purse. 'Twelve sovereigns, as usual.'

'What would His Lordship prefer – coin or livestock?'

'In this instance, let's make coin,' he declared and, turning his horse, he rode out, leaving Cornall to handle the paperwork.

Cornall dismounted, reached into his saddle-bag and pulled out a quill and small bottle of ink, which he handed to me. I threw the purse to Grace, which she caught and opened. I opened the bottle of ink and dipped the quill in as Cornall opened the ledger, held it for me and pointed to the relevant column.

'Twelve sovereigns, to the penny,' said Grace.

I looked at the column and, seeing the correct amount, I signed. Taking the now quite-worn letter of introduction, he handed it to me with a sneer and, without saying a word, left.

'Grace, why does he hate us so?' I asked after he had gone.

'Nought so queer as folk,' she said, tossing the purse back to me.

CHAPTER 24

I left the following day for Hoghton Tower once more. Again I decided to ride through the night and I rested only for short periods. Though having no stock with me I still had to stop for feed for Orlando, but nonetheless I made good time.

This time when I arrived at Hoghton Tower, it was to an exceptionally sombre atmosphere. Mark and Harry came out of the yard to greet me, obviously surprised since I was not expected.

'His Lordship died,' they said solemnly.

'My dear Master Wickham!' declared Roger Anderson walking out of the kitchen.

'Roger!' I said greeting him, 'I am sorry to hear of His Lordship, God rest his soul.'

To my surprise he embraced me. 'Indeed, indeed. What brings you to this sad estate?'

I looked at him. He knew. 'I understand there is a clearing sale … and I have twelve sovereigns of my master's coin.'

He nodded sympathetically. 'Meat is meat for ravens and so trade is trade. But Tom, you will always be a friend of Hoghton.'

'Thank you, Roger. And where is Will?'

'He resides at Lea Hall and works for the Hesketh family these last two months. Mark will send word.'

'Consider it done, Mr Anderson,' said Mark.

Harry took Orlando into the stable and Mark rode off to Lea Hall. Roger and I wandered into the kitchens and I asked about the wellbeing of another friend. 'And young Susie?'

'Ah!' he sighed sadly, 'I feared you would ask. Sadly she passed away.'

'How?' I asked, inwardly shocked.

'I will let your friend tell you that sorry tale.' He sighed and, putting his arm round me, squeezed my shoulder.

'Cook! We have a guest!' he called as we entered the great kitchen.

'Master Wickham, how good to see you,' she said, turning around with her ruddy face and podgy smile.

I was sitting in the kitchen eating a plate of eggs and ham, kindly prepared by dear Cook, when Will came in. I stood up and he rushed towards me. 'My dear friend!' he said grasping me in a tight embrace and I him.

'Mark tells me you are here to scavenge for Lord Lousy?' he grumbled, sitting down to wait on me finishing my food.

'Sad, but true. There is, however, a silver lining. I get to see my true friends.'

Cook brought over a cup of small beer for Will.

'Are you hungry, Master William?'

'Kindness be your heartbeat but, thank you, no, dear Cook.'

I had noticed the kitchen staff were gone and the pantry thin, to say the least.

'Things have changed, Will,' I said throwing a glance around the kitchen.

Will sat back and rubbed his face. 'They have, they have, and you heard of the arrest?'

Assuming he meant Campion, which he did, I nodded. Campion and friends were not good things to talk of.

'That pretty much pulled the rug from under the feet of Hoghton,' he said, drumming his fingers on the table.

I looked to Will with the penetration of brotherhood. 'Tell me of Susie?' I asked, failing to conceal my sadness.

Will leant forward, dropping his elbows on the table, and buried his head in his hands.

'Susie! She was truly the fairy's midwife,' he said, lifting his head and breathing in for strength. 'Remember the tincture from mushroom that her brother made?

'How could I forget?' I said with an ironic smile.

'Indeed, one trip in Queen Mabb's speeding chariot was enough for me, too!'

'To be sure.'

'Sadly, not for Susie. It appeared she kept tippling at it and, after her encounter with that savage Topcliffe, she drank it like wine.'

'I thought as much when I saw her last, but she was very much alive.'

Then Will told me the tragic tale of how she deteriorated and, not three weeks after my last departure, she went missing. A great search was made around the grounds but to no avail.

'The following morning, why I know not, but I went to Houghton Bottom and there I found her in a small brook lying face up looking at the sky, flowers in her hand, eyes wide open and as dead as dead can be.'

'Oh Will, God rest her soul.'

'Yes! If the churlish vicar would've allowed it!'

'Did he not?'

'I said to him, "Lay her in the earth, and from her fair heart may violets spring"!'

'He thought she had profaned death's journey?'

Will nodded.

'Where does she lie?'

Will's eyes welled up with tears. 'I know not! But a ministering angel shall dear Susannah be, when that vicar lies howling,' he choked, turning his empty cup over on the table and pondering the tragedy.

There was silence. Will cleared his throat. 'How are my parents, brothers and sister?' he asked by way of distraction.

'They are well but in hard times. They do not come to us any more for transport. They borrow the sadler's horse and cart if need be. Truly I have not seen a lot of them.'

'Quiney, Fieldy and Tyler?'

'Fieldy has taken an apprenticeship with a printer in London, and Quiney and Tyler finished school last August. What they do now, I'm not sure.'

We both sat back and searched for words.

'What do you at the Hesketh family?'

'Teach the children and make plays with their players.'

There was more silence.

'Will, that night of the feast? It was a wondrous night and all that has passed since has been … not so wondrous.'

Will looked to me and, smiling the most delicious smile ever, he spoke so quietly and sensuously. 'Then we alone, shall hold that night special in our hearts and one day, I'll share it with the world. A night begotten from a single breath, drawn and blown by only the fairies, you, and I.'

Sir Richard walked into the kitchen. We both stood. 'Don't get up. Good to see you, Tom. Come to pick the bones?'

'Sadly, my master is a bit of a gannet.'

Sir Richard sat down and put his feet up on the table. 'Well, the clearing sale is all of the dregs.'

'Demetrius and Lysander?' I asked.

'Gone to Hesketh, and I take Hermia and Helena to Appleby with their progeny next week. And fine progeny, too, thanks to you, dear Tom.'

'Better price at Chiswick!' I said.

Sir Richard simply threw a glance at Will.

'North is better for de Hoghtons,' said Will.

I got the message.

'My late brother had two fine holsteiners,' Sir Richard said.

'Fine beasts,' I replied.

'Have a look tomorrow. Make an offer. There are some standards, work horses, not too bad. Sorry, most of the good stock is gone.'

'Thank you, Your Lordship.'

'Pish! Cook, can we make a bed for young Tom?'

'Certainly, Sir.'

Will put his hand up, too.

'And one for Will.'

'Sir.'

'Only retaining Cook and Mr Anderson in the house at this current time,' said Richard, as he stood up and shook our hands.

'Dawn, in the east paddock?'

'Sir,' I said.

Richard about-faced and left as smartly as he had arrived.

'Will you take the stock back to Lousy?' Will asked.

'He wants me to turn some profit for him.'

'Chiswick?'

I nodded.

'Take me, too!' he said excitedly, sitting forward on his chair.

'What will you do for a ride?'

'I still have Moot.'

'Indeed you do. You have money?'

'I have saved two pounds and a shilling.'

'I ride hard and rough with little rest and less food.'

'Then you'll take me?'

'Hesketh's?' I asked rhetorically.

'I'll send word; they'll understand.'

'So long as you keep up, I would love to have your company.'

Will blew his auburn hair back from his face and smiled that seductive smile. What I did not realise was that this was the first (and least subtle) of many subversive gambits he would contrive to pursue a secret motive. Later in life, to those who knew him well enough, this was to become his stock in trade.

It was the fifth hour. Day was just breaking when Will and I saddled up in the stables. We rode down to the east paddock, where a low-hanging mist lay scattered around over a light crispy frost. At the paddock gate, we pulled up to look back at the house. It was a sad but majestic sight as the fresh sun illuminated the lonely castle on its naked hill, which, in turn, floated on an ethereal pillow of pink mist.

I had a bag of feed with me to occupy the horses whilst Will tied them off with the halters I had given him. However, first I needed their attention. I put my fingers in my mouth and blew a very loud sharp whistle, which quite shocked Will. Sure enough, the herd came galloping over.

'How do you do that?' he asked.

I showed him my fingers and their placement in the lips. Will mimicked and tried but he could not get it.

'Where did you learn that?'

Suddenly there was another whistle in the distance from behind Will.

'You did that without moving your lips!' he laughed.

I pointed to the source of the whistle. It was Sir Richard and Mark on the Holsteiners coming at full gallop towards us.

'He did!' I said pointing.

Will tried again but still could not quite get the sound.

'Good morning, boys. Cold enough for you?'

'Players like to stay warm and sleep in, Sir.'

'Well, Will when you are, you can!' he laughed.

Mark fed the horses, and, as I picked stock, Will haltered them and tied them to a fence post.

'Only one to a post, Will,' I called.

'Verily.'

After a half-hour, I had a row of six good, solid standard breeds, four geldings and two mares, probably worth only pound a piece in Chiswick. Now, the Holsteiner mares. I looked into their teeth. Fine beasts and tall at probably sixteen hands.

'Seven years old,' I declared.

'I believe only four,' stuttered Richard, looking to Mark who nodded so obsequiously it made me chuckle.

'Six at the very least!' I laughed and looked the horses up and down.

'Two pounds the standards and five pounds for the Holsteiners. Twenty-two pound the lot! What say you?' said Sir Richard.

'Hell will freeze over before a blind man would pay that!' I laughed.

Will was a little shocked at my brazen attitude, since this was a side of me he didn't know, and it had toughened up even more recently.

'Fifteen the lot, and that's a good price,' said Richard.

I was wondering what my price would be when Will made a subtle signal with his hands, which I figured to be the figure nine.

'Ten shillings a standard and three pound each for these two. Nine pounds the lot.'

'Oh … no, no, no. Twelve pounds. That is it. I cannot take a penny less.'

I decided I would call his bluff.

'Richard, this is not my coin and I have a duty to keep. I will be passing the family seat of Lord Gregory, so I must hold my price.'

I had no idea where the seat of Lord Gregory was but I knew him to be a great horse trader.

Richard capitulated with a deep sigh. 'Times are hard and you have learnt well. Nine it is.'

I showed my hand. He slapped it.

'The west yard, settle up and hand over. Come, Mark.'

He mounted up and rode off, slightly put out, I would say.

'How did you know he would take nine pounds?'

'I heard him chatting prices with Mark and Harry yesterday. But how did you know about Lord Gregory?'

'I didn't. I guessed.'

Will guffawed. 'I don't believe it,' he said. 'The Gregory seat is Banbury, two days south from here. He holds a large stock that he turns over constantly.'

After paying Sir Richard, we took charge of the two Holsteiners – Cowslip and Barley they were called. I bought four bags of oats for a shilling, which we loaded on the standards. I took the front, leading Cowslip whilst Will brought up the rear on Barley and leading Moot. The standards travelled loose between us. It was slow going at first, till Will got the hang of driving a herd but, by the end of the third day, we had reached Aylesbury, which was an easy day and a half from Chiswick. As we approached Aylesbury, the road became increasingly busy. It was market day.

The middle of town was heaving with stock and folk carrying baskets of chickens, ducks and woodcock. Men pushed handcarts loaded with bundles of turnips, kale, fine red carrots. But the most trying were the women with baskets of annoyingly aromatic bread hot from the oven. It was a job to keep our herd together. I have to say Will did good work and soon conquered finger whistling. I had to think fast. We needed a pen to hold our stock and some feed, for we had one more feed left for the herd.

I whistled to one of the market boys who were marking empty pens. He came over, clutching his chalk-board and squinting through the sun.

'I need a pen. I have ten beasts.'

'All pens be booked. Thee selling today or morrow?'

'Neither. Passing through.'

Wretched boy laughed. 'Then get thee gone. This here's for traders.'

He looked at Will trying to control the herd. 'Real traders, that is!'

There was another whistle and the boy turned round. Someone pointed at us, waved at the boy and whistled once more. It was Lord Gregory.

'You have friends in the right places,' groaned the boy and, beckoning us to follow, he fought his way through the throng to an empty holding pen. We put all our stock inside and dismounted as Lord Gregory fought his way through the sea of farmers.

'Tom Wickham. Anywhere you don't turn up?'

'The queen's palace,' I laughed.

'Given time, you will,' smiled Lord Gregory.

'Selling or buying, Your Lordship?'

'Cattle buying. You?'

'We're just on our way to Chiswick. This is my friend, Will.'

Will put out his hand. 'William Shakespeare,' said Will, shaking Lord Gregory's hand.

'What have you got? Let's see. Six standards and those are a pair of Holsteiners. And what's that?' he said, pointing to poor Moot.

'My master seeks a good profit.'

'Well, sell those standards today here. They are short of workers, and then get gone to Chiswick. If you can get to the auction there by midday the morrow, you will get a very good price for those – possibly six pounds a beast, eight if you are lucky.'

Lord Gregory turned around, whistled back at the boy and made him some hand signals. The boy signalled back and jotted on his board.

'Get those to the ring at eleven and be at the nail straight after,' he smiled.

'Once more, I owe you, Sir,' I said.

And certainly we did owe. The standards went into the ring owing my master ten shillings and, blow me to dust, the bidding started at fifteen shillings! In shorter breath than a fresh foal, the bids passed the pound mark, then to twenty-five shillings! Finally all done at forty shillings a beast! That was a staggering twenty pounds the lot!

Normally I would wait for things to quieten down before settlement but if we were to make Chiswick as Lord Gregory suggested, we needed to move. After waiting patiently in line at the nail, I showed my letter, signed off my stock and collected payment. I set off at once with Will and the remaining stock. I put Will back on to Moot to keep the sale beasts fresh. At an appropriate point, we pulled up and I took off my saddle. Will was intrigued as I opened up the stitching under the pommel. After stowing eighteen of the nineteen pounds and ten shillings I had after the commissions, I stitched it back up and re-mounted.

'I am impressed, Tom,' said Will.

'Look poor, move fast and with God's grace, the robbers will not notice thee,' I said.

We let the horses drink at a shallow ford and gave them the last of the feed we carried. Then we rode full tilt through the night to Chiswick. Three miles short at Acton village we stopped. Day was breaking and we were all tired. There was an old farmer moving his milk herd, so I greeted him and, for a penny, was able to buy feed, agistment for the morning and a barn in which to lay our heads.

'We'd be obliged if you wake us at noon,' I said.

'Waking thee at midday!'

'And I'll pay another fourpence to wash down our horses,' I added.

'For the auction at Chiswick,' he said with a smile.

'Aye,' I said, carrying the last bit of tack to the corner of the barn where we had made our bed.

Will and I lay down and in no time we were sound asleep. In fact, we were in such a deep sleep the very next thing I knew was my foot being kicked by the old farmer. I woke up, went into the yard and plunged my head into the trough.

'Wah!' It was cold but good. Then I looked up and saw Barley and Cowslip tied to a pillar, looking not only clean but their coats with a beautiful sheen to them.

'Look good, eh?' said the old farmer.

'What did you do?'

'Bit of milk makes 'em shine!'

The cheeky beggar, I thought. I thanked him and went to raise Will.

We reached Chiswick at the second hour after midday, just in time for the last book and pen.

'You all right to run Barley in the ring?' I quickly asked Will.

'Absolutely, my friend,' smiled Will, albeit a touch nervously.

They were put in an early lot and, only minutes later, Will and I were leading the two beauties round the ring. With their fine gait, high heads and shiny coats I was sure we would get a good price. The bidding kicked in at four pounds. This was good; we kept running around the ring. The bidding went to eight pounds. Will stopped in the centre as I turned a figure of eight. I flicked Cowslip's rein. She reared, beat her hooves then, bless her, she settled to a stand, calm as a millpond. I bowed to great applause as the bidding topped ten pounds! Stone bidding topped out, all done at ten pounds, twelve and six! Twenty pounds and twenty-five shillings the pair!

We took a room that night and were well fed. I felt we had earned it. After costs, I was going to take a sum of thirty-five pounds to Lord Lucy, a profit of twenty-three pounds for doing nothing.

That night Will spent much of the evening sitting on the window ledge, using the light of the moon to write.

'Let's to London the morrow?' he said, looking out of the window.

I was already in bed and ready to sink into the land of nod.

'I have to get back to Stratford,' I said, turning over.

'A day or two. What would be the difference?'

'I am carrying nearly forty pounds in coin. London is thick with vagabonds and thieves, or so I am told.'

'We are two and I have a sword.'

I sat up. 'The livery fees are expensive. It will cost too much.'

'Paddock the beasts here and go by river?'

It was tempting.

'We can call on Fieldy.'

'You know where he is?'

'No, you do. You said he was taking a printer's apprenticeship.'

'London is a big place, Will, and I never got an address!'

'Come on! We can but try!'

'Very well, but paddock the horses here and take a boat.'

I put out my hand and Will slapped it.

At dawn I was up and sitting in the window ledge sewing the coin into my waist-band. Since I was sewing the coin from the saddle too, I had had to enlarge it with a bit of sacking. It took me a while, but my childhood was spent mending tack and had given me nimble fingers, so I did a neat job in the early light. I finished and was admiring my work when, looking round, I saw that Will was awake and watching me.

'You know how to look after coin,' said Will.

'Especially when coin is not mine and my skin depends on its safe passage! Good morning to you, too, Will.'

'Yes, good morning.'

We dressed and, after some food, we set about finding a paddock for the horses. It wasn't hard. We found one behind the inn costing a penny-halfpenny a beast, thruppence a day, so sixpence, for two. Damn it, same paddock in Stratford could be had for a penny!

From the inn, we walked the short walk down to the jetty and, after a bit of a haggle, we found a lighter to take us down river for fourpence. What a journey that was for fourpence!

As we travelled closer and closer to London, the houses on the river became bigger and bigger. Sumptuous they were, with many floors and perfect gardens right down to the river bank. We must have passed a dozen Charlecotes. They were so beautiful and all with at least two-score gardeners working. Will sat up on the bow of the boat, breathing in everything with the intensity and capacity of a great stallion's chest.

'Where you boys from?' asked the lighterman.

'Stratford' I told him.

'Where's that?'

'North-west.'

'Nothing north of Watford, is there?' he laughed.

'Only the world,' I said.

'So what you come to the big smoke for?'

'See a friend.'

'Where he be?'

'Not sure.'

'He got a trade?'

'Apprentice printer.'

'You'll want Blackfriars.'

'Why do you call it the big smoke?' asked Will, looking back to us.

The lighterman jerked his chin in the direction of London, and there, several bends away in the river, was a thick smoke hanging in the air that was obviously over London. As we travelled on I realised this river took a pounding from a population far greater than our little Stratford. Indeed, suddenly the smell accosted us like the tongues of a dozen over enthusiastic hounds.

'What's that?' asked Will, hankie to his nose and pointing to a series of great buildings on the north bank.

'The Palace of Westminster, the Hall, the Abbey and the Parliament. Thought that's where thee might have been headed, see King Henry's sword in the Abbey.'

'Blackfriars for us,' I said.

'Good. Wise man would keep away from there next few days.'

'For why?' I asked.

'The trial.'

'What trial?' asked Will.

'Jesuit – on the morrow.'

Will's ears pricked up. I looked at him and shook my head nervously. A look of determination came over his face and I moved up the boat to silently remonstrate with him.

'In God's name, Will! No,' I whispered through gritted teeth.

Will said nothing and continued to stare at the foreboding edifice of Crown and State as we sailed quietly past. We sailed up to the next bend and, as we rounded, the great city came into view, albeit still a good distance away. It was incredible: the boats, hundreds of them, all going to and fro, sailing, rowing – even punting. Smoke stacks belched, nourishing a dark mist that hung over the city, like the thinning feathers of a mother hen sat on her young. And there, in the distance, a bridge! A bridge that was unimaginable! It was nothing short of a whole city crossing the river. There were whole buildings all the way across, some four floors high. I stood with Will on the bow of the lighter, watching, grinning, breathing as our bodies tingled with excitement.

'Where be the Tower of London?' called Will back to the lighterman.

'Beyond the bridge. Thee no want never to be took there; last journey for anyone, that's for sure.'

He looked at his direction, then muttered once more under his breath, 'Thee'll smell it before you ever see it.'

It was indeed a breathtaking sight. As we arrived closer, the sounds got louder, too. People calling, livestock baying, builders hammering, hooves pounding, and the perpetual noise of wagon wheels grinding over cobbled streets. It was similar to Stratford but just so very much bigger, louder and three times as absorbing. The boat moved closer to the edge and I could see one of the city walls coming up on the north bank.

'What's on the south bank?' I asked, pointing to the other end of the distant bridge.

'Southwark, if thee wants to be tickled by a bit of bear-baiting, or get a bit of the other … tickled.'

The boat started to close in on a wharf.

'Blackfriars; this is where thee will find the printing trade.'

We paid the boatman and set foot for the first time in the great city. It was as busy as cattle herds at market but with people. No one seemed to notice our presence at all. Rushing smells invaded our nostrils, both sweet and sour. Goodness, I thought. Stratford smelled, but this was potent to say the least.

'Act like we have been here all our lives,' I whispered to Will.

Carrying some forty pounds sewn into my attire, I did not want Will or I to be seen as fresh colts ready to be skinned by the nearest trickster. Will was on it and he appeared an old hand as he quickly accosted a man pushing a handcart laden with books.

'Good day, fine Sir. My friend and I look for the premises of my friend, William Ponsonby. Know thee?'

Without even stopping or looking at us, he answered. 'St Pauls, the churchyard,' he said, pointing in a northerly direction.

'Who is this William Ponsonby?' I asked Will.

'Publisher of books.'

'So you know him?' I asked.

'No.'

'How do you know of him?'

'His name is in books,'

'What books?'

'Hoghton library.'

We wound our way up the narrow streets, navigating spittle, excrement and urine as we weaved in and out of the stream of people. There were men of business, all of whom bore goods and, if not goods, they bore urgency and purpose, or simply fine clothes. The women, too. Did I mention them? There were more cherries than blossom. I never saw so many attractive women. Everyone was in a hurry, though; no one sauntered, so we did the same, applying haste and purpose to our stride! But in front of the great cathedral we were reduced to young colts once more; we stood open-mouthed, gaping at the awe-inspiring building that is Saint Paul's. And yes, in two shakes of a filly's tail, we were approached by two men.

'Guide you round the city, sirs?' said one toothless street warrior, whilst the other viewed us like a salivating hound watches a gormless hen.

We were newcomers to the big smoke but not fools. Will took his gaze from the great edifice and looked directly into the men's eyes, placing his hands on his hips.

'Get thee gone idle sirs, before I show thee the sight down river of the bridge!' said Will, sounding like he owned the very ground upon which we stood.

The two vagabonds looked at each other. Realising we were not the soft touch they anticipated, they took their leave as silently and obsequiously as they could.

'There, it's all in the intonation. This way I think?' said Will pointing. He strode off in the direction of a line of shops.

'But why to this shop, Will?'

'I'm sure they will know where to find Fieldy. London is a big place but the world is a small one, and that's for sure.'

Will walked on and looked all the premises up and down quite meticulously. His gaze stopped at one particular shop front with lot of books in the window. Above the window in gold letters was the name, William Ponsonby, so we entered.

A bell secured to the door announced our arrival but nevertheless Will entered as though the premises were his own. As Will perused the books up on display, a man came from the back. Feigning my interest, I limply glanced over the artifacts of literature, paper, quills, inks and ledgers.

'May I be of service, sirs?'

'Are you the proprietor?' I asked, as Will continued his browse.

'I am.'

'Mr Ponsonby, my friend and I seek Master Richard Field?'

'I do not know anyone of that name.'

There was silence and the look on his face suggested to me he was indeed lying.

Will turned around, a book in hand. 'What will thou want for thee?' he asked, holding the book up.

'*Hecatompathia; Passionate Century of Love*, Thomas Watson, published only a week.'

'I read the title but not the price.'

'Crown,' smiled the man curtly.

I have to say Will did a poor job of containing his shock but, nonetheless, he took out a sovereign and handed it to the man, who took it and went for change.

'John Bishops, end of this row. There you will find the young man you seek,' he muttered as he handed Will fifteen shillings in change.

Will and I glanced at each other, not sure what to say. We bid him thanks and left but at the door he spoke again.

'Little that seems so, is rarely so. Never did a foul hound alight on a book of love, let alone buy it. Who are thee and from whence you hail?'

We stopped and turned around.

'William Shakespeare and my friend, Tom Wickham. We are from Stratford near Warwick.'

Mr Ponsonby mused the muse of a tired man.

'You would not have been the first spies I had in this shop, nor the youngest.'

He sighed heavily and, without looking up from his ledger, waved us gone.

We left and followed his instructions to the end of the row, but there was no shop, only an alleyway so we walked down it. We came upon a yard with the gates half-closed, but the word 'J. Bish' was apparent, so we concluded the ending 'ops' was on the other gate and entered. We had hardly crossed the yard before we heard the cry.

'Will!'

Long and loud it rang out!

Fieldy ran out of a doorway wearing an apron and covered in ink! He leapt through the air into Will's arms and they embraced. He put a hand out for me and ruffled my hair.

'Tom! What brings you both?' he asked, standing back and looking at us with admiration. We explained about the horses and told him how we thought we would come to the big smoke and seek out our friend.

'How did you find me?'

We told him about Ponsonby and what a strange reception we had, and Fieldy beckoned us into the print room. 'Shh! This is not a Stratford paddock. London walls have ears,' he said.

Inside we saw the great press and the plates he had been inking up. All around our heads hung sheets of uncut pages, drying and displaying their beautiful text. Will looked all around; awestruck and excited, he breathed in the smells of ink, wood, paper and vellum.

'Ponsonby thought we were spies,' said Will, gently reading the suspended pages.

'Surely!'

'Spying what?'

'They still search the printers of the Jesuit's text.'

'Is Ponsonby a Papist?' asked Will.

'No, Will. But how many people in England do you think know how to use one of those?' said Fieldy, pointing at the press.

Will shrugged.

'About forty people and, of those forty, how many do you think can leave no trace of what they printed?'

Will nodded, now a touch wiser

'Ten,' said Fieldy.

'So every printer knows,' Will uttered quietly.

'How come he's not been betrayed?' I asked.

Will looked to me. 'Guilt by knowledge and association.'

Then he looked back to Fieldy. 'Is William Hartley one of them?'

'Will!' snapped Fieldy, this time really vexed.

'I hear there is a trial tomorrow of …?'

'Enough! God in heaven's name, stay away from that!'

A man entered the room and stood by the press holding a spanner. I nudged Fieldy.

'He is friend,' sighed Fieldy, giving a nod in the man's direction, who then turned to the press and started to make adjustments.

'The morrow I will to Westminster Hall … to see King Henry's sword,' declared Will.

'It's in the Abbey, and do not go there at all! Tom, do us both a favour, and take him to Shoreditch instead.'

'What's in Shoreditch?'

'Yes what, Dickie?' said Will.

'They have built a new playhouse, Will.'

'A house just for plays?'

Fieldy nodded and we both saw Will taken. Hopefully, this would distract him from Westminster Hall.

'Sure tis not just a yard for drinking, whoring or bear-baiting, only serving the occasional play?' asked Will suspiciously.

'Just plays!' stated Fieldy, quite emphatically.

'Well, that will be a dream come true. We will all go – old friends to the car of Thespie!'

He clapped his hands and, putting his arms around Fieldy and I, gripped us hard, seeming both happy and distracted.

'Afternoon.'

'What?'

'Plays are in the afternoon.'

'This afternoon then!'

'I have to work.'

'Then Tom and I will go.'

'Good,' said a relieved Fieldy.

We all smiled.

'But still to Westminster the morrow,' he added.

Fieldy pulled away.

'Stay away, no good can come!' he said. 'I've seen the busy sight on the hill by Posterngate. Believe me, ignorance is bliss.'

Fieldy then looked to the man adjusting the press and whispered to Will, 'If you must, talk with him. He will tell you all you need to know. Just keep away from the hall. Now I have beds to ink before Mr Bishop returns from his lunch.'

I looked at Will and nudged him to take our leave.

'Shoreditch, come Will,' I said.

'Stay at my rooms, if you will,' said Fieldy,'

'Where?' I asked.

'Above Ponsonby,' smiled Fieldy.

I laughed. The irony was not lost on me.

'How do we find Shoreditch?' I asked.

'Go east, down Cheapside, Bishopsgate, then Bishopsgate Street to Shoreditch. You'll find it,' said Fieldy, picking up his inking pad.

The man adjusting the press looked at us and smiled as we left. Will wanted to stop and talk to him but I pressed him on. It was an educational walk down Cheapside seeing all the different trades and people rushing around the city. At Bishopsgate itself we took a bit of a shudder; Will subtly pointed out a sight accompanied by a foul stench and the monotonous song of blowfly. From their inopportune vantage point above the gate, some rascals' decapitated heads leered down at us with worm-ridden eye sockets.

'Welcome to London,' said Will, as we moved swiftly on.

CHAPTER 25

We arrived at Shoreditch and there was quite a throng surrounding not one but two playhouses – each about a furlong apart. One was called 'The Theatre' and the other – near a street called Curtain Close – was called 'The Curtain', sensibly enough.

The play was about to start in The Curtain. We paid a penny for seats rather than a ha'penny to be with the riff-raff, or groundlings as they were referred to. The play got under way but it was a terrible bore. The actors were slow at recalling their lines and very poor at declaiming them. The humour was non-existent, the story incomprehensible and soon there were cat-calls from the groundlings. I looked to Will, who was sitting, arms folded and frowning.

'Enjoying the play?' I whispered.

'Get thee gone. Is this the best they can do?'

At that point there was, in the distance, quite a roar from the other theatre. Will noticed it, too. And when a third big roar went up, he nudged me in a hint to take our leave, which we did, as did others.

There was a very big noise coming from The Theatre so, approaching the doors, we became quite excited. However, the beggars had seen us coming and for arriving late it cost us a farthing over the normal penny.

'Here they come!' declaimed a man on stage.

'Yes, I am the thief behind the curtain!' the comic actor went on as we took a seat.

Everyone looked to Will, me and the other latecomers. It appeared this was a ruse of The Theatre to steal the audience from The Curtain. The actor, who was comically dressed and made up, pointed straight to us and addressed Will and I directly.

'Sirs! You are my new-found friends! I had a wager with my old friends, these poor and deprived groundlings, that, indeed, if we did cheer loud enough, you sirs, to this theatre, like ravens to a gibbet, would fly!'

Will stood up and bowed to the actor and he returned the compliment, which was followed by a great cheer and applause from all, myself included.

'Now we will begin our story! The famous victories of Henry V of England!'

He wielded his hand and an army of actors took to the stage and he his exit. The play that followed was certainly entertaining with some fine battle scenes; one in particular I have a notion may have got out of hand at one point. Some parts of the play did sag and falter but then the funny man would come on and play sorcerer to the audience and bring the temperament up once more.

At the end, we all gave a rousing applause and cheered the actors hard. Will was in his element, without a doubt. He looked as if he would never stop applauding or take his leave.

'What do you think?' I shouted above the noise of applause and cheers.

'Good, good. Never seen such a blossom of play and zeal,' he shouted back.

Then he nudged me. 'I can do better!' he grinned, and left while everyone was still standing and cheering.

I followed as Will left the theatre and made his way to the back of the staging part of the building. He rapped sharply at the door. It was opened by a young boy about fourteen years old.

'Can I serve thee?' he asked.

'I would talk with the proprietor,' said Will.

'That would be Mr James Burbage, my father.'

'Burbage of Stratford?

'Yes.'

'We must speak!'

'If you insist.'

The boy ushered us in and we meandered through actors undressing, as they laughed, sparred and argued among the smells of body, wine and facepaint.

'I'll warn,' the boy said. 'He's in a foul mood.'

'But the theatre is full. Surely …'

'He has had a request to tour the provinces, from the secretary of state himself.'

'So why the foul mood?' I wondered out loud.

'For "request", read "instructed",' Will whispered.

We saw the funny man, or clown they called him. Will stopped briefly and shook his hand.

'Thank you, thank you. A fine performance,' said Will with a smile.

The clown was quite affable. 'I am obliged to you, young sir – Richard Tarlton.'

'And I you, for such mirth and command – William Shakespeare.'

'Anon,' he said with a bow, and we carried on.

We were taken to a small room where Mr Burbage sat, counting coin and entering it into a ledger with a clerk. As we entered, he put the bag of coin into a strong box and the clerk closed the ledger.

'Speak!' he said, without looking up.

'Two men of Stratford would talk with you, Father.'

'Thank you, Richard,' he said, and young Richard left.

'Sir, you are a Stratford man?' said Will, by way of greeting.

'What of it?'

'Family by birth?'

'Yes, yes, brother Henry. Speak! What do you want?' said Burbage looking up and giving us a sour once-over.

'I wish to be employed here, Sir,' said Will with somewhat over-confident self-assurance.

'Do you?' said Mr Burbage and then he stood waiting, for what I wasn't sure.

'Sir?' said Will, puzzled.

'You been schooled?' Burbage snapped.

'King Edward's in Stratford.'

'When did you leave?'

'Three years since.'

'University?'

Will sniggered. 'Oh, no, Sir.'

'What's funny?' asked Burbage pointedly.

This was not going well. Will was embarrassed.

'You haven't been to university, so you can't write plays for me. What can you do?'

'Direct players, Sir.'

Mr Burbage took a deep breath and turned to the clerk. 'Why does every half-educated idiot think they can salvage their life by directing players?'

'Beats me, Sir,' agreed the clerk, tutting.

'Richard!' shouted Mr Burbage.

Richard appeared at the door. 'Show these ... boys out!'

Well, that was a shock and a wake-up call. At the door Richard was just about to close it when he looked at the somewhat-shattered Will.

'Father likes a reputation. Make a reputation for yourself and you will never find greater loyalty in this business.'

The door closed. We turned around and were about to walk away when I saw the man who adjusted the press at John Bishop's.

'Did you enjoy the play?' he asked with a smile.

'We did,' said Will.

'But you did not enjoy the audience with the proprietor?' The man grinned again.

'I don't believe we..?' pondered Will.

'John Hewitt, but you can call me Weldon.'

We shook hands and I went to introduce ourselves but he bid us not. He knew who we were.

'Burbage is an ill-tempered old beast but he is an honest trader who hides a heart of gold beneath his dragon breath.'

'Indeed,' said Will.

'Night is falling and I am hungry,' Weldon declared and we nodded in agreement.

Weldon signalled that we follow him. There were a lot of inns on this road but Weldon seemed to know exactly which one he was headed for. We entered an inn called the White Hart and he went straight to a quiet alcove at the rear.

'The food is good here and I am known, so it is safe.'

'Safe from what? I asked.

'Unfamiliar eyes and ears.'

Will and I sat down a little perplexed as a maid bought a jug of beer and three cups.

'This is not Stratford or Lancashire,' said Weldon quietly.

We looked at him intently.

'Things tolerated there are not tolerated here,' he said.

We both realised we had been somewhat innocent about the state of toleration and Popery.

'I heard you mention Bill Hartley,' said Weldon.

'Yes, I met him with ...' started Will but Weldon quickly raised his hand to suggest no mention of names or places.

'A kind man and he and his ... friend. They admired my work,' said Will.

'You write?'

Will nodded.

'Well, if those two men admired your work, your day will come and, when it does, it will certainly be,' said Weldon clearly impressed.

'Be what?' I asked, but Weldon and Will would only smile.

'Bill taught me all I know about printing. Alas, now he languishes in Marshelsea, as we speak.'

'Marshelsea?' I asked.

'Prison,' whispered Will.

Weldon asked for food and it was duly brought: ham, cheese and oysters and an orange. Ever concerned about money, I expressed concern as to cost but Weldon insisted he would pick up the reckoning, so I picked up an oyster.

'His friend?' asked Will.

'The Tower, and I, too, would advise against the morrow.'

Will thought for a moment. ''Tis a trial. There is chance of justice,' he wondered aloud.

Weldon looked at us and started to peel the orange with a singular sense of purpose. 'Reckon?' he said, breaking the peeled orange.

Will and I looked at each other, and then Weldon spoke again.

'Trial's a sham. If the Virgin Mother were on the stand, this hall of justice could get a conviction for whoring,' he said sarcastically.

I have to add that at this time, whilst I was eating and enjoying some much-needed supper, I was distinctly uneasy about the company and the discussions. I cared for none of it one way or another, moral coward I might be, but in this life I seek only to earn my way and live a common existence. My dear friend was different and all knowledge he drank like a thirsty horse, sucking into his belly gallon upon gallon of the invigorating waters.

'There was a public disputation, which I attended,' said Weldon.

'How?' asked a curious Will.

'Serving clerk, of one at court,' he uttered guardedly.

'Who?' persisted Will in a whisper.

Again Weldon said nothing. He looked Will straight in the eye, handed us each a third of the peeled orange, and then spoke. 'Though physically he was a sorry sight from his wracking, I did see him stand four long hours, barely able to lift his wrenched arms. Despite being denied paper, pen, chair or table, did he run rings around his tormentors?

'He showed their pretence at learning to be little short of the babbling nonsense of foolish clowns. Though amusing, I realised this joust procured him a fate that was sealed in all but process. And that will be this morrow coming when Crown and State will, indeed, reveal what what is, is.'

He popped sweet segments of orange into his mouth, to work against the bitterness of this tale. Will pondered the words of Weldon and poured some more beer, as did I. We three sat and drank in silence for a while, till Weldon spoke once more. 'Settle the reckoning I will, then be away. You stay with Richard?'

'Yes,' I said. We shook his hand warmly.

'Make way before the inns close. All the riff-raff, vagabonds and madmen take to the streets in that hour,' he said and bid us goodbye.

In the end, I was sad to see him go, a man of great courage and sentiment. Will and I shared another jug of ale, then we made our way back to Fieldy's digs. The walk was fine and event-free but falling into the streets were many men thick with drink. Sure as Weldon's words, by the time we rapped on Fieldy's door, the sound of the streets had changed. No longer industrious men going about their business, now the streets were filled with the sound of baying dogs in search of lame foals. We were, indeed, glad to be on the correct side of an iron-studded oak door. Fieldy had a small room above the Ponsonby shop, which was, I think, doubling up as storage room, for it was full of books.

'Penny a week,' said Fieldy as he pushed his possessions off the bed so that we could all fit into it.

A small high-set window in the roof let a thin beam of moonlight drift its soft hue across the room. I sat with Fieldy, telling him about the plays and how we were duped from one theatre to another. He was amused, since he had had neither time nor coin to visit a playhouse.

'I am off to sleep. I will be at the works at the fifth hour,' Fieldy finally announced as he sleepily slipped into the bed.

'Me, too. Will, we are back to Chiswick and from there to Stratford without refreshment. I suggest we all sleep?'

Ever in pursuit of erudition, Will continued to read the stored books by the light of the single moonbeam. I ignored him and, in two short breaths, was in the bed falling into a deep sleep.

I was nudged awake at the fifth hour by Fieldy, who was up, dressed and putting away the dozen or so books that Will had made use of throughout the night.

'Will is gone, Tom,' he uttered in consternation.

I sat up quick. 'No!' I started.

'Tom, I have to work and leave you to our friend,' said Fieldy apologetically.

'Yes, yes, I … umm, Dicky, my britches?'

'They are heavy?' he noted, handing them to me.

'Heavy with Lord Lucy's profit.'

'How much?'

'Thirty-five pounds,' I said, wiping the sleep from my eyes.

'You been walking around with thirty-five pounds on your person?'

'Yes,' I said, buttoning up my jerkin.

'You are a brave man.'

'Or foolish,' I replied.

'No, brave; fool is out there and you have to find him.'

We left the little lodgings but were headed in different directions.

'Tom, Will and you, together or separate, always welcome in my lodgings. Never take a room in an inn.'

'Thank you, Dick,' I said and we shook hard and embraced.

'Keep our friend out of trouble; he has a nose for it.'

'I will,' I said and we parted, he to the printers and I to Blackfriars wharf.

I asked the boatmen if a lone young man had taken a boat to Westminster but they all said no. Wondering what to do, I bought bread and cheese from a street trader for a farthing and sat on the wharf munching it. Did I dare get a boat to Westminster or should I just say to hell with my selfish friend and journey back to Chiswick, on to Stratford and never look back?

The choice was never in question. I could not abandon him; he was my friend, albeit a foolish one.

Eventually, I braved myself and took a boat to the Westminster pier. The boatman asked no question and I sat on the bow and paid him no attention. I disembarked giving him two pennies, and, seeing a thin but certain crowd heading in one particular direction, I followed. Outside the great hall of Westminster, there was a thick gathering with mounted horsemen parading in and around the waiting throng.

I was just wandering towards what I assumed was the main entrance to the hall, when I was suddenly grabbed from behind. It was quite an act. Before I had time to scream, resist or even see who my assailants were, I was launched into a carriage. I thudded into the seat and a rapier was instantly held at my throat. The carriage was solid with heavy curtains. I looked to where a smart young man sat gripping the weapon. Next to him sat a tall and imperious woman whom I recognised at once as Lady Montague. Another man on her other side leant forward and searched me. He pulled out my letter from Lord Lucy and handed it to Her Ladyship.

'No weapon, Ladyship. Fair amount of coin sewn in that waistband,' he said.

Her Ladyship looked at the letter and then handed it back to me.

'Glad you did not use my letter to come here. Is it safe?'

'Yes, Your Ladyship,' I replied sheepishly.

There was silence as she thought what to say as she was certainly angry.

'What in heaven's name are you doing here?' she finally demanded, visibly distracted but with a tone of relief.

'Put up your sword,' she whispered to the man.

'I am looking for Will,' I said, adjusting my attire.

'William is here?' she exclaimed.

She turned to her swordsmen but both kept eyes on me.

'Find him. He's young. He'll be on his own.'

The swordsman jumped out of the carriage and slammed the door.

'Why are you carrying so much money?' she asked.

'I've been trading horses for Lord Lucy, Ladyship. It is his coin.'

'And you go gallivanting around this city with it stitched to your person?'

I nodded shamefully.

She smiled. 'Clever; not such a big a fool as your friend.'

The door opened and in leapt the swordsman.

'Ladyship, just saw him enter the hall,' he said sitting back down.

'Sure?' she asked.

'Skinny young man on his own, dressed like he doesn't have a pot to piss in, clutching a book.'

'That's him,' I said.

'Where are your horses?'

'Chiswick.'

'Boys, take me to the west entrance. I will get out there. Take this man to Chiswick and return directly.'

The swordsman stepped out, leapt up with the driver and in an instant, we were moving. She leant forward slightly and looked me in the eye.

'You, young man, will wait in Chiswick for your friend, whilst I see he stays out of danger,' she stated with an impressive degree of authority.

At what I assumed was the western entrance, we stopped and a footman opened the carriage door. Her Ladyship disembarked and was greeted by a man whom I took to be important, on account of his silken embroidered coat, with a gold chain heavy enough to pay a king's ransom.

The carriage door shut and once more we were off. It was quite a long journey to Chiswick. Try as I might to engage my 'companion' with conversation, he smiled kindly but not once did he utter a single word. At Chiswick the carriage slowed. The man drew back the curtain and, seeing the inn behind which were the paddocks with our horses, I pointed. The man banged the top of the carriage and stuck his hand out pointing to the inn.

We pulled up. The swordsman hopped down and opened the carriage door for me. I have to say, as guards go, they seemed most cordial – though not people you would want to cross swords with. I stepped out. They bowed, smiled, doffed their hats and left.

I went to the livery at the back of the inn, gathered our tack and bags and whistled for Orlando. He responded and galloped hightail across the paddock with Moot not far behind.

I took the chance to give them a good feed and a groom, ready for the journey home. I settled the reckoning with the innkeeper and wondered what I would do next. Sitting on the road outside the inn watching for the carriage to return, I realised it had been a long journey. So, back again and out once more would be some hours. It might be nightfall before Will returned. I was worrying whether he may turn up at all, when I saw him walk up the road from the river wharf. He walked towards me and, despite holding his head high and standing strong, looked ashen-faced, sad and heartbroken.

'I am sorry,' he uttered quiet and dry.

'Forgiven,' I said, forcing a smile.

'I had to …' he said trying to explain, but his eyes welled up red and teary.

'No need to tell me now. We have a long ride,' I said, putting my hand on his shoulder and squeezing it gently.

We mounted up and rode. Just as we passed Acton village and on the Oxford Road, however, blow me, it started to rain. Not a downpour that forced us to take cover, just a solid drizzle that made the journey cold and horrible.

At Beaconsfield, we gave up and took cover in the inn. We did not bother with an upstairs bed as they had a small smithy at the back of their modest livery and the fire was going a storm. We dried off and slept with the horses, all for tuppence each, including feed for the horses and bread and pottage for us. Will had still not said a word and, though I was used to his long periods of quiet, where he would stare into infinity for an aeon, this time it was long, deep and very intense. What had happened back at Westminster Hall I did not know but it had undeniably been affecting.

Around midnight, the weather cleared and there was a bright moon, so I woke Will and suggested we move on. Dawn rose just before Oxford, and on the west Wycombe Road we took a rest at Stokenchurch. The horses were tired and in need of some feed, water and grazing. As we watered the horses at the village trough, Will spoke for the first time in almost a day.

'There never was greater determination to convict a more innocent man, Tom.'

'Condemned to death?'

'With two compatriots, to be hung, drawn and quartered nine days from today.'

'God take their souls, Will.'

'For sure. That's a horrible death, Tom.'

'It is, Will. Did you meet with Her Ladyship?'

'Lady Montague entered as I reached the door of the great hall and she … joined me … I sat with her and her compatriot. Whom he was I don't know. Her Ladyship said nothing the entire time.'

'She is a good friend to you, Will.'

Will nodded with a touch of humiliation. Truth was, I did not know what to say. I was just a simple boy of Equus and a yearling in this great land. For others, the pursuit of power, position and influence was the sole carriage of their life. Is it so bad to ignore things which one cannot affect, in any way shape or form?

'Remember him that night?' said Will.

'In Hoghton? I do indeed,' I replied, making up a meagre feedbag for the horses. I handed one to Will for Moot.

'When I saw him yesterday, he was wretched. Barely able to stand and smell he did, probably not been near a basin since his capture. He was weak and worn; they had crushed his body as best they could without taking his life. But plague to them, his spirit lay undiminished, stronger than ever. He answered back all their accusations with the speed and dexterity of a swallow in flight around the eaves.

'All present thought the absurd and scurrilous charge of treason would surely fall. Then they bought in this man, witness they said, to his plot to assassinate our queen. This man, a poet and play writer too, no less. Anthony Munday was his name. I watched his eyes dart around not only to see who would witness him, but also to take direction. His testimony was comic in the realms of Tarlton! But it was sufficient for the jury.'

'I am sorry, Will. He was a good man. Any honest man could see that.'

Will looked to me despondently, and said: 'In condemning us, you condemn all your own ancestors, all our ancient bishops and kings, all that was once the glory of England – the island of saints, and the most devoted child of the See of Peter.

'That's what he said when they condemned him to death.'

We rode on, Will letting Moot follow me so as to read his book. We passed through Oxford, which Will barely noticed, reading all the way without looking up. Even stopping for two turnpikes and required to show my letter, he still read on. We made it to Stratford halfway through the following day. Clopping into the livery, we were greeted by Grace and, unexpectedly, Anne Hathaway with her brother Bartholomew, who, though pleased to see us, looked somewhat out of sorts. We dismounted, and I took both horses to the trough.

Will approached Anne tentatively. It was heart-warming to see them struggle with the need to embrace, their inner truths not yet declared. They held back, taut, like a storm-cloud holds its charge, waiting for a suitable point on which to alight and release its dazzling strike.

'William, how are you?' said Anne softly, with a slight stammer and simultaneously shedding a tear.

'As well as the world allows. But you, I cannot say same. What is with thee?' asked Will as he picked a single tear from her cheek with his finger.

'Our father is dead four days,' said Bartholomew, who, though only a couple of years older than Anne, had all the deportment of an austere and aged uncle.

'Dear Richard! My sorrow and God rest his soul,' uttered Will.

Reaching out, he took hold and squeezed Anne and her brother's hands.

'We have just returned the cartage used to convey his body to his internment,' said Bartholomew.

'My friends, my sorrow to both of you,' whispered Will, releasing Bartholomew's hand, but not Anne's.

Bartholomew cleared his throat and Anne pulled her hand from Will's.

'And you, William, tired you are I can see, but there is something else, am I right?' asked Anne looking deep into his eyes.

Will, too, looked into her eyes, but he said nothing.

'Our stepmother is attendant on us, my sister,' stated Bartholomew rather formally. 'We must take our leave. These two travellers have only just arrived and surely need rest and food.'

'Yes, of course,' said Anne with a smile that remained attached to Will.

'Sister, please take my purse and reckon the account with Miss Wickham,' demanded Bartholomew, clearing his throat.

'Yes, brother, of course,' she said, putting out her hand without moving her eyes.

Bartholomew sighed and put his purse in her hand.

Anne went inside with Grace to settle the reckoning. I took the tack off the horses whilst Nym Granger gave them feed and a brush. Bartholomew approached Will, gripping his hands with sweaty reticence. 'Master Shakespeare?' he asked tentatively.

'Sir,' smiled Will.

'My stepmother tells me my sister has affection for thee, and I would see her in exultation, not agony, does thee ...?'

'Have affection for your sister, Mr Hathaway?' interrupted Will quite softly.

'I should not ask, but I do, out of the affection I have for my sister.'

'Yes, I do,' said Will.

Bartholomew nodded formally, gripping his coat like a nervous vicar trying to display his authority. 'In that case, mother

... stepmother, asks me to say, you are free to call at Hewlands whenever you wish, Sir,' he declared. 'With either I or my stepmother in attendance, of course.'

'Of course,' said Will.

Anne came out of the stables, crossed the yard and, handing back her brother's purse, she took her brother's arm.

'Thank you, Tom. Your aunt was most obliging, for which my brother and I are grateful. We shall now take our leave.'

She cast her eyes back to Will, who bowed long and deep to her.

'My prayers for your father, Miss Anne,' said Will.

'Thank you and I hope your journey is ended well.'

'Journeys end in lovers meeting, a very wise man's son did say,' said Will.

Anne shied away, covering her blushing face; Bartholomew cleared his throat; and they both turned and left.

Will put his hand on my shoulder and squeezing it, he whispered,

Oft have I railed against love in many ways,
But pardon love I honour now thy power:
For were my Palace Greek Pyramids,
Cupid should there erect a stately bower.
And in my Palace sing his sugared songs,
And Venus doves myself will finely feed:
And nurse her sparrows and her milk white Swans.
Yea, in my restless bosom should they breed.
And thou dear Lady sacred and divine,
Shalt have thy place within my heart assigned:
Thy picture yea thy fiery darting eien,
I'll carry painted in my grieved mind.
The chief's coulters shall be scarlet blood,
Which Cupid pricketh from my woeful heart:
And tears coming shall further forth my good,
To paint thy glories according their desert.
I now am changed from what I want to be,
Cupid is God, And there is none but he.

Gosh! That quite set me aback, such poise and elegance could dear Will recite a poem.

'Did you write that?'

'No! Thomas Watson,' he sighed.

'You men must have need of food,' called Grace.

Will and I both turned to Grace and grinned. We were as hungry as a road-worn army.

'I have fresh bread, spicy roast rooks and greens.'

Heaven-sent Grace, always there to care and love.

'Will, you must stay and eat for sure but your family you must go and see forthwith. They long for your news.'

'And I, too, my family, Grace.'

We ate and over the meal Will intimated concern about his predicament of no employment. He knew the pressure to return to the glove shop would be high. I could also see the impending fate of Campion was also weighing heavy on his mind.

'Grace, do my parents know of the fate of … the Jesuit?'

'I believe so, Master Shakespeare, though I try not to concern myself with such affairs.'

Will nodded knowingly and carried on eating.

'I must go to Charlecote,' I thought aloud.

'His steward comes each day at four and asks of thee,' said Grace.

'All the more reason I should go to him,' I said.

After we had eaten, I went to Charlecote on a fresh horse and Will to Henley Street, on foot.

I rendered my coin to the steward, who entered it in the ledger and was duly impressed. Cornall came in, making his presence known, and I noticed he had a woman playing his shadow, a fat little dumpling with a face like a bowl of sour milk. I signed and returned my now very-worn letter from His Lordship. I looked up and, out of the corner of my eye, caught them touching hands and whispering, her squished little eyes darting from Orlando to me. So, Cornall had found himself a woman, and they, I suspect, probably had an eye on the livery position. I was walking across the yard and about to mount up for home when His Lordship rode in on Rafsaan.

'Wickham! I have missed your reckoning. How did you do?'

'A profit of twenty-five pounds, Your Lordship,' I said.

'Good, very good.'

He dismounted and a stable boy took Rafsaan away.

'Most agreeable mount I ever had, can't remember where I found him,' he mused as the ever-handsome Rafsaan was led away.

I would love to have reminded the pompous bastard. Not only did he know; he also knew I knew! Besides, there are more important things in life: a roof, food and dry beds.

'Oh well, good, good. Well, back to work, sure your aunt has need of you.'

'As pleases you, My Lord,' I said, as he walked away.

Riding out I noticed a new long drive was being constructed to the rear of the house. It looked like they were turning the house to face the other direction. It certainly did add a certain grandness.

CHAPTER 26

In the following days I settled back into livery routine: haulage, horse delivery and pickup. Such old hands we were, it revolved like a well-greased wagon wheel. I did, however, warn Grace about Cornall, his woman and the possible consequences.

'I had noticed as much, but thought best not to trouble you,' she said. 'As long as this place runs as true as a bow-man's shaft, there is little they can do.'

The Shakespeare household was a dismal place in the days before Campion's time of execution. Will returned to assisting his father. His particular talent was pattern-cutting, and his hand was as placed and as mathematically precise as an astronomer mapping the universe.

I was walking horses down Rother Street when I noticed an agitated John Shakespeare striding along wearing his work apron, which was unusual. I thought little more of it. I tied off my charges at the trough and waited for pick-up, which came soon enough. I was walking back to Ely Street when again I saw John Shakespeare walking back to Henley Street, anxious and in a determined stride. Passing the Sadlers' bakery I had a notion to drop in.

'Master Wickham, glad to see you,' said Judith as I entered.

I tilted my head and raised an eyebrow.

'William is missing,' she whispered like it was some state secret.

'Since when?' I asked, slightly irritated that no one had told me.

Hamnet come through with a sack of flour. 'Two days,' he said.

Now I was angry. I said nothing and left the shop. I knew exactly where he was. I ran back to Ely Street as fast as I could. I entered the gate and standing in the middle of the yard was Grace.

'John Shakespeare is looking for William. Have you seen him?'

'Can you cover me for two days, Grace?'

'Yes.'

'Nym!' I shouted.

'Sir!'

'Orlando, I need him ready to ride!'

'He's gone to Tyburn, hasn't he?' whispered Grace.

I looked at her and said nothing.

'Go, find him. I'll keep cover,' she said.

I rushed inside and picked up a cloak and my medicine kit. Nym had Orlando saddled and ready to go. I pulled the knife out and unstitched the medicine pouch. I took out Lady Montague's letter, which Grace took from me and briefly read.

'Where did you get this?' asked Grace, quite shocked.

'She gave it to me,' I said.

'If His Lordship …'

We both looked at each other and said nothing as I put it in my jerkin.

Under the hour, I was on the road to Oxford and from there to London. This was normally two days hard ride. I had half a day and one night. I did it, but how I don't know. I remember little of the journey, other than Orlando lost a shoe the far side of Oxford near West Wycombe. At midnight it started to rain hard. We had both been walking a while. I had worn out my boots and my feet were sore and bloody.

At a small hamlet, under an open barn, an old man sat in chair watching the rain. His face was worn and devoid of expression, his smile having been consumed by his weathered skin a hundred years ago. Seeing our plight, he waved us into a smithy, next to where he sat. The fire was burning low but still had some heat.

'Thee up late,' I said by way of greeting.

'Expecting,' he said.

'Whom you expecting?'

'Death,' he said.

'Whose?' I asked foolishly.

'Mine, but no visit this night,' he sighed.

'Thee a smithy?' I asked exhausted.

The man shook his head.

'Son, sleeping,' he said, pointing to a cottage nearby.

He looked at my sore and bloody feet, and then to the state of Orlando.

'Follow,' he said.

Raising his weary body from his chair, he walked to the rear and went to a cupboard. Opening it, he shuffled methodically through some jars.

'Thee need to rest a while, mend feet. Feed, heal, then travel,' he said, pausing at a pot of ointment and taking it from the shelf.

I shook my wet and exhausted head and mustered a smile.

'Cannot, must go. I have a friend in grave trouble.'

The old man looked at me.

'Wife, law or State?' he said pointing to my bloody feet, and then threw me the ointment, which I caught.

'State,' I said in a singular tone looking him straight in the eye.

With his weathered hand, the old man gestured to me to use the ointment, and, as I slowly peeled off my boots, he went out the back.

I had just finished pasting the green, sweet and herbal-smelling ointment on my feet and was wondering what he was up to when he re-appeared. He was leading a saddled-up standard bred and threw me a pair of boots, which I also caught.

'Get thee on thy calling. When thee return, thy horse be shoed and rested.'

I smiled and went to thank him profusely but he merely waved me be gone, so be gone I was. Into the night I galloped, thankful for the rain in retreat, a fresh horse and soothed feet.

I approached the village of Tyburn about a half-hour before dawn and silhouetted against the dawn was the scaffold. Village of Tyburn, they called it, though no one lived here. Only a mad man would. The place stank of death and rotting flesh; and there were puddles of stale and congealed blood. The only morning birdcall was that of hungry ravens waiting to scavenge their next meal.

A small brook, where horses watered, was so close to the scaffold it must have run with blood on a busy day. I could not believe what a morass of death I had walked into; the only sound in my head was a thousand screaming souls. The scaffold, or the tree as they called it, was a big affair, triangular, permanent, and built with knowledgeable purpose. There was a fireplace built beside which was being fed and stoked as two men hoisted a large cauldron of water on to it. The sun burst through the leafless trees and various people started to gather in the surrounding mud. I looked around for Will. I could not see him but the light was still poor.

'Mind your horse for a penny, Sir?' said a small voice.

I looked down and there was a small barefooted boy in the most pathetic excuse for clothing I had ever seen.

'Mind it for a halfpenny, Sir,' said another little guttersnipe, equally poorly clothed.

I dismounted as other boys rushed up to enter the horse-minding auction. I went to the first boy. 'You were first and I'll give you tuppence' I said.

The other boys all groaned but in a second rushed off to the next horseman.

I tied my horse off to a post for the boy was too small to control him. 'Stay with him – no feed, no water,' I said.

'Well handled,' said a voice.

I turned around. There was a young man in a white doublet and dark hose. 'You kin?' he asked.

'No, but I search my kin.'

'You not local?'

'Warwick,' I said quietly.

He nodded. I gently put out my hand to shake. The man imperceptibly shook his head.

'No names, no introductions, today,' he whispered, throwing a subtle glance around.

To our right there was a growing noise of traffic, and the man turned to its direction. He crossed himself, reached into his doublet and pulled out a rosary, kissed it and went towards the approaching throng. What happened next was strange. It was like the snatches of visions and memories I had from Puca's tincture, but a dark side. Here the tincture was death, driven by the crushing force of a State that masqueraded in a blank mask of false justice.

In the distance the traffic approached from London. Down the Tyburn road came horsemen, people, cries, tears and moans; drawn to it were more people. I was starting to wonder if, indeed, I had been stupid and Will was not here. I looked hither and thither, desperately inspecting every face twice to convince myself it was not Will. Every rear view I queried. Was it his shape? Then, as the crowd gathered and moved in unison, I noticed a figure standing alone. The increasing crowd was buffeting the figure as it moved in reverse with the approaching cortège of militia and its associated retinue.

I ran over and, in no time I, too, was consumed by the crowd – a strange random mixture of sensation seekers, officials and the devoted. We jostled in the mud as the cortege approached. I reached the figure; it was indeed Will. I grabbed him and he immediately grabbed my arm clenching it tight. He did not turn; he knew it was me.

We both watched as the horses dragged three fence hurdles past us, to which were strapped the poor wretches for execution. The only one I recognised was the holy father, Edmund Campion. He was a sorry state compared with the last time I saw him – battered, shredded and beaten, he looked almost too exhausted to die.

Jammed between the swaying people, we were picked up and moved about by the crowd as it pressed forward like a herd of worried horses. The motion stopped and we all swayed softly in front of the scaffold as would a sea of lost souls, lapping at the side of a doomed ship.

The wretches were dragged up to the scaffold and they were joined by the man whom both Will and I recognised at once: Richard Topcliffe. As the three men stood, they were violently stripped naked and ropes placed around their necks whilst Topcliffe read out their names and warrants. The other two were priests called Sherwin and Briant. Once more, Topcliffe's vocal cords cut the air – yes, I knew that voice!

'Hopefully, this will remind your Pope, that first bishop of the synagogue of Satan, that the excommunication of our queen was a mistake!'

'My queen, your queen. I pray for her,' called Campion.

Topcliffe waved to the executioners and the naked bodies were hauled aloft.

Silence engulfed Will and I; motion slowed to the most definitive detail. We wanted to look away but being there made us strange co-conspirators to this savage act and we had to watch. The men struggled with their dignity but, as the pain took over, they kicked and struggled on their ropes. Topcliffe gave another signal; the executioners grabbed the men's genitals and, with a single wipe of a knife, they cut them off and cast them aside. Struggling to suppress a retching in my gullet, I was frozen to the spot! There were gasps of sickness from the crowd. As the bleeding men struggled on their ropes, the gripping pain was soul-numbing in its truth.

After what seemed an interminable time of suffering, Topcliffe gave another signal and once more the executioners stepped forward. This time with swords and with the flash of the sun catching their blades, they opened the men's stomachs and spewed bright, glistening scarlet blood across the grey and white hues that surrounded. Their innards fell to the ground like bloody wet cord and were scooped up and launched into the cauldron. Yet still the tragic figures struggled at the end of their ropes.

Their movements became weaker, another signal, and the men were cut down and, upon falling to the floor, were decapitated most savagely. There was a parting in the crowd and the man I had seen earlier, his white doublet now covered in blood and his face as white as his doublet had been, staggered away from the scaffold. Sound started to reappear in my head with mutterings of the Hail Mary.

Will and I stared dazed and aghast at the three heads laying there on the scaffold awash with blood. Half-naked executioners stepped forward and hacked up the remaining bodies, throwing the body parts into the cauldron. An arm severed and flung into the cauldron caught on the lip. Bubbling water and flames charring the fingers gave the limb a twitching motion, rendering a foul image of someone clawing at the edge of hell itself.

Suddenly Topcliffe looked in our direction and he certainly recognised us, but it seemed he could not remember from where. He turned away and spoke to a soldier but before he could look back to us, I grabbed opportunity by the throat and pulled Will away.

I whisked Will to my horse very smartly and, grabbing the gutter snipe, I showed him a shilling. 'You never saw us.'

He nodded once and snatched the coin. 'Take the Oxford road,' he whispered, pointing with his chin to the trees.

Will and I leapt on the horse and together we made our getaway.

I looked back and could see the small boy giving the soldier wrong directions, which in turn the soldier gave to two horsemen who took off down Tyburn lane.

By the time we returned to the smithy it was a night and a day, for two up on the horse, we could only walk. For the entire ride all I could think of was Campion's naked disembowelled body and severed head. A man with whom we had supped, into whose bowl I had dipped my bread, and whose eloquent memory could recite text 300 years old. A man whose spirit had done nothing but to seek, soothe and understand.

I dismounted; Will too. We looked at each other for a few moments but what possibly could either of us say.

Will then looked to the horse. 'This is not your horse?' he declared, with utter banality.

'My horse,' said the smithy.

Will about-turned and faced the smithy, a middle-aged stocky man. I explained the story but he raised his hand to stop me. 'Shoeing your beast and loan of my horse, one shilling and sixpence.'

I took money from my purse and paid him.

'How is your father?' I asked.

'Dead, yesterday morning, sat in that chair there, he was.'

'Death has been busy these last few days,' I muttered as I put my purse away.

Two up on a thankfully rested Orlando, we headed home. However, just before Oxford, we were stopped at a turnpike by the military. We dismounted, nervous but also astounded that this was the first time we had been stopped. The soldiers seemed mostly taken up with the rabbit they were roasting over a really quite feeble fire.

'What'll we do, Tom,' whispered Will, as someone looking like the captain walked over.

'Leave it to me,' I whispered back.

The captain was quite well spoken. 'What name and business,' he said.

I bowed courteously, reached into my doublet and pulled out Lady Montague's letter. 'Sir,' I said presenting it.

The captain took the letter and read it, and, after a quick inspection to see if the seal was genuine, handed it back.

'Very good,' he said and went back to the pathetic warmth of the fire.

Well, that was easy, we thought as we re-mounted and carried on. Will put his hand into my jerkin and removed the letter. 'How did you get this?' he asked, surprised.

'You mean when?' I said.

'When then?'

'She gave it to me after Corpus Christi.'

'Why didn't you tell me?'

'What to tell? It's not as if you tell me everything, is it?' I said as Will pushed the letter back into my jerkin. 'At least I had it when we needed it.'

Will agreed. On we sauntered and he started to snooze on my shoulder. A few miles further on, I noticed there was a horse about four furlongs behind us. I did not think it was a robber because he kept a constant distance, but I did feel we were being followed.

'Will, wake up.' I said, prodding him.

'What?'

'Don't look. I think we have picked up a shadow.'

'What'll we do?'

'Pretend to look at Orlando's hoof and tell me what you see, about four furlongs behind us.'

Will took a look down at Orlando's hoof, this way and that, and straightened up. 'Yes, man on a horse, about four furlongs back. So?'

'He's been there the last hour. We're two-up. He should have passed us by now.'

'See what you mean. What'll we do?'

'Keep going for the moment, see what happens.'

About a half-hour later, we rounded a bend and there was a small hamlet. At a crossroads, as chance would have it, there was a bridge on which two boys sat with a horse. I broke into a trot and, to the surprise of Will and the boys on the bridge, I left the road and went into the shallow brook under the bridge. I leapt off Orlando.

'Stay here,' I said to a confused Will.

I ran up to the bridge and looking to see if our shadow had rounded the bend, which he hadn't, I held my last shilling up to the boys.

'Ride your horse two mile out and back again,' I asked.

No contest; they snatched the shiny shilling and were off. I grabbed a grass, shoved it in my mouth and lay on the bridge wall. With ears twitching, I waited and sure enough I heard our shadow round the corner. All I needed was Will and Orlando to stay as quite as a dead mouse. I heard the hooves break into a trot and approach rapidly, then stop beside me.

'I say,' said the rider.

I sat up and looked at the man on the horse. He seemed benign, noble but not wealthy I would guess. All I wanted was a good look at him and the brand on his horse's arse.

'Sir?' I said, shielding a non-existent sun from my eyes.

'Two chaps on a horse?'

I pointed in the direction the boys had taken off. The man looked down and, seeing the fresh hoof marks, carried on after them. I watched him go and committed to my memory the triple-diamond brand on the horse.

As soon as he was out of sight, I reckoned we had just enough time to make pace down the other road, which we did. I have no idea who the shadow was. I thought I had seen that brand before but could not remember where. Whoever it was, as far as I was concerned, was out of sight and out of mind and definitely out of our hair.

We reached the livery at daybreak, where a very anxious Grace awaited us. She approached me, took the horses and whispered frantically. 'He's here?'

'Who?' I whispered back.

It could not be the shadow, could it?

'Somerville!'

'Johnny!?' said Will, suddenly excited.

'In your bed; he turned up at midnight …' said Grace.

Will did not wait, he ran inside and up the treads to my bed.

Grace looked worried. 'Quite drunk he was, and sobbed about … that priest for most of the night. Thomas, get him away from here before His Lordship or stewards show up.'

'Grace, he's gone, believe me,' I said frantically and sprinted into the tack-room and up the treads, where Johnny launched himself at me.

'Tom, young Tom, I hear you were there, too! God in heaven!'

So soaked with drink he was, the inebriation was permanent. Gripping me hard in an embrace, his tears ran down my neck. 'Sorry,' he said releasing me, and wiping the snot from my collar.

'Johnny, who told you we were there?'

'What's it matter, Tom?' said Will, trying to support Johnny.

'Johnny?' I repeated.

'My old chum, Henry Walpole, was there. He told me about you and Will. He knew not who you were but I knew from his description, t'was you both!'

'We only just got back! Where were you?'

'Tom, Cuz is upset. Leave him alone.'

Johnny's drunken tone changed from sentimental to angry. 'It's that usurping queen that should be quartered!' he growled.

'Shut up!' I snapped, barely subduing my irritation.

There was the sound of hooves in the yard. My heart leapt. Grace's head appeared at the top of the treads. 'Cornall!'

'Get under the bedding and stay there!' I whispered angrily, pointing at them like naughty children.

I came out into the yard having stripped off my shirt and quickly smeared some saddle wax on my hands. 'Mr Cornall.'

'Mr Wickham, Miss Wickham.'

'Can we be of service?'

'We are short of feed at Charlecote.'

'How much you need?'

'Dozen crushed oats.'

'We have a dozen. I'll bring them over.'

'Obliged,' he said and thankfully departed.

I went back upstairs and called the all clear. Johnny and Will sheepishly appeared from under my bedding.

'Johnny, you cannot stay here,' I said.

'Father won't have him,' said Will.

'Pish, Johnny knows when he's not wanted.'

'Where's your horse?'

'In your stable, I think.'

'Sorry, Johnny. You have to go,' I sighed, with genuine remorse.

Johnny suppressed his drink-soaked tears, hugged Will, and then me and went downstairs.

'Wonderful Miss Wickham, could you possibly avail me of my steed,' we heard him say, his gentlemanly diction still raising a smile from us.

'Sorry, Will,' I said, exhausted or shamed; I could not rightly tell.

Will collapsed back on to my bed, stared at the ceiling and, with tears streaming from his eyes, he listened to the languid clip-clop of Johnny departing on his tired old nag. I gave myself occasion to contemplate the brand on the mount of our shadow. Was it Topcliffe? Or at Tyburn, Banbury, Chiswick? It was tantalisingly annoying, but I had seen it.

CHAPTER 27

In the following weeks, Will went to ground and spoke little of what had happened. I did not know how he had taken himself to Tyburn in the first place, but Johnny was definitely involved. The man in the white doublet, was he the Henry Walpole Johnny spoke of? Or was he the man that had followed us? I felt these were questions best left unanswered and so I just got on with work.

Slowly Will recovered, spending time out at Hewlands when he was not working for his father. I worked on but always with one eye out for a triple-diamond brand on any strange horse.

One late afternoon, I was by the river slow walking a lame horse when I saw Will sitting on the bank. I tied off the horse and sat next to my friend.

Will said nothing, just launched stones into the river. Suddenly he buried his head in his hands and then looked up. He gazed out across the river and spoke as if to the passing water.

'Is life but a walking shadow? A poor player, that struts and frets his hour upon the stage, and then is heard no more; is it a tale told by an idiot, full of sound and fury, signifying nothing?'

Will launched another stone. It flew heaven sent, then crashed into the water, shattering a reflected cloud into myriad fast-moving circles.

I rubbed his shoulder. 'Even shadows need a body from which to be begotten,' I said.

He turned to me and smiled. 'I was told the pen is mightier than the sword, but Topcliffe proved them wrong,' he said.

'How is Anne?' I asked.

Will threw another stone, creating a pattern of cross ripples to the ripples of the previous stone. 'Tom, I think I do love her.'

This was telling me what I already knew. I grinned kindly. 'So what is this thing called, love?' I asked.

'That's terrible,' he said with a giggle.

'At least I raised a smile from you. Is that not the point of poetry?'

Will said nothing and, elbows rested on his knees, he watched the sky like a cat looking to where it will leap. Then he stood up.

'Love is a smoke made with the fumes of sighs; Being purged, a fire sparkling in lover's eyes; Being vexed, a sea nourished with lovers' tears; What is it else? A madness most discreet, A choking gall, and a preserving sweet.'

'Is that Watson?' I asked, knowing full well it wasn't.

He looked to me and sighed heavily. 'No, it's Shakespeare.'

'Then like this river, let it flow,' I said, throwing a stick into the current and we watched it gently carried away.

Looking at each other, the tiredness of the last six months pulled on our souls, much like wet clothes from the heaviest rain.

'Lend me a bed this night, Tom?'

'Of course.'

Arms around one another, we walked the short walk to the livery and he lay in my rough bed of bag and straw. There we both slept till I woke and set about my chores. Will appeared the in yard at about the eighth hour.

'Good morning Tom, Grace.'

We had already been up since the sixth.

'There is bread on the table but I am afraid that is all,' said Grace.

'I have no hunger but thank you, Grace,' he replied.

'Will, I am off to Shottery for stock feed from Fulk Sandells. Do you wish to accompany me?'

Will smiled, 'Yes, I would like that.'

I shafted Heavens Gate into the sturdy old dung tup and we set off. It was hard for Will, passing through Wilmcote, his mother's lost paddocks and, worst of all, the unfinished house they lost in their financial mire.

Fulk was an elderly man, brash and with a humour as sharp as a young colt's kick and as wicked as a palfrey in season. His farmhouse was walled with a heavily gated yard; he kept a lot of feed which, to the resourceful thief, held as much value as hard coin.

The yard was in a lane between Shottery and Wilmcote.

'I do not know this place, Tom.'

'Does what he does and keeps clear from the rest,' I said.

I jumped off the cart and grabbed the heavy iron ring hanging on the great studded gate and banged it heartily. 'Fulkeee!' I called, and then banged some more. Still there was no sound.

'Early in the day, he does drink some of an evening.'

I banged some more on the gates, then more.

'Fulkee!'

'Who bangs there on my gate?'

'Fulk, it's Tom Wickham.'

'Tom!'

There was a grind, a clang and a crash as he moved the bolts, and the gates released its gravel-shod groan of old iron against ancient wood.

'If I had a penny for every time I opened these gates. Ha! When I die, call on God for I would be the perfect gatekeeper of hell, eh? Imagine?'

Fulk struck a pose as if he were the keeper of the gates of hell.

'Who's this? Fool farmer hanged himself on expectation of plenty? Get in and roast your goose on that fire! Oh, you are the gentleman who short-changed a French whore? Come in, come in, theft is theft! Whether from a whore or a king.'

Will was in a fit of giggles, and so was I.

'Too firking cold here for hell. What do you want?'

'Dozen sacks of crushed oats.'

'A crown! But to you Tom, four shillings. What's this laughter? Who's your friend?'

'Will.'

'Pleased to meet you, Will. You a horseman?'

'No, I am a teacher.'

'Not a teacher; he's a poet and writer of plays.'

'The one courting Miss Anne at the Whatleys?'

Will flushed and a wicked smile came over the face of Fulk.

'Ohh! Did wonder who'd been sniffin' around young Anne.'

Fulk nudged me hard and laughed a most lascivious and lecherous laugh. Then he cleared his rustic old throat, became all serious and put a fatherly arm around Will and walked him into the yard. He cheekily called to me like a common servant.

'Boy, bring the cart in!' He laughed and turned his attention back to the giggling Will.

'Never a finer maid will you find in all the lanes. Maid she is, I can vouch, not that I tried my luck. Old family friend, see? Don't be letting her go, you be sure? Now, I can give you some good advice on married life.'

'That I would be keen to hear,' said Will trying to contain his laughter.

'Oh, but first …'

Letting go of Will, he limply skipped over to the wall of the building, untied his britches and let loose a stream of steaming urine.

Will looked to me and silently guffawed. Fulk walked back with a lordly gait, disseminating his advice with the knowledge of a thrice-wed vicar.

'Now, in married life, first, don't drink too much – provokes the desire but robs the performance. Second, in the marital bed, never release wind, neither fore or aft, and never pick thy nose. Wives do not like this, I can personally verify.'

'I thank thee for this advice, Sir.'

Fulk bowed his thanks.

'Nothing of it. Now! A dozen sacks! Coin first!'

I threw a purse of four shilling which he duly caught.

'And at four shillings you can load the wretched things yourselves.'

I knew the mirth of a meeting with Fulk would put some humour back into Will. I did notice, though, that Anne was the first person who really saw exactly what Will needed. Her devotion was always quiet, contained. She was frighteningly observant and never feared a decision, no matter how hard, painful or unpalatable it might be.

Together with her brother and stepmother, she continued their father's great passion, the garden. She knew much about it and as the season advanced she would walk her increasingly beloved William through the plants and herbs, reciting her detailed knowledge of their uses.

Anne looked after him so patiently, never pushing him or haranguing him, as many women, including his dear mother, would have done. Even when it strained her more traditional brother, with a reassuring smile she would simply say, 'Things come to those who wait.'

It was a cold, sad Christmas that year but one day, in the late spring of 1582, Bartholomew arrived in the yard.

'Good day to you, Mr Hathaway. How can we be of service?' I said, placing my broom against the wall.

'Good day, Master Wickham. I require a horse for a day.'

I nodded. 'Indeed, how do you ride?'

'I'm sorry … I am not sure I understand?'

'Are you a good rider? Not good? Are you carrying baggage?'

'Of course, understanding you now. I confess I am not a good rider, being more partial to walking – better for body and soul.'

Moot was tied up at the trough so I pointed to him. 'Moot is quiet and does not scare easily,' I said.

Bartholomew seemed unimpressed. Poor Moot, no great looker but a dependable mount. 'I think I need something a little more …'

'Where are you headed?'

'Tredington.'

'No distance. Take the cart?'

'A cart would not be appropriate.'

'Tell me the purpose of your trip and maybe I can help you better,' I said.

Bartholomew shifted from foot to foot. 'It's of a personal nature,' he uttered.

Nym came out of the stables leading a finely groomed Orlando with plaited mane and his head held high.

'Now! That horse would suit very well!' he said with pleasured excitement.

'So you wish to impress a lady,' I declared.

Bartholomew winced. 'I never mentioned such a ...'

'Mr Hathaway, you didn't need to. Orlando is my personal mount and whilst he is available, for an agreeable sum, he is powerful and needs a firm hand.'

'It would be marvellous if I could ... if you were to accompany me on the other ... horse?'

'Certainly, two horse fees and my time.'

'Oh?'

I sighed.

'Two shillings and sixpence.'

'Could you make it two shillings?' he simpered.

'I could, but you're under the spell of love, so umm?' I declared with a small grin.

'Two and six is agreed,' he sighed.

'When?' I asked.

'Tomorrow morning at the eighth. At the farm?'

'Till then,' I said and, picking up my broom, I went back to my chores.

Bartholomew paused before leaving. 'Your friend,' he asked.

'Will?' I replied, whilst sweeping.

'He spends much time at our farm, scribbling.'

'Scribbling?'

'Yes, scribbling. My stepmother seems happy with this but I am unsure. Have you any idea what his intentions are?

'Best ask Will yourself?' I said, still sweeping.

'I do but he always quotes ... poetry. Biblical quotes I can comprehend but latter-day poets, alas I am lost.'

I stopped sweeping, but in truth I did not know how to respond. There was an awkward pause so I cordially shrugged at our emotional impotency and he left.

The following morning I turned up at Hewlands on Orlando with Moot on a lead. The front door opened and I was greeted by Joan. with her youngest children huddled around her.

'Good morning to you, Mrs Hathaway.'

'Good morning, Mr Wickham,' said Joan softly. 'Anne is helping her brother dress.'

308

'Well, I am at his disposal. How is Will?'

'Presently he sleeps in the upstairs room,' she said ushering me into the parlour. 'He spends most of the night occupied … in his thoughts … it's the quietest time.'

Joan offered me a seat on the settle beside the fire, upon which lay a dozen or so paper sheets in a hand that had to be Will's. I longed to pick them up but there was a tension around the subject of my friend, so I ignored them.

'I will ask Anne if my stepson is ready,' said Joan awkwardly.

She left the room, followed by the children, so I picked up the sheets and shuffled through them. A play, and a bloody one, too. On one page I read a maid, Philomela, is savagely raped by her brother-in-law and he cuts out her tongue to prevent her telling. I was shocked. 'The Tragedy of Tereus and Philomela' was the title.

Hearing their return, I hastily put the sheets back where I found them. Anne walked in. I rose and, bowing, I greeted her.

'Tom,' she said.

'Miss Anne,' I replied.

She was followed by her brother, still struggling with his collar but dressed like a gentleman.

'I await your order, sir,' I said and bowed very formally.

I noticed that Anne discretely picked up Will's sheets and held them to her body like a precious child.

'Shall we, Mr Wickham?' said Bartholomew, as Joan opened the door.

'Please, call me Tom,' I said.

Bartholomew looked at me and smiled. 'Very well, Tom,' he said and walked out the door.

'But call me Bart and I will be upset,' he continued as he turned down the path.

I put Bartholomew on Orlando and took a leading rein on Moot. By the time we reached Tredington, Orlando would be used to this inexperienced rider. It was an entertaining ride as I noticed that Bartholomew was practising something in words and poise. Every so often, if he caught me turning around, he became embarrassed; it was my notion that he was going to request a betrothal.

At the edge of the village, I released the rein and followed Bartholomew to the house where he was heading, which turned out to be a smart recently built manor with porch.

'Fabric merchants,' Bartholomew whispered back to me.

At the door he dismounted and hammered the knocker with several beats of flowery self-importance. I held on to the horses whilst Bartholomew repeated his knocks.

There were footsteps within.

'Such fancy knocking proclaimeth the approach of vanity, whose pride of heart swelleth at an empty sound!' pronounced a prosaic voice from within.

The door was opened by a man dressed in the distinct clothing of a Puritan. He smirked as he looked the smiling Bartholomew up and down. 'Enter, you are expected. You will be received in the parlour,' he said.

Bartholomew walked nervously in.

'Servant can wait outside,' said the Puritan shutting the door.

I took out a brush to give Orlando and Moot a light groom, wondering why he had even bothered with a fine horse. Nevertheless, a short while later, I heard the return of footsteps and, when the door opened, sure enough Bartholomew appeared with a smile as bright as a drunk at a cockfight.

'We are betrothed,' he whispered, as the door was closed behind him.

I dropped Bartholomew off at Hewlands and he pushed the half-crown into my hand and rushed into the house, announcing the news to all. I listened to all the screams of delight whilst I reset the tack of Orlando and Moot for the journey back.

'I hear Anne's brother is betrothed,' said Will.

I turned around and there he stood at the door of the stable. He looked tired, dishevelled, his hair a mess, his shirt open and stained with ink.

'Isabella Hancocks, of Tredington,' I replied, as I pulled a girth one notch tighter.

'I'm not familiar with her,' said Will.

'Fabric merchants and they're Puritans,' I told him.

Will sighed and rolled his eyes. 'Bartholomew is quite a ...'

His voice faded, he breathed in.

'And ... I hear John's brother has been ...' Again he tailed off and wiped his nose with an ink-stained hand.

I guessed he was referring to Thomas Cottom who, with a plethora of other poor deluded priests, had been recently executed.

'If you mean Thomas Cottom, yes, in May,' I said with little emotion, almost curt.

Will thought and sighed. 'Mercy, should drop as gentle rain from heaven; it is higher than the crown, a quality of God himself,' he said.

'That's Aquinas?' I asked, still adjusting tack.

'Not quite,' sighed Will.

I stopped what I was doing, turned and looked to him. The only thing that gave me any hope was that my dear Stratford friend was at least covered in ink and had a bunch of quills stuck in his waistband.

'I have a job,' Will announced with a touch of feigned joy.

'What doing?' I asked.

'One day in the week, teaching children in Temple Grafton. I still cut the odd pattern for father, keeps mother ... happy.'

'Good,' I smiled.

This was awkward. I knew John Shakespeare was still in a deep well of trouble. However, as I concentrated on furthering my reputation for good horses, any routine in my friend's life was good.

'Will, I must be on my way,' I said and mounted Orlando.

'Hand me Moot?' I asked.

Will picked up Moot's lead, gripped my thigh hard and looked me in the eye.

'Vengeance is in my heart, death in my hand. Blood and revenge are hammering in my head,' he declared and then, relaxing his grip, he laughed and waved me goodbye.

Looking down at the inky impression Will's hand had left on my britches, I wondered where my friend was heading, but though I cared, I did not have the time to worry.

CHAPTER 28

The summer was busy. It went by at the speed of a horse in flames and was profitable, too. Grace and I managed nearly seven pounds in saved coin. Bartholomew had been in several times for some discrete riding lessons. It seemed his betrothed was a competent horsewoman and more was expected of him.

Bartholomew's marriage was held at St Gregory's church in Tredington in the second week of November. It made him very proud because the church was nearly 500 years old and had the tallest spire in the whole of Warwickshire. His bride, Isabella Hancocks, came from a family some of whom said were drifting to the more austere side of Puritanism.

The livery had been engaged to provide two carts for friends from Stratford to attend the marriage. I drove one and Grace the other, bringing Moot on a lead as a spare horse. Thomas Whittington, a shepherd who all his life had worked devotedly for their late father, conveyed the Hathaway family from Shottery to the church. After the service, I understood there was to be a procession to the Hancocks' house, where a wedding feast would be offered to all the guests.

It was quite a cross-section of folk there. The Hancocks, it appeared, were very well connected in the neighbouring county of Oxfordshire. In fact, in retrospect, it was a strange mix of past, present and future. The present was there in the form of the young emerging merchant classes, who, benefiting from their allegiance to the new ways, took every opportunity to display their wealth.

The future – now they were a worry – a new breed of religious hardtack, Puritans. They dressed in solemn austere clothes and stuck to their mandates like dog poop to a boot. It did occur to me that if these people were to ever take control of the State, life could become very harsh.

Then there were those from the past, sitting by the wall, their women discreetly running rosaries through their hands. Poor Papists secretly clinging to their bloodied faith like withering flowers in autumn and oblivious of the bonfire at the end of the lawn.

The Hathaway family arrived, and a very proud Bartholomew dismounted from the cart as his sister and stepmother straightened and brushed his clothes. Friends welcomed him and gathered round whilst his stepbrothers lined up behind him, discussing the most formal way to clutch a bible.

I looked around and there, among the herd of society, unseen by anyone and floating like the sole note of a flute high above the music, Will stood out in his singularity. Whilst Bartholomew and family took their place by the altar, Fulk dropped me a wink as I stood with other servants at the back.

Bartholomew's bride entered the church, escorted by her Puritan adviser. She was not what I would call beautiful. The next thing I knew Will was standing behind the pillar to my left and nudged me as she walked towards the altar.

'Sturdy beast,' he whispered as I tried not to laugh.

The service got under way but, about halfway through, there was the most extraordinary incident. The church door burst open with a boom and in marched a man, plainly a Puritan and with a dark haggard face. His severity alone parted the congregation. He stood in the middle and, waving his finger aloft, declaimed to the nuptial couple, 'Verily niece, thou hast been buffeted by Satan in the form of this … farmer! He is not one of the faithful and this vanity is a travesty of the Lord!' he yelled.

There was total silence as he stood proud, waiting, but for what, no one was quite sure. Bartholomew took control and, whilst his bride endured – looking not too happy – he calmly approached the proud and defiant uncle. Bartholomew calmly and quietly whispered something in his ear. The uncle appeared to listen, and then recoiled facing Bartholomew eye-to-eye.

'Shan't!' was all he said.

Bartholomew responded by taking him firmly by the shoulder and elbow, and frog-marched him out of the church, down the path. What happened next was quite a shock. Instead of returning calmly, Bartholomew rushed back into the church and, as he thrust the door shut, there was a gunshot and a musket ball slammed into the door.

There was near hysteria inside but, with great presence, Bartholomew calmed everyone, before electing to go out once more to deal with the situation. I, and some of the other servants, went to back him up but when the door was opened, having reloaded very quickly, all we saw was the barrel of the musket being lined up once more. We all dived for cover as Bartholomew once more shut the door, followed by another explosive report and again a musket ball struck the oak.

This time, Bartholomew wasted no time rushing out. As the uncle frantically tried to load a third time, Bartholomew's fist landed firmly in his face. We all caught up and gathered behind the heroic bridegroom whilst John and Fulk soothed a disturbed vicar with a brandy flask.

Bartholomew straightened his cuffs and cleared his throat.

'I have never witnessed such behaviour in a house of God,' Bartholomew shouted at the still-dazed and bloody uncle. 'Begone! Never darken your family's door again!'

We all applauded as Isabella rushed up and, standing breathlessly in front of Bartholomew, saluted him with a deep long curtsy. He returned the honour, with a long deep bow.

Bartholomew then stood and addressed those gathered.

'I will not have any marriage before God desecrated by anyone, whatever the reason. And, none more so than when it is the last wedding of the year and, indeed, ours,' he stated with heartfelt affection, offering Isabella his hand.

I noticed those words had an interesting effect on Will. He immediately looked to Anne and her to him. As the nuptial couple walked back to the church, through an arbour of applause, they paused at the door. Bartholomew smiled. He touched the two musket balls embedded in the oak and Isabella kissed him.

'Make a first-rate warden, eh?' said Fulk, removing the brandy flask from the vicar as they re-entered the church.

After the service, the procession to the house was full of talk and laughter. This was a wedding few would forget. For all us cart drivers and horse minders, a fire had been lit in the yard and a table of very welcome food laid out. The wedding guests were entertained inside the family house with a large feast but I gather it was short of wine, on account of the family's religious divisions.

Much of the talk inside was, of course, about the raging uncle and his musket. Bartholomew, having taken control of the situation so decisively, found himself placed on quite a pedestal of pride. I did notice the 'adviser' skulk around, in and out of the house, all the while dropping disparaging comments. As night fell, candles were lit and the carousing celebrations carried on. Though the family had been abstemious with wedding wine, their friends and relatives were forewarned and subsequently well charged with supplies. Will came out of the house alone; he leant on the edge of the cart and smiled to me as Grace approached.

'How are you keeping, Master William,' asked Grace, as she put a blanket over the horse to stave off the now-dropping temperature.

'I have been keeping well, Mistress Wickham.'

'Your mother did ask after you in the market the other day. I do confess, I could not tell her.'

'I will visit them tonight,' he muttered guiltily.

I looked to Will; he had a distance in his eyes. 'Did you talk with their family, inside,' I asked.

Will shook his head and pushed the dirt with his foot.

'You must have spoken with someone,' I asked, pushing him.

'They have some interesting books,' he said. 'I took the chance to leaf through them. 'Tom, when you travel back to town, would you take me?'

'I'll be late,' I said. 'Take Moot. Leave him in the yard. Nym is there.'

'Thank you, Tom.'

'When will you go?'

'Now,' he sighed.

Will looked to the house where he caught the eye of Anne, who sat inside by a candlelit window. She smiled softly to him and he gently waved back. I untied Moot and brought him round. I had no saddle, just a bridle, so I begged Will to go with care but Moot was quiet so I was not worried.

'Is all well, my friend?' I asked discretely, as I gave him a leg up. I handed him the reins and looked up into his eyes – still distant they were, but briefly he looked to me.

'Why is this the last marriage of the year?' he asked.

'Grace? Why is this the last marriage of the year?' I asked, turning to her.

Will twitched as the words left my mouth.

'There are no marriages in advent. It's less than three weeks to the start. Must read banns for three weeks, see?' she said, nonchalantly filling a nose bag for the horse.

'Will?' I wondered aloud.

'I must go.'

He looked around to the door as three men chatted loudly on the porch. 'This is not for me, this kind of … babel,' he whispered.

Will rode off into the night. I turned to look at the window where Miss Anne had been sitting but now it was empty.

'Miss Anne be like Miss Isabella,' Grace said quietly.

'Like what?' I asked stupidly.

Grace approached and spoke softly in my ear.

'Women will always see things that men never will and more to the good.'

She looked me eye-to-eye and, noticing I was not picking up on her hints, she twisted my cheek.

'Nephew, they are both with child.'

My heart dropped like a bucket into a well, part plummet, part fresh, part fear, but all depth.

I knew the newly wedded couple were going to reside at Tredington so, when an errand boy asked me to attend Miss Hathaway at Hewlands, I expected it to be about cartage for Bartholomew's possessions to his nuptial home. However, when I arrived there was a distinct air of conspiracy. The house was empty, which was unusual, and I was ushered into the parlour by Will, who was looking in better sorts than I had seen previously.

'They are all at Tredington, helping Bartholomew and his wife,' Will said.

'What service do they need from us?' I asked a little confused.

'I need your service, not they,' said Will.

'Oh?'

'Anne is …'

'With child?' I interrupted.

'How do you know?'

'Grace told me at the wedding.'

'But even I didn't know?'

'No one did, Will, but women will always see things that men never do.'

Will was surprised.

'Wedding or lawyer?' I asked.

'Wedding,' said Will, feigning indignation.

He stood up. 'I have to get a special licence, too late for banns and other church law stuff,' he stated in a tone that I could only describe as strangely relaxed.

'Simple enough, is it not?' I wondered curiously.

'I, we, don't want any fuss, small and sweet, a whisper in the wind, all bloomed and plucked before anyone knows, especially Bartholomew.'

'Trinity?'

Will shuddered. 'Cannot.'

'For why?'

'Vicar Haycroft.'

I realised what he meant. After what the vicar did at his sister's funeral, the pain was still deep.

'Besides, only a Roman Nuptial Mass holds the dignity that Anne's love deserves.'

'Is she Catholic?'

'Shh. As much as any of us.'

The poet in Will was clear, but for myself I could not see why it mattered in front of whom you said 'I do'.

'We want Frith to marry us.'

'Frith?' I repeated, rhetorically.

'We need a bond and a special licence that allows us to marry without the three weeks of crying the banns and legitimacy to wed in Temple Grafton.'

'Why bother with banns and licence if you choose the ancient rite?' I asked.

'Frith will obey the law of God but he is most insistent we also obey the law of the land,' replied Will.

'Good then,' I said, not really bothered either way. 'When?'

'Friday.'

'Friday?'

'Sunday is St Andrew's day, the start of Advent. No marriages till after Christmas. The size of Anne's belly will put our child's legitimacy in question.'

'Yes, Will, but it is Monday.'

I looked Will in the eye, which glistened with a clandestine magic.

'You aren't telling any family, are you?' I said.

Will continued to smile and slowly shook his head.

'The morrow, fifth hour, meet me here with a mount. We shall go to Worcester and I will attend the Consistory Court,' he whispered conspiratorially.

'Yes, that ...' I said, agreeing but not having a clue as to what he was talking about.

Will stood up and embraced me. 'As reliable as that old horse,' he smiled.

'Heavens Gate?'

'Yes, that one.'

'Thank you, Tom,' came Anne's soft voice.

She had appeared on the threshold of the pantry, looking utterly beguiling with a basket of herbs in her hand. The scent enveloped us as she stood there.

'Last of the season,' she said, holding up a ragged bunch of thyme and inhaling the fragrance.

CHAPTER 29

It was getting cold; the chill of winter seemed to be arriving early. Thankfully there was no freeze. Ice plays havoc with the beasts' hooves. Will was up and ready, clutching food wrapped in a napkin by dear Anne for our journey, and we set off a little after the fifth hour. It took us about four hours. It was a delightful ride, a clear sky with the sun flickering through bare trees providing intermittent warmth to soothe our faces.

Riding into Worcester through St Martins Gate was very pleasant. It was early in the week with the town quietly going about its business. There was a trough outside the cathedral's west front and so we tied up there. We wandered around to the chapter house to see if a clerk or steward could be located. After talking to a few clergy, we took their directions. Through the chapter house, cloisters, the old school, cross the east transept and exiting a door, we arrived at the west front once more. Frustrated by this situation and seeing a man sweeping the steps of the cathedral, Will took it in hand. 'Wait here, Tom.'

I watched as he walked over and, out of my earshot, greeted the sweeper like an old friend. They seemed to have quite a protracted discussion. I could see Will listening intently, nodding, and then laughing, and the sweeper laughing, too. Finally, the sweeper started to point specifically, so I assumed we were getting good directions. They shook hands and Will trotted back over to me.

'If lost always ask one who serves,' he said. 'We have to go back to the chapter house: there they hold the Consistory Court.

'Apparently, Bishop Whitgift is notoriously drunk after midday and his clerk is deaf as a post with poor eyesight. And they have a volatile case at the moment – a family trying to stop a marriage, or some such thing. It seems that it is quite protracted, so he was wishing us good luck.'

We found the Consistory Court. In fact, we heard it before anything. Down the stone corridor it echoed, like I imagined the Day of Judgement would sound. We turned up at the great carved doors but were prevented from entering by a court bailiff.

'Court is in session gentlemen,' he said politely to a background of screams and yells from within.

'What kind of session is this?' Will whispered.

There was another scream, a long wail and a collapse of some kind, and then a gavel hitting wood.

'Adjourned!' came a yell from inside.

'Our turn?' I said, looking at Will.

The door opened and a man physically dragged a woman from the court as she sobbed in quite a dramatic fashion. They were followed by a smug young couple victoriously gripping a marriage licence. Judging by their clothes, it would seem they were very much a class apart.

'Wonder what their story is?' whispered Will.

'NEXT!' came a call from the bailiff.

'Never let the truth get in the way of a good tale,' muttered Will as we walked in.

The bishop sat high up on a carved wooden throne, central behind a table long enough for a hundred to feast at. At one end of the table sat an elderly clerk amid a series of ledgers, quills and ink wells.

We both stood at the table and looked up at Bishop Whitgift, who was plainly weary.

'Gentlemen, it has been a tiresome morning and we are in need of lunch. I will adjourn till the second hour.'

'Court is adjourned!' shouted the bailiff, and with that they all up stood and left, leaving Will and I standing in this great, damp old hall listening as doors groaned and scraped, before finally booming shut.

'That is four hours for lunch?' I said to Will.

'What do you expect when you combine the legal profession with the church?' Will sighed.

We returned to the horses to give them some feed, and I gave them a light rubdown – more to pass the time than anything. Will undid the little cloth bundle that Anne had given him and laid it out quite fastidiously on top of the wall. There was some bread, cheese, two apples and pieces of cold bacon. We enjoyed our little lunch, and then took a walk along the bank of the Severn. It was a beautiful view, its glassy artery snaking its way through the county.

'How do you become very good at something, Tom?'

'Do it all day, every day, for as long as you can.'

'Like you with the horses? Like my father with the gloves?'

'I suppose,' I answered.

I was not sure what this was about. He was deep within himself and knew the answers before asking the question.

Eventually at the second hour, we found ourselves again in the great stone echo chamber that was the Consistory Court. We stood patiently before the table, waiting on the bishop and his clerk.

'Court in session. All rise!' shouted the bailiff.

The booming noise of doors and the breaking of wind, combined with accompanying echoes, heralded the entrance of the bishop and his clerk. They both tottered across the hall to their seats with a distinctly post liquid-lunch meander.

'What have they done?' slurred the bishop, sitting heavily into his throne, and sending up a cloud of dust from the cushions.

'Nothing, Your Excellency,' replied Will.

'Must have done something; you're here.'

'Special marriage licence and dispensation from the banns,' interrupted the bailiff.

'Why?'

'Maid is with child,' said the bailiff.

'So, you have done something, haven't you? Even if it is just satisfy your lust!' said the bishop, raising his eyebrows and spilling dribble from his wine-soaked grin.

Will simply bowed in submission, trying not to laugh.

'What is the date, Clerk?'

The clerk did not react.

'Clerk! Date!' shouted the bailiff.

The clerk looked up, clearly bemused, and placed his hand to his ear.

'Deaf, mad and drunk?' whispered Will as I tried so desperately to contain my laughter.

'Clerk! His Most Reverend Excellency asked you the date!' shouted the bailiff.

'Of what?'

'This day!' shouted back the bailiff who, it would seem, was not only used to this but also quite tired of it, too. Given the echo, deafness and wine, this was going to be a protracted event.

The clerk shuffled methodically through his papers.

'Twenty-seventh day of the eleventh month, year of our lord, fifteen hundred and eighty two!'

'Three days from the start of Advent, St Andrews Day and the end of marriages for the year! Thus, too late for the reading of banns across the parish. Special marriage licence required,' stated the slurry Bishop.

'Excellency,' said Will in agreement.

'Special licence granted. Clerk, enter it so.'

The clerk looked up again and placed his hand to his ear.

'Think we could be a while?' I whispered to Will.

After much shouting by both the bailiff and the bishop, the clerk understood and opened the correct ledger.

'Groom's name?' he asked, hand poised with quill and still optimistically holding his hand to his ear.

'William Shakespeare,' declared Will in a clear enunciated tone that still battled with the echoes.

Nevertheless, Will repeated it very slowly as the clerk entered it into the ledger, even more slowly.

'Bride?' he asked looking up, his eyelids quite heavy from drink.

He looked as though he may nod off any second and, indeed, suddenly the bishop did, simultaneously releasing wind.

'Hathaway,' said Will, rolling his eyes.

The clerk grinned and wobbled on his elbow.

'We know you had her away. You told us she is with child,' snorted the clerk.

'No! Her name is Hathaway, Anne,' snapped Will.

'So you had it away with Anne who works where?'

'No, she is … she works for the Whatley family in Temple Grafton but her name is Hathaway.'

The bishop snored on his throne. I looked to the bailiff, who simply rolled his eyes in return.

'Whatleys? We did them this morning. Screamed so loud they did – very rude people. So you are Whatleys? Did we not finish that one, Bailiff?' said the clerk.

Will suddenly lost possession of himself. He pulled at his hair and walked towards the clerk.

'No! I am William Shakespeare of Henley Street, Stratford Upon Avon. My troth is pledged to Anne Hathaway, who works for Whatleys of Temple Grafton. She resides in Shottery, the next village, and we wish to wed in Temple Grafton. Please try to comprehend this before we all die!'

Will placed his hands on the table in front of the clerk, whose face I have to say was a picture of wine and hearing-loss induced confusion. The clerk looked this way and that way, and noting the bishop snoring, he changed from confusion to severity.

'Point of order, Mr Bailiff?' said the clerk, not taking his eyes off Will.

The bishop stirred and the bailiff cleared his throat.

'Order in court!' he declared.

Will returned to his place in front of the bishop with me.

'Where are we?' said the bishop, sitting up.

'Second session of the day, Excellency,' informed the bailiff.

'Not those wretched Whatelys?' he worried.

'This gentleman has had his way with Anne Whatley and needs a special licence,' said the clerk.

'What's the date?'

I could not believe this! We were about to go full circle, but thankfully the bailiff stepped in.

'Excellency, we have established the need for a special licence and clerk is just writing it out now.'

'Good, good. Can we adjourn then?' asked the Bishop.

'Clerk, is the marriage entered?' asked the bailiff.

The clerk was lost in the slow act of making the entries. Will and I did wonder what on earth he was actually entering.

'Clerk is in the process, Excellency,' the bailiff informed the bishop.

Will looked to me.

'If breath was ever bated,' he sighed, as we watched the clerk go about his business as if it were a slow tooth extraction.

After slow and eloquent use of the quill, fastidious blotting, and careful shutting of inkwells, the clerk closed the ledger and held the licence copy in his hand, smiling through his droopy eyelids. We all breathed a sigh of relief and the bailiff went to take the copy to pass to Will. But the clerk moved it from reach, and then dropped a piece of cannon shot on us. 'Surety?' asked the clerk.

'Surety?' queried Will.

'Oh, surety?' said the bishop sitting up, waking and raising a buttock to release wind.

'What surety?' said Will in a distinct tone of apprehension.

'In the event that the banns not being read, an aggrieved suitor, parent, or troth plighted unknown, is in a position to take legal action against his Most Reverend Excellency Bishop Whitgift. Therefore, this Consistory Court requires a surety to ensure indemnity for his Most Reverend Excellency Bishop Whitgift.'

There was total silence.

'Very good, bailiff,' muttered the bishop.

'How much?' asked a concerned Will.

'How much?' the bailiff asked the bishop.

'Clerk, how much?' the bishop asked the clerk.

The clerk's attention was taken by the bishop in a way that you may well have thought he had only just walked into the room.

'Excellency?' he inquired, looking to the bishop.

'How much?' repeated the bishop.

'What?' said the clerk, holding both hands to his ears.

'Surety!' snapped the bishop, who was getting outwardly as irritated as we were internally.

'Oh, one moment,' he said and then started what resulted in an extensive search through the various ledgers.

'Yes, here we are,' he stated, concentrating on one particular page of one of the smaller ledgers. He looked up.

'Forty pounds.'

I can safely say, if Her Majesty the Queen walked in naked as the day she was born, Will and I would not have been more shocked!

'Present your property deeds, sign the surety and we are done,' said the clerk benignly.

'Excellency, I have no property. I cannot produce deeds. I am a man of simple means, and this is a large sum,' stammered Will.

'Then you have one day to find someone who will. Court is adjourned,' declared the bishop, bringing down his gavel and missing the stud.

'Court is adjourned! All rise for his Most Reverend Excellency Bishop Whitgift,' boomed the bailiff. And with that, they left!

Will and I stood there stunned to our boots, the humour of the situation having evaporated quicker than water on a hot shoe.

Walking back to the trough, Will was in a daze and quite wobbly on his feet.

'What am I to do? I cannot ask Father; he is in debt. Bartholomew? He would drop off the globe.'

'We'll find a way,' I said optimistically.

As we rode back to Shottery, Will's predicament was ground to our bones by a fierce cold wind. We pulled our jerkins close to us and wished we had been better prepared for the bitterness.

In the house, Anne was sitting at the parlour table with John Richardson.

Anne leapt up and flung her arms around Will.

'I spoke with Father Frith, and he is ready and attendant on us,' she whispered sweetly into his ear.

'John,' I said shaking his hand.

'And I understand congratulations to you, William,' said John.

Will looked to Anne.

'I had to tell someone,' she said coyly.

'Sad that dear Richard is not with us,' said John.

'Indeed, and thank you,' said Will quietly.

There was silence on our part, which concerned Anne.

'Will, what is the matter?'

'Don't tell us you have a mad musket-wielding uncle!' quipped John.

'No. The bishop will not grant a licence without surety.'

'That is a worry,' gasped a shocked Anne.

'How much? I am good for twenty pounds,' declared John breezily.

'They want forty.' said Will, somewhat embarrassed.

John looked wide-eyed at both of us and grinned. 'I'll ask Fulk to stand twenty!'

'Would he ... ?' stammered Anne.

'Richard Hathaway is the only honest man we ever did business with, save young Tom here. Dick was the best, a kind and generous soul whom, if we cannot repay in death what he gave us in life, then we did not deserve it in the first place.'

Will shook his hand warmly and I, too. Anne embraced John.

'When do you need it,' said John.

'Tomorrow?' said Will.

'Right!' he said, surprised but not fazed. 'Tomorrow, fifth hour, Fulk's yard.'

We all nodded in stunned thanks as John smiled and left.

The following day turned out not only to be more absurd than the previous day's trip, but also one of the most drunken days of my life. Will and I met up at Fulk's yard. It was a chilly day with a crisp sunrise but this time we were well rugged up, so it was going to be a warmer ride than the previous. Hearing us arrive, Fulk briefly came out of the house. 'Tie up and come in,' he shouted and went back inside.

Will looked to me. 'We should really ride, to get there before their four-hour liquid lunching,' he said.

'I'll get them moving,' I reassured him as we dismounted and tied off our mounts.

Rubbing our hands for warmth, we walked over to the house and entered the front door. We were immediately hit by the smell of wood smoke, old wine, cheese and unwashed dogs. This mature aroma was mixed with a fresh aroma of simmering spices, pears and other fruits.

The fire was going well and, hanging over it, was a pot that Fulk stirred with great care. 'Mr William!' he shouted.

'Mr Sandells,' replied Will.

'You've met John Richardson, good friend of mine and your late father-in-law to be, as it were? He tells me of a family problem.'

'Indeed, Sir, and has kindly agreed to assist.'

'And so have I.'

'Thank you, Sir, from the bottom …'

'Shut up. No speeches. Richard Hathaway, the kindest most generous-hearted man I ever knew, whereas I am a tight-fisted drunken fool!' said Fulk, stirring the pot.

'I am sure not, Sir,' said Will.

'What do you know?' he snapped.

'I did not …'

'Don't care what you did, doesn't, do or whatever! All you need to know is that this day, I am prepared to make an exception to my appalling personality, on account of Dick's memory – and his delightful daughter.'

'I thank you, Sir,' said Will.

Fulk nodded to Will's thanks, and continued to stir gently.

'And! Tell Bartholomew t'was not me who informed Isabella's mad uncle,' said Fulk. 'That little Puritan she has for "advice"? T'was him.'

'Indeed I will. So! Well, shall we ride?' said Will optimistically.

John said nothing but picked up a couple of goblets and went over to Fulk.

'Just get warmed up a bit before we ride. Tis a cold day,' said Fulk, pouring some heated wine into the goblets.

He grabbed two other goblets and, filling those as well with red steaming-hot wine, he handed one to each of us.

'What's in it?' asked Will.

'Some excellent red wine from Italy, French brandy, juice of a Spanish lemon, spices of the Far East, apples and honey from down the road!'

'No mushrooms?' I asked.

'Why the dickens would I want to put mushrooms in?' muttered Fulk, and then raised his goblet towards Will.

'Marriage!' And with that Fulk downed it in one!

We had a sip or two, it was strong stuff. I looked to John who had also emptied his goblet but with less gusto.

'Shall we ride then?' said Will, putting down his goblet.

'Haven't finished ya drink, Will!' declared Fulk.

'It is quite a distance we have to ride,'

'How many times you been to Worcester, Will?'

'Including yesterday, once,' said Will.

'John and I have done the journey more times than my dog has licked its balls. Shut up and drink – not letting this go to waste,' he said, pouring himself another.

Will looked to me rather concerned. I shrugged and downed my goblet of very delicious hot wine, which certainly lit a warm fire in the tummy. John took out some bread and cut it up as our cups were charged up once more. I stuffed down bread in a vain attempt to soak up the wine.

An hour later, the pot was done and so, quite frankly, were Will and I. Our heads were swimming with intoxication and the sun had been up less than an hour. On the other hand, John and Fulk seemed positively energised by the wine. Fulk went to a cupboard opened a drawer, pulled out some title deeds and sifted through what must have been a dozen or so. He took two and stuffed them into his doublet; then, picking up a flask of brandy, he walked out into the yard.

We all mounted up but Will and I were a little woozy getting up into our saddles.

'Young today, think they can handle it. Dear, oh dear,' whispered Fulk to John.

He chuckled to himself and deftly cantered out of the yard.

It was quite a job keeping up with them. In fact, safe to say, they were the best riders I have ridden with. Fulk and John passed the flask between them most of the journey whilst Will and I sobered up as best we could.

When we arrived at the trough at the west front of the cathedral, both Will and I simultaneously dismounted and plunged our heads into the icy water, much to the amusement of John and Fulk.

'Get used to it boys. It's all life has to offer, believe me!' laughed Fulk, who for all the drink he had put into himself seemed remarkably composed, as did John.

Once more we found ourselves in front of the table of the Consistory Court, but this time things were different. Fulk and John greeted the bishop as old friends. After a furtive discussion with him about a price for their feed and the availability of French brandy, Fulk and John produced their property deeds for the clerk. With a nod, a wink and a circulating brandy flask, they signed one ledger after another. The confused clerk was then slapped heartily on the back by Fulk, as John took the copy of the licence off him. John handed it to me but I noticed it was riddled with errors. I was about to point these out when Will snatched it from me, his elbow firmly planted in my ribs.

Outside at the trough, we triumphantly untied our horses, Will's precious licence safely stowed in his doublet.

'I cannot thank you enough.' said Will.

'We won't be riding back with you,' said John.

'Oh?' said Will, expressing surprise.

'There is business to do here. We are lunching with the bishop,' said Fulk, touching his ruddy nose with a knowing wink.

I suddenly realised there was a whole strata of subversive trade that put brogging in the shade.

Will watched John and Fulk walk off, and then turned to me.

'Blessed Campion. They swapped his way for this way? Not sure whether to laugh, cry or scream?' Will pondered out loud with a heavy sigh as he mounted up.

The ride back to Stratford was cold but with the licence next to Will's heart, we were as warm as toasted peascods.

CHAPTER 30

In what I saw as a sign of his rapidly growing ability to wrong-foot the world with his growing grasp of people, Will, within a few days, had arranged a fully legal clandestine marriage with a Catholic Nuptial Mass. Vicar John Frith, who was to conduct it, was also a master of the subtle art of politic and, indeed, he had taught much to us both. Frith, quietly of the Old Faith, managed to keep the State satisfied he was a good vicar of duty to our queen. Will and Anne were adamant how they wanted to marry. They decided on a very late hour for privacy and safety, as all would be in bed.

Ordinarily, a wedding was a great family event of celebration. Will knew this full well and he recognised excluding parents and cousins would bring consequences. This, however, was Will, and nothing about Will was ordinary.

The night of the 29th of November, at just past the midnight hour walking into the 30th of the month, I entered the old Saxon church of Temple Grafton. The soft round arches, musty aroma and poor state of repair offered an ancient atmosphere of comfort, like lying one's head in the lap of a loving grandmother whilst she gently strokes your hair. A crack in the wall had allowed ivy to work its way in and wind itself around the old pulpit. A hole in the roof had let in rain and a puddle glistened near the altar.

Vicar Frith had lopped down a large rosemary bush and strewn it on the floor to soak up the last of the puddle. He had arranged what must have been three-dozen candles around the apse, some in candlesticks, others balanced in fractured masonry. They flickered gently, lighting the bed of rosemary and the surrounding water-damaged wall paintings.

Vicar Frith was kneeling in the apse, deep in solemn prayer and unmoved by my entering the church. It was a quiet autumnal night with no breeze outside and, chance would be, it was a cloudless sky with a new moon. The picture was quite moving as I stood in the empty church, waiting for the nuptials to take place. I looked around at the fading wall paintings; in most churches they had been compulsorily destroyed. These were probably too damaged by damp and neglect for the authorities to bother with. There was the Madonna and child, the resurrection of Jesus and then there was, all too appropriate, the massacre of the holy innocents. As their faces caught the flickering candles it was as though, in the twilight of their ephemeral existence, they had come to witness the marriage of Anne and Will, before finally fading into the mists of history.

I waited patiently, as I had no idea who was coming. After a few minutes, Vicar Frith came out of his prayer, gently rose and approached the altar. It was then I realised that only I was to witness this marriage, save two small boys who suddenly broke into plainsong of such sweetness that instantly caused tears to spring from my eyes. Frith pulled a rope and a small window high up in the wall opened and the moon shone in a light that sparkled through the airborne dust like the magic sprinkles of an angel.

Will and Anne rose from their knees, all the time unseen in the darkness of the transept and, and as the boys sang, the young lovers walked solemnly into the light. I had never seen any girl look so beautiful, having only ever set eyes on Anne in plain and austere collar, bonnet and work dress. Here, she wore gown of autumnal-coloured cloth that hung wonderfully on her. With no bonnet, her hair was down and hung to her waist in a luscious loose plait, into which were woven honeysuckle and hellebores climbing up to a crown of camellias around her head. Will wore an open white shirt and brown leather jerkin, grey hose, leather britches and boots. He looked the very essence of a bard. At the altar, they both knelt and Will stretched out his left hand towards it and, looking to Anne, whispered, 'I am the Elm, and thou the honeysuckle, come let thine arm entwine me.'

Anne stretched out her right arm and, with a gentle smile, she wound it around Will's; their fingers entwined and stretched out to God. As the heat of the candles grew, the bees wax, the old stone, the rosemary and the honeysuckle produced a profusion of perfumes that lifted the air with a scent I could only describe as sacred.

Anne and Will only had breath for one another. Anne never took her left hand off her womb or her eyes off Will; nor did he take his off her. Vicar John Frith read the old Roman marriage rite with a tender solemnity that I had never heard before and have never heard since. The Latin rite fluttered from his lips like the soft caresses of a mother's hand on her firstborn child. Anne and Will answered their vows with a deep softness in their voices, as though their very souls whispered to the world on this most blessed night.

As they exchanged rings, I saw the most intense connection in each other's eyes. And, as they kissed, I felt as if I would never marry or find love. Why? I do not know. Maybe I had just witnessed something so special – something that comes to precious few and I neither had the love nor sacrifice in my heart to give to another in such a selfless way.

I, too, knelt as John conducted the Nuptial Mass. Will and Anne took bread, followed by the two boys. I assumed, as a known Protestant in practice I was not included, so held myself back, but Frith stood waiting for me, beckoning me forward with nothing more than the love in his smile. I moved forward and dropped to my knees.

'Corpus Christi,' he whispered.

'Amen,' I choked and opened my mouth.

Frith placed the host on my tongue. I closed my mouth and returned to the darkness of the knave where the depictions of the massacre of the holy innocents caught my eye. I silently wept as those paintings re-lit my memories of Campion's gruesome execution, and the others – people who sought only to worship freely that which they had held so precious in their hearts.

When the service was over, Will and Anne walked serenely out of the church to where I had a small cart waiting. I had taken the precaution of wrapping the horse's hooves tightly with sack-cloth for a silent journey. After waving a heaven-sent goodbye to John Frith, I silently conveyed the inseparable couple down the moonlit lanes to Shottery.

The rest of the night they spent at Hewlands farmhouse, upstairs in the family nuptial bed. Joan had taken the children to friends and left the house free.

I spent what was left of the night lying in a field near a large oak tree not far from Stratford. I let the horse loose to graze. Despite being late in the year, it was not too cold and I wanted to retain as much of this night as I could. The moon dropped below the horizon at about the third hour. Wrapped tight in a blanket, I lay in the cart watching the most colossal display of stars move their mighty body around the great heaven above.

CHAPTER 31

The four months following the marriage were quiet and I saw very little of the young couple. It was unusual for a groom to live with the bride's family but Will and Anne both lived at Hewlands. Bartholomew took charge of the farm whilst Anne helped her stepmother look after her younger siblings. Will tried on occasion to work for his father but it was a tense situation at Henley Street. It was in late March when there was an event that at first seemed to be a catastrophe, but in retrospect it was like a lit fuse of future, and even bigger, detonations.

I was woken by the distinctive smell of smoke and some loud crackling noises. I leapt out of bed to hop downstairs and check the smithy fire, but I was confident it was fine. Rushing into the yard I saw the sun was rising, but not only was it two hours early, it was in the west. Stratford was on fire. I threw open the livery gates just as Grace caught up with me. There was already a throng of people rushing to the western quarter of town carrying buckets. Nym appeared from his quarters in the stalls.

'Grab all the buckets, Nym,' called Grace.

We had six in all and with two each we joined the rush towards the fire, keeping as close to the river as we could. Crackling like musket-fire, embers dropped on us here and there. We saw two lines of people between the river and the fire, filling and emptying buckets.

Arriving with our six buckets, we put them into the lines but were encouraged to help out at the hot end.

The main fire was big, hot and terrifying, like a great dragon devouring its way through the town, street by street. Around us there were constant screams and shouts of all descriptions; some frightened women, some hysterical children, and others were men giving instructions. The most penetrating sounds were screams too blood-curdling to assign a gender to as, somewhere in the stampede of flames, some poor bastards burnt to death.

Grace and I realised it was too hot to get close enough for our buckets to have any quenching effect. The fire was like a horse or cattle stampede and I knew the only way to stop stampede beasts was to give them nowhere to go.

I shouted to one man whom I recognised as a town night watchman. He seemed to be directing the firefighters. 'We need a break!' I called.

'No time to rest,' he barked back.

Grace looked to me and, passing an empty bucket, she rolled her eyes. She left the line and approached the watchman.

'Get back in the line!' he screamed.

'We need a break' she shouted.

'Rest when fire's out!' he yelled back, pointing and ordering her back in line.

This was going nowhere fast. I left the line and joined Grace but the idiot ran to us and, grabbing me, he remonstrated.

'Get back, get back!' he kept saying as Grace also tried to stop him pushing me back to the line. Nym, bless him, pitched in as well.

'A fire break! We need a fire break!' screamed Grace as she suddenly grabbed the man by his jerkin and, to his shock, physically spun him around to face the path of raging fire.

'There, look!' she yelled. 'Two streets down, make a break in the buildings. Stop the spread, otherwise it'll be on the high street by dawn.'

The watchman calmed down, more out of bewilderment than anything.

I turned to Nym.

'Get Heavens Gate, the yoke and all the rope we have.'

Nym took off to Ely Street. Concerned that a fight was breaking out amongst the firefighters, other men rushed over, and with them appeared John Shakespeare.

'John!' I called.

'Tom!'

'John, we need horses, strong horses, ropes and hooks. We have to make a break in West Street!' I said forcefully.

For once in his life, John didn't dither and he and the other men immediately organised themselves to do my bidding. Grace and I headed for West Street, followed by two of the night watchmen.

The direction of the fire was clear and this was the chance we had to stop it in its tracks. We just had to pull down four of the buildings in front of us. In West Street there was a line of old timber storage buildings that not only would burn a treat if they caught, but who the hell would mind if we pulled them down? They had lain empty the year and were as rickety as an old codger anyway.

Nym arrived with Heavens Gate and so, grabbing some onlookers, I organised them to help Nym yoke and line him up. Someone rushed up with a first-class grappling hook. Who this stranger was I don't know, but we attached the hook to a rope and he hurled it with great accuracy through the first-floor window of one of the buildings. I commanded Heavens Gate to pull. He pulled, and a great window-frame came clean out, landing in the street with a spectacular but useless crash.

'Lower truss, get the lower truss!' a voice shouted.

Running towards us, we both recognised Henry Burbage.

He ran forward and, freeing the hook from the window frame, kicked in a front door, disappeared for a few moments and placed the hook around something, somewhere. I could not see.

'Now pull!' he called, running back out.

I flicked Heavens Gate and he gave an almighty pull, and unbelievably a huge truss came away from its ground. It shot out through the door and instantly the whole front of the building came crashing down.

The fire was still getting close and we had to get the other three buildings down. At that moment, John Shakespeare and a few others showed up with two other cart horses, some more rope and hooks. Suddenly, we had a demolition crew and, working in unison, Grace got stuck in with Harry Burbage and helped him place the ropes and hooks. John helped me with our three-horse pulling team and soon we had the fronts off and were working on the hanging floors. The street was a mass of plaster, brick and timber, which the human bucket chain doused with water. As the sun rose, the fire reached our break and thankfully had nowhere to go. Blackened, dirty, coughing, sweaty and smoky, we all stood in the rubble and watched our victory over the fire. I turned around surveying all the rescuers and helpers. It had truly been a job. Even Grace, standing beside the great Heavens Gate, had a smile on her face. Looking at me she gripped her hands in front in a victory sign. I returned the sign and looked back to the fire which was well beaten.

Then, like a punch from nowhere, my ears took a hit from a loud boom! There was a crash and suddenly we were all struck by a great thrusting cloud of hot dust. Coughing and spewing in soot and plaster dust, I was flung to the ground and my head spun like a whirligig! I pulled myself up, but in the cloud I could not see a thing. There were shouts and screams and, as the dust cleared, the sun shone where a minute ago had been the gable end of a building.

My heart raced like a bolting stallion.

'Grace!' I called as I staggered to where she had been standing. Two of the horses pulled themselves out of the rubble of a wall that had spontaneously collapsed, it having been weakened by our firebreak demolition.

'Oh no! No!' I screamed, as I staggered over the rubble, realising that Heavens Gate and Grace had taken the full weight of the collapse. I clawed frantically at the mess but was soon restrained by Harry and John.

'No, you can't!' I screamed with all the strength my smoke-filled chest could muster.

It was useless. She was there in front of me. She looked unharmed but upon trying to lift her head I found a large piece of masonry had penetrated the back of her skull. Heavens Gate lay twitching but both front legs were broken and he lay pathetically whinnying, unable to move. Their heads were close together. I slumped down beside them both and put my head in my hands, tears welling in my eyes. Gathering my strength, I looked up and, holding back my tears, I saw a man with a pail of water. I beckoned to him to bring it over. Using my shirt I took water and cleaned poor Grace's face as men with shovels gently started to dig her out.

When she was extracted, I washed Heavens Gate's head and waited for someone to arrive with a firearm, which they did eventually. After much discussion as to how to load the weapon correctly, they were ready to put the old man-of-war out of his misery. I wetted his philtrum and lying close, I breathed gently into his nostrils. There was a loud report, an air shock, and he breathed no more. I wiped my face with my bloody shirt and staggered to my feet. Standing there, with Heavens Gate's blood on my face and Grace's on my hands, I looked at the dying fire and was painfully aware that I was now alone in the world.

Grace's burial was horrible – out of town and in heavy rain. Lord Lucy sent a clerk. Mary could not face it, but John was there. Will came, but he looked terrible and barely spoke to his father. He ran off back to Shottery as soon as decorum allowed.

To add insult to injury, various groups loyal to Lord Lucy blamed the fire on Catholic sympathisers. Lord Lucy's searches continued, including the Shakespeare house. Thank heavens, Will was not there, for his animosity to Lord Lucy was growing.

Lord Lucy had petitioned the Privy Council, who sent one hundred pounds to the fire rebuilding fund, further cementing his position as the loyalist's loyalist. His Lordship's fundraising did also have a fortuitous irony in his favour; he owned the buildings we had pulled down.

CHAPTER 32

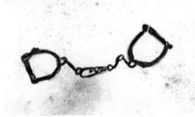

The functioning of the livery was down to me now; however, Nym Granger was an excellent steward to my foreman. Though we had no mandate officially, it seemed to be left this way by Lord Lucy. We stayed on top of everything, earned good coin and received no complaints, so we were mercifully left to ourselves. However, Regan, that trollop of Cornall's, did keep popping in once a week or so, always on some spurious pretext with a view to getting us thrown out.

Meanwhile at Hewlands, in the third week of May, Anne gave birth to a fine little girl. I was now so busy with the livery that I was a world away and heard the news from the Sadlers. I was at the bakery picking up bread, when Judith came rushing in. She ran past me and whispered excitedly into Hamnet's ear, then turning to me she realised I was not just another customer.

'Oh!' she squeaked and Hamnet raised an eyebrow.

'Hello, Mrs Sadler.'

'Judith, please. Your friend became a father,' she informed me warmly.

I nodded a smile. If I were to be truthful to my heart, I felt the twang of jealousy that I was not first privy to the news. 'Girl or boy,' I asked.

'Girl. She is to be called Susannah, after …'

'A woman of purity and virtue, falsely accused by her elders, book of Daniel,' I interjected.

'Young Tom, your Bible knowledge impresses me,' replied Judith.

I forced a smile to my face and bowed my head in appreciation.

'Good day to you both,' and taking my three loaves, I left the shop.

I saw Mary Shakespeare cross the street with little Edmund.

'Good morning, Mrs Shakespeare. Would it be in order to offer congratulations?'

'Thank you, young Thomas. Indeed it would. I am now a grandmother.'

'Joyful news.'

'It is, it is. Now that he has a family, maybe you Thomas, as close friend to our son and this family, can persuade William to return to work for his father. He is sorely missed and certainly needed.'

'I will indeed do my best.'

'Good day to you, Thomas. Come Edmund.'

They carried on towards the bakery, whilst I made a swift pace back to Ely Street. It did occur to me that Will was currently in a bit of a spot, feeling pressure from two sides. Anne was good and gave him space but how long would that last? A man has to provide for his family.

In an act of acquiescence to State and church, Anne persuaded Will to have little Susannah baptised in Trinity. Will did not need much persuasion, seeing the opportunity to repair some of the damage done by their clandestine marriage.

'Tom, our love belongs to whom we choose, but children, they belong to the world,' he said diplomatically, when I asked why he capitulated to the baptism but not marriage.

The christening celebration was a riotous affair at Henley Street, with Will being finally forgiven for his nuptial secrecy and Anne accepted into the Shakespeare household with bygones left to a healthy respect. Quiney and Tyler were there and then, quite a surprise, Fieldy put in an appearance on a rare visit from the big smoke.

I was half-expecting cousin Johnny to appear but he did not; talking of which, there was plenty to drink, and I noticed Will availed himself more than was probably appropriate for a young father. When Anne quietly requested him to desist, he snatched away and, putting an arm around Tyler, downed his cup. I could see this was not good.

Towards the end of the celebration in a quiet corner of the pantry there was intense discussion between Anne, John and Mary. Will was lolling by the fire, quite drunk, when I inadvertently entered. It was clear from all of them that I should retreat, which I did.

Later, as the afternoon waned, I found Anne in Mary's garden soothing little Susannah to sleep. 'All well?' I whispered.

Anne turned round to me and forcing a smile to her tired face she said, 'Yes.'

'I'm bidding goodbye. I have the late feeds to do,' I said awkwardly.

Anne looked to me, and then over my shoulder, to make sure we were alone.

'His parents want him to work in the glove shop. They are relentless. Will just writes and burns manuscripts almost hourly. He drinks too much. I am worried, Tom.'

'When I next go to Chiswick, I will contact Lady Montague.'

'Who be she?' asked Anne, still soothing Susannah.

'A friend to Will – a good friend.'

'Thank you, Tom,' Anne smiled.

Before I did finally leave, I helped a rather drunk Will on to the back of a cart. Anne, with baby Susannah, took the reins and, in the face of some opposition from the Sadlers and family, with great dignity she resolutely drove her daughter and husband back to Hewlands.

That's what I loved about Anne; this diminutive woman had the internal strength of a plough horse, the loyalty of an Arabian and poise of a Holsteiner.

In the next few months I did little trading, a few beasts locally but no big trades for the Chiswick ring. Besides, being now responsible for the livery, I was not yet confident enough to leave young Nym Granger in charge; but that was about to change. It was early October when Lord Lucy made an uncharacteristic appearance. He rode into the livery with Cornall, two militia men and an intense sense of purpose.

'Wickham, we need a cart and pair now!' he demanded, leaping from his mount.

'And three spare!' he added, landing on the ground.

'Yes, Your Lordship.' I turned and called to Nym Granger, who rushed out of the tack-room.

'Master Granger, get the two-by-two cart and both cobs.'

'Master Wickham,' he replied and called to two stable boys.

They set about the task whilst I went to the stalls and brought out three good standard-breds, fresh and strong. I tied them to the trough and checked all their shoes.

'May I ask Your Lordship where and for how long?'

'Why, you spying for someone?' he snapped.

'Your Lordship, if the ground is hard I will leave these shoes as is; if your going be soft, I will put in some stud nails for grip. If longer than a week, I will give you a repair bag.'

He tilted his head feeling a touch foolish, and muttered a guilty reply.

'Yes, yes, of course, your … loyalty … it has always been good,' he said, and sniffed with that irritating superiority that was the privilege of gentry.

We soon had His Lordship's request prepared and ready to leave. Cornall took from his horse some chain and locks and threw them on to the cart where they landed with an ominous metallic thud. Well, if I had wondered what this trip was about, I certainly knew now.

'Who will be driving the cart, Your Lordship?'

He looked around really quite surprised that a driver had not magically appeared to serve him. 'Um oh, yes, um, you can,' he said.

'I'll get my things, Your Lordship.'

'Don't have time for that,' he sneered to a smirking Cornall.

With that, they rode out of the livery.

'Follow,' called His Lordship.

I leapt on, took the reins and followed.

'Hold the fort for me, Nym,' I called, as he ran after me and threw me up some bread and a cloak.

'She'll be good,' he reassured me.

I caught up with the little military cortege and soon realised we were heading north.

After some wet travelling, I was certainly glad of the cloak. To my worry, however, we were arriving at the village of Edstone, home of the Somervilles, and sure enough at their front door. I can definitively say at this point, I was ready to pass bricks out of my rear end. I kept as calm and as cool as I could. The militia banged on the door but there was no answer.

'Open in the name of the queen!' they yelled again and again.

Eventually, an elderly man walking beside a small palfrey, loaded with two sacks of feed, informed us of their whereabouts.

'They for Banbury gone.'

'You say to London to assassinate the queen?' barked Lord Lucy.

'No, Banbury – the market,' said the man.

'It has been heard John Somerville seeks to bring harm to our queen. Have you heard such a thing?'

'Dunno, may have done. Always talking nonsense when he has drink in him, does that Somerville,' the man answered meekly.

'We are here to stop this treason; in the name of Her Majesty I appropriate that feed,' stated His Lordship, pointing to the man's sacks.

Cornall jumped down and chucked the sacks of feed on my cart. I kept my cap down and said nothing.

'Hey! They cost fourpence!' bemoaned the man, as Cornall remounted.

'Put your request in writing and you will be recompensed,' said Lord Lucy.

'I can't write,' yelled the man as we took off along the Banbury Road.

'We may call you as a witness,' Lord lucy called over his shoulder, as the man stood in the middle of the road, alone and violated.

We travelled onwards, calling from inn to inn in search of Somerville and at one, just outside Banbury, we found him. Lord Lucy's militia dragged him out kicking and yelling in his customary way. Dear Beth stood at the door dumbfounded.

347

'What the flaming heck is you arresting my good person for?' demanded Johnny.

The militia said nothing but dragged him across the yard.

'Since when was vending a couple of old nags at market a crime?'

Cornall came out with two pistols, Johnny's broken sword and some papers.

'Well equipped for the deed, Your Lordship,' stated Cornall as he popped them into a bag.

'What the dickens are you talking about?' demanded Johnny.

'Weapons and a list of accomplices,' Cornall told Lord Lucy.

'Self-protection in case we get robbed and list of friends to bludge off, to save inn fees!' declared an exasperated and still struggling Johnny.

'Why are you staying at this inn, and not this friend here!' demanded Cornall, holding up the list and pointing to a name on it.

'Because the last time I had too much to drink and, in the black of night, did accidentally relieve myself in the ladies boudoir! In heaven's name, how did a brain your size ever master the skill of reading!'

I could not believe this. Johnny, even in the face of such a situation, found a funny story to tell and a comic insult to throw!

'Now come along. You are all mistaken, let me go!'

'No! We are not! I am Sir Thomas Lucy, Justice of the Peace for all of Warwickshire and Her Majesty's steward! You sir, John Somerville, are accused of high treason. We have witness to your intent! Assassin!' shouted Lord Lucy, pointing into the very depth of Johnny's being.

All movement ceased. Breath dropped from Johnny's gallop like a dead horse hits the ground. Looking at Lord Lucy, he was suddenly aware of the gravity of his situation and his face went a whiter shade of pale.

'Oh, my God. I am a dead man on account of wine and fools,' he uttered.

They chained his wrists and feet then threw him into the back of the cart. I hoped and prayed he would not recognise me.

They locked his hands to one of the bars and then threw his belongings and the sack of evidence on after him. The others remounted and about faced. I turned the cart and followed. Beth ran after and placed a blown kiss upon poor Johnny as they took, what they both knew, was surely their last sight of each other.

As we left the inn behind us, Johnny moved this way and that, trying to get comfortable in the cart.

'I know this cart?' he muttered to himself. 'Methinks, many years ago, me did travel to see the Coventry plays by this very transport.'

I said nothing, kept my head down. Lord Lucy and Cornall were in the lead with the two militia men in the rear.

'My jailer is young Tom, is it not?' he whispered quietly under his breath.

'Aye,' I whispered back hoarsely yet hopefully imperceptibly to nearby ears.

'Who would have thought? I'll not betray thee. I am a dead man,' he sniffed quietly.

'I'm sorry, sir,' I whispered.

'Don't you be sorry, Tom. This drunken fool's fault, not yours. But they'll not take dear Johnny's life. Johnny's life is his own, to live or give as he please. Oh hell, not this world I'll miss; it's me dear Beth.'

Sitting in the best position he could, he spent the next few hours trying to contain his tears, every now and again muttering of his love for Beth.

Stopping only twice for small sleep, feed, rest and water, we rolled into Charlecote at an unseemly hour. Drunk with sleep, ironically, Johnny was dragged to the stables where he was chained up and thrown some bread and a flask of small beer.

The house steward came rushing out of the house pulling on his clothes.

'Your Lordship, you have a Mr Thomas Wilkes staying with you.'

A very sleepy Lord Lucy looked at the steward with his weary eyes

'And who is Mr Thomas Wilkes?'

'Clerk of the Privy Council, Your Lordship,' he said with a breath of awe. 'He carries a warrant for the arrest of one Edward Arden.'

'Indeed.'

'Sir, he sleeps now but is most concerned to move as soon as is possible.'

'Wickham, have we fresh horses in Ely Street?'

'Yes, Your Lordship.'

'Rest up four hours and return by the ninth. Go.'

'Lordship,' I answered and picked up my reins.

Thankfully, the horses knew the way back to Ely Street, so with reins wrapped tightly around my fingers, I was able to get some sleep for part of the journey.

I drove into the livery and Nym had just risen to prepare first feeds.

'Mr Wickham, sir?'

'Not now, put fresh horses in the shafts and wake me at the eighth,' I said, getting off the cart and staggering towards my quarters.

'Tom, I should say ...'

'Nym, shut up! Do as I ask and ask nothing of me!'

Hunger and tiredness had the better of me. My temper had snapped and I walked inside, climbed the treads and dropped on to my sack. There was an uncharacteristic smell of stale wine about the place, and someone in my bed, damn it.

'Will?' I shook a sleepy and drink-soaked Will.

He suddenly sat bolt upright and rubbed his face. He looked terrible.

'Is it true?' he said.

'Is what?'

'Johnny.'

'Yes, and in four hours they are arresting your uncle, Edward.'

'Cousin, not uncle.'

'Fine, cousin! Will, I need to sleep.'

Will stood up and stomped out down the steps in a fit of umbrage. I was too tired for it. I put my head down and was gone!

It was the eighth hour when I was woken by Nym and, goodness, did I have to battle to get myself vertical? Downstairs Nym had some pottage swimming in barley and bread. I fell upon it. Hot food by sweet Jesus; this was most welcome.

'Nym! Thank you. Mmm ... who taught you how to make this?'

'Your aunt. I tried to tell you about Mr William.'

I held up my hand, my mouth too full.

'It is I who apologises to you. I was in bad humour,' I said.

'No need. Fresh beasts in the shafts ready to go when you are.'

'Thank you, Nym,' I replied.

No sooner had I mounted the cart than I looked up and saw Lord Lucy and his retinue already waiting in the gateway. A man slid off the back of Cornall's horse.

'This is Mr Wilkes. He will travel with you. He doesn't ride,' declared Lord Lucy.

He was a small man, well groomed and tidy with quality clothes. He had few lines in his face and had hands that had never touched anything rougher than a book or a lady's bosom.

Cornall dropped another bag of chains and locks on to the cart, and Mr Wilkes climbed up and sat down beside me, barely acknowledging my existence. The retinue moved off and I followed, trying not to let on that I was quite familiar with the route. So much so that when, at a crossroads, they were not sure which road to take, I had to really sit on my tongue to not tell them. Eventually we arrived at Park Hall, near Orton on the far side of Warwick, a pretty house, gracious but not pompous, grand but not ostentatious. It had a soothing brook at the southern end of the lawn with cherry trees dotted around that must have been a charming sight in blossom. Against the deep red brick there were scattered masses of wild honeysuckle that also would have been spectacular in summer profusion.

As soon as we arrived, there were screams and shouts from within. Cornall dismounted, sprinted around the house and, as Edward Arden tried to run out of the kitchen door, Cornall reached it first and, kicking it shut, struck Arden in the face. Another man tried to run down the rear lawn but, with Arden unconscious, Cornall was free to apprehend him, too, which he did very quickly. Another man at the front door was picked up by the two militia men. Mr Wilkes walked up to him as he was dragged across the lawn.

'Francis Throgmorton!? Secretary of State will be pleased,' he smirked joyfully, and pointed to the cart.

The men brought him over, chucked him on to the cart and chained him up. Cornall brought over a bruised and bloody Edward Arden and the other person.

'What happened?' asked Lord Lucy.

'Ran into a door, Your Lordship,' declared Cornall.

'Idiot.'

'Who are you?' asked Mr Wilkes.

'Edward Arden' he said, spitting out a tooth.

'Not you, him!'

'I'm the gardener,' said the quivering man.

'Let's see your hands?' demanded Lord Lucy.

The man showed his lily-white flawless digits.

'Priest! Name?' said Lord Lucy.

'Hall,' he whimpered.

'Bring him along,' said Wilkes, as he took out and then unrolled his warrant, which he then read to them.

All three were chained up on the cart and we set off once more. After an hour, I realised we were not going to Charlecote but to Warwick, where Lord Lucy was Justice of the Peace. Arriving at the West Gate, we entered Warwick. A gent with some friends rode up and greeted Lord Lucy. The man was distinctly important, for Lord Lucy dismounted and bowed to him. The man walked around the cart with His Lordship, stopping to sneer at Arden.

'This upstart is still going and still enjoying the other!' he said laughing at Arden.

'Devil take you, Dudley,' muttered Arden through his broken teeth.

'Put them in the castle dungeon,' said Dudley. He waved me and the militia to follow his men, and in turn, Lord Lucy and Dudley followed us.

The castle, next to the river, was a neglected wreck of an affair. It was old, very old, and had little maintenance in two lifetimes. It stank of mildew and rotten excrement. There was a part they called Caesar's tower and there in the basement, fit for neither man nor beast, was a waterlogged dungeon. Since the doors no longer functioned effectively, the poor wretches locked to my cart were chained to rings inside.

On the way out into the main courtyard, Lord Lucy looked around the deteriorating structure. 'Good building. Norman, strong. You should make repairs,' he said.

'Would have been able to afford to if that wealthy wench had wed me!' snapped Dudley under his breath.

Which wealthy wench was that I wondered? A very rich one surely, looking at the size and state of the place.

I was ordered back to Charlecote that night, so off I went with a bit of food supplied to me by Dudley's steward.

The last words I heard as I departed were from Dudley to Lord Lucy and Wilkes.

'I want every connection with this squalid family found, searched and interrogated,' he said. 'I want every ledger, book and scrap of paper they own read and logged. If there is one-eighth of a sixteenth of disloyalty, arrest them.'

I tapped gently on the kitchen garden door of Henley Street a touch after midnight. The door was opened by Mary, who was a little surprised to say the least. 'Thomas, what is it?' she said with concern.

I slid in the door, blew out her candle and, shutting the door, I gently put my finger to my lips.

'Is it Will?' she gasped, sitting down.

I shook my head and at that moment we were joined by John.

'Where is Will?' I asked.

'Hewlands. Thomas, what is going on?' he said reaching for a candle to light.

'Please do not light the candle and pray be seated, Sir.'

'We heard about Johnny,' said John with a deep sigh.

'Aye, he is held at Charlecote,' I said.

'No, they have taken him to the tower this morning,' said John.

Now I was surprised.

'It seems it is us who bear the news, Tom,' said John, raising an eyebrow.

'John, Sir; Mary, Madam; your cousin Edward Arden, his friend Francis Throgmorton and a priest have been arrested this morning and are held in Warwick Castle.'

'Dudley! Damn his eyes!' gasped Mary putting her hand to her mouth.

'Yes. He was there,' I said.

'He wanted to marry Her Majesty. A penniless whore would not marry that murdering piece of waste!' snapped John.

So now I knew the 'wealthy wench' Dudley referred to. I looked at John and Mary directly and they me. There was a silence as they waited for what I had to say.

'They are going to search every family connection of Arden for incriminating evidence of disloyalty. Sir, Madam, I beg thee, make your house clean.'

'What are you implying, Thomas?' said John, becoming rather defensive.

'John, I know about printers, their wares and the movements of some texts and persons. That is all I will say. I will now take my leave and crave you forget I ever visited this night. As I did, indeed, forget your visit, Sir – one summer breakfast.'

They both nodded compliance and thanks. John put his hands on Mary's shoulder and squeezed her softly. Gently she stroked the agate stone of his alderman ring. Looking at their pale and stricken faces lit only by the moonlight, I bowed and left as quietly as I had arrived.

The fallout continued and, with a larger armed retinue, Lucy and Dudley tore apart the surrounding Arden family and associates. Thankfully, Dudley preferred to use his own men, so I was able to lie low in the livery, keeping the horses groomed and tack polished.

Will kept his head low at Hewlands but he was getting increasingly agitated by the whole episode. I would call round from time to time but he would not speak with me. Anne had the patience of a saint, and she supported Will with a dowry she had received upon their marriage. A few pounds, she told me. Not enough for a house but enough for some time.

I was at Charlecote when the horrible news arrived. I was settling a horse in the stall where Johnny had been chained up. Flicking the straw around, something under the muck caught my eye; it was leather, but not tack. I picked away the compacted muck and found a book. Wiping the muck off, I knew exactly what it was, *Publius*

Ovidius Naso: 'Sixteen hundred years old and we are still reading him eh? Where'll your bloody gloves be in ten years, let alone fifteen hundred! Our Will is going to write, I can smell it. And, he'll be like this man, still read by all in a thousand years.'

Dear Johnny's words still echoed in my ear, driven by love and passion, yet tinged with sadness and alcohol. I heard sound of Cornall's distinctive pace. I dropped the book and, with my fork, pushed it back into the straw.

Cornall pushed his ugly face through the stall bars. 'Dead! Those treasonous Arden bastards are all dead!' he sneered.

'God save the queen,' I said.

'God save the queen,' he replied, and then with a wink and cocky smile, he walked out.

I retrieved the book and, opening it I found in the cover a pathetic inscription – Johnny's last words smeared in his own blood: 'Fair Cuz, live, love and write.'

CHAPTER 33

If the foul execution of Campion was the rack that twisted Will's soul to breaking point, the arrest and death of his beloved Johnny was the turn that snapped the ratchet. The subsequent flying spindle sent young Will's spirit screaming for vengeance. For the man we all loved so much, a call of death most brutal never came closer. God watched over all of us that cold November afternoon, when he sent the ice early. It froze the river; it froze the trees; it turned the grass to crisp shards of crunching teeth. It froze my fear, soul and heart enough to let me do and say things that in the gentle warmth of summer would have been unimaginable.

At three o'clock, a freeze had started to descend and, by the warmth of the fire, I busied myself repairing harnesses. The door opened. I looked up and standing in the doorway was Anne. She suddenly side-stepped and flattened herself against the wall, as if trying to hide.

'Anne?' I inquired.

A loose window blew open and the snatch of light revealed her face was quite pallid, and I knew the cold was not the cause.

'Anne, what's going on?' I persisted.

'I think hhh … he's gone to, to, to … to kill Lord Lucy.'

'What? Who?' I asked with nervous rhetoric.

Not only was this a serious situation, but I instinctively knew the answer. I grabbed Anne's shoulders and shook her once. 'Which way?'

'Th … th … th … the old, dd … drive.'

Throwing off my apron, grabbing my doublet and, for some strange reason I cannot explain, the crossbow, I rushed into the yard. As luck would have it, Nym Granger had just come in on the sharp and speedy Flyte and was now tacking up Orlando for some exercise.

I leapt up on to Orlando.

'He took my father's rapier!' Anne quickly added, without a stammer.

'Nym! Follow!' I cried.

I turned Orlando around on his hind legs and I looked straight into Anne's eyes. 'Go to Hewlands! Stay there. Wait, and not a word to anyone!'

She nodded once.

'Come Nym!' I yelled and spurred Orlando out of the yard.

We tore down Ely Street and headed for Cloptons Bridge.

Nym Granger did well to keep up, as Flyte was a good horse but not as fast as Orlando. We annihilated the five miles lying between Stratford and Charlecote in what seemed like one quarter of the hour.

Not wanting to be spotted entering the park, I took a cut around some turnip paddocks that lay alongside a small copse. That, in turn, fronted the bit of the Avon that ran through the Charlecote parkland. By the time we reached the edge of the park grounds, like a torturer's cold metal grip, the freeze was really starting to take a hold. Day was gone, and a ghostly blue tint from the full moon of a cloudless sky illuminated the frozen countryside with a light of betrayal, for those embarking on ill-advised deeds.

We came out of the copse and there, in the park, less than five furlongs from Charlecote house itself, I could make out the image of a figure in a single-minded stride. The deer, just introduced to the property by Lord Lucy, looked up in a state of confusion, not sure whether to take fright or expect feed.

We hightailed it towards the striding figure. Will was in a state of high agitation and gripping his father's rapier. He was dressed only in hose, an open shirt doublet and wore only one boot. When I caught up, Will was quite hard to stop. I leapt off Orlando and, running into Will's path, I had to stop him with both hands. This was madness; he was striding towards Charlecote as fired up as a cavalry charge at full tilt.

'Will, Will, in God's holy name what are you doing?' I pleaded.

He stopped, leaning into my hands, his tear-worn eyes clearly fixed on the house in the distance. 'Who lives by the sword will die by the sword and he by mine!' Will growled.

Nym stood nervously in the background, holding Flyte and Orlando. I shook Will, trying to get him to come to, but he was in an oblivion of suffering.

'A quill is sharper than a sword! You told me that!' I remonstrated.

'Fye!' he spat.

'Open men's hearts with your pen, not your sword.'

'That's good,' he slurred, with a momentary smile.

'Your wife said that,' I simpered.

'She's a poet.'

'No! She is your wife and mother of your child. This, is a poet,' I said thrusting, Johnny's book into his hand.

Will recognised it, and it seemed to have a calming effect. Suddenly there was the sound of splashing near the house accompanied by the baying of dogs.

'Mister Wickam!' called Nym, in a nervous whisper.

I looked around to the river crossing in front of the house as four horsemen came thrashing across, sending forth a moonlit spray of incandescence.

'Oh, my God in heaven!' I gasped. It was Lord Lucy, his steward Cornall and some men. Nym and I had cause to be on his property but William had no cause at all. If ever we needed a cause fast, it was now. Will dropped the rapier and caressed the book. I picked up the rapier and threw it into the river. Will looked to the approaching horses and loping mastiffs.

'Don't get us all killed!' I silently raged to him.

The deer looked on, still expectant of feed. The approaching horseman descended into a dip in the paddock. Seizing the moment, I grabbed the crossbow and with two God-given seconds, I cocked it and shot one of the deer which fell to the ground. I cast aside the weapon and turned to look at a terrified Nym, as Will stuffed the book into a pocket inside his doublet.

'Follow my word or we three will mount the gallows before the week is out,' I stated categorically.

The thundering hooves approached and suddenly, like demons of the Apocalypse ascending from a frozen hell, the horsemen rose out of the paddock depression with Lord Lucy at their head on Rafsaan.

In moments too quick to call, we were surrounded by the four men gripping the reins of their black heaving horses. They scuffed and strutted around us, kicking up chunks of frozen earth. The accompanying dogs went straight for the fallen deer and tore it apart in seconds. I silently gripped my bladder as breath of the snorting horses bellowed out of their nostrils like the steam of hell itself. I stood by Will, who hung his head, seemingly still oblivious to what was going on around him.

'Wickham?!' shouted Lord Lucy incredulously.

My Lord,' I replied.

'What in the devil's name is going on?'

Cornall cried out, 'Poachers, My Lord!' as he tried to force the dogs off their prize.

'Indeed, Sir. Your steward is correct,' I concurred.

'Nym Granger and I discovered this wretch helping himself to your bounty, My Lord.'

All eyes now moved to Will who dropped to the ground with his head hanging in his lap. The steward's men dismounted and picked up the distraught Will. They offered him to Lord Lucy, who peered down imperiously. He leant forward on his pommel and studied Will closely for some moments.

'Heavy with drink, My Lord,' said one.

'You seem ill-furnished for poaching,' Lord Lucy declared.

Will looked up and made an effort to pull himself together. 'Sir,' he muttered.

'Do you know who I am?' he demanded.

'Lord Lucy,' Will whispered, nodding his head.

'Then! It isn't "Sir", is it? It's Your Lordship or My Lord,' Lord Lucy snapped.

'Yes, My Lord,' whispered Will.

'You know who I am, but I have no idea who you are. So who the bloody hell are you?'

'William ...'

I had to interrupt. Shakespeares were known to be of the Arden family and Arden of Somerville. We could not risk a union being made

'Shakeshaft; William Shakeshaft, My Lord,' I quickly said. 'A known blaggard and dishonest creature if ever I ...'

'Shut up, Wickham!'

Shuddering, I breathed as deeply and as quietly, as I could. Lord Lucy now addressed Will as Shakeshaft. My ruse seemed to have been accepted. Thankfully, Will was taking the ruse as well.

'I was hungry,' Will whispered, with a convincing undertone of remorse.

'May well be, Shakeshaft. It is the start of what I believe to be a long and cold winter. But if you are hungry, you come to my kitchens and take the scraps that are available for those in such plight. Do not kill and steal my property!'

I thought this was His Lordship being forgiving and we were in a clearing paddock. But I was wrong.

Lord Lucy dismounted and Cornall followed suit. His Lordship moved towards Will, waving away the men holding him. Will stood composed watching him approach. Lord Lucy looked him up and down.

'You have misplaced a boot?'

'In the ditch I fear, pursuing my quarry,' said Will and he pointed to the now masticated deer.

'My quarry,' corrected Lucy.

'Your quarry, My Lord,' retorted Will in instant submission.

Lord Lucy looked around the landscape. The freeze was setting hard and had thankfully covered the tracks we'd made in the dew.

'Where did you approach?' he inquired.

Will pointed in the direction of Tredington.

'There, My Lord.'

Lord Lucy raised his chin and, looking along his nose at Will, he placed his forefinger on Will's chin and pushed it this way, then that.

At this moment, I wondered if we were believed. Lucy's smile was thick with the lather of suspicion.

'You're familiar to me,' he quizzed.

Will said nothing and, where he could, looked at the ground. Lucy raised Will's head with his hand, ironically gloved by the skill of Will's father. He stared once more into Will's eyes.

As those eyes locked, I now remember this as the single most defining moment in Will's life; he was one breath from the gallows. All that would keep him alive would be his wit, intelligence and poetic sensitivity brought to bear on the slightest nuance of a reaction. A paltry twitch in a cheek, muscle or eyelid could unmask him. This was to be the performance of his life. This was the moment in time the young man departed and poetry's greatest alchemist arrived.

'Arden. You have the look of one of they. You cannot be, of course, but, there is a look – in the eyes.' As Lord Lucy studied him, sadistic and taunting, I knew the merest flinch of vengeful emotion from Will and all would be lost.

'They are related to that popish assassin John Somerville. He had that look you have. He had that look in his eyes. Coward hung himself rather than face his fate like a man; bloody Papists for you,' he drawled sadistically.

Will's face was a masterpiece of composure, with a hint of submissive fear.

'Edward Arden – should have seen him struggle at the end of his rope,' he mused, with a sick chortle.

I could see Will start to shake with rapidly freezing lips and reddening eyes. Whether it was fear, the cold or shear theatrical genius, even I could not rightly tell. Lord Lucy walked back to his horse and straightened his gloves.

'Beat this thief,' he demanded casually.

Cornall waved to the two men, one of whom grabbed a leather-wrapped steel-tipped cane from his horse.

'Not them. You, Wickham. Beat Shakeshaft like the blaggard and dishonest creature you tell me he is.'

A cannon loosed a shot in my heart! If I did not take the stick and do His Lordship's bidding without the faintest betrayal of sympathy, our lie could be lost.

Lord Lucy remounted his horse and waited. I do not remember seeing the cane tossed to me, but I caught it nonetheless. In two strides, I ran over and struck my beloved friend across the face; he went down like the deer I felled earlier. I then hit and hit and hit my dear, dear friend in a frenzy of passion surpassed only by the passion with which I despised the whole Crown and Government that brought me to this foul moment. After what seemed like the bloodiest eternity, I eventually heard the only welcome word uttered that night.

'Enough!' called the rotten Lord Lousy.

Sweating and panting I looked down on my bruised and bloody friend, then handed the blood-smeared cane back to its owner.

'Leave him on the Tredington road,' ordered Lord Lucy.

The steward's men lifted Will between their horses and dragged him off in a posture of the crucified Christ. Cornall dismounted to recover the crossbow and, tying a lanyard to the remains of the deer, he and Lord Lucy galloped back to Charlecote house dragging it behind, pursued by the dogs. The eyes of that sorry deer as it was dragged away stayed with me the night, even more so than my bloody friend being hauled away. I stood, praying to God almighty that my friend would survive.

'What now, Mr Wickham?' stuttered a somewhat pole-axed Nym Granger.

Without replying, I pulled myself on to Orlando and took off back to Stratford.

Nym followed and, as we galloped down the old drive, I explained we had to get someone to pick Will up before the late hour or he would surely die. Of course, if we were seen ourselves, the truth would be out. We needed a small miracle.

Unbelievably, prayers were answered. When we hit the Stratford road a miracle did come in the shape of Judith and Hamnet Sadler. With horse and cart, they had been collecting flour from the mill in Tredington, baking being a nocturnal activity. I pulled up their cart and begged them to do God's work and about face their cart and go back to Tredington, where they might find in a ditch, a friend in distress. Confused but convinced by my unusual plea, they obliged.

Nym, I told to go back to the livery and perform the late feeds, whilst I headed for Hewlands.

'Nym! Find another crossbow, too,' I yelled as I took off to hightail it to Hewlands.

I arrived at the Hathaway house and quickly stabled Orlando out of sight. I rushed out of the clamp-like cold and into the cottage. Anne sat by the fire on her favourite settle feeding young Susannah from her breast. Guiding her nipple into the little mouth, she rocked in a nervous fashion, more for her comfort than the child's. She looked up at me, biting her lip, trying not to cry, wanting to know but not wanting to hear. Closing my eyes, I clasped my hands together in a gesture of prayer to signify all was well but not yet home and washed. 'Are we alone?' I asked.

She nodded.

'Will they return?' I said, checking curtains.

Anne shook her head. 'They are in Coventry for my sister's birthday.'

'Thank God. Do you have some water on the fire?' I whispered.

Anne froze for a moment. She nodded and pointed to a cauldron on the fire.

'Fresh linen?' I uttered.

'To bandage?' she whispered with subdued panic.

'Ointment?' I added.

She breathed deeply, and then rose from the settle and her demeanour changed as she mentally mounted her survival steed. She became cold, hard and devilishly practical with sword-like precision. Quietly, she stopped Susannah's feed and placed her in a small rocking crib near the fire. She gently tucked her in and, taking a twisted bit of linen, squeezed milk from her breast onto it and placed it with Susannah, who sucked at it sleepily. Facing the wall, Anne composed her clothes and wiped her tears. 'Is Will on his way?' she asked, turning around.

I told her the Saddlers were conveying him, and she turned to face me. 'Are his injuries bad?' she asked.

I could only nod.

'Get the blanket and bolster from Mother's chamber and place it on the table,' she demanded curtly.

I obliged and she busied herself clearing the table, preparing a bowl for hot water and fresh linen strips for bandaging. She fetched a tub of ointment, a mixture of wormwood and common groundsel boiled in pig fat. Father's green grease, she called it, handed down through her family, the most potent healer of cuts and preventer of infections. I smelt it and, ironically, it was exactly the same ointment the old man had given for my feet on the way to London – the last time I had bailed out Will.

We had only just finished organising our makeshift surgery when the door burst open. In a rush of freezing air, lit by the brightest moon, in staggered Judith and Hamnet with a very white and bloody Will, wrapped in flour sacks. Instantly, with a grip as tight as a scavenger's daughter, Anne seized control of herself.

I helped Hamnet carry Will and lift him on the table, and then started to peel off the sacks and what was left of his clothes. Anne immediately picked out her best silver needles and ordered Judith to pour boiling water on them in the only silver salver they had. As the layers came off, the injuries I had inflicted became horribly visible, a multitude of welts, abrasions and broken skin, now erupting into swellings, bruises and weeping gapes.

The delicate skill of Anne's needlepoint was put to good use, as two of the wounds could only be held together by thread. Slowly, she and Judith gently toiled over her poor husband. As they turned him this way and that, Will would wrench and clench, gripping the pain.

At one point, Anne could take no more and, bursting into tears, she screamed, 'I hate … this!'

Will's eyes immediately snapped open and looked straight into Anne's with the most troubled fear in his heart. He tried to reach her with his hand. Anne knelt beside him and gently wiped her tears with his hand.

'Not you … just … this,' she recanted.

Standing up once more, she breathed in, composed herself and went back to work. 'Judith, more hot water, please,' she demanded.

Whilst the women worked on, Hamnet knelt and prayed. I on the other hand, sick that I had inflicted every suffering wound, decided to see to the welfare of Judith and Hamnet's horses. As I rubbed them down, I silently prayed that infection would not visit my friend.

It was about the second hour when finally all was done. Bandaged and wrapped in blankets, Will was laid in front of the fire close to his daughter. There, fed with a hot herbal tincture boiled up by Anne, he fell into a deep sleep. The rest of the night both he and Susannah were watched over by Anne sitting on the settle sewing her needlepoint.

I left Hewlands after Judith and Hamnet. To my relief, Anne never asked me to give an account of what happened. Little knowledge was always considered safest. By the time I fell into my bed, it was past the fourth hour. Thankfully, Nym had fed and stabled all the horses and in the morning he rose and performed my duties as well as his. Even though I was able to sleep till a good hour, all was not yet over.

CHAPTER 34

It was midday, and thankfully fine sunshine had thawed our frozen world. The sharp clip of horses' shoes across the cobbled yard heralded a visit to the livery by its owner and his steward, Cornall. I signalled Nym to take charge of their horses, which he duly obliged. His Lordshp walked over to me with a knowing swagger that made me realise I was in trouble.

'Good day to you, My Lord' I said with the customary bow. Lord Lucy looked about the yard.

'Quite a beating you gave that thieving Shakeshaft,' he said.

'A thief is a thief, My Lord,' I replied, as obsequiously as I could. 'I trust the punishment I meted out was satisfactory.'

He didn't reply, merely grunted. He thought for a moment and then looked to the sky. 'Wasn't in the ditch this morning,' he mused.

'Must have took himself to his abode,' I speculated, with all the detached interest I could muster.

'I thought that, too, but that was quite a beating. I expected the bloody wretch to die in that ditch last night.'

'He was fortunate,' I replied, realising this was not a casual fat-chewing of the events; this was an interrogation.

'Or maybe he had assistance from friends?' said Lord Lucy.

'Or a good samaritan,' I countered, trying to control my rushing fear.

'That's what I thought. We went to Tredington, Mr Cornall and I. No word of a Shakeshaft anywhere.' Lord Lucy gave a whimsical but loaded grin.

'He only said he came from that direction, My Lord,' I replied.

'I thought that, too.'

His Lordship lingered on my answer; again looking at the sky, then to Nym, and back at me.

'You said you knew him?'

'Only by reputation, sir. From where he hails, I am not sure.'

Lord Lucy seemed to accept this but he was clearly not yet done.

'His crossbow puzzled me. Mr Cornall noted it resembled one hanging in the tack-room here,' he stated pointedly.

Fortunately, Nym had done as I had asked the previous night and replaced the missing weapon.

'Many crossbows, My Lord – a common weapon,' I replied nervously. 'The one in the tack-room still hangs there. I'll have Mr Granger retrieve it.'

'No, Mr Cornall will.'

Lord Lucy waved to his steward, who went to the tack-room. There was a tension as we waited for Mr Cornall to bring the said weapon, or news of its absence. The weapon duly arrived and was briefly inspected by His Lordship, who sniffed the sniff of irritating, but only temporary, defeat.

'Shakeshaft wasn't carrying any bolts though. Strange to go poaching with a crossbow and one bolt?'

This was relentless; I shrugged rather than answer logically to such plain provocation.

'And, the way he was dressed puzzled me too. Did it puzzle you?' he asked, looking me straight in the eye.

'The dress of a hungry and desperate man, My Lord?' I replied.

'Yes, I thought that too, but hungry and desperate for what? And under the drink?'

I said nothing, for to answer was to keep digging the hole I was in.

'What if he wasn't a poacher? What if he was an Arden or a Somerville, and what if he was helped by friends?'

'I don't follow, My Lord,' I queried with gut-wrenching internal panic.

'If he was coming for me, that means he may have had friends who lurked nearby, ready to assist in an escape – *secundum caedes?*'

'*Secundum …?*' I stuttered.

I was now horribly on the back foot and I did not know enough Latin.

'After the killing,' Lord Lucy snapped.

'You think he may have been an assassin, My Lord?'

'What do you think?'

'I apprehended a poacher, or so I thought.'

'There are two kinds of assassins, Mr Wickham: foolish and intelligent. Both dangerous, but they have different accomplices. The foolish assassin's accomplices will try to prevent; whilst the intelligent may conspire and assist. As my servant, if you are attacked, I will see to it your attacker is found and punished. Since, as your lord and master, an attack on you, is an attack on me. I, too, am a servant. I am a servant of Her Majesty Queen Elizabeth, and an attack on me is an attack on our glorious monarch. A very serious matter indeed. So, any lies that conceal an attempted attack on my person, whether foolish or intelligent, are *lunctum praesumo*, that is, joint venture.'

'Am I accused, My Lord?' I uttered in submission.

I had no option but to be this direct and stare the devil in the eye. There was a deathly pause that seemed a lifetime of a thousand years.

'Only this Shakeshaft can verify if I have been lied to. I will enter it into court records. He has taken a punishment of beating for poachery, served upon my judgement.'

'Sir,' I nodded.

'However, there is now a situation I will not tolerate. I can only have servants of unspeakable loyalty. If you can bring Shakeshaft before me, for further interrogation, I may be persuaded otherwise. Till then, gather your belongings and leave.'

His Lordship about-faced and went to his horse. Cornall put the crossbow in my hands and followed.

'Mr Cornall, take an inventory of all feed, money and livestock on the premises.'

'Shall I start with that horse there, My Lord!' Cornall asked, pointing directly to Orlando.

'Wherever, said Lord Lucy, turning his horse.

The sky fell upon me with the crushing force of a brick wall. I had no document, I had no proof this was my horse. That pointing finger stabbed dead all the time, knowledge, love and tenacity I had imbued in that beautiful beast.

'Very good, My Lord,' Cornall replied with a freshly self-important grin.

Lord Lucy left as I stood in a trance, quite dizzy, as if I was going to fall to the ground. The next thing I felt was the turgid breath of Cornall close to my ear.

'You both came closer to the gallows than a dog's tongue to its prick. Mr Shakeshaft would be advised to take cover for a good while.' He sniffed, then hoiking, spat onto the cobblestones.

'Pen and paper?' he added.

'Didn't know you could write,' I pondered in my dazed state.

'Lot of things you don't know,' he said.

'Nym, get Mr Cornall what he needs,' I called hoarsely.

In the tack-room, I picked up some clothes and rolled them into my cloak. I had eight pounds saved; it lay in a purse secreted in the brick work beside the fire, but Cornall walked in, so it was going to have to stay there. However, I had to take the medicine pouch; the contents of that were too dangerous. I picked it up as casually as I could.

'What's that?' demanded Cornall.

'Medicines for horses,'

'Belongs here,' he snapped.

I sighed desperately.

'At least let me have some means to pay my way?' I pleaded, hoping he would not spot my heart in my mouth and beating nine to the dozen.

Cornall snatched the pouch from me and emptied it out on the table. Provocatively he lined up the oils, ointments, bandages, needles and blades.

'I'm a fair man ... so we'll share it,' he said.

I nodded with feigned appreciation. Cornall suddenly laughed and threw the empty pouch at me. 'Your share!'

'Thanks,' I muttered, as my heart moved from my mouth back to my chest.

'Now get out!' he growled.

I wandered across to Orlando and stroked him for the last time.

I turned to Cornall as he stood at the door.

'At least get a good price for him.'

'Probably go for glue,' he laughed re-entering the tack-room.

I breathed down Orlando's nostril and soothed him. I wasn't worried about his future; he was a fine steed and would be quickly spotted by any discerning horseman. I was just gutted at losing him. However, there are many horses but you only have one life and, after the last twenty-four hours, I was thankful to walk away with mine.

I walked out of the livery for the last time, my home since birth. I didn't feel it mattered that much. With Father dead and Grace dead, what was I walking away from? Other than a bed, food and work, there was little to hold me there. So into the night I walked with nothing more than my bedroll and a few possessions. I knew there was still a lot of tension over the Arden affair, so I gave the Sadlers and Henley Street a wide berth.

I spent that night in a hedgerow, which was excruciating. My head was crushed with the cold. I barely slept. At dawn, cold and desperate, I travelled on and quietly let myself into Father John Frith's bothy, at the back of his church in Temple Grafton. My boots were worn through and, with bloody feet, hungry, damp and wretched, I collapsed on a sack of herbs surrounded by Frith's other wounded creatures of the woodlands.

It only now dawned on me that in ten short hours I had gone from a young man with prospects, to a vagrant. Sadness I felt, yes. Self-pity? Not really. Anger at the behaviour of my Stratford friend, who effectively placed me in this predicament? That was harder; but there was a passion in Will that was ... so God-given. All it needed was a spillway and the sluice pulled, then it would flow like an overshot mill. That much I knew. So, no, it was not his fault. The anger was most with myself for knowing truth and not being able to walk away from it.

The door opened and daylight blinded me. 'At last, he stirs,' said a gentle voice.

I had slept so long I was not even aware a day and a night had passed.

'Father Frith?' I asked trying to recognise his silhouette.

He closed the door and lit a tallow candle. I looked to my feet; they had been dressed and bandaged. Then I realised I was not sleeping on the one sack that I thought I had set down on, but a large straw-filled linen bag and with blankets.

'How long have I been here?' I asked, with a touch of panic.

'Four days,' he answered casually.

'What?'

Father Frith took a stool and, sitting down in front of me, opened a small straw-box, out of which he took a pottery vessel. Upon removing the lid, steam ascended into the air like a candescent angel of mercy. It was the most welcome aroma of pottage I have ever smelled. He handed it to me. I cupped it in my hands for few moments, savouring the warmth and regenerating aroma.

'Spoon?' said Father Frith.

He handed me a spoon and I slowly started to eat. I had an urge to attack it like a mad dog but I wanted to taste every moment of this simple but life-saving food.

'How could I sleep so long,' I muttered, slurping the delicious food.

'You suffered great shock, not just to your body but to your heart and soul, too. You needed time to recover.'

'When did you find me?'

'I didn't. I was in here when you entered and collapsed on the floor.'

It was only then I realised how little I could actually recollect after I had left Ely Street.

'How is … my … Stratford friend?' I asked somewhat nervously.

'He is recovered well, this last fortnight.'

'Fortnight! Two whole weeks?'

'Yes, he will be glad to hear of you. He was concerned.'

My spoon froze mid-air and, stunned, I stared into the almost-empty pottage pot. It hung there, like some mysterious alchemist's vessel of time. Sweet chirps from Frith's wounded birds brought me back to earth. I thought I had been but one night in the hedges, after leaving Ely Street, but it seems like it was a lot more.

Later that evening Will appeared at the bothy door. 'Tom,' he whispered.

I was still dozing a bit but I woke, sat up and rubbed my eyes.

'You must come to Hewlands, someone ...,' he paused for a moment, '... wishes to speak with us.'

'How are you, Will?' I asked with a tinge of sarcasm.

Will said nothing. I noticed he still had some dry wounds and he held a walking stick. I had certainly done some damage. I could see the forefinger of his right hand was bound to his second finger. He looked around, purposely avoiding my eye.

'Thomas, I owe you my life, and indeed I owe you, yours. My friend, who supped with Arabian princes, made love to a French noblewoman, had position, food, money, a bed, and now I have made you a ...'

'... vagrant,' I said with an ironic grin.

'No ... not while there is breath in my body, *meus frater in lacte*,' he whispered, hoarsely.

Will looked me straight in the eye with the most intense craving for forgiveness. I could do nothing but stand and embrace him. 'I am still that man. You owe me nothing, except that which you give with love and love alone.'

I felt relief enter his body like a fresh flush of spring water.

'Your hand?' I asked, pointing to the bandages on his right hand.

'The fingers ... broke, but they will mend, or so I am told,' he muttered, looking around the shelves of injured birds within their cages.

I said nothing. Will turned his eyes back to mine. 'At least I can't cut Father's patterns any more,' he quipped.

'You ... can still write?' I inquired, nervously.

'In a scratchy way; but then ... I write with my heart, not a pen ... so,' he said, with a gentle smile.

After giving our thanks to Father Frith, we walked over to Hewlands, Will still limping a little. Once there, they made me comfortable in the stable loft. Whilst waiting for what, or whoever, it was that wanted to speak with us, Will was reserved with details. I spent time in the house. Joan and the other children made for a busy abode, which was good cover, since I gathered Lord Lucy was still not satisfied and the more recusants and traitors he 'brought to justice' the more 'favour' he received from the State and Crown.

I was sitting in the parlour and cuddling little Susannah whilst Will read Johnny's book of Ovid, when there came a knock at the door. It was Will's father and mother, closely followed by John Richardson.

There was a long face on all of them and Mary was mopping her tears with a hankie. Will stood up and limped to the table.

'Mother, Father, Mr Richardson?' he asked politely.

Anne entered the room, drying her hands and curtsied in respect.

'I am still unaware of what happened, or how you came to be thus, William, but things seem to indicate it be best if you left the town for a while,' stammered his father, as Mary wept.

Will nodded.

'I have been a fool, Father,' he whispered.

'Lord Strange is in Oxford and heading south-west,' said John Richardson.

'He is?' uttered Will hoarsely.

'Missive is, he will take you on, apprentice player, two shillings a week,' said John Richardson.

There was silence. We all looked at each other awkwardly. A king could live off that if, of course, the king didn't eat.

'And my friend – I have some debt to him, Mr Richardson,' Will pleaded.

'Lord Strange will take him, too, if he wishes. Groom, one shilling a week,' he said, a little embarrassed.

A shilling a week! Wow. Well, it was more than no shilling a week, I thought to myself.

Mary put her arms around Will and held him tightly. 'I love you, son,' she wept.

'I you too, Mother.'

'One other thing,' said John Richardson. Mary released her son.

'Lord Strange says if you ever be under the influence of drink in his service, you are gone.'

Will nodded, imperceptibly but definitively. I noticed John Richardson throw a conspiring glance to Anne, and she returned it.

'We must away,' said John.

Mary pushed a purse of coin into Will's hand and kissed him before being pulled away by Will's father.

'We expect to see our granddaughter regularly,' he said, smiling to Anne and stroking Susannah's forehead as she slept in my arms.

'You shall, my father, my mother,' she replied sweetly, and held the door for them as they left.

John Richardson stood for moment as the Shakespeares departed down the path.

'Tom, Nym bought some feed from me yesterday, for Cornall.'

'He and Regan running the yard now?' I asked.

'Yes, Nym asked me to give you this.'

John handed me a purse and, before I could say anything, he left. Of course it was my purse. I gently handed the sleeping Susannah to Anne and opened the purse; there was my eight pounds savings to the shilling. I pulled out a crown and rushed out the door and caught up with John Richardson at the gate.

'Sir, please. Give this to Nym. Tell him if ever he needs my help, if I can, I will.'

He took the crown, smiled and, without a word, tipped his hat to me and rode away. I noticed that he met up with another horseman, who had been waiting at the corner and on the withers of his horse was a brand mark, three diamonds.

'Hold, Sir!' I called and ran to them.

They stopped and, as I ran in front, they both looked at me from their horses with fixed grins.

'You, Sir, I know you,' I said, pointing at the stranger. It was that shadow himself.

'You have a sharp recall, Sir, and if you hadn't given me the slip, I'd have offered Her Ladyship's help sooner.'

'That was over a year gone,' I said, truly not believing he could have taken so long to find us.

'Shall we say, events delayed us for a while? You still have her letter?'

'I do, Sir,' I replied.

'Good, keep it safe and use it wisely,' he said and, smiling once more, they rode off.

It left me quite dizzy. This conspiratorial world that I tried so hard to avoid seemed utterly intent on following me.

Back in the cottage, closing the door was strange. It was like the door shut on a great part of our lives, but the three of us knew in our hearts another great door was opening.

'It's a walk to Oxford!' sighed Will.

'Do you still have Moot in the paddock?' I asked Joan.

'We do, but is he not the property of …'

'Unbranded, never on the inventory,' I said.

Anne raised an eyebrow and looked to Will.

'What the eye doesn't see, the heart doesn't know, especially one as cold and wretched as Lord Thomas Lousy's,' smiled Will.

Anne reached out and cuddled her beloved Will.

'I may be away some time,' said Will, looking into her eyes.

'I know,' she replied with her most beguiling smile.

'I'll return,' he said.

'I know,' she answered, slowly placing her soft lips on his.

As they kissed, Will took a folded paper from his pocket and pushed it gently into Anne's hand. Only in later years, did I find out the content of that note, which she held to her person and was buried with.

> Those lips that Love's own hand did make
> Breathed forth the sound that said 'I hate'
> To me that languish'd for her sake;
> But when she saw my woeful state,
> Straight in her heart did mercy come,
> Chiding that tongue that ever sweet
> Was used in giving gentle doom,
> And taught it thus anew to greet:
> 'I hate' she alter'd with an end,

My Stratford Friend

That follow'd it as gentle day
Doth follow night, who like a fiend
From heaven to hell is flown away;
'I hate' from hate away she threw,
And saved my life, saying 'not you.'

End of Book 1

Lightning Source UK Ltd.
Milton Keynes UK
UKOW04f0936130715

255075UK00001B/3/P

9 780992 592202